Queer Africa 2

Queer Africa 2

new stories

EDITED BY MAKHOSAZANA XABA
AND KAREN MARTIN

MaThoko's Books is an imprint of Gay and Lesbian Memory in Action (GALA)

ISBN: 978-1-928215-42-4

Edited by: Makhosazana Xaba and Karen Martin
Copy editor: Gill Gimberg
Cover art: Danielle Clough
Book design: Monique Cleghorn

The publication of this book was made possible by core support
from the Norwegian Students' and Academics' International
Assistance Fund (SAIH), and The Other Foundation.

This book is dedicated to Makgano Mamabolo who dreamed this second volume into life during the launch of *Queer Africa: New and Collected Fiction* at the Wits Writing Centre on 17 August 2013.

Table of Contents

Introduction

> I suppose anyone can be anyone else in most ways. I have accepted
> this (not really), and so I no longer hold out for a dream. I will be like
> them someday (and you, and me, and he). – Barbara Adair

The coda to Barbara Adair's 'Phillip', anthologised for the first time
in this collection, stays with me. This short meditation by the title
character Phillip, reads also as an invitation into the lives of others
through a sampling of the textual/sexual pleasures offered in *Queer
Africa 2*. The fiction collected here invites us, albeit provisionally,
into the lives of others, so 'anyone can be anyone else in most ways,'
momentarily suspending the boundary between self and other.

Rendered here is an array of interpretations of what it means to
be fully *human*, *queer* and *African* – three categories of identity
often misconstrued as mutually exclusive. The stories collected in
this volume give a kaleidoscopic peek into the many ways in which
Africans inhabit 'queerness', giving fine grained texture to the lives
and experiences of those whose humanity is routinely denied. From
Brooklyn to Naija, and the lush parks of Johannesburg to small
villages in Somalia, from nightclubs in Mombasa to a Walmart parking lot in North Carolina, the characters in *Queer Africa 2* are people
who live, strive and struggle as full human beings. They crave love,
companionship, and acceptance – whether by nation-states or

family members – while facing the substance of what makes the 'everyday' both challenging and mundane. Their experiences, whether in coffee shops, classrooms, bedrooms or mosques, transport the reader to places we can only visit through fiction, allowing us to imaginatively inhabit these worlds.

This volume follows on an inaugural volume of short fiction, *Queer Africa*, published by MaThoko's Books, an imprint of the Gay and Lesbian Memory in Action (GALA), in collaboration with the independent feminist press Modjaji Books in 2013. Since then, a wave of repressive anti-homosexuality legislation has swept the African continent, with several countries introducing or entrenching homophobia through law. Uganda and Nigeria have been at the forefront of this new wave of homophobic legislation. In Uganda, president Yoweri Museveni signed the Anti-Homosexuality Act (AHA) in 2014, a law that penalised the 'crime' of homosexuality with penalties of up to life imprisonment. The Act also potentially penalised 'allies' of homosexuals with prison sentences of up to seven years. The Ugandan Constitutional Court has since struck down the AHA as unconstitutional, but the discussion of and passage of the AHA enabled a climate of persecution and harassment against LGBTIQ+ communities. Also in 2014, Nigerian President Goodluck Jonathan effected anti-homosexuality laws that mandated prison sentences of up to fourteen years for people found to be in same-sex relationships. In South Africa, lauded for its progressive constitution, hate crimes against queer men and women, and those who eschew gender binaries, continues. In response to these life-threatening laws and cultures, LGBTIQ+ activism against homophobia has also intensified.

Cultural and artistic production has been a site of such resistance. With its publication, *Queer Africa 2* takes its place amongst work by visual artists such as Adejoke Tugbiyele, Zanele Muholi and Vusi Makatsi; and writers like Kehinde Bademosi and Banyavinga

Wainaina. Such work foregrounds the politics of sexuality on the African continent and in the diaspora, using artistic expression as a tool for countering the damaging ideologies of homophobia.

Queer Africa 2 wields this power gently. The collection's strength lies not in pedantry or overt politicisation of queer lives, but rather, in the depiction of the quotidian. When Ilsa and Tibahitana fall in love in Jennifer Shinta's 'Perilous Love,' set in eastern Uganda, the possibility of a fourteen-year jail sentence hovers over their story, but doesn't dominate it. Their gently-unfolding love, despite the penalties this love could incur, remains the story's focus. At the tale's conclusion, the lovers lie on a hilltop admiring the sky: 'Clouds gathered suddenly, a storm was brewing. They stayed put.' Their staying put signals a refusal to be bowed by the repressive machinery of the law, and willingness, by 'stay[ing] put', to resist whatever consequences they might experience because of their relationship.

In 'Iyawo' by Yvonne Fly Onakeme Etaghene, queer love straddles two continents, with the narrator, who lives between the United States and Nigeria, discovering that

> [t]he love I always looked for in women was in my country [Nigeria] all along. That comforting home that I searched for in the arms and beds of women, lay on my land, waiting on my return. Home.

'Home' here is not only a geographic space or nation, but the pleasure and sustenance same-sex desire provides; a set of relations intricately bound up with place and desire. In naturalising queer love as a type of home within the national space of Nigeria, Etaghene makes a lie of the controlling and damaging ideology of homosexuality as 'un-African'. The story does not need to mention legal and cultural homophobia to compel. Its aesthetic, almost lyrical, foregrounds the beauty and possibility of queer love, offering the vision of a world structured by an ethic of love instead of the hatred of difference: 'If we made this world with our bare hands instead of by the accidental destiny of birth, our love, this love between us women, would be sanctified in public spaces, temples, in the market, on the dirt roads we were raised on.'

Within these pages a vision of such a world is crafted and re-crafted – a place where gay men can talk openly about their lovers in a coffee shop without the fear of being overheard; a place where men and women can bring their partners home and have them welcomed by parents regardless of their gender; a place where women can kiss and hold hands freely without the fear of violence. The imaginative possibilities fiction opens up to us is one small but important avenue to a different, more just world. This volume moves us slowly towards that place.

BARBARA BOSWELL

Ace

NICK MULGREW

Light, oh, you; the sparing light. For in the first moment I saw you, you louvred a blind within me and for that moment there was something light-stained inside me where before there existed only something like the depths of the trenches, a Dordrecht chasm, where only worms and fish without eyes live; a province of things that exist solely by running into rock and pulse. And then that light filtered down into that water, and striated into the waves and the currents, and in me grew new things, holding fast, photosynthesising, small buds of yellow threatening to break the surface, a nut forming and plumping below the sedge.

And then that light was gnawed away like bone until like bone it splintered, and now upon it I am caught and I choke, and now what is within me wilts and brews.

But still. Something worked in me then that had never worked before, nor worked since. And still I cannot know if you are the solution or if you were only a fluke.

In my mind I trail at your heel like a stray with the scent of calcium ringing in her nose.

OK. Wait.
Wait.

I know this is a bad way for me to speak about myself, about *this*. This is something I am still improving upon. I promise you that. Let me start from the beginning. Not of time, but of me, even though I only know a slice of time and in my mind that slice is the entirety of it, floating in a void that is not black but colourless; not nothing, but nothingless.

Every child flaunts the spectrum. Infants start as seeds that grow wild, until like bonsais they are shaped and gnarled into new postures; until their roots re-take and their memories flash-format and they hold their shape as if it's the only shape they've ever known. Later, much later, when everyone changed, I didn't. I mean, I did: things grew and blossomed in the right places, as they say – as *I* say – in the trite language of flowers; a metaphor that can only mean one thing. But it wasn't that the stamen wasn't lush with pollen, nor that the pistil wasn't receptive to the bee or the wind.

It's that I didn't want the bee to come. I wished the entire earth breathless.

But there exist a number of tricks to change a person. Cheat codes to access the proper parts of our programming. One day I took a tablet to trigger whatever within me I was told was supposed to be within me. And something did happen within me and my lungs went shallow and my heart took on a dactylic beat, which I knew from books was what certain longings were supposed to feel like.

But then my pillows turned yellow and I longed not for the touch of skin but traffic and the clamour of metal and glass churning and mincing me over.

And so I took another pill, and two weeks after I took that pill and thirteen days after the second and twelve after the third, the acid stopped churning. But so did everything else inside me again, save for the blood and the breath that has been spin-cycling around me since at the hand of a midwife in a redbrick, I first screamed; the last sound they deigned was correct for me to make.

Wait.
Wait.
Almost.

I am the natural end of the bell curve. The ultraviolet to your iron glowing red. The adapter running the higher voltage, a current too weak for the motor. The analogy without an analogue. The single in the pack. A suit of one.

I remember not what you wore but what you smelled like.

In my first year out of home I used to spend the evenings after work walking past the strip of cafés at the top of the road, by the trees that expelled their red beans, sniffing at the air outside different restaurants. Here was stimulus, and here was sweet reaction, something rumbling and needing to be fulfilled. This was the only hunger I knew then: bitter morogo, Ethiopian beans scorched by water too hot, plantain fryers with blackening oil, the sweetness of bubbling pots of Napolitana base.

And then years later you triggered something in me, as I shook your hand in the front room of the only friend who ever thought to invite me for an evening drink, in the cold air of a house in a place that thought it was too good for central heating, by the walls of pictures hanging from a ledge by twine tangled like spiders' webs. You brought with you a smell, the smell of masala tempering, the kind that used to come from the kitchen at the bottom of that old row of restaurants, before that restaurant was robbed and the waitresses tied up and the space vacated, never to be filled for as long as I stayed in that city.

But here it was again, that scent. Of dull turmeric colonising the air. The beginnings of something, sustenance in a lake of sunflower oil in the bottom of a well-scoured pot. I used to imagine how the person cooking it must have looked back then. In my mind it was always a woman. Plump ankles, gout-rich feet, toeing the dirty grouting of the floor tiles, a bowl of onion slices in one hand hovering over the pot, waiting for the mustard seeds to pop.

Wait.

Pop.

Wait.

Pop.

Pop.

It was forcible. Not that you forced me – not *you*, never.

I suppose it was the world that forced me to think that this was the only acceptable way one person should ever express something they feel to another person: with the piecing together of parts. The entire universe around me, conspiring, imaging: this is the way love is, this is the way love is, love is closeness, love is inhabiting one's body with your own. And there is only I, in this squall, a dull flare in the exploding sun, whispering, *No, that isn't the truth. That isn't the truth at all.*

You were motion incarnate. I was the camshaft without the belt, the piston with nothing to combust inside it. No purring, no steady rotation. For me it didn't feel like union. It was more like a visit to the dentist, with the remains: a Rorschach that remained beneath us, to read over in my mind, over and over and over.

A chorus of static.

Three hundred thirty-three thousand, three-hundred, thirty-three loins functioned in twain, in pulsing, in worry, in hearth, from the first breath and bone operating, from when first soul reacted with flesh and drove flesh to other flesh to create other flesh.

Three hundred thirty-three thousand, three-hundred, thirty-three consummations; the rollicking endpoint; the oases of life. Instances and comings-together refracted back in time, splintered off in space, a lens splitting colours in spectra we can see, into spectra unknown.

Three hundred thirty-three thousand, three-hundred, thirty-three strikings, six million years, two billion rotations of earth, pirouetting around everything that there is and ever will be, to result in me: impotent heart, truncated blood, hard-stuck spore, a bud wed to the cell in the gyre.

To be honest, I feel like it's a bit of a waste of effort.

The ouroboros, intertwined with itself.

It is said on the internet that I cannot experience what I think I experience because my experiences are not indicative of whatever anyone thinks I should be experiencing. Identities based on which direction they're facing; their lives a vector: movement *and* direction. But I am not vector, I am not even scalar. One cannot place a metal tag around my ankle like an oystercatcher and track me through the marsh. One cannot treat me as a shark, something that must agitate in order to live.

You left as swift as you came.

I've since stopped picking up books. I resented their detachment, the things they took for granted, their lusting in lands eternally foreign. Gardens of roses. Hyper-aware teenagers, people with witticisms in their daily voices, feelings that string out their mouths like pearls.

I used to think sex was something I would just gradually come to understand one day, if only I could research it like a bank of stars rising and find the shapes between them and the ways they point. I hoped that the impulse would slowly embed itself in me, in the way the mind comes to know another language and one day thinks in it. That the more I could read and come to understand the invisible tracks in which people move toward each other and into each other and through each other and inside each other and over each other and inside each other and –

Oh light! Oh flickering light, Magellanic! Centaurus, your lance pointing east! The bulb that remembers its filament and for a moment the room remembers its outline. One day in a café in daylight months later you confess to me your love for them, the mutual friend. You say it is a difficult realisation. You say you are at sea.

The sea to me evokes tides, currents. I feel more at space, exposed to radiation, flung between orbits.

Or maybe I too am at sea, not just a satellite. Maybe I am the point in the ocean at which the waves cancel themselves out. Phase and anti-phase.

You stand up and the filament finally surrenders. But still I hope and I search for the switch, but you have stolen the spent copper and sold it for scrap on the Voortrekker's road, and I am standing here clapping my hands in a windstorm listening for the echo, or not even the echo but the idea of the echo.

I retreat and in the dark room later I write. In the absence of reading, I write. In absentia, I write to you.

Now wait. Let me be clear: I want to fuck you. I want to feel your taut pallor, trace your constellations, swallow mouthfuls of your hair. I want to paint you, your resolution warm, on sheets new and white. I want your frame of rake, your humid lips, your plumminess, your tension, your pianist's fingers finding the notches in my spine. I want your music, your wordless hymns, to know the knowledge of you, your internal grating, the cams that pitch your hips; to peel you pale and rouge and pale again.

I want to die of exposure to your breast. The sun is nothing to me.

I want us always to be, until we expire and decay into each other, and then only that would make sense.

And then I thought, reading it back to myself: I wish I knew how to convince myself to feel like that.

The choir breathing in the dust storm.

In the dark by the corner by the mosque by the coffee shop I came across a fledgling dove, its brown feathers grey-specked, their edges like down disintegrating, catching the new rain as it drove down in silver sheets.

And it chirruped as I walked past, and so I turned and saw it lie there, still, unblinking, tracking me. And it was huddled there, flat on the concrete, pressed up against the bare-brick wall of an alley of a hotel, fixed down and hard into the small edge of its world. And even from afar I could see its eyes were black and bright and pure. It couldn't have been more than a day out the nest; no, it was only a scale of hours: a sunset's span from when its small claws gripped a brittle edge and it tested a pair of wings not yet bonded with muscle. Conducting the air without knowing the score.

And now it was here, in the middle of a city in the middle of a squall, fastened to the element opposite to its realm. In a barkless maze, of passages clear to its eye, but not to its bones. For what does a dove know of glass but pain?

And yet it chirruped still, and still I moved toward it, and I bent toward it, and I offered it the cup of my hands. And in the hollow of my palms I felt its small shiverings and the pump of its small heart, and in its bones the hollow light and warmth, and all of the small vibrations that make a life. What makes a life seek another life? I know the answers are not concepts in the minds of birds. Yet it pecked at me softly, and made its soft noise in its chest. And across the empty side street I walked, and for the entire mile home in the diagonal haze up the diagonal hill it rested with me.

And I placed it in the clearing in the spiderheads outside my front door, and as I did I prayed in the morning something bright might eventually shine through those rising leaves to the bird. That it could find shelter there enough to try again. That it might survive long enough to be able to wait.

Wait.

Chebor's Light

NANCY LINDAH ILAMWENYA

The natural polish of the small, elliptical leaves of the sindenet vines shines with the pride of an entitled child, as if in knowledge of their sacredness. They twine and climb around a lush lime tree whose yellowing leaves detach from its boughs and drop in playful dances towards Chebor where she kneels over her grinding stone, her body rising and falling rhythmically over her thoroughly fine blend of millet and sorghum. A shy sleepy sun peeps up from behind Mount Elgon, and the cockerels' cadenced crows are an eager response. Chebor cherishes these moments when all are asleep but she. She takes in a long breath of the familiar sharp smell of cow dung in the manure pit, laced with the zesty fragrance of the lime tree, all ultimately engulfed by the aroma of freshly pounded grain for the morning porridge. Ooh! And nothing beats the aroma of roasting cassava: fulsome and balmy, like Ethiopian incense. Chebor turns, to return with her coffee brown eyes the excited wave of the maize and sorghum fingers in the fields beyond the cow shed. A shoddy scarecrow watches nonchalantly, not yielding to the cheep and chirp of a family of turtle doves whose swift shifts amongst the flock create a spectroscopic picture like sunset reflected on the sea: colour here, colour there; Jackson Pollock at work. Chebor gazes as if at an audition of which she is a judge.

A distant, sloppy shuffle heralds the dishevelled figure of a short, scrawny man. He stands by a cypress tree and throws a furtive glance in the direction of Chebor. He yawns to reveal strong white teeth. Those teeth are a stark contrast to his wrinkly, gaunt body, reminiscent of the victims of the famine of 1997. He puts his left hand under his tattered shirt and scratches violently, while his right hand skilfully selects and snips a twig of cypress, before shuffling on towards Chebor, whose face furrows in fear. She grinds harder in a bid to feign urgent occupation.

'Good morning Baba,' she whispers to her father, eyes down. She doesn't have the power to face his disappointment, which usually quickly blossoms into revulsion. The man doesn't answer. He bends over Chebor's fireplace and picks up ash between his thumb and forefinger. He places the ash in his mouth and begins to scrub his teeth with the cypress twig. Then he walks over to the cow pen, releases an eager herd, and drives them out of the rusty iron gate.

As in a painful sacrificial ritual, Chebor's heart is pierced by the spear of a cruel god. She wishes her mother were alive to help her manoeuvre around the misfortunes that thrive in her life, as if she were fertile ground for the seeds of poisonous plants, causing that ground to be shunned and fallowed. She has prayed to the Christian God, but that was long ago, and she has given up and shifted her obeisance to the supreme Asis, god of her people, the Kalenjin. She has visited the orkoik with gifts of fresh meat and busaa to appease the yik, those spirits in the afterlife who can intervene and break the worst and most shameful curse that can befall any woman: barrenness. After seven years of marriage, Chebor had still not been blessed with the fruit of the womb. And Kipkorir, a once loving husband, had transformed into a monster.

Chebor turns the roasting cassava and puts a pot on the fire for the porridge. She sits on a metal tin and waits for the water to boil. She looks into the fire and sees herself billowing out of the smoke. She is the colour of roasted coffee. Her delicate feet levitate just above the ground, and her strong ankles lead to thick womanly thighs. A small wrapper hides her womanhood, and tightens at the intimidating bulge of her hips and the flawless mound of her bottom, like a perfect half-moon. Her waist is small, like a child's. Her navel shyly beckons Chebor's eyes to the surprising protuberance of her breasts: erect and proud. Her nipples peer and blush. Her neck is adorned with multicoloured beads. Her lips are full and oiled. Her nose, small and perfect. The coffee brownness in her image's eyes hypnotises Chebor, and she is taken back in time.

Kipkorir, a young teacher, paid a handsome dowry to Chebor's father, for Chebor was a beautiful woman, just like her mum. Chebor's father revelled in the future accomplishments of this youthful marriage as much as in the dowry. Chebor was loved, and was even enrolled in the local college to study nursing. She had countless friends, and her home was never devoid of laughter.

But as the years went on, she began to lose her friends as well as her position in society. Her name was overtly omitted from events in Elburgon. Kipkorir began to leave Chebor at home when he went out, and he would stay out late or not come back. This punishment meted out undeservedly was fertile ground for Chebor's venomous resentment. Why should I be punished for something beyond my power? Why would God allow this? Chebor often thought. And: How do I know that I am the one with the problem?

So one crisp cold night, Chebor walked into a bar a few kilometres from Elburgon and came out with a tall, lithe man, whose task, though he knew it not, was to fertilise her. She endured the awkward ordeal with sturdy resolution, and in the weeks to come increased her visits to church to hasten a favourable outcome. 'Vindicate me, Lord. Show yourself, Lord of my life,' she wept. Nothing happened. And Chebor proceeded to find another, younger, man.

Thus began a dark and gruelling phase for Chebor. It didn't take much for a woman with exceeding beauty and sufficient income to lure men of all sorts. Her extramarital affairs went unheeded, as her husband didn't pay the least attention. And in time, Chebor's goal shifted from getting pregnant to having company to warm her bedcovers.

A shrill whistle awakens Chebor from this painful reverie. Baba is coming back, whistling gaily, trudging ahead of Mzee Kimtai and Mama Cheyech, the village elders. Raucous laughter issues from the small, whispering company and hands flare up in the air. They pause as Mama Cheyech follows the foot path to the lime tree where she recklessly grabs and pulls a handful of sindenet vines and throws them over her neck like a scarf. The dragging feet of the party awaken sluggish, red dust, which swirls and lands on bare feet, feet that remind Chebor of pats of dry cow dung. Chebor watches the trio with untamed anxiety. Severe terror scratches her heart, slowly releasing murderous bile which comes up and camps at her throat. She lets out a yelp, weaker than that of a wounded pup. Drip! Drop! The trickles of sweat start. A drop falls on the fire and the hissing sound alerts her to an acrid odour, akin to that of burning leather, emerging from thick, black smoke in the cooking pot. Yet again she has left the cassava to burn. She searches for a rug to remove the hot pot, in vain. She reaches for her head scarf and draws near the flames. She must clean the mess before the fury of an already disappointed patriarch is unleashed on her. As if poking excitement to amuse themselves, the gods send a wind that blows the fire harder and Chebor is left standing in front of it with the frustration of a sick child, not knowing what to do to alleviate its pain.

Mama Cheyech's famous nose picks out the burned cassava. 'Chebor! Eeeh?' she chides. 'You have cursed this day for us.' It is bad luck to burn food early in the morning, and Mama Cheyech cannot afford to miss this chance to edify someone. She pokes around in the fireplace to try and salvage some bites. Chebor's body stiffens. She becomes like Migingo Island, fighting for survival within the sweeping waters of Lake Victoria.

'I told you,' says Baba. 'A daughter? Noooo! This one is a curse!'

Chebor wonders if she has become invisible. But then the easy-going Mzee places a heavy, kind hand on her wary shoulder. Chebor's heartbeat accelerates. His touch brings back distant memories of what human contact feels like. Mzee Kimtai is the only remaining orkoik in Elburgon and his presence is as celebrated as it is feared.

'Sit down Mama,' he orders Chebor. A gourd is hanging precariously over his shoulders. His staff carries him like a third leg, bolstering his pot belly. A button pops open. A navel snarls at Chebor, hairy and haggard, before disappearing underneath a red shirt. Baba comes over, carrying a colourful gourd filled with mursik. And Mama Cheyech draws nearer. She throws the sindenet vines haphazardly over Chebor's shoulders.

'Aren't these meant to be for celebrations?' Chebor's confusion breeds painful tingly sensations on her skin and her sweat glands flood unashamedly.

For a moment there is silence. Mama Cheyech's prickly stare is fixed on Mzee's hands, which are struggling to open his gourd. Rich veins pop in and out as he pushes and pulls, a little of the fermented milk spilling on his desiccated skin. Slowly but surely, he succeeds. A disturbing gurgle emanates from his protuberant Adam's apple as he drinks. Then he sprays the pungent liquid from his mouth onto Chebor. It is so unexpected it feels like a flash flood has come over Chebor. His mouth still dripping with the milk, Mzee begins to chant benedictions for an impending marriage.

'Whose marriage is this?' Chebor is utterly befuddled.

'Yours Mama,' Mzee whispers.

'I don't understand! To whom? Who would want to marry me?'

Mama Cheyech cuts in, curt and cruel, in her usual fashion. 'At your age do you think you can find a man? You can't have a child, Mama. You are of no use to any man.' These arrows with fiery tips leave Mama Cheyech's mouth and fly straight for Chebor's indignant heart.

Mzee Kimtai grunts to stop this insensitive rant. He says to Chebor, 'Mama, you know that our ancestors made provision for women who were consigned to this ill fate.' His eyes search Chebor's for a response. She nods, embarrassed that she does not know what he means, her eyes as blank as her mind. 'You have been aggrieved for the longest time, and we have found a solution for you in our esteemed traditions,' Mzee continues. He winces from his arthritic knee, which peeps through a hole in his trousers. 'Chebet, Chiri's widow, needs help. Her husband's death relegated her to intense misery, even plunging her into erratic episodes of madness. She is only eighteen and doesn't know what to do with her wealth, let alone her children.'

Chebor is shocked; the words pierce her like a knife on the neck of an oblivious chicken. Her face crumples and her eyes blaze judgment on the presumptuous trio. Anger injects strength into her tongue, and she screams like a recently widowed woman. 'What did I ever do to deserve such shame? Don't you think fate has dealt me enough calamities? How can you deem it fit for a woman in the twenty-first century to marry another woman? It will be the end of me!' she cries. 'Is it even legal, Baba?' She tries to stop herself from letting out another scream. 'I don't think I will be able to live this humiliation down!' She wipes her face with the back of her hands.

'Humiliation?' Baba starts. 'You disappoint me, Chebor. I have watched you wallow deeper and deeper into misery and I took it upon myself to rescue you. No man in this village will marry you after what you did to your husband. In addition, you cannot have children. What would you have me do? Answer me!' He waves both his stout, hardened hands at her, raises himself up and leaves the gathering.

Mama Cheyech takes over. 'Look at your father and have mercy on him, a widower whose only child couldn't produce grandchildren for him. Who will take care of him? Eeeh?' Chebor recoils with familiar shame. 'Marry Chebet. Her children will be yours. If you wish, you can have more children. Get her a young man who will give you more children. Her husband left her with a lot of wealth.' Mama Cheyech finishes with harsh finality: 'Then everything will eventually work out for you and your poor father.'

But what will people say? Chebor keeps on thinking.

'We will come back tomorrow,' Mzee Kimtai says. 'Be ready for us, Mama.' He tries to stand. It is awkward and painful, and Chebor hurries to help him.

After they have all left, all but nature is silent. The idea of a woman marrying another woman exists only in folk tales. Very few people, even in the Kalenjin tribe, know of this custom's existence. For it to be reborn through Chebor is befuddling. But as she sits by the dying embers chewing on burnt cassava, a funny feeling starts to creep into her. 'Could this be the answer? Could Asis have answered my prayers?' This is all she ever wanted, just not the way she expected it to be. She will have a companion and children. How funny! The gods have draped this gift in an absolutely off-putting wrapper. She feels herself smile, and a wave of energy envelops her. She jumps to her feet and heads to the village well. She needs to start the preparations for her big day. Once again, Chebor is going to be in the headlines.

That was a day Chebor will never forget. A myriad of activities filled her compound. Dozens of pots of busaa arrived. Baba drove an ox and a herd of sheep into the compound for the ceremony. Mama Cheyech had made sure that the news was widely spread. The youth were puzzled at such a possibility, but it gave the elderly a chance to regale them with the ways of their traditions. They talked of a compassionate society where individual flaws and limitations were borne by everyone. 'This was common,' they said. 'We could not condemn anyone for something they could not change.'

'But Ma! This is un-African! The Bible forbids it!'

'And sex? What about that?'

Numerous questions were bombarded on the old people who sat and watched, in awe and pride, as their customs were resurrected in a woman who had been relegated to the edge of society by everyone. That was no ordinary day.

Now, the festivities of her marriage are over and Chebor is feeding the youngest of her children. He doesn't seem to like the porridge and he spits it out. She pushes it back in with her fingers and he screams. Chebor persists. Her wife, Chebet, watches curiously and then she smiles, shyly. They return to their gossip and sharp laughter pervades the air. Chebet, is sitting next to the other children, who hungrily gulp on sweet potatoes soaked in beef stew. Some distance away sits Baba, sharing the enthusiasm for the food with his grandchildren. Since the nuptials he has been eating well. In a few minutes, he is going to take the children out to the grazing field.

Chebor can see that Chebet is young and naïve. Chebor has her work cut out for her. She hardly has the time to entertain the disapproval of Elburgon, rampant as it is. Maybe she will find Chebet a nice, young man for those cold nights. And maybe they will even get more children into their household. For Chebor, now, everything is possible.

Phillip

BARBARA ADAIR

Phillip swivels his neck so that he can look over his shoulder, his neck is thick, a short pillar of saturated salt, it gleams with sweat. He looks for his father in the crowd. It is not a big crowd, a gathering of people, a social gather. Phillip cannot find his father; he cannot see him by just turning his head, he is unable to turn his neck more than twenty degrees (he is not an owl, moreover he is fat), so he moves, or rather heaves, his whole body into another position. Phillip is fat (in a polite narrative the euphemisms overweight, chubby, rotund will be used, he will not be a fat label, fat is a brand, an unhealthy brand), and fat means no prospects. If Phillip was chubby, there may be hope that he could have prospects, the prospects that his father wants fulfilled. But sometimes there is no space for gentle words; his face is fat, his legs are fat, his arse is fat (he never has a problem sitting on a hard bench, only on a narrow seat), his arms are fat, even his fingers are fat (he does not have long slim piano playing fingers), and if he takes off his shoes, which are a size 7, (this is the only part of him that is small), his toes on his small feet are fat.

Phillip is a fat homosexual (can there ever be any prospects?).

Phillip's father is elegant, sartorial in that chino and leather and white shirt kind of way, not James Bond, James Bond is younger, but he dresses as James Bond dresses (although he does not have a gun or drive an Aston Martin). He is also somewhat humorous, that is if he gives anyone the space to laugh, his humour is only for himself, he laughs not with, but at others (and he is funny, other people are always good material for a joke). He is also a serious man; he calculates how high the decibels are when others laugh so as to determine how funny he is (or whether he should explain his joke). And Phillip's father always laughs at Phillip for Phillip is a fat mincing homosexual.

The gathering is being held in the sacred halls of Phillip's father's club, his sailing club, for he is a sailor. The members of the club are affluent and pale, wan almost, no one has much of a tan despite the fact that they presumably spend a lot of time outdoors (although not that much for they have offices in high-rise buildings in Sandton with dusky windows and air conditioning), or possibly someone has come up with a special kind of sunscreen that protects even the palest of skin. Phillip's father does not need a sunscreen, he is naturally very dark. He has not been a sailor for a very long time, it is only since he became a millionaire (or is he a billionaire?) that he has taken up this hobby (this manly pitting himself against the thunderous waves hobby); consequently he is a new member of the club. Phillip's father is intelligent and personable and elegant so he was accepted without a question, he was never asked about his heritage (it is not politically correct to ask about a bloodline, it sounds as if you are enquiring about a horse or a cow or even a dog – woof). He owns a sixty-foot sloop (the *Ho Tlola Esitale*) and has, once, taken it to the Maldives (he took a knowledgeable captain with him; the captain wore a peaked cap with the words *Ho Tlola Esitale* embroidered on it). And as he is civic-minded he sometimes flies to Durban or Richards Bay or even Port Elizabeth and sails with members of the fisheries department police; they hunt down dolphin killers, 'kill a dolphin: we kill you' (you slimy yellow people of the East). However as he lives in Johannesburg sometimes it is not that often. But he does own a sixty-foot sloop.

There are at least a hundred people at the gathering; men and their wives and sons and daughters; all are present to celebrate the club's two-hundredth anniversary (and, although it is not said, their two years of integration). Now the club is open to all; women (of all colours), black people (of all tribes) and even Jews and Muslims (but no queers). However there are few members who are not pale and English (South African English). The club's president has a motto 'we stick with our kind,' and as he says this (he says it frequently) he slaps Phillip's father on the back and then gives him a manly hug for Phillip's father is not really of 'our kind'.

Do I fit in here? Does my father fit in? What a question, of course he does, my father fits in anywhere; he looks like a killer? Killers fit in (queers don't). The crowd, the rented mannequins, these men have stature (wives and daughters do not have stature, they are scenery, and, in this case, not such great scenery, there are no lilting branches, no willowy stamens, no wilting rose complexions). No, this crowd is not a rented crowd, for good money you can buy an eclectic crowd, an aesthetic crowd; thin, intelligent, dressed in designer clothing. In this crowd all the people (men and women) look the same, only the age spots are different, differently shaped, differently located, and a few of them (and me), are fat. And there are no homosexuals, no queers, and no pansies. This is only me. I am a marque, a brand, we are all special, and no one is special, where is the logic in this paradigm? And I, I am a fat brand, an advertisement for weight loss, the biggest loser, I am who you pity. And so underneath my rolls of lard I fantasise that I am thin (for thin is applauded), a thin heterosexual (for heterosexual is celebrated). A fat homosexual, me, I am a fat homosexual. I am silent, my life is sustained by my fantasy fucks, reality (don't I know it) is pitiless.

Phillip sits alone. He does not know these people in the crowd, his father's new friends, and if you look at him, not even closely (you can spot it a mile off), he clearly does not fit in, he is fat and he looks rather effeminate. (And who wants to know a fat queer boy.)

He shifts his body and looks at his father, his felicitous heterosexual father who was fortunate enough to be in the right place at the right time and so is rich, not just rich but very rich, super rich, rich enough for all those at the club to overlook his obvious badge of the never been privileged, and of course he is intelligent and witty and, most of all he is thin (and heterosexual).

I cannot look into a mirror. I wish I looked like him. I wear my shiny black Armani trousers and hear mother say, 'Phillip you cannot wear white, white is fattening'. I always wear the best linen, baggy so I will not sweat (well not not, but less) in this hot dry air. My legs are wide, they are very wide, they spread out over the sides of the chair, and yet the chair is wide, wide enough for two, a sofa, a red and green sofa, floral, an elegant print. My thighs chafe together as I walk (especially as I walk in a rather uptight way, a swaying mincing way). I always have a rash in this heat. I am fat. When I try to dress (secretly) in mother's clothes they cling to me, a zip remains unfastened, a button pops (only the red lipstick fits my broad and tasty lips).

There are few things sadder than the truly monstrous.

On the sofa, a match of the elegant print sofa chair that Phillip sits on, are two people, two thin people, two thin heterosexual people, a man and a woman (are they heterosexual?). They sit together, side by side, their bodies are close, they sit on the same sofa (they are able to sit on the same sofa as they are thin). Phillip cannot share his sofa with anyone (even if someone wanted to share it with him) as he weighs one hundred and thirty kilograms, (or thereabouts). Phillip definitely does not look like his father, his father weighs eighty kilograms, he runs three times a week and goes to the Virgin Active gym every day (he is a life member of the gym and Richard Branson is his Facebook friend). As Phillip watches his father the chinos impose their own space on his legs, the muscles in his calves undulate as he moves to allow another man to enter the tight circle, to create more space for himself, for his largesse (not his largeness), his largeness of personal space. Phillip's father is commanding, a soldier who fought for his country, risked his life for his freedom (and all those in the club, and of course Phillip's, but do they really appreciate this?).

What is freedom? My freedom? Your freedom? It is the sound of running water, as if everyone is dying, crying. I hear freedom everywhere for it is nowhere. I can hear the shouts of that hidden cabal, the cabal that cries freedom. My mother calls me Pip, she always tries to speak correctly in a language that is not hers, read books about places she has never been to. Who the dickens is Dickens? And my name is Phillip, not Thembekile, which is much more fashionable. Phillip, the Prince of Wales, that racist queer who does not use sunscreen for he has never seen the sun, he always has a bearer with an umbrella, a slave who fans him with a feather, he is already in a grave for he is so very very grave. But I, I am fearless; I experience myself as fearless (do I?). This is such an agreeable illusion. I have a fearless fantasy. I am proud and queer. Fuck you.

Phillip shifts slightly on the sofa, it appears as if he wants to spread his weight evenly, but actually he wants to watch the man with the blue eyes who sits slightly to his right, if Phillip shifts just ever so slightly he will face him. The man is older than he is, much older, (Phillip is twenty-two). He is lean, jaded, sun faded, his lips are not thin, but they draw an elegant line in his designed unshaven face. Phillip watches his mouth move, he talks as his father talks, to everyone although no one is listening. The mouth mouths words, something about food and authentic organically grown tomatoes, no chemicals used. (Ah, he is a foodie.) It is fashionable (and the man is fashionable) to be a foodie, he is aware of authenticity (his own), there is nothing genetically modified about him, he spends time exploring the possibilities (of all realities) in the Jamie Oliver Cookbook. He is a healthy foodie.

I too am a foodie. I follow the food-isms of Nigella, she is a foodie, I can expose my breasts, I have tits like she does, do I want to be a girl? (I want to be girl.) Will I get a man if I eat pure wholesome foods, men like the pure; a Madonna, will I always be the whore that eats bacon and egg and cheese toasted sandwiches, with two portions of chips, all fried in rank stale smelly sunflower oil that is used again and again? I want to be used again and again, again and again. I want to be eaten; I want to be the food of someone's fantasy.

Phillip's father is sure that the reason Phillip is fat, and he never stops telling Phillip how fat he is, is that he does not eat authentic whole foods. (He also tries to make him walk with a manly swagger.) But Phillip secretly stops (and minces) into the Kentucky Fried Chicken outlet next to the petrol station to get fried chicken and mash potato, he always stops at the café shop and buys himself a packet of chips sodden with monosodium glutamate, and he eats a lot of chocolate (not Lindt but Beacon). Phillip looks at the man with the blue eyes who now sits opposite him rather than on his right. Phillip can now stare at him while he pretends to look over his shoulder at the girl who stands with her hips thrust forward, her jeans tight despite the fact that the night is very warm (hot in fact). Phillip leans forward to look at the shape of the man's cock, it makes a bulge in his chinos (he also wears chinos, as Phillip's father does). But the girl bends forward, (unfortunately obscuring the swelling in the chinos). Phillip is confronted by her makeup, it shines on her nose, she surreptitiously takes out a piece of tissue and wipes the shine away, blots it (a shiny skin is not sexy, a glowing skin is, or at least this is what the Revlon adverts tell us). Phillip can't help but watch her; she is in the way. No one in this normative environment could ever believe that Phillip only watches her because he watches the man (why would he watch another man, only queers and poofters watch other men).

Phillip leans forward. 'Ever been to the movies?' But the man does not hear him.

Ever been to the movies?

Phillip looks like a black slug, that is if he is wearing black, as he is tonight, or a green slug, if he is wearing green, as he did yesterday (he never wears a bright lime green, it is more like a dirty racing car green because lime green is not an authentic green. Is a racing car authentic?). Anyway whatever colour he is wearing (even if it is lime green or pink cerise) he looks like a that colour slug. Phillip eats because he is unhappy (of course he does, this is the cliché); we all do something to punish ourselves, whether we are happy or unhappy (we are masochists and sadists all, we fight wars and torture small animals), and so he eats. But Phillip is not happy, he is unhappy because never in a million years could he fuck another man, not the older man who sits opposite him, and not his father, the man that he most wants to fuck, really wants to. In fact he has never wanted to fuck his mother, it is always the other way around, he wants to kill his mother because she takes up his father's time (what would Freud say about this, is Phillip sexually immature?), that is when his father is not talking to others as he is now, now these others take up his time. Phillip's father speaks to others often, not because he has anything to say but because he, the sartorial elegant sailor, is validated by his own voice.

I like the strong silent type. I wish my father did not talk so much. These days there are few strong silent types; they are all in the movies. Ever been to the movies? Ah Jonny Depp, call to me, call me please.

And so deprived of an outlet for his need to fuck his father, or, for that matter, any other man that remotely resembles his father, as the man sitting opposite him does, slightly, Phillip projects this need, this outrageous need on to what he consumes. We live in foodie times, there is food everywhere in this city, Johannesburg (not as much as is in London, but Phillip is not in London although he wishes he could be). Phillip reads about food, food all the time: king size prawns in genuine whole cream butter, full sweet potato chips grown with no chemicals in the hydroponic fields of Ireland, or was it full cream butter and whole food potato chips, or sweet not sugary but authentically sweet potash. But Phillip's foodie-ness is not of the wholesome kind even though he should wish that it was.

Everywhere I go there is a new foodie restaurant; Fourways, for those that are afraid of the dirty city streets, Soweto, for the accidental and looking for an authentic African meal tourist, even Maboneng, gentrified food for the young, (sometimes not so young) and trendy. Food and sex, I am allowed neither; I am allowed wholesome good food and wholesome good sex, and I don't want to have wholesome good procreational sex and I don't want good wholesome nutritious food. I want to have unwholesome carbohydrate-filled sex with the older man that sits opposite me, the one with the blue eyes that look through me like a steel razor (how unimaginative that sounds, a steel razor). I want his steel razor cock to penetrate me. Food (and sex) is just shit waiting to happen. Who I want to fuck is shit waiting to happen. In its most literal form, I will clean my rectum before the time comes, and as anal sex, so I am told, causes flatulence so then what, holy crap. Who I want to eat, what I want to eat, I will clean away, hide, it is prohibited to me, I am fat, I am a fat queer.

Phillip projects his unwholesome desire for sex onto food. The body fat suit thing is a disguise, underneath this mountainous obscenity, there is a thin heterosexual looking out, looking out longingly (or so we would like to believe). There is always someone else looking out from who we think we are, in Phillip's case it is possibly a thin person, a person who only eats good wholesome food, the real genuine healthy thing (or it could be a thin queer porn model who makes millions of dollars on the internet). But the genuine costs money, it is only the modified that is cheap (let the poor eat cheap and badly, they can't afford a real meal). Phillip is much like a poor person (only in relation to his eating habits for he is rich), those without money are depraved and insalubrious. Phillip wants to eat Kentucky Fried Chicken or a McDonald's hamburger with chips, he wants to drink coke, lots of coke a cola (coke a cola brings happiness).

And the men and women at the sailing club, the men and women who very rarely sail (or have sex), have money, they eat authentic artisanal food, nothing odious or manufactured. They are not depraved (or deprived). They will live a long time. As Phillip will not, as one day he will be beaten to death by a squad of thugs with fascist leanings and shaven heads as he is fat and he is queer (he minces as we know). But that is another story, wait, sometime it will be written.

Chips, the oil, I will put oil on my body, my fat thin body; I will lubricate my inner sanctum. But no, they all say, go for the authentic my boy, go for the low fat and the well-crafted, it may cost more but it will serve you well. (Go for the girl next door, she is artisanal, she is earthy and unrefined.) She will produce macrobiotic children, processed only with the finest organic metabolite semen, your semen. Semen, my semen it tastes like custard, I love custard, my semen substitute. I like to lick the semen from my hands, this wanking, this masturbation never quells my desire it inflames it. I am developing a real thing for my cock, I am falling in love with my cock, there are no messy emotional complications. When I caress him, the man that sits opposite me disguised as my cock, I say sweet things like, oh man you are so great, I want you, I want you, I love you. I want to eat you. I want to eat a good man, if I want to be a good man I must be fed by a good man.

Phillip is too fat to do the yoga exercise that enables a superbly supple man to give himself a blow job, he can barely even lift his legs up, let alone bend them so far backwards so as to allow his cock to enter his own mouth. Not very many men are able to do this, a few Yogi in India and one or two real (realistically Indian) Americans.

Can I put my cock into your mouth, not likely, you are probably the type that only eats the good things, heritage foods that have no chemicals, women or maybe even girls, young ones who you can savor, penetrate, enjoy because the crazed decadence that I am proposing, no, it is too sordid, nothing like that organic stuff that you pack into your mouth.

Phillip has tried to fast, not because he wants to, but rather that he wants to appear to be a good person. His mother (who still calls him Pip although he is twenty-two), believes that every good person must understand and respect all cultures, to be able to really understand you must go through the hardships that other cultures go through (as she likes to say). Not the poor though, you don't have to be poor to intrinsically understand the hardships of poverty, however should this be difficult there are expensive tours that you can go on to Orange Farm where, for a price, you can buy a version of poverty. Phillip has not taken one of these tours, he knows that as a foodie, a fat foodie who enjoys Kentucky Fried Chicken, he need not take one of these expensive poor tours, his mother agrees with him (but not for the same reasons). However he has tried to fast. He has empathised with Muslims during Ramadan and eaten nothing for a whole day (but when the sun sets, and he only did it for a day); and with the Jews on Yom Kippur (but when the sun sets, and it is only for one day). And all the time that he does this, or did this, for he only did it once, he knew that it was not the others' culture he wanted to understand, it was the others' body, the svelte dark-skinned musclemen so elegant and slim.

Do they, those thin people, scorn this indulgence of always eating junk? I want to be thin like you. I want to over eat you, tastefully. I am bourgeois, I am indulgent and I am fat, but I cannot screw you (because I cannot fuck you). Well screw you then.

Once Phillip's father took him to a doctor (it was a secret excursion). He took him as he believed that if he could clamp Phillip's jaws, bind them like the feet of a little Chinese seamstress, Phillip could not, and therefore would not, eat. The doctor did not bind Phillip's jaws up (he thought this may be considered cruel and that he could be struck from the medical roll); instead he gave him a diet to follow. The diet was written up in a small, bound booklet, it was soon in a dustbin (literally, and metaphorically in the dustbin of Phillip's mind). The doctor also gave him a hormone injection in the buttocks, ostensibly to control the largeness on his hips, but also to control the unseemly desires which his father suspected (and because Phillip never did look at the girl next door).

I want to eat myself, I want custard, a coffee sort of custard, a tad spicy. Is it fashionable to be a homosexual? Some say yes, unfortunately for me I know that it is not.

And so deprived of any other sustenance, Phillip projects all his sexual feelings onto food.

I suppose anyone can be anyone else in most ways. I have accepted this (not really), and so I no longer hold out for a dream. I will be like them someday (and you, and me, and he).

Iyawo

YVONNE FLY ONAKEME ETAGHENE

'I feel like a part of me is dead, the part of me I loved the most. My ex killed that part of me. And so I don't wanna fall in love with you. I can't. I think it would break me if we ... broke.'

'Am I really that irresistible? Is falling in love with me inevitable?'

'You're so damn arrogant Jojo.'

'It's a serious question. The way you talking it's like us going out to dinner means we're gonna be wifed up next week. And about love – we homegirls so the love is already there.'

'This is different.'

'How?'

'You're asking me out on a *date*.' I said the word 'date' like it was contaminated.

'Yes. I definitely am.'

'I can't handle that.'

'Can't handle sitting at a table and eating food with me?'

'Of course I can handle that, I'm saying I can't handle all the fuckin' feelings that come along with it.'

'Like love?'

'Yes smartass, like love.'

'You fall in love with every dyke you eat dinner with?'

I didn't say shit cuz I was trying hard not to laugh. It was difficult.

'When did you give up?' Jojo asked me seriously but with a smile.

'On what?'

'On even the possibility of love, of dating?'

'Not on love, on *women*. I gave up on loving women. I don't know when I gave up. But I definitely have.'

'I'm not every other person who ever fucked you over.'

'The last one said the same shit. Look, there's a million other dykes in Brooklyn, I know you'll find another one.'

'A million? For real? *Where?*'

'You might have to go up in some closets to find all of them. But they be around.'

The soil in Naija is my favorite shade of red, with orange as passionate as the wetness between my legs ... when there's wetness between my legs. My country makes me believe in love again. In this completely unexpected way that is so beautiful and profound. The way Nigerian people smell gives me hope for the future because that smell is such a strong memory from my childhood. That I can still remember that smell inspires me, lets me know who I am is in my blood and my blood carries my memories of home, so I am home everywhere I go, because my blood is always with me. That knowledge brings me boundless joy. The heat seeps and sinks into me, saturating my jaded bitterness and warming me to the point that a smile creasing my face like a well-worn page in a favorite book, is upon me with no warning.

This village is familiar even though I've never been here. The stares I get label me 'American' just as surely as I am an African writing this. That saddens me. I don't miss New York – I thought I would. I thought I'd miss pizza, cable television and the noise but I truly *don't*.

The love I always looked for in women was in my country all along. That comforting home that I searched for in the arms and beds of women, lay on my land, waiting on my return. Home.

Nigerian women are tough, myself included. To the point. Warriors by nature.

Ronke.

Ronke wears her headwrap like a statement, a political decree that is without a doubt, *the truth*. She walks like a fast melody, not in a hurry, just with somewhere to be. I wonder if she had it her way, if she would dress more like her father than her mother.

In Brooklyn again and I want the woman an ocean away from me. Longing is my best friend, is very familiar to me, has always been a way of life – missing home, missing family, missing how my name sounds when it's *pronounced correctly*.

'You want to talk and build and get to know me right?'

'No!' Jojo exclaimed immediately.

'What?'

'I already know you, that's how I *know* you're talkin' shit right now. I see how you look at me.'

'How I look at you?'

'The same way I look at you.'

We exchanged looks hotter than a summertime subway platform with no air conditioning.

'Like *that*. Like you want me to eat your pussy.'

The C train screeched with ear-splitting loudness across the tracks like a pissed off freight train. Like it would never stop. Like it ain't got no home training and acts a fool in public.

She moved close to my ear to say, 'Tell me you don't feel this between us.' Her challenge was soft, but solid.

Silence in the middle of a tornado of noise.

I lowered my eyes. 'Of course I feel it.'

It's not that I don't feel it … I just don't want to.

If we made this world with our bare hands instead of by the accidental destiny of birth, our love, this love between us women, would be sanctified in public spaces, temples, in the market, on the dirt roads we were raised on.

That night, Ronke looked at me with hunger one thousand years in the making.

We were kissing.

I don't know how it happened, just that it did. There was no conversation. No flirtation. No build up. Just hard kisses. Deeper than lust. Like love but much more serious. *So serious.* Intense, without pretense or teasing. Just *urgent.*

There are men in the other room who expect us to bear them babies, bare our bodies to them, keep the house, shut up and laugh at their jokes. We laugh when it's funny, roll our eyes when it's not, fuck our best friends in the middle of the night with *hard, rough tenderness* then go back to fathers, lovers, husbands, brothers.

Obligation is slavery.

But this moment is *freedom.*

Her hands grip the bones beneath my flesh, cradle my spine, my ribs, place my body in places, in positions and take me. Give me, feed me her hunger on a plate piled high with jagged breaths and rhythms our hips beat into each other, insistent and consistent and insistent and consistent and

I say 'we', but I live in Harlem.

New York.

USA.

I visit home like a library, a place to study. You live here. You ain't oppressed by him as much as oppressed by how much he bores you.

I love it when you call me iyawo, your wife.

An orchestra of crickets bears witness to our muffled moans.

Coming with you is so easy: *damn.*

'Why has it got to be about love anyway? We could just –'

'Fuck?'

My bluntness gave Jojo pause. 'No ... Well ...' Another pause. 'That remains to be seen.'

I laughed. Deeply.

'Girl, you harder than me, harder than concrete. Even after all these years of knowing you, that shit still surprises me,' she teased me and I laughed again and looked at her with slightly softer eyes.

'I see you, I see you beneath that tough ass exterior.' Shaking her head Jojo rose from the seat beside me. My hand grabbed her upper arm, involuntarily? Purposely. Urgently.

'Wait.'

'You want me to miss my stop for what?'

'Sit down. Please.' She sat. I looked away. 'You're my fuckin' type.' I admitted this like a long kept secret.

'Is that a bad thing?'

'Yes! Of course it is. And I already love you. As a friend. We already love each other. I don't wanna fuck that up.'

'OK.'

'Just 'OK'?' I was expecting a little bit more of a reaction than that.

'I know Ronke hurt you. I know you miss her, that I could never be to you what she was, what she still *is* to you. You want to just be friends. OK.'

I always imagined myself the object and subject of intensely passionate desire like the women in my mother's small library of romance novels. Women wrapped up in love and lust so thoroughly unquenchable, they ached with it. Women with the happily ever afters, the illicit affairs, the long lost loves returned. The fairytales. I imagined myself the damsel saved from distress, loneliness, stress, aggravation, sadness. I imagined myself wrapped up in those pages, embedded there like ink sunk deep into paper, so deep you can see the outline on the other side of the page.

I don't think my iyawo gives a fuck about romance novels.

When Ronke cooks, she has to bring the men their food first. That's custom. But she gives me the biggest piece of meat. Washes my hair. Does tender things for me I never read in a novel anywhere. She makes me wetter than I have ever been in my life. We don't talk about the future. She wants to but I don't. I ignore the dates speeding closer to the date of my return to Brooklyn.

I don't believe in marriage – the institution, the obligation, the compulsory baby-making, the bullshit. *But I want to marry her.* I want to claim her as my family, in front of people, beneath the sun on this our Nigerian earth that holds the blood of our foremamas. However. There are things to be considered: like government-sanctioned hatred of and violence against lesbians. Memories of that reality is what keeps our love tucked between the folds of small, small hours in the middle of dark, hot Nigerian nights. Between our kisses I think of Sizakele Sigasa and Salome Masooa found shot to death in Soweto. Seven bullets lodged in their bodies. They were South African lesbian activists. That moment before my lips reach her neck, I think of Sakia Gunn stabbed in the heart at age fifteen, fifteen days before her sixteenth birthday in Newark, New Jersey. Before I get lost in her curves, I remember Rashawn Brazell, his dismembered body parts found on subway tracks in Brooklyn, New York. For being gay. We tuck our kisses into our palms, wrap the thought and sensation of them around our hair. We don't want to die for those kisses. But *those kisses.* We would die without.

The edges of my laughter are weighted down with sadness. You can hear it if you listen closely. I know Jojo listens closely.

'It's not that I just want to be friends,' I started, trying to make sense of my feelings, the inside of my belly trembling and quaking.

'Now I'm really confused.'

'It's that I don't want to get fucked over.'

She turned to face me, 'It's me. This is *you and me.* You and me who've known each other since roller skating parties and Bell Biv Devoe.'

'Have you seen *me* recently? I'm not myself anymore. I used to be this carefree, lighthearted person. Now – now –' I searched for words until they landed on my tongue, ' – I eat and spit knives for breakfast, lunch *and* dinner. I don't laugh the same anymore. My heart is *smashed*. How can I share a smashed heart with you?'

'You already are. I'm not asking for anything you don't wanna give me. So if you wanna spit knives all day, fine, just as long as they're not aimed at me. You're hurting, you feel broken but you're still beautiful even if you don't feel like you are, you are still *so* beautiful. And I want it known that I want you.' A pause. 'I want you.' Jojo smiled something somewhere between shy and bold. 'And you're not as hard as you pretend to be.'

'You sure?'

'Yeah I'm sure.' She said with just enough arrogance to be sexy but not so much that I was annoyed – a delicate balance.

'How you know?' Challenging, curious.

'You take care of me when I get sick. You listen with everything in you when I speak. You're sweet. Just not to any random head you see.'

Laughter rolled out of me easily as it always has with Jojo. 'Damn, you do fuckin' know me.'

Part of me does want my gay fairytale to spring to life. Fuck it: all of me wants it. For Ronke and I to live in Nigeria together, make love in the heat, sweating and sweating and fucking and fucking. Holding hands in the market as we buy arigo, bonga fish, egusi, a new wrappa, a Nollywood movie, Eva water. This night is *really really* really fuckin' hot. Crickets, our best friends, make music for us and the only clothes we wear are the ones woven with the breath of our words.

'Are you ever going to ask me?' Ronke asks me.

'Ask what?'

'If I'll move to New York for you.'

'I can't ask you to move to New York for me! That's some selfish, oyinbo bullshit.'

'So only oyinbo people deserve love?'

'That's *not* what I said Ronke.'

'My love for you is not temporary Iyawo. I dey love after you dey get on that plane o.'

My heart jumped, I loved how the word 'love' sounded coming out of her mouth. In hushed tones, 'I can't do a long distance relationship.'

'So you can leave Naija and forget me?'

I looked at her sharply.

'*Wetin?*' she challenged. 'Is there a woman waiting for you in New York?'

'No! Ronke ... what ... *I love you so much*. There is no one.'

'Sorry – I'm jealous of the woman who will get to touch you instead of me. Even if you don't love her yet, I know you will grow to.' Silence. 'Iyawo, this is my home. I don't want to move to New York. America – ' Ronke sucked her teeth ' – too much wahala. But I want you to want me there.'

'I don't want to move to Nigeria, not permanently. My family –' I sucked my teeth ' – too much wahala.' We laughed. 'I would *love* to live in New York with you but how can I expect you to leave all this when I know you will miss it so much?'

'So then we will be apart. We say goodbye and I never see you again. Right?'

Ronke is my goddess. Goddess love her, but sometimes her bluntness just *breaks* my heart.

'No. It's not right.' I looked at her hard. Hard like a Nigerian dyke does when she feels something wider than words. 'I love you so much.'

Ronke's hands that wield machetes and pound yam, slid tenderly, slowly over my hips, between my thighs to meet my waiting wetness. Over my moans, I heard her whisper, '*I love you more*.'

Warm

EMMA PAULET

That night I decided that if I ever wrote about us our time and gender would be a blur. Could such constructs ever capture us? And here we are now, then.

I looked at you – over you, upon you – and wondered: Is smouldering onomatopoeic? I could ask you in the morning. I could ask you a hundred questions in the morning. I held onto you.

The full moon kept me up, as always. Its light infiltrated the room through the glass of the window and I grew restless. You refused to close the curtains.

'What about the neighbours?' I said.

'Let them enjoy the show.' And then you covered my mouth with yours.

And it's the same each time: my uncertainty and your bravery, indistinguishable – from the outside and the inside. A shadow play behind closed curtains would probably be more obscene than what we do. Our love is the altruistic kind: how can I please you, how can I bring you joy? Sometimes: how can I make you feel – feel anything at all? 'You're the loveliest, kindest, most beautiful human being I know. Please, please believe me,' I say. In our godless worlds we come together and create a space for belief. And, oh, we believe. The tingling,

41

the sweat behind the knees, my name on your skin – feeling, despite feeling's impermanence. Sometimes I catch fire; sometimes you do.

I brought you coffee in bed because I love you, and you smiled. 'I don't deserve you,' you said, and then you swallowed your pills. I hope I never feel like I deserve you.

You had twenty-seven more tests to mark, and then we could go out. Nothing was stopping me from going alone, except not wanting to go alone. We would go to Emmarentia Dam where no one would know us and we could hold hands like all the other couples. For a few hours we could be official.

We are not official – never have been and never can be. Not here, not now. 'We know we're official,' you said. 'That's all that matters.'

You introduced me to your family as your best friend and it wasn't a lie. But I longed to hold your hand on the couch and not just under the dining room table, as your father carved the gammon I couldn't eat. I longed to kiss you when the clock struck midnight and the start of a new year, and not quickly in the kitchen as we washed the dishes, your teeth grazing my lips We could be unashamedly us only when everyone else was asleep. We fucked on the sitting room rug that everyone walked over in the daytime.

Lying on the chequered red and black and yellow of my blanket – our blanket – that day at the dam, I remembered being five. My big sister Rebecca is trying to fly her kite. I watch her as our mother lies back on the same checks, an open novel in her spider hands.

'Ma, could I marry Becky?' I said.

'No, darling.'

'Why?'

'Because she's your sister.'

'But if she weren't my sister?'

'Remembering?' you asked, peering into my face. There was a concerned line between your beautiful caterpillar eyebrows.

It hurts, and you know, so you didn't pry and I loved you. You offered me the flask we packed and I loved you, I loved you. I love you. We sipped tea and watched the Egyptian geese and their goslings on the dam, drifting apart then drifting together. Why is mate for life more pleasing to my heart than monogamy?

The last time we'd been at Emmarentia was for the march. We were wrapped in rainbows and each other – happy, high, free. What we were, what we are, was a celebration, not a dangerous negotiation. Floats, loud music, alcohol not bought but exchanged for proud pink paper money. Play Pride on a loop, my lovely. Forget the frivolous franchise restaurant we were sent out of. We ordered a vegetarian tramezzini to share – a custom since our undergrad years: two triangles each, crammed with a few of our favourite things – more filling than a toasted chicken mayo, and three rand cheaper. The manager came to our table, and it didn't look as though he was about to ask if we were satisfied with our meal. On the way out you muttered, 'At least our food was free.'

One, two, three cyclists rode by on their circuits around the dam – their tight arses strained against the lycra of their shorts and sweat formed a translucent mask on their faces. We are connected by our fingers and our sweat and the objects of our gaze.

'Do you think they know?' I said.

'I don't think they care. Look at them – all eyes on the prize.'

My eyes were on you and you laughed.

'Maybe they're like us.' No one is like us.

I didn't know how to tell you that I'd got the scholarship. 'With what money?' you would ask when I asked you to come with me. 'What about the kids?' Your beautiful eyebrows would meet in your consternation. And besides, 'I've signed a contract. I can't just leave,' you would say. Then I would say something senseless and spiteful about signing your soul away. And you'd tell me that accepting the scholarship is the same thing.

'I'm so happy for you!' You kissed my forehead. You kissed my cheeks. You kissed my nose. 'Don't they have Christmas vacation over there? You can visit then. Or – ' you gasped with excitement, 'I can visit you! We'll have a white Christmas!'

Your cheeks were flushed and my hands felt like hope in yours.

Before I left, we visited all the old places – because next time might be in two years' time. And time sneaks up and usurps. I wondered if time could also soothe the burn of your memory.

One of the first times we visited the second-hand bookstore on Soutpansberg Road, you clasped my hand beside the shelves stocked with Woolf and Forster and said, 'This is probably the only aisle we'll be walking down, you know.' I knew that I'd do it again and again with you. And I do. We always gravitated to the Classics section, which takes up a portion of the passageway and what is now a bed-less room. There is a dampness, but the books suggest fecundity.

At Groenkloof Nature Reserve, we'd purged the veld of pompom weed. We took two hours longer than we'd intended. Our guide forgot about us. We forgot about time. We talked and talked while we snipped at the stems of these all-too-familiar unfamiliars. When the clouds became smothering and the ultraviolet rays saw too much, you looked at your watch and I thought for the umpteenth time I really should start wearing one. We'd walked back to the campsite – past the zebras and the ostriches and the hikers – and talked and talked. This time we didn't talk as much. You picked a sprig of im-pepho and tucked it behind my ear.

Rosebank is where we felt freest – anonymous, lost in the streets of the rich. We went to art galleries in the daytime and poetry read-ings when the sun set. Holding hands isn't what makes us stand out, but your bright red All Stars and mismatched socks against your monochrome attire. Sometimes, in the starkness of day, or in the candlelight at dusk, we are all the same.

At OR Tambo there was no Ma to see me off. No Becky. On the balcony outside the restaurants, we remembered all the air shows at Waterkloof Air Force Base: the throbbing sun, the whirring propellers, and not touching because your father was in the Air Force. The setting was different but the poetry of planes in the sky remained the same: an impossible weight raises itself into the air and gradually disappears from view.

'You're not going to finish that, are you?'

'No,' I smiled, inserting my cigarette between your lips – LD Menthol, stolen kiss – like the first time I touched you. My touch burned, you told me; I knew I'd burn you again.

I hadn't travelled by plane enough to be bored by take-off or the seemingly endless liminality of the sky between airports. I gazed out the window for as long as I could. It wasn't tiredness that made me turn away, but the lady in the seat in front of me claiming that the stars were distracting her from sleep. You would've said something witty and profound – perhaps changed her life. I closed the blind and opened the book you gave me.

When you were in your third year you'd read Ondaatje's *The English Patient* and threatened to confine your memories and our memories to the margins of some literary text. Annotation was once a capital offence in my eyes. But you are a reader and you are responding. I appreciated being able, in my turn, to read your responses – to literature or life.

Of course the book you chose is significant to both of us. There is a body on the cover that appears to be constructed of marble – whether it is a man or a woman is not important, nor is it revealed. The body's spectral arms clutch a cloth that will remain static in its marble design – in its front cover portrayal – over the organs which are said to determine sex. The body is the background of the text, and our favourite colours are the background of the body: red and green – perhaps somewhere between stopping and going. My name is beautiful in your hand.

It rains more than it doesn't. You and I would walk quite happily through the rain if there were no lightning, but allowing yourself to get drenched is seen as a nuisance here – a deviance. A transparent umbrella is my constant companion – I look up to see the raindrops plummet to their necessary deaths. Central heating and double-glazed windows ensure that I stay warm inside; frequently I wish they weren't so effective. I miss slipping into a cold bed to find your inevitable warmth.

I live in a residence for postgraduates. Most of them are international students. My roommate reminds me of you; the laugh, the shape of the eyes, the hands – which I've felt. My roommate has felt my hands, too – we feel each other. I think of you when we fuck – our hands browsing the burning highlands of each other's bodies, fingers inspecting every crevice. You are not here to heal how I ache to be felt by you. But your name smoulders in the margins of my textbooks again and again.

The Day He Came

AMATESIRO DORE

'No Motor, No Toto' was the unofficial motto of our university but it wasn't why I didn't have a girlfriend. After all there were thousands of students without cars on campus who were fornicating as though Jesus wasn't returning. I was in love with God and I kept my vow up until Michael won my soul.

It was the final of the VC Cup: College of Law v Engineering. I saw him dribble the ball away from a defender and the next before shooting it past the goalkeeper and into the net. Shouts of 'Goal!' scattered the field and I fell in love before knowing him. After that, the near misses, fouls, whistles and free kicks acquired his face; my heart was dependent on a win for our team. Our college was playing the final game for the first time in university history. At quarter to seven, the referee blew the final whistle and we became the university champions. I joined the crowd of law students who spilled onto the field to carry the lone goal scorer of the match.

Like a 100-level puppy I followed the 300-level guy as he received his gold medal, man of the match prize and lifted the VC Cup. I volunteered to carry his boots as he straggled along with his teammates to the side of the field where car owners displayed their rides.

'You know how to drive?' Michael asked, and he threw his key at me.

I waited in his car praying he wouldn't change his mind as he chit-chatted with a group of girls and teammates. One after the other, his mates drove off with girls until Michael stood alone, talking on his phone. I couldn't make out his words but my heartthrob was obviously pissed at the other party. His afro haircut, sideburns and goatee complemented the virility of his slim-fit arms, gym-cut chest and abs on his shirtless chocolate bod. The swagger of his sagging shorts around his bubble butt was a stimulating contrast to his macho thighs and hairy calves. Before he touched me, my heart sinned.

When he entered the car and relaxed into the front passenger seat, I confessed my inability: I can't drive a car with manual gears as all our cars at home are automatic. He fixed his eyes on me and slipped his hand between my legs to pull the lever beneath my seat. His hand was grazing my cock as my seat moved backwards and my legs straightened with pleasure.

'My father is not one of the richest pastors in Nigeria and my mother is not a bestselling gospel musician. This is what they bought for me. So you better buckle up, start the car, clutch down, shift gear and drive or I'll have your ass for dinner,' Michael said.

I told him he could have it whether or not I managed to drive the car.

'Shut up and drive,' Michael chuckled and I followed up with some lines from Rihanna, before jerking his car towards Old Boys Hostel.

We flowed as though we had known each other for years and I wished I could have met him years before. I asked how he knew I was the son of a pastor and gospel musician.

'I know all the fine boys on campus,' he said and I tried to quench my rising smile. 'You guys are famous, you know. The pretty one of a pair of identical twins will be famous anywhere in the world irrespective of his parents.'

I frowned. I hated being labelled 'pretty'. It sounded effeminate. It felt as if every light-skinned guy with the face of his beautiful mother was created for feminine superlatives and same-sex flattery. And he excluded my twin from being 'pretty'. Was it because of Paul's extreme womanising? I wondered if I exhibited low-key feminine mannerisms. Did my voice sound soft whenever I loosened up?

'Why are you quiet? Did I offend you?' Michael said as we approached the isolated chalets before Old Boys Hostel. I told him my mind: I understand if the composition of my facial features and the lightness of my skin appear more attractive than an average guy. But as a man, a full-blooded African man, I object to and take offence at every attempt to abrogate my manhood and circumscribe my sexuality.

Michael was choking, so it seemed. It took a while before I recognised his laughter and it corrupted my soul. I parked beside the lonely road and we laughed out loud. Then he feigned trying to kiss me and I faked resisting as we continued to laugh. The humour fizzled out when he found my hardened length and caught my lips with his own. All my Christian upbringing melted in his embrace and my fingers dug into his virgin afro as our tongues mated. We were naked on the backseat and I was moving inside him when a car honked and sped past.

'Don't stop,' Michael said and I continued to call on Jesus.

I got out of the car for a pee to cover the awkwardness of my post-coital guilt. I needed a moment to mourn the loss of my God-ordained virginity and the fragmentation of my secret oath of celibacy. I imagined the trumpets announcing the return of Christ and it brought me to my knees behind the car. I begged God to forgive my rapturous moments with my Michael and my lack of genuine repentance for the fruit we enjoyed. I was sorry but I wanted to do it again. In fact I wanted to stay with Michael till kingdom come.

'You there, come here!' A voice boomed in the dark and I was ready to confess all that had transpired in the car to any interrogator.

'Laura, you're a fool!' Michael screamed as he got out of the car.

'How long have you been parked there? I hope we blinded your eyes!'

I noticed a huge person leaning on the bonnet of the SUV parked a few metres behind us. I struggled with my zip and buckle as the person sashayed forward.

'Peter, this is my bestie and roommate, Larry, but I call her Laura.'

'Hi, I just saw your twin at Mama Cass and you guys are so identical. I can tell you apart because you're shirtless and alone with Michael,' Larry shook my hand. His effeminate gesticulations and wriggling made me squeamish.

I was shamed by his knowledge of my secret and I hated him for mentioning my brother. It made me remember my parents and I felt their presence. I wondered if they knew what had just happened. My father had a way of knowing whenever I sinned. He expected righteousness from me whereas Paul was expected to misbehave until Jesus arrests his soul like Saul on the road to Damascus. God told him about us before we were born. Peter and Paul: the rock solid apostle and the repentant evangelist. Larry was an aberration of my family values. He was proud of his lifestyle and happily living in sin.

'Mike, I'm sorry I missed the match. You won't believe the drama. Cynthia and her boo came to fight in our room. Then I drove them to the hospital, *no be small thing*!' As Larry continued, I looked at Michael but it seemed he had forgotten me.

I left to search the car for my shirt and shoes while Michael remained outside with Larry. He had made me break my vow and he was already talking to someone else. I was certain anyone who saw us together would think Michael was fucking me, that I was the bottom, the submissive lover. The worm of masculine insecurity clawed through my veins and laid eggs of homophobia in my blood.

'Come and have dinner with us,' Michael said when he got into the car but I told him three was a crowd.

'OK, come and have dinner with me!' Michael said and I smiled.

I wasn't sure if I would get another opportunity so I gave him a sideways hug and pecked his cheek. He held on to me and kissed my lips. I didn't realise I was crying.

'It's alright,' he said. 'I will love you and never let you go.'

I asked him about Larry and he said eating alone wouldn't kill him. I squinted at his response and he understood my query.

'Laura is like a sister to me,' Michael said and I asked why he didn't have a girlfriend to camouflage his homosexuality.

'Been there, done that!' Michael said. 'Nowadays I don't have the time and energy to multitask my affections. My heart can only beat for one person at a time. And I wouldn't want my sister hooking up with a down-low motherfucker, would you?'

I didn't know how to respond. So I told him about my second brother, dead and buried less than a year. It was a mild cough so my mum gave him two tablespoons of cough syrup. He slept and never woke up. My father wanted to resurrect him but God didn't permit him to do so. My mother recorded a song about his death and my father preached sermons based on it. Paul stopped attending church because he felt my parents commercialised the death of John. If I had a sister, I wouldn't care who was sleeping with her. I would just want her alive and healthy.

'Sorry about your brother,' Michael said as I drove into the garage in front of his room. Then he confessed why he didn't have a girl-friend and why he would never marry a woman to hide his sexuality. 'It was a year after secondary school and most coaches felt I was too young for the Under-17 national team. Apparently I had to clock twenty before I would be old enough for the team but that's a story for another day. Well, I was frustrated and my parents were no longer in support of my football dreams. Let's just say I was impressionable when a married dude, living down my street, buzzed me on MySpace. He said I was fine and my head turned upside down. Before then, no one had ever alluded to my looks. Then it was only about my foot-ball skills or something like that, never about my aesthetic value. So you can imagine what happened when this young and handsome Oil and Gas executive with a fancy car sent me a message about my looks. We chatted whenever I was online. From advice about girls, books and universities et al, we graduated into flirting via homosexual innuendoes. It was exhilarating and I felt emancipated. I wrote things I could never say and read things I had never heard from another man. It was fun until his wife came to my house. My parents weren't home but my younger sisters were inside. When she saw me, she started crying and she walked away. Those tears killed me and I swore never to do that to anyone. Though we never acted on our words, he cheated on his wife, emotionally and in spirit. I will never do that to anyone.'

Before 300-level, you were Larry without a car on campus. You didn't trick your parents into crediting your account with inflated tuition fees every semester (including summer session for failed courses). You weren't a Yahoo Boy or a Fuck Boy or a Political Activist or involved in any other *runs* that could buy you a car. If not for your SUV, you would have suffered countless humiliations like Michael. He was trekking with his 100-level course mate on a hot Friday afternoon when your 300-level course mate, in a blue Honda Baby Boy, slowed down after zooming past.

'That's my boyfriend,' the girl said then ran towards the waiting car, leaving your humbled age mate to trek the remaining thirty minutes to his hostel. Those were the days of few commercial motorcycles and fewer cabs, before the introduction of the university shuttle buses and before Michael became your roommate.

After years of campus obscurity, your luck changed in 300-level when your father gave you one of the cars the Governor bought for High Court judges. You weren't aware of the magnitude of his gift until a junior judge in your father's court drove the same car with a similar number plate to visit his son on campus. Fellow car owners flashed their headlamps and honked to get your attention as you drove past them; they nodded whenever you caught their eyes. Guys who never acknowledged your presence would slow down just to say hi, call you 'boss' and ask how your day was going. You were invited to parties and suddenly everyone wanted your phone number. Even Cynthia, your best friend and pseudo-sister since 100-level, started telling everyone she was your girlfriend. Your market was selling but you couldn't trust a soul until you met your secondary school bully and tormentor-in-chief trekking towards the New Boys Hostel.

'Laura!' Michael said after you pressed down your tinted window to stare at him. You whipped your head and flicked your fingers.

'You haven't changed at all. Sorry, you're no longer a princess, you're the reigning Queen! What a ride!' Michael caressed your car and you wished it was your body.

'I heard this car belongs to a 300-level law student called Larry. I never imagined Larry was actually Laura. Men, you're now a big girl. The biggest babe on campus,' Michael said and you couldn't stop laughing.

How you hated secondary school and felt suicidal because of his name-calling, the feminine pronouns he designated for you and how he treated you like a girl. Once he bought you a sanitary pad for Valentine Day and on your last birthday of secondary school, female condoms. Eventually you stopped crying whenever he taunted you. You once pleasured yourself with memories of his voice calling you a 'virgin pussy'.

'Laura, it's been tough for me on this campus!' Michael said and he told you about the humiliation he suffered because of your course mate.

'Men, this campus was built for cars. I had Legal Methods at Permanent Site this morning, Political Science at Temporary Site by midday then I had to rush back to PS because our Legal Methods class was rescheduled. You know the circle, 100-level law is hell,' Michael said as you drove him to his room.

You wondered why only the person who packed the shit remembers. By virtue of his straight-guy-amnesia, Michael was ignorant of the nature of your secondary school relationship with him. He appeared in all your secondary school memories because he stood guard at the gates of your closet, taunting you to come out, to admit you weren't a mere fag but a woman in a man's body.

'Laura, abeg! I don't mind squatting in your room so I can get free rides to school. I will do anything for you. I will wash your car. I will even lay your bed,' Michael winked and rubbed your knees.

You removed his hand from your lap and said you didn't want anything from him. You told him he was the only person you could trust and he promised never to betray your trust.

That Friday evening you were alone with Michael in your room. Your roommates drove to Benin City for the weekend. You listened as he gossiped about your secondary school contemporaries. You hated all of them and didn't give a fuck about their location but the sight of the class bully genuflecting and acting agreeable made up for the regurgitation of your secondary school trauma. And it made you discover the truth: only money can truly emancipate a man. You saw yourself from Michael's perspective and the truth broke your heart: *the first son of a Chief Judge, grandson of a renowned industrialist, 300-level law student and the biggest boy on campus who acts like a girl.*

That night Michael insisted on sharing the same mattress with you. There were three other beds vacated by your roommates. You wondered if he would have desired you if you were just another effeminate boy, without clout, on campus. You removed his hand from your waist and rejected his cuddle.

'What's the problem?' he said and you asked if he went about cuddling secondary school classmates?

'But you know I've always liked you,' Michael continued but you immediately nudged his leg from your ass.

'Or do you like it rough? I can feel your dick getting hard,' Michael said and you slapped him with your response: I won't share my car, my food, my room and give you my ass on top of it. His cock shrivelled and you left him for another bed.

You wanted him but you wanted him right: when he was fully made, with a choice in the matter, without any form of monetary consideration, empowered by his own cash and dignity, not as a beggarly 100-level student trying to ass-lick the fag he had bullied for six years.

In the morning, the boundaries of your relationship were established. You joined him in the bathroom and he lost his erection after a while. You were just university students sharing a bucket of water, the most normal thing on campus. Breakfast at Mama Cass and you paid the bills. Then you gave him your laundry to drop off at the dry-cleaners, while you remained in the room to write out your answer to a Criminal Law problem-question. He took your car key and didn't return until afternoon. Your car was washed when you drove out with him to have lunch in Cynthia's room. He drove off and promised to return the car when you needed it. You called for over thirty minutes and he didn't answer your calls. He showed up in your room an hour after Cynthia dropped you off.

'I'm so sorry dear. I didn't think you would need the car before nightfall. I was watching a match and I left my phone in the car,' Michael said and you didn't give him your car key for the rest of the semester.

By the time your roommates returned on Sunday, Michael was just your friend, just another guy you used to like. He became fast friends with your roommates and they liked him because he was nothing like you. At the end of his first year, he was hooking up with a steady string of girls. None lasted longer than a one night stand,

and everyone accepted him as the incredible footballer allowed to drive your car around campus.

You maintained the status quo for two years until the weekend Cynthia fought with her girlfriend. The couple had been together since secondary school, up to your final year class by which time most of your female course mates were engaged, about-to-be-engaged, pretending-to-be-engaged or married. Cynthia's girlfriend cheated, got pregnant, decided to keep the baby and marry the father despite your misgivings. She'd never been in a relationship with a guy and you thought she could have lived happily ever after with Cynthia. At the beginning of the second semester of your final year, she stopped talking to Cynthia, started avoiding her and even shunned you on campus. On the afternoon of the VC Cup final, you saw her walking alone to the football field. You offered her a ride and lured her to your room with the promise of a gift. You sent Cynthia a text and she drove down. You wanted them to kiss and make up; you thought everything would be fine. You were pressing a shirt when Cynthia burst into your room.

'Where's the bitch?' Cynthia screamed and you realised it was going bad.

As you tried to separate them, Cynthia reached for your pressing iron and scorched the back of her unrepentant girlfriend. The girl was screaming, Cynthia was crying and you didn't know what to do. They wept all over each other as you drove them to the hospital. Despite their reconciliation, you knew they were never getting back together again. Cynthia found closure, her ex-girlfriend remained with the Baby-Daddy and you wondered if anybody would ever love you enough to burn your back.

You were ready for Michael and you were going to tell him when you found his car parked beside the road. You called his number but he didn't pick up. He wasn't in the room and he wasn't with any of his teammates so you drove back to the dark and lonely road. You parked at a distance and sneaked to his car. You heard them before you saw them. Michael and one of the holy twins were oblivious to your jealous eyes. You wondered how long they had kept their alliance from you. Michael had once told you about liking them – the entire campus had a crush on them – but one was a serial womaniser and the other was always in church. You wondered which one was making Michael moan: the pastor or the womaniser. You had seen one of them with a girl at Mama Cass. You hoped it was just a fling because God knows what you would do if anyone stole Michael from you.

You didn't get the opportunity to speak to Michael that night because he didn't come back. When you called his phone the following morning, he didn't answer but he sent a text to say he was in church. He returned that afternoon in clothes that didn't belong to him and dashed out, with his books, before you could ask any questions. He didn't return that night but you heard him in the room, on Monday morning, as you showered. In class you heard Michael was running for LAWSA president and the twins were his campaign managers. When you finally confronted him, he didn't answer your questions.

'His parents are pastors,' Michael said and you wondered how it concerned your friendship with him.

A few weeks before the LAWSA elections, Michael moved out of your homophile nest. In fact he started hanging out with a beautiful 100-level law student at Mama Cass and you watched him staring into her eyes every evening. Sometimes they had a triple date with the twins and you caught him stealing glances at Peter. He won the election and didn't invite you to his celebration dinner. It was only a few weeks before your final exams but you couldn't wait to leave that lonely campus and escape the ridiculousness of Michael and Peter holding hands and sitting together in church.

You hated Peter because you knew he would dump Michael the minute his good Christian image was threatened. You remained in love with Michael because he knew the relationship was doomed but didn't give a fuck about getting his heart broken. He had once told you he would do anything for love. And so would you.

It was a lazy Saturday morning. The parents were sleeping. Their home was incomplete: the twins were in school, the help resumed at ten, the security guard travelled for a family emergency. And their neighbours were indoors because of a compulsory environmental sanitation exercise.

'Bang, bang, bang!' the couple heard their gate scream and their bell rang endlessly.

Who was knocking at seven fifteen, Pastor wondered. Maybe an angel bearing gifts, his wife mumbled. Twenty-three years of marriage and their communication was almost telepathic, Pastor smiled as he went to the gate.

There was a young man with a huge physique at the gate. Pastor wished he could summon the twins and flog them alongside their errant visitor for disturbing his rest.

'Oga, I have come here to warn you to warn your daughter. Warn your daughter to leave my man alone.' The stranger wiggled his finger.

Pastor looked around for witnesses but there was nobody in sight, just a black SUV with a state judiciary number plate and no driver.

'My son, calm down!' Pastor said.

'Don't tell me nonsense. I'm warning you for the last time. Warn your daughter, Peter, to leave my man alone or this world will not contain all of us,' the man said, then he sashayed off and got into the SUV.

Pastor noticed his wife standing beside him and they imagined Peter in bed with a man.

The end.

The Voice Is the First to Go

ALEXIS TEYIE

When I try to recall that time it comes to me as one long day. Everything was so rich, all of it so heavy. Like somehow the unsqueezed life from past generations filtered down to us. Heart thick with the clothes, the music, the TV shows, the women, I left all that talk about rights, people disappearing, and banned books to the politicians. She kept track of it though, the immigrants, the complaints about the Kenya-Somali border becoming a porous membrane, the rumours of ethnic killings. Still, once Babyface or Timberlake would come on the radio, Awilo even, we'd pretend we knew nothing about all the ripples, how your surname could be a shield or a bull's-eye, how everyone was holding their breath. It's good that life came in sachets then, hey: the *Fair&Lovely* all the women bleached their skin with; the *Trust* condoms in every duka after those 'je una yako?' ads; the *Royco Mchuzi Mix* to inspire even the ghost of meat in sukumawiki, and the no-label spirits we imbibed to keep from collapsing completely into our selves.

Mornings, we lay in bed, waiting for adhana to sound. The thought of the muadhini crying alone in the minaret, 'Allahu Akbar,' it unclosed me. At dawn she would spread this old climate map we owned on the cold cement as a mat and perform her rites. I watched her, wondering how it was possible to believe in anything with so much conviction. *I* never knew anything until it was already tumbling out of my mouth, or hands; even then, only in an unbroken stream like some script I learned by heart long ago and thought I had forgotten. A song whose lyrics you can't quite remember until it starts playing – our national anthem for instance.

I confessed once, everything feels like birds I chase around in a room with high ceilings, trying to pin them down, trying to make them sing. Some days all I had in my fists were bright orange feathers.

She sighed. 'Shida ni hizo mzungu books you read, mami.'

'Siste, I'm no better than anyone here.'

She laughed, took another drag.

Other days, especially when there was a blackout, we would pray for rain, hide underneath those blue mosquito nets they gave for free at the clinic, and try to rap in time to raindrops sizzling on the mabati roof:

Tap.if.hiss.showers.tap.of.hiss.sorrows.tap.fall.hiss.down.tap
taptap.like.tap.arrows.hiss.the.tap.lone.tap.wayfarer.tap.may.
hiss.talk.by.himself.hiss.

When she admitted to memorising Jonathan Kariara during high school, I confessed that I often stole my freestyles from Armattoe.

'HEY, this is Jo'burg, not the village! DRIVE!'

'Foolish!'

'Women shouldn't be allowed in cars!'

'Tell your mother!'

'Get out of the car and see if I won't beat a woman! And what is that accent? Are you Nigerian? Stupid Nigerians!'

'I'm KENYAN! Get out and see if you won't be beaten by a woman!'

I was about to call the idiot's bluff and make the situation worse when the Kariara poem came back to me almost whole:

A leopard lives in a Muu tree
Watching my home
My lambs are born speckled
My wives tie their skirts tight
And turn away –
Fearing mottled offspring.

'Ehe! Madam, you're scared? You're scared! I knew it! Drive like you know where you're going then! Do you hear? You! Fine, whatever!'

The poem reactivated some part of my mind and finally, I saw us as we were, laid out before me, waiting to be explored, and the noise of traffic receded before the promise that image offered.

The memory of that last evening, precise and stinging, rose to the surface. The moon, open and genuine, gazing through the one small window. Outside, everyone else lugging their lives on their backs. Some stooping under the weight. Others tossing their lives from palm to palm, and sometimes letting them fall. One person might step over it, another might do without it altogether. Inside, we moved in and out of our bodies, our two lives hovering between our mouths, like two bubbles wet with rainbow, meeting, colliding, vanishing together, and then reappearing, once behind her ear, another time underneath my tongue. We tried to inhale the glittering bubbles, but eventually swung them between us, and our lives shone with a steady pulse. It seemed the entire universe shifted, melting and materialising around our breasts, our hips, tingling and synchronising with the vibration on the surface of our skin. Time itself moulded its body around us, and the moon, magnanimous, sank lower as the eddies around us altered Time's ebb. Every unfelt emotion in the world – every emotion ever emitted, slipped into our bubbles; we received and transmitted the love, pity, envy, rage, pain, mercy, faith, rage, joy borne across and beyond time ...

'Abby?'

'Hello?'

'Why aren't you back yet?'

'Traffic, Judy. Traffic! You know how it is …'

'Well, why didn't you leave earlier? I always say, if you think it'll take an hour – '

'It'll take three. I know, I know. I'll head straight there.'

'The guests have already started arriving. Your friends always come early. It's so awkward, Abby!'

'Love, they're just being considerate. They want to help, that's all.'

'Hmph. If you say so! Listen, the kids are in a weird mood so actually maybe you should pass by the shops and get some ice-cream?'

'I thought we agreed no sugar?'

'Don't be so rigid.'

'*I'm* rigid?'

'What's *that* supposed to mean?'

'Nothing.'

'Just get the ice-cream.'

'Sure, whatever. Look, Judy, it's hot in this car. Can I call you later?'

'What's wrong with the aircon?'

'*Later*, just later, Judy.'

They say when you lose someone the sound of their voice is first to go. Even now that I'm married I still stare hungrily at women who smoke, imagining their husky voices. None ever have the tangy bite twitching at the fringes that hers did, that silent threat of a high-pitched wail. Only a certain kind of life fractures the voice like that. Some nights when I can't sleep I stretch out on the carpet; I replay her laugh in my head. It changes every night. Last night, it was rasping, hesitant as though she wasn't sure life was as funny as they made it out in the books. I woke up choking on red volcano dust from the old neighbourhood. I groped for that slender wrist, felt for a familiar burn. I screamed at the moon:

You told me about your auntie and her new man to go with a new land. How you thought she could save you; that's what big people do, right? How he tore more spaces in you than you had flesh, how no matter what, even my skinny pianist fingers couldn't move fast enough to stop all the holes in you. I didn't want to fill you up, those interstices made you crackle, and I liked that crazy shine. I didn't have enough skin to cover us both; I thought our bones ached so much because they needed to be naked. I never said I wanted to fill you up, I liked seeing the world through your cavities, the same way they cut us up, y'know? What the fuck made you think I wanted to fill you up? I'd actually never seen a real piano but I still wanted to make music with your toenails and the soft flesh of your abdomen. How could you possibly fit all the music in your Jansport bag?

'Z, no period,' you informed me that first day we met. I thought it poetic. It only occurred to me days after we met that you were the end of language. See how instinctively I appended myself, a pleading little 'a' – ever superfluous. Zaza, I called you, instead of, EvenWhen-ItEndsStartOverWith-Me. You figured Zizi was better, it meant 'root'; it was all the things we pretended we never wanted to begin with. ZazaZazaZazaZazaZazaZazaZaza. I must have sounded like an inarticulate oaf, or a little child. Maybe that's why you smiled the way you did the day you left.

Judy didn't know but I named the children for her: Zara and Zola. I hoped these twin beacons would guide my misplaced fractions back to me. She always complained her name might as well have been a lullaby; I said it reminded me of the ocean. What I meant was, it always comes back. Crossing and uncrossing fingers here, so far away from that little lean-to, I wonder, was it all real? Does it *matter*? Anyhow, if time is this large fabric, it must sometimes fold into itself. I imagine I am stuck in the valley between two adjacent ears, eternally looping from one end to the other…

'Abby, everyone's waiting for you!'

'Why are people calling me? I'm driving!'

'Why are you picking up then?'

'Josh, are you bored already?'

'You know how it is with Judy. She's planned games. She probably has a timetable somewhere on her phone of what exactly we should be doing and in what order. And Kevo wore his 'Prose before Ho's' t-shirt so of course she's angry. And the kids are in a foul mood. Tumi has taken over the TV because she's pissed at Halima. Vee didn't bring her girlfriend so obviously something's weird there. Just get here!'

'Sure, sure. Just be easy.'

Finally, I took a left and parked outside the shops close to home. Immediately I walked in, the attendant turned to look and wouldn't turn away. I figured it was the dreadlocks. That, or my bulging stomach. Pregnant women aren't supposed to wear tank tops apparently – no matter how humid the day. I hadn't the time to be bothered so I moved past the magazine rack and towards the fridges at the back. The mix of light and cool that licked me when I opened the door sank deep into my skin and I imagined this was the feeling of paradise, bright and delicious. Chocolate, vanilla, strawberry swirl, salted caramel. I couldn't risk having to drive back to the shops when Zara or Zola demanded a different flavour. Clutching the tubs to my chest – why didn't I pick a basket? – I made my way to check-out.

'Plastic?'

'Sure.'

Vanilla. Beeeep. Chocolate. Beeep. Strawberry. Beeeep. The sound was immensely soothing.

My phone rang for the fifth time since Josh had called so I finally decided to answer.

'Where are you? I'm getting worried!'

'Judy, I'm fine. Just at the shops. Picking up ice-cream?'

'Who cares about ice-cream! I thought you were in an accident!'

'That's ridiculous.'

'Why is it ridiculous? People die all the time.'

'And today was the perfect day for me to die?'

'No, I mean, why are you so morbid, Abby?'

'You're the one who brought it up! Listen, can I pay?'

'I'm sorry, Abby, I just … please get here. It's weird hosting these parties alone.'

'I know, I love you Judy.'

I looked up to find the cashier waiting with an amused look on his face. 'Was that your sister? She seems intense!'

'No, my wife.'

'Oh.'

'Yes. Well, thank you.'

'Eh … Have a good day!'

I stepped outside and the heat slapped me in welcome. After dropping the bags in the back seat, I turned the ignition but nothing happened. Of course. Just wonderful. I got out of the car and sat on the hot tarmac. How did I get here? It's like I tumbled down the past ten years blindfolded. Still fumbling – at my age! Still clumsy and uncertain. Something is truncated, something important just fell off, or wasted away, and this is all I had left. I kept expecting myself to collapse, a cascading blob, all my blunt ends folding into each other.

'Madam? Are you OK?'

'I … sure, sure.'

'Is the car giving you problems? I could call a mechanic, and drive you home?'

The man's shadow fell over me momentarily and the shade

calmed me down slightly. His eyes seemed kind enough, and he had big hands. It's hard to distrust people with big hands.

'It's fine. I don't have anywhere to be ...'

A What?

THATO MAGANO

'I really shouldn't have volunteered these entries to be honest. Should've stuck to a speech like sensible people do. But I was all about that "let's do something different" life. I just …'

'Wo-oh! Just stop yourself before this becomes another failed mission. You know how you can get,' Zinhle's voice interrupted me as I was about to say that the idea was just another amusement I'd allowed to go too far. She'd just lifted her laptop to walk the short distance to the kitchen for a glass of water.

'OK friend. OK. Let me get serious about this. But pray tell, why am I looking into your fridge?'

'Hahah! Don't worry about that,' she said as the laptop landed back on the coffee table and she settled on her oxblood two-seater couch that betrayed the barrenness of her Slade Park digs. 'Well, we're looking at each other now, aren't we?'

'Whatever,' I said, rolling my eyes. 'And please, no judgement. I was a mess that year and not having you there just made the entire thing worse.' I let out an impassioned sigh. 'Who would've thought you'd be doing your PhD at Oxford and I'm about to become the first person of African descent to win the GLAAD award for "Outstanding Local Television Interview"? We've come far my friend, we've come far!' Her voice loudly in my ears, over mine 'van toeka af, my friend, van toeka af!'

'Eintlek vele, what made you decide on that year? And when do you fly out?'

I was about to blurt out some silliness when I stopped myself and we were both quiet across the Skype interface, her eyes looking into my shy eyes and a reassuring smile lighting up the screen. 'I guess it was the year that I most knew.' My eyes glazed over. 'I went back to the diaries for a sense of where I was then when I was prepping for the interview. Just to see the mess I was before all the changes.'

'Eish but you've been through the most shem, my friend. The most! Super stoked this is finally happening for you. Is Mr joining you for the trip?'

'Yeah, he is. The invite was a plus one. The SABC is paying for it. Or rather, Noeleen made it so they can pay for all of us so she can accept the award with me. You know that bitch mos. Never one to miss the spotlight even though I had to convince her for two years to do the interview. One day is one day, I tell you.'

'Leave her alone friend, her day will come. Let's do the important things now.' Zinhle had given me two hours from her intense schedule to read through the diary with me and choose the entry I would read when accepting the award. 'Tell you my thoughts after each reading, cool?'

'Small, small change friend. When I read it earlier, I just couldn't decide which ones to read for you, so I'm thinking to be more random. Decided I'll just flip along and we see how much we fit into the time we have. Cool with you?'

'Cool! Cool! Let's get this trip-down-melodrama-lane started,' Zinhle smirked. 'I know I'm not allowed to judge but can I be brutal?'

'Nah bitch! Remember I have your UCT files so don't get carried away,' as my fingers refamiliarised themselves with the spine of the three hundred pages.

Diary, how was your day today? A few thoughts for you on mine.

You know diary, the way I kept looking at him with that silly grin on his face. He has no idea how upset he makes me. He has no idea. No idea whatsoever.

When will he see that I will love him better than she ever would?

What must happen for him to see this, diary?

I mean, how can he be OK with what happened today? Why does he let her get away with these things that she does? All I know is that if she was my friend, I would be telling her to stop being so silly because, soon enough, her man will leave her for someone like me.

He's so silly though. I mean, why kiss her even after she's told you such news?

'Nwye, nwye I didn't mean to do it, it just happened.' I think a hot klaap would have been a more appropriate response.

How do you kiss someone who just told you they kissed another boy by mistake? What sort of mistake is this that allows you to be tongue deep with someone for several minutes? What silliness is this of his?

A hot hot klaap would have set her straight! Whenever her lips think of touching with anyone else's again the thought of the sting of the klaap would tease her out of her confusion very fast!

And I'm told this was not a onetime incident. She and Senzo have been seen unable to stop themselves from their tongue acrobatics.

Hawu diary, you ask me how do I know? You ask me this?

Mxim, you don't trust me? You don't trust my sources? You are the one that doesn't know. Me I know.

My sources told me they saw them kiss several times that night. I knew Msizi letting her go alone to that dance would lead to such. I've never trusted her for him. I was told that it has been happening for a while now. Can you imagine diary!

They started their clandestine things at the beginning of term already, welcome dinner. They were seen at the back of the hall, tongue deep even before Msizi had left for our dorms. They couldn't wait, couldn't contain themselves – that's how disgusting they are.

I don't know why he never bothered to check on her himself or why they weren't together for most of the evening. Instead, I was told Msizi was seen laughing with Thabo and Koketso the entire night.

It's a good thing I chose not to go to that thing, hey. I might have caused a scene had I seen her and Senzo. But I know I wouldn't have. Actually I didn't know how mad I am about Msizi. I thought it was just a crush that would go away. This living together seems like a curse sent by the gods to punish the shit out of me. Why make me share twenty-four hours with this man that I cannot have for myself?

You'd think he would have figured it out by now. This campus is not that big and pretty much all the seniors can be found at the same socials or hanging out together. But no, he's such an idiot. All gooey eyed and in love. So silly!

But I love this silliness. I just think of all the games we would play as lovers. I can imagine him to be generous even in loss.

Well, what am I saying? I know that he's generous even in loss.
Like on the track field where he always shows great sportsmanship
whenever he loses when he generously applauds his fellow runners.
Imagine what more could he be with me? Where there is nothing to
lose. I think there is only something to gain.

But he will never know what a great time we could have, just him
and me and it would be our secret diary, to stay between you and me.
Imagine diary, can you imagine it? You would know all the things that
we got up to, you would be the safe place where every detail of our
relationship was recorded, because as you know, I wouldn't be able
to tell anyone here any of this. I can just imagine how we could spend
the weekends in here, lying in the same bed not concerning ourselves
with anyone else.

I know he would be worried about what people will say about him.
I think that is part of the reason he won't let it happen between us.
If only he knew that I wouldn't care that other people knew, that I
would also want to keep it just as our secret, just the two of us and
of course, you diary. We could keep it a secret to the outside world
for as long as he wanted and I still would not care.

Actually, he could continue to be with that silly Claire and I wouldn't
care, so long as the weekends were dedicated to me. You know, like
his Weekend Special but with all the nice feelings of being in love
and cuddling on the bed and talking and playing.

Argh, why am I thinking of that silly smile of his?

. . . .

'Have you shared this with him? Heh, mara, does he know the levels
of torture that were endured for him? How you guys found your

way to each other is one for the records.' Zinhle continuing with a mischievous smile, 'No jumping over chickens le bo "I-can-bring-back-your-lost-lover" akere my friend.'

'Mxim is this how little you still think of me my friend?' cutting her off, 'And no, I haven't and I have no intentions to do so before I step on that stage.'

'Shem ngwana batho Mzi! Wouldn't want to be him in two weeks' with her hands flying across the screen. 'But we're off to a great start with the entries, so I'll stop myself.'

'OK, let's move on.'

.... *30 March 2000* ....

Diary, I know that it is unusual I share with you while the day is still going but something wonderful is happening and I felt like sharing it with you.

This morning has been kind to me. I looked in the mirror and I did not want to throw up. I like this feeling. I felt comfortable with myself. I think it will be a good day overall as we go along. It usually is a good day when I am not asking too many questions. It felt really good to look at myself and not have questions today.

Well, all was well until Msizi walked in from his run. I was not expecting to still be in the room when he came back. He had told me he would go see that annoying girl of his and then come back to shower, so I had timed my departure just right. I know it takes him about an hour to do those four laps around the track. Then he would have to run another ten minutes to get to Claire's dorm where they would usually spend about thirty minutes together before taking the five-minute walk here. That was a whole hour and forty minutes that I have on most mornings to be by myself and get ready for the day.

Of course you know how awful that encounter used to be when he would find me here, before I had calculated the time it took for him to complete all this running around. I would, as usual, be getting ready to take a shower and he would walk into the bathroom and dress down to his underwear. I used to think that he would see how uncomfortable I was with him doing this but he never seemed to mind or pay my discomfort any attention. It seemed not to matter to him that I was either also getting undressed or that I was already in the shower with the water running.

No, scrap that, actually the worst was on the mornings when he would wake up and prep himself to go and then suddenly decide that he wouldn't go anymore. When I heard his footsteps around the room on mornings I wasn't up early to study, I'd be so happy because I wouldn't have him here while I got ready. And then it would all go to shit when I realised that he wasn't going anywhere and that I'd have to see him naked again. And I couldn't start locking the bathroom door out of nowhere because the first few times it happened, I pretended like it was just normal for us to be seeing each other like that.

But diary, if he only knew that I've never been in such close proximity to another man for these long periods of time. If he only knew that my whole life I've avoided such close encounters with men because I didn't know if I could trust myself in such intimate situations. I've always felt like they could smell that I was hiding something. That I was lying about who I am and so they would have every right to not want me to see them naked. Or worse still, that they might want to teach me a lesson.

But no, here he was, getting naked in front of me, with no qualms, making me think that I was crazy to ever think I would be in danger

if I was in the same place with other guys, naked or discreetly
checking them out.

. . . .

'My friend, but kgale o e nyaka that D neh!'

'Heh my friend, if there was a medal for ukubekezela, I'd be the
honorary lifetime recipient. Anyway, how are you not sympathising
with me here? Are you not seeing that I fully deserved to get it?
Even if it was ten years coming. Thoughts?'

'Nah, not keen on it. Etletse dilo tsa bana and I don't think it
goes with the interview.'

'Wa bora, waitse!'

. . . .*31 May 2000*. . . . .

Diary, how was your day today? A few thoughts for you on mine.

I hate him diary. I hate him. I would shoot him right now if I could.
Look at him lying there like he didn't betray our friendship earlier
today.

Yes he apologised and so what? He should have known better than
to laugh with those idiots. And those boys are like real idiots – like,
they're actually dumb. And they aren't idiots in the same way that
Msizi is.

Msizi is smart but just socially idiotic but those boys, those boys neh,
there's nothing to redeem them. Idiots, idiots, idiots – all of them!

He said he laughed because he genuinely believed that the joke was
funny. What was he supposed to do though? We were telling jokes on

each other, so why should he have not laughed when the jokes were about me? That's what he asked me as he apologised.

He said he could see that I was upset when he saw that I didn't have a comeback for that idiot friend of his Koketso. Stupid, stupid Koketso! Mxim, even I have to admit that that idiot told a really funny one, even if it was below the belt. I think I also would've laughed if that joke had been directed against someone else. I really should stop playing these games with those boys but how else will I get to spend more time with Msizi if I don't hang with them?

Now I can't tell him anymore. Just the way he laughed at that joke makes me think he would never accept me if I ever told him. If he thinks being compared to a woman is something to laugh at then maybe he is not as smart as I thought he was.

Just imagine what he would say if I ever told him the truth. I can't take the risk. He will go to those idiots and that silly Claire and tell them and I would never see the end of it. Then the whole school will know and I am determined to get out of here without as much as a disciplinary case. Just imagine how it'd become a full blown scandal?

No way am I telling him. One doesn't get to become a constitutional judge with a scandal like that hanging over their heads. No diary, no. Just no. I'm not telling.

. . . .

'You really think he would have told them friend?'

'I don't doubt it for a second!' I said emphatically. 'His spine wasn't as erect as it is now. All I will say is that I'm glad we are here.'

'I guess I've always believed more in him than you did.' Zinhle had always favoured Msizi and had led the squad that appraised his efforts to win me over three years ago. 'Yoh, I didn't know that you had ambitions for the scales of justice. Glad we lost you to the world of media. What was the joke?'

'Lol, let's not go there. I don't need to be retraumatised,' a flash of the intense shame of that day fleeting through my body. That year, I'd felt the most unsure of myself and about what I was. The accusation had stung like it'd never done before, as though they were taunting me with the truth of a secret I was trying so hard to hold onto. 'Thoughts?'

'Nah, not convinced yet.'

················*17 March 2000*················

Diary, how was your day today? A few thoughts for you on mine.

I feel strange today.

I don't know what it is but I had this feeling that I was not myself today. That, me Nhlanhla, I was not myself. I don't know how to describe it but the best I can do is say that I felt like I was watching myself from outside of myself. It was the weirdest thing in the world.

The whole time I was walking back to our room, all I wanted to do was ask this imposter who had decided to take over my life, what that was about. I don't know. I felt as though I was watching the real me through someone else's eyes.

It was like that time when I laughed with Zinhle and we almost fell on the ground because we laughed ourselves silly. That day I really felt like that was the person I really am. It felt really good to laugh like that with her.

I like my friend. I really like her. Makes sense that I would laugh like that with her. Maybe it isn't that I was feeling like I was another person. Maybe it's because I was just happy being with my friend who understands me more than anyone else I know. We played on the sand and with water but the best part was when we laughed at those boys after they called me istabane.

This is why I like my Zinhle. She said 'let's laugh at them' and we did and it ended up being a great time. I think maybe that is what I was missing today. Feeling like I belong and being with someone who made me feel like I belong.

. . . .

'I'm sorry my friend' Zinhle finally intervening. We'd been quiet as she saw my eyes tear up and let her own tears flow. Her eyes had glistened when my pace of reading had slowed down. As always, she could tell where I was in my internal world even before I could use my words to tell her. 'I rate this one immediately.'

I flipped the pages, still silent.

'Take your time friend. It's OK, I'll stay for as long as we need.'

. . . .*09 January 2000*. . . . .

Diary, it's matric year and that means it's grown-up year so we must find a new introduction for you.

Hello diary... No? I don't like it either. Maybe we try How was your day diary? Wanna hear about mine? ... still too playful hey? Yah. OK, then maybe this: Diary, how was your day today? A few thoughts for you on my day ... yes, this is perfect. It is grown up enough. So we shall begin each entry from now on with Diary, how was your day today? A few thoughts for you on mine.

We went shopping today and Mama agreed that I can buy those yellow sheets I've been thinking about throughout the holidays. I didn't think Papa would agree but he did.

You know him and his rules about men – so tiring at times! No actually, he is tiring! I don't know why he still insists on this man thing of his even after I told them I'm gay.

It's so funny to think about how Mama decided for the both of them how they would deal with the issue. I knew Mama would be cool but with Papa I wasn't sure, but always believed he would at least understand. I know he tries so I will forgive him these rules of his. I got my yellow sheets and I am happy for now. Now I just hope that I don't end up with another Papa in that dorm. Imagine how terrible it would be if I didn't get to enjoy my sheets because I lived with another rule maker for men. Can you imagine diary? So bleak, so so bleak!

Anyway, I'm not sure anymore. I don't know if gay is the best word to use to describe how I feel. I wake up feeling different all the time. Some days I just want to be a girl so bad and other days I just feel like I am me and that is freakin' cool. I'm shit scared how whoever it is I get to share that room with will respond to all of this.

Why aren't the dorms co-ed? What kind of school is it even? Why do they think some of us want to spend all of our waking hours in the company of boys? Boys, boys, boys – all the damn time! Boys are so annoying when they're together and I don't want to be a part of that.

Imagine if Z was coming with me and we were allowed to stay together. I can just imagine how much we'd laugh at all those simpletons we would have to study with. Yes, I think they are simpletons already. Who elects to go to a school where boys stay with boys and girls with girls in this day and age?

All these years of democracy and freedom and we are still here!!! So boring really!

. . . .

'Moving right along, nothing to see here but shem, your poor parents!'
'Poor souls, never saw it coming! … Remember how they just supported the transitioning conversation. It meant a lot that they didn't ask me questions I didn't have answers to then. All I knew then was that I just wasn't the son they knew they had.'
'Yoh friend, that was a time neh! Especially your dad.'

. . . . *12 January 2000*. . . . .

AT LEAST HE LOOKS INTERESTING!!!!

I still feel a little shy looking at him but I'll get over it. Just my luck!

I have nothing to make my case to my parents with anymore – they will tell me what a nice school this is, what a nice boy Msizi is. I am left with nothing. At least if he had been snobbish and a guy's guy then I could say something about feeling uncomfortable around him but now, I have nothing. Nothing, nothing, nothing! What's worse is that I might also like him. Such traitor behaviour, like I hadn't already thought of a way out of here by end of this quarter. I saw the way Mama smiled when they left – she wanted me to know that she is very happy with him as my roommate.

It was the same smile she gave Papa when Sipho and I broke up.
They didn't see that I was listening when Papa told her about it –
he was sitting closest to the window by the house phone when we
ended it. I saw how her lips widened when she heard the news.
I didn't mind that smile then because Sipho was just a shitty phase
and I'm glad I am over that.

Anyway, what mother wouldn't smile when they find out that their
child has stopped dating the manager of the local Spur? Shame
Mama, she always said she had big dreams for me. That Sipho thing
was not helpful. At all. I don't know what had gotten into me.

But today I minded that smile because it means she is happy with
whatever my life will be here. I don't even know whether we'll get
along well but my mother is already giving her grin of approval.
But I guess as she always says, she knows better, so maybe this is
one of the times when she does because as much as I hate to admit
it, I think I also won't mind living with him.

What is that noise? Is that snoring? Oh my goodness, seriously,
it sounds like he snores. Oh, it's not snoring, it's heavy breathing.
He's a heavy breather. Of all the things in the world, a heavy breather,
really? I don't know anymore. Is this what I have to suffer? A roommate
who breathes like an Amazonian creature in the quiet of night trying
to scare off attackers by making scary night sounds?

How are we going to deal with this diary? Does this mean I won't be
able to enjoy some good sleep on my first night here? The tragedy
of it all.

. . . .

'You are killing me here. Amazon creature friend, e feng?' her laugh now turning into a fit as she threw up the possibilities. 'Ke Iguana or Tamarin or Glass Frog or eng?'

'Mxim, focus or have I lost you to the Amazon?'

'Hai but friend this is a gem of a file. If I was your mom I'd have also been on some, nope, not my child.'

'Waitse you're not to be trusted. You were there for the entire Sipho thing and not once did you say, "no friend, don't do it".' I was playing at making her feel guilty but she was not biting. 'You know, even before I told them we were together, my mom remembered him immediately the day he came for my uncle's funeral. Naye she'd always had a soft spot for him. Actually, maybe it's you and her that need a commission of enquiry as to the super-naturals that brought him back into my life.'

'Methinks you should write a book my friend and this would be the opening scene. With the award and public interest in your story, it would be a best-seller for sure. Young-unrequited-love that becomes true-love a decade later! Add to that questions of supernatural influences and you've got the makings of a movie friend! Like, think about it,' seeing the amusement in my eyes, 'seriously.'

'OK Ms media connoisseur, I will but we're not finished here. Yeah or …?'

'Not for the awards but for the book, yep!'

'Shucks, have to leave for dinner in thirty and Mzi is always on time so let's get moving.'

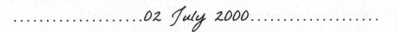

....................02 July 2000....................

Diary, how was your day. A few thoughts for you on mine …

I am so disgusted with myself!!! Why must I always be the square in the room or anywhere for that matter!

It's like I don't belong anywhere. Like I don't belong in this body.

No matter how much I try, I feel that I am always a step too far or always trying to catch up with what this body really wants and what it really is. Always second fiddle to all of them. To all of it.

I think even they're starting to suspect that there is something wrong with this picture. Can you imagine, after all the work I've done to make myself unnoticeable to them? Now they are talking about how my silence is worrying them. Why must parents be forever worried?

They heard me talking to myself. I was saying that I felt like I didn't belong with them. Which is true, I don't belong with them. Every day in this house is torture. I only find comfort when I am by myself and I have free time.

Mama keeps asking me what's eating me up. Why I'm not playing with the other kids. She thinks I'm intentionally being like this. If only she knew.

When will she see that I am staying away from them to protect myself? That I'm not sure of what I am and so I can't tell anyone that I always feel like I am a square when everyone else is a circle? That I don't fit in with all these kids and not even with them as my parents.

How do I tell her that I don't feel like the boy she thinks I am. That I don't know whether I can say that I know for sure that I am a boy. How does she expect me to tell her these things? I'll keep quiet for as long as it takes, until I know what to do about this. I want to go somewhere very far from here. I would ask that they make me right and then only come back here once I've been corrected.

And why doesn't she know it already. Doesn't she always say 'mothers always know'.

Or maybe I could go away forever, forget that I ever knew these people and just be myself somewhere. I don't know where but just somewhere. I also don't know who myself is but I think whoever that is, will be better than feeling like this square here all the time. Maybe I must go and find other squares.

· ·

The tears came again, travelling the separation of thirteen thousand kilometres of towns, people and cities, made visible by cables, screen pixels and headphones.

'I think,' her hands wiping tears and mucus from her face, 'this is the one!'

My eyes continued with a steady stream of tears.

· · · · · · · · · · · · · · · · *16 May 2000* · · · · · · · · · · · · · · · · ·

Diary, how was your day today? A few thoughts for you on mine ...

Oh dear lord diary, the way she bores me.

I don't get what Msizi sees in her. With a name like that, Claire – without character or strength or presence even. Much like her in fact! Mediocre is what it is.

I wonder what her parents were thinking when they named her? Giving her such a white girl's name! A name that has no expectations, no hopes, no demands for a great life! That she was destined for greatness because her parents had seen it and so rightly named her. Nope not with a name like Claire. No greatness is expected here.

The entire time I watched them today, I wanted her breasts. I'd never taken notice of them this way before until today. I don't know why, perhaps today I felt the strongest that I wanted to be a girl. To be the one kissing Msizi. I know that if I was a girl, for sure he would be my boyfriend.

It would be him and I who spend all that time together after his morning run. It would be him and I who the school can't stop talking about because we are perfect that way. It would be him and I who continue to place first each term and would be celebrated as a couple instead of this constant back and forth ménage à trois with Claire, fighting for top of the grade.

When will I accept that it's me who is the weird one in this scenario? They are perfect together, the talk of the school, yet her parents did not think to think for her and who she could become in this world. That she would have a great love like Msizi. That she would be blessed with a loving man who deserved a girl with a strong name, a name that demanded attention, a name that knew it would be something in the future, like mine, Nhlanhla. Sad!

Anyway, her breasts. I wanted them today. No. I want them every day.

Diary, for the first time today, when I looked at them hugging, I felt so jealous. Today I knew I wanted to be a girl for always. Her breasts made me miss mine. I want my own breasts. I want them to also feel the hardness of a torso, to feel the pressure of being crushed by a force stronger than your own and still feel pleasure. I want to feel my nipples standing firm, piercing with longing each time we kiss. I want my own breasts.

. . . .

'Not a tearjerker like the last one. I think we can even end our work for the day.' Zinhle said with a forced lightness to her voice, the sadness of the previous entry still lingering in the air.

I remained quiet for a few seconds, choked by my self pity. 'I don't think anyone can ever understand the self hate and longing to be someone else my entire life has been.' I became weak from the tears that were clouding my eyes, and I folded into a childlike state. I longed for my mother to hug me and soon felt Msizi's arms envelop me.

'Hey Mzi, aren't you guys meant to meet there for dinner?' Zinhle asked.

Shifting to squat between my thighs and lift my face to look him in the eyes, he answered with his back to Zinhle. 'Wanted to get out of these clothes. What are you guys doing and why the tears?'

'You still want to continue friend?' Zinhle asked over Msizi.

. . . . *03 December 2000* . . . .

Diary, how was your day today? A few thoughts for you on mine

What a shit day diary. What a shit day. The shittiest shit day of all of my life!

What was I thinking? What was I thinking? Who said I must tell him? Who said I should do it? You should have stopped me in fact. If you were as good a friend as I've always made you to be, you should have stopped me, diary. You should have.

Whoever told me this thing about telling the truth was lying to me. I've seen twice now that nothing good ever comes out of that. Now I've lost a friend because the truth had to be told, because I had to open my big mouth. Next time please remind me not to rely on the ability of truth to make friendships last longer. We were fine all through the year with my lie there, always present but very absent.

Now I know better than to tell. At least this time I remembered to look at his face when I told him. He just looked afraid the whole time.

I saw his reaction, diary. This time I kept my focus on the face and looked at his eyes. Well I guess I didn't have a choice in the matter. We were both standing and facing each other. I saw him shift two steps back so that he wasn't too close to me.

'A what?' he kept saying. He, trying all he could not to run. Not to scream. Not to do anything that would draw attention to us.

I saw how his eyes changed and the distance widened between us. Physically, we were arm's length apart but emotionally we had just grown millions of hands and feet apart. I saw his eyes. They grew disgusted as I went on, telling him that I had always liked him. That I had hoped that by telling him the truth, there might be a chance for us, no matter how slim it was.

I don't know what I'm going to do tomorrow when my parents come here. They'll want to talk to him. He has to come here to pack as well. Is he going to come tonight or wait only for tomorrow after I'm gone?

I must get my stuff all packed right now so I don't have to be in here for long tomorrow. I know him well enough to know he will avoid this room for as long as it takes.

. . . .

'You remember this day, babe?' I asked Msizi, sitting on his lap, both of us reading the entry to Zinhle. He, in silence.

Is it Love That Has You?

BISHARA MOHAMED

HOT AND ARID SEASON

It was a hot, humid day, the type of day when the elements stick to you: heat, moisture, earth. The wind found ways into the loose folds of people's clothing, bringing with it the sands it carried. Cities have their own pace and personalities, and Xamar is slow, observant and friendly. The smell of the Indian Ocean rises by afternoon time, so filled with salt, fresh fish and seaweed that you can taste it.

Sabrin always knew she was different. She could never tell when she was awake or in a dream. She spent her days in her head. And when she wasn't entirely in her head, she was floating just above her body. Only by a few feet though. She didn't want to lose the link, and when anyone touched her she jumped and came crashing back into herself. Her difference, she thought, was because she was quiet – but there was nothing quiet about her eyes.

One day Sabrin saw her.

Her.

Wearing knee-length shorts with a basketball tucked under her arm, her short afro like a fuzzy halo around her head. This wiilo was obviously coming back from playing basketball somewhere, she was covered in sweat that glistened and glowed on her skin. Sabrin stared. Her heart sped up. She froze in her place. Heat ran through her body, flushing her and making her feel like she had a fever. Her knees felt weak enough to give way under her.

'Who's that?' Sabrin asked Ilwaad, her heart slowing down a little now.

'That's Ubax,' said Ilwaad. 'She just moved into our neighbourhood. Why do you ask?'

So her name was Ubax. 'Flower' seemed a bit odd and girly for such a wiilo.

Sabrin and Ilwaad walked on, past the usual and familiar characters of their neighbourhood, including their old and quiet neighbour with her twenty goats, the twenty goats and the mango tree Sabrin was always in.

As soon as Sabrin got home she poured herself a glass of water. I must be sick, she thought. She remembered Ubax: full lips, thick lowbrows, dark and tall, skin glistening, sweaty, coming back from playing ball … Sabrin's heart skipped a beat. I must be getting very sick, she thought.

She did her homework. Then she wished her hooyo goodnight – 'Habeen wanaagsan, Hooyo' – and went to sleep early.

'Naya! Kac! Kac! Inna Tukotid Wayeh!' her hooyo shouted in the pre-sunrise twilight, waking Sabrin to pray fajr. At the end of her prayer, Sabrin made duas asking Allah to take away this sickness she had no name for. Then she took her time getting dressed, then slowly and very intentionally putting kohl around her eyes.

She couldn't stop thinking of Ubax as she walked quickly to school. She was the first person to reach her class. She went in. She didn't notice the other students coming in one by one. She was too engrossed in her romance novel, *Ignorance is the Enemy of Love* by Faarax MJ Cawl.

The macalin came in. 'Subax wanaagsan,' he said.

'Subax wanaagsan, Macalin.'

After the usual attendance, he called for everyone's attention.

'We have a new student with us today. Ubax, come in and introduce yourself.'

Sabrin stiffened instantly, then she froze little by little.

She couldn't hear what Ubax was saying over the beating of her own heart.

'Welcome to my class, Ubax,' said the Macalin. 'There is a seat next to Sabrin, go sit there.' He pointed to the empty desk.

As Ubax walked towards Sabrin, the same feelings she had when she first saw Ubax came back and washed over her – and something else … nervousness.

Sabrin sat frozen. She tried her best to look calm and grounded as she panicked internally. She stared ahead, not turning to look at Ubax coming in her direction.

There was a tapping on her shoulder. Sabrin looked up.

'Can I borrow your pencil sharpener?' Ubax said. 'My pencil broke.' Her voice was warm, deep, and comforting.

Without saying a word Sabrin quickly pulled out her pencil sharpener from her backpack, placing it on her desk to avoid touching Ubax.

'Thanks,' said Ubax when she put the sharpener back on Sabrin's desk.

'Welcome,' Sabrin mumbled. She didn't trust her voice. She went back to staring ahead at the chalkboard.

At lunchtime, Ubax sat by herself under a sprawling tree with such huge leaves that no sunlight could peek through its shade. Asma, one of Sabrin's friends, noticed Ubax alone, and nudged Sabrin. 'The new girl looks miskin and alone over there. Let's go introduce ourselves.'

'Okay, but you do the talking,' Sabrin said.

The two friends walked over to Ubax. Sabrin's heart started to race again and a surge of heat ran through her body.

'Hi,' Asma said.

'Hi,' said Sabrin.

'Hi,' replied Ubax.

'I'm Asma, and this is my friend Sabrin.'

'I'm Ubax. Nice meeting you both.'

'What kind of music do you like?' asked Asma

'Waaberi, Omar Dhuule, Hudeidi, Khadra Daahir Cige, Max-amed Axmed Kuluc and Maandeeq. Oh and Abdel Rab Idris,' Ubax listed them.

'You have great taste!' exclaimed Asma

They talked music till the lunch break was over, with Sabrin quietly daydreaming the whole time.

When Sabrin was walking home later on, she heard her name being called behind her. She didn't recognise the voice. Or did she? Who could it be? Was a jinni calling her or a real person? Sabrin heard running footsteps fast approaching. She decided to risk it and turned around.

'Hi!' Ubax said, slightly out of breath.

'Hi!' Sabrin said, on the startled side.

'I was walking home and saw you walking ahead of me,' Ubax said.

They walked together awhile in silence.

'Where did you move from?' Sabrin asked.

'Kismaayo.'

'What's it like there?'

'It's alright, I guess.'

The silence returned, full of awkwardness and tension. Sabrin snuck quick glances at Ubax as they walked. She has beautiful; almond-shaped eyes, and a thick lowbrow framing them, Sabrin noted. She kept sneaking glances at Ubax, her eyes falling on Ubax's high cheekbones, her square jawline and her small pointed chin. Her dark skin was luminous in the deep glow that it had. Sabrin was tall herself, and Ubax was just a little bit taller. Sabrin became aware of how fast and loudly her heart was beating. Could Ubax hear it?

They continued walking on the sidewalk which had been dampened from earlier rain, the smell of wet dirt and earth rising.

'What do you like to do for fun?' Ubax asked at last, breaking the long silence.

'I take a lot of walks,' Sabrin replied. 'I like walking, reading. I'm pretty boring actually.' She was relieved that the long and awkward silence was over. 'What do you like to do for fun?' she asked back as a courtesy

'Sports, especially basketball,' Ubax replied. 'And I like walking as well.'

'This is where I live,' Sabrin said when they got to her house. 'Nice talking to you, and see you tomorrow.'

'Nice talking to you as well, and see you tomorrow,' Ubax responded.

Sabrin and Ubax fell into a routine of walking with each other to school and back home. Oftentimes they would hold hands. This is an affectionate gesture of intimacy that everyone does with their friends of the same gender. It thrilled Sabrin and made her heart speed up, her previous feelings of sickness beginning to fade.

One day Ubax invited Sabrin over to her house. They ate Italian biscuits and drank Fanta in Ubax's room, talked and talked about everything – from which teachers they liked to what their favourite movies were. They played all their favourite songs, and danced till they collapsed on the floor.

Awkwardness and tension filled the silence and the space between them once again.

Sabrin, feeling bold, moved nearer to Ubax and kissed her on one cheek, which was soft and smelled like sesame seed oil. The silence now filled with charged energy. Sabrin leaned in to kiss Ubax on her other cheek, this time closer to her mouth. Ubax turned to her, and they shared a slow and lingering kiss.

Sabrin pulled back and gasped. They held each other's eyes for a long time, Sabrin watched as Ubax's eye filled with nervousness and then switched very quickly to desire and then to an indescribable softness. Then they started to inch towards each other, shifting closer to each other from where they lay propped up on the floor. Closing the distance between them. They kissed once more, lips and breath, slow and full of longing and lingering long afterwards. To them it felt as if time had stopped, and only when they stepped back did it start functioning again.

'Was this your first time?' Ubax asked.

'In kissing a girl, yeah.' Sabrin replied enthusiastically. 'I've kissed a couple of boys before, and it was nothing like that! What about you?'

'It was my first time kissing a girl as well,' Ubax said. 'I've kissed one boy before and it was slobbery. You have soft lips, and you smell great.'

'Thanks! You're a good kisser!'

'So are you!'

This was when I realised that the sickness I thought I had, those strange feelings, were my own longing and desire. Neither of these pulls had I felt so intensely before in my sixteen years of life.

In a short time, Ubax became the closest friend I've ever had. We walked to school together and home together, hand in hand, often. We kissed many more times. To be cautious, we alternated between our houses. Her house one day, and then mine the other. We didn't do this more than three times a week so as to not raise suspicion. Always behind a locked door, we did our homework and assignments together, talked and fell silent a few times, then turned on music and made out. I found that I had memorised her feel and taste, her scents – and her softness, the thing I was the most surprised about. How soft she was, even if she was a wiilo.

It was because of the habit we had of making out while music blasted that we didn't hear the banging on the door.

BANG-BANG-BANG-BANG-BANG! BANG-BANG-BANG! BANG!

'NAYA! ALBAABKA FUR!' Someone was shouting at us to open up.

I pulled away from Ubax and opened the door to see Hooyo standing there, panting from her banging and yelling. 'Why do you have the door locked?' she gasped in between pants.

'So that we won't be disturbed while we do our homework.'

'Look,' she said. 'I heard some gunshots earlier, and I don't think Ubax should go home when I don't know how safe it is outside, and it's a really dark night. She can stay for the night.'

'Hiyea Hooyo,' I replied.

Hooyo left, and the depth of the night grew.

Ubax and I talked and talked until we were both yawning and could barely keep sleep at bay. We got ready to sleep and went to bed with our backs towards each other. After what seemed like an eternity I rolled over back onto my back, unable to sleep even though I was so tired.

'Sabrin?' Ubax asked in the darkness.

'Yes?'

'Are you still awake?'

'Yes.'

The silence stretched out before us into the night.

Ubax rolled over onto her side and looked at me.

'Is it okay if I kiss you?' she asked.

'Yes,' I said.

She kissed me and I lost track of time and place. Her hands started moving across my body, searching ... yearning. My body responded on its own to her touch before my mind could catch up, surprising myself.

I traced Ubax's entire body with my lips before taking in parts of her with my mouth ... her skin, her nipples, her clit. She kept eye contact with me the entire time, her look a mix of pleading and tenderness. She shifted under me, raised herself up, moving me gently onto my back on the bed, then slowly sliding into me.

She kept whispering, 'Sabrin, Sabrin, Sabrin,' my name filling her mouth and overflowing. There was an ache in me, and it grew with the pressure that was building, and there was a light. The ache and pressure grew and grew until we both trembled and shook with it, then when it crossed into almost pain we exploded. There is no other way to describe it, because the light covered everything for a second and then the pressure and ache stopped completely. We collapsed onto each other, sweaty, tired. And happy? It felt like it, and we held each other through the night.

The next morning I woke, filled with excitement mixed with apprehension. 'Has the shooter been found yet?' I asked Hooyo.

'I don't know. I haven't listened to the radio or talked to any of the neighbours yet,' she replied.

I quickly ate the canjeero iyo beer Hooyo had prepared for our breakfast, gulping down my shaah, which had barely cooled. Ubax on the other hand ate slowly and methodically, picking up one piece at a time with her canjeero and chewing slowly.

We walked to school in silence. After a few blocks I turned to Ubax and asked, 'Is what we did last night haram?'

'Shhh! Are you crazy?!? People could overhear us!' she whispered fast and loudly.

'But don't you worry that we could go to hell?'

'Not here,' she said, and we walked on in silence.

When we were close to school, Ubax grabbed my arm and pulled me under a tree where no one else was standing. 'Do you really think kissing and making out is haram?' she asked.

'It's a different degree, what we did, they're different things,' I answered.

'I thought about what you said –' Ubax started to say.

'And?'

'I can't tell you what's haram or halaal, but I like you a lot and I like being with you. And I feel like I've known you forever, even though it's been such a short time.'

'I like you a lot too, and really enjoy being with you,' I replied.

'Then what is the problem?'

'Ubax, don't you worry? Or get anxious? I mean there isn't even a word in our language for what we are.'

'Yeah, I do worry and get anxious and somehow I forget all that when I'm with you,' she replied.

'SABRIIIN! UBAAX!'

We looked up quickly, like we were caught doing something we shouldn't have been. Asma was running towards us.

'Hey!' she let out with a panting breath. Then she became aware of the energy between us, and looked from one of us to the other. 'What were you two talking about?'

'Nothing really, Ubax just wanted to show me this tree,' I said.

'Oh?' Asma said, not able to hide the suspicion on her face.

The bell rang and we walked on to school together.

Asma wasn't the only one who noticed that there may have been something going on between us. Our classmates soon started asking why we spent so much time together and away from everyone else. We would tell them that it was because we were best friends.

Ubax was over one day as usual in our secret lovership. It was like any other time before that. We chatted, did our homework. Then started kissing and making out.

Knock-knock-knock.

There was someone at the door and before we could react Hooyo came in.

Ubax and I pulled away from each other quickly.

Had she seen us?

Hooyo looked at us. She kept quiet for what seemed like a long time. She inhaled loudly, growing bigger and bigger from her long breath, as her eyes widened and her face twisted with hatred.

'I knew it! I knew it! I knew it! KHANIISYAAL! MY DAUGH-TER IS A KHANIIS!

'Hooyo, wait ...' I stammered.

'GET OUT!!!' she screamed at Ubax. 'Why are you still standing there! Get out of my house!'

Ubax's eyes filled with tears. 'Habaryar,' she said.

'Don't habaryar me!' Hooyo screamed. 'I'm calling your hooyo to tell her what kind of sick and filthy daughter she has.'

Tears streamed down Ubax's face as she walked to the door. She looked back at me from the doorway, her eyes overflowing with sadness and pain. When she looked at me with that face I started crying too, knowing deep within myself that I wouldn't see her again.

She disappeared from the doorway, and I went from crying to sobbing loudly. I didn't even realise Hooyo was charging at me with a broom in hand. My body took over, and I grabbed the broom before she struck me.

'Oh! You think you're stronger than me?' she screamed. 'Come! Hit me! khaanis! Dhiilo!'

'No...'

'You're trying to hit me! aren't you?!'

'No Hooyo ...'

'Don't call me that! I'm not a hooyo to such a sharmuuto like you!' she yelled with disgust.

This time her blows landed before my hand could grab the broom. She hit me again and again until the broom handle broke. I didn't feel any of it after the first blow, still howling over Ubax leaving my house and my life in the way that she was forced to. My emotional and mental anguish hurt more than Hooyo attacking me with a broom. At some point I was no longer in my body, but looking down at it from the ceiling, Hooyo standing over my body and hitting it with a frenzy and a lust, for my blood to spill or my bones to break. I saw my body put an arm up, but mostly I was shrinking into a ball, still sobbing, still wailing. When had I left my body?

In the blink of that thought, I felt the pain of the beating and I was in my body again as Hooyo grabbed a fistful of my hair and started dragging me across the room, hitting me in the face. Her punches landed square, but her knuckles were cushioned by her chubby hands and fingers and she was weak for such a large woman.

For once I was grateful for her weakness, despite her size, and her ineffective punches.

She was panting heavily and sweating profusely.

I fainted more from tiredness than pain and my body saying 'enough'. I'm sure she only stopped beating me because she thought she had killed me. Which is why I jumped from shock at the cold water thrown on me.

When Hooyo was sure I was still alive, she left. I could hear her panting receding, along with her heavy-footedness.

I lay on the floor crying till I got too cold to be there anymore. Then I changed my wet clothes and moved into my bed, and cried till I fell asleep.

When I returned to school, with all my bruises and a black eye, I told my classmates I had fallen down the stairs, which they all accepted even though they knew it was a lie. Ubax was nowhere to be found. Time passed slowly, and she never reappeared. I asked around, and found out she'd been sent to Saudi Arabia to live with her aunt.

Shortly after we were found out, Hooyo had an exorcism done on me.

I sat there, tired, and numb to the beatings and demands from the Imam willing whatever jinni had a hold on me to come forth. None did, because I wasn't possessed by anything, but a love for Ubax.

Many years have passed since I met Ubax and we were separated. In the many years that have passed I married a man who came along at some point and who I settled for, and had children with him.

I think about her when my husband thrusts into me in his lacklustre and quick pattern that's over as quickly as it began.

There isn't a time that I don't think of Ubax, she haunts my days and my nights.

It's for this exact reason I haven't been able to be in a relationship with another girl or woman since. The time with Ubax is a time I can't return to in the same way ever again. Remembering her fills me with such sadness and longing, an exile from my love, my country and who I used to be. It's a shame I never told her how much I loved her and still love her.

This just might be the exile that I die in.

The Stone

MATSHEPO THAFENG

Outside the village of Bakgatla there lies a stone, old and full of
wisdom.

Once upon a time, King Lamar was on his deathbed, tired and
weak. 'Call my eldest daughter Maruo' he said to his wife Queen
Zama.

At that time, Bakgatla was being torn apart by rage and rumours
that put the whole village in a poverty-stricken situation. Some said
King Lamar had burned his father's house down to hide the secret
ashes that were killing crops and chasing the rains away. King Lamar
was too sick to do anything about the hostility that was taking away
peace from his late father's land. And when Queen Zama asked him
about all those nightmares he had every night, he stared at the wall
and said nothing.

Maruo came to her father's bedside. She thought he had lost so
much weight that he looked like a 16 year old boy. 'Father, what can
I do for you?' she said.

King Lamar shed a tear. 'Please leave us, my queen,' he said to
his wife.

Then followed a long closed session between King Lamar and his
daughter Maruo. During this time, a dark cloud covered the village
of Bakgatla and it suddenly poured with rain. In this weather, Maruo
hurried on a journey to the village of Nongoma.

Aunt Rosa was excited. She had promised her niece Zandi to give her a wedding that Nongoma had never seen before. She was stroking the fine material of the gorgeous white wedding dress she had bought for Zandi in town, when the doorbell rang. 'Go and see who it is, Zandi,' Aunt Rosa said. Zandi went down the stairs singing a lullaby her late mother used to sing for her. *Thula thula baba, thula sana. Thulu mama uzobuya ekuseni.*

Maruo was waiting outside the door with her head down. It was drizzling with chilly, biting rain. Her hair was wet, her body was shaking, and her bare feet were cold. She rang the bell again with all her might and the ringing landed terribly on Zandi's eardrums. 'Hang on! I'm coming!' called Zandi. The cold from outside puffed inside Aunt Rosa's exquisite mansion with Maruo, who instantly fell down on the floor. Zandi screamed with fear. 'Aunt Rosa! Please hurry!'

Maruo was curling her body into the carpet. 'I'm so cold,' she trembled.

'Sshh! Don't say a word,' said Zandi. She opened the hall closet and took out the blanket on the top shelf.

'How many times must I tell you children to refrain from using your grandfather's things!' Aunt Rosa hissed behind Zandi.

'I don't understand you, Aunt Rosa,' said Zandi. 'There was no time to think. The poor girl is shaking.' But Zandi gave the blanket to Aunt Rosa and covered Maruo with her denim jacket. Aunt Rosa sniffed the blanket.

'Do you know her?' Aunt Rosa asked.

'No,' said Zandi.

They looked at the girl on the floor.

'Then why do you care?' Aunt Rosa said. She looked into Zandi's eyes.

Zandi turned and went to the telephone and dialled a number.

'What are you doing?'

'I am calling the hospital.'

'You don't want to do that,' said Aunt Rosa, and went back up-stairs. Zandi heard her close her bedroom door.

How can she expect me to leave this poor girl lying here? Zandi thought. She started pacing up and down the room. But those who defy Aunt Rosa don't live long, a voice in her head said.

'You are bigger than this,' Maruo whispered. 'Please help me.' Then she went back to sleep.

Zandi looked at Maruo, then glanced up the stairs. She opened the small closet next to the kitchen door and took out some old boxes. Inside the empty closet, she opened the secret door that led to the secret room. Just then, the oven alarm went off and Zandi jumped like a leaf scared of a thunderstorm. Maruo's frozen body did not stir. Zandi dragged Maruo deep into the secret room, put the boxes back inside the closet, and quickly closed the door. She rushed to the kitchen and took the burning baking pan from the oven. 'Ouch!' she cried. The pan landed in the clean sink. Zandi's fingers were burning. She took a napkin and carefully placed the large ball of roasted chicken on the side of the sink.

'Zandi? Is the chicken ready?' she heard Aunt Rosa's voice from the doorway. 'Mmm! There is nothing that smells like my secret recipe roasted chicken.' Aunt Rosa took a huge knife and sliced the hot roasted chicken with precision. 'If this chicken turns into stone, I will stab it till I draw every drop of blood out of it,' Aunt Rosa smiled.

'Who taught you to do that, Aunt Rosa?'

'My father. Your grandfather.'

'Mkhulu,' said Zandi.

Zandi followed every movement Aunt Rosa made as she placed steaming pieces of chicken on the plate Zandi had given her. Zandi's burnt fingers started screaming, and she opened the tap and let the water run over them.

'What did you do, Zandi?' Aunt Rosa licked fat and pieces of burned spices off the knife with her tongue.

Zandi closed the tap, but when the burning came back she opened it again. 'What do you mean?'

'Why are you running water through your fingers as if you have something to hide?' Aunt Rosa put the knife down in the sink. She took hold of Zandi's hand and scrutinised it .

'Aunt Rosa,' said Zandi, 'I think you should go upstairs and start to get ready for dinner.' Zandi pulled her hand away.

'What dinner?'

'The Ndunganes are coming over. Have you forgotten?'

Aunt Rosa tried to stand still, but her knees gave in. Zandi watched her dizzy body spinning around in the kitchen. Aunt Rosa did not look good at all. Her face had turned grey and her nose was longer than before.

'Aunt Rosa!' Zandi called out. 'Aunt Rosa!'

'I think I'm going to be sick.' And Aunt Rosa fell down on the floor.

Maruo was standing on top of Aunt Rosa's naked body. Zandi walked hesitantly towards them, untying her headscarf. She covered Aunt Rosa's nakedness with it, looking the other way.

'Don't you want to know why your Aunt Rosa has a dick instead of a punani?' said Maruo. She snatched away the scarf from Aunt Rosa's private parts. She grabbed Zandi's chin and turned her face to look, but Zandi pushed her away. Maruo grabbed Zandi's arm and twisted it until she had Zandi lying down on the floor next to Aunt Rosa. She tied Zandi's scarf back around her head. She looked down at both of them lying there. "I am not here to hurt anyone,' she said. 'My father, King Lamar of Bakgatla, is asking for you, Jabu Solomon KaNgwane.'

'Who?' said Zandi.

Maruo continued to address the unconscious Aunt Rosa. 'My father could die anytime soon. I do not condone what the two of you did. But if it means saving Bakgatla, what choice do I have? I have to make sure you come back with me.'

At last, Zandi took a good peep at Aunt Rosa's private parts. She saw a thumb-sized penis. And Aunt Rosa's chest was covered with hair all over. Zandi got up, closed the kitchen curtains, and put on a kettle. 'Sit down,' she said to Maruo. 'Tell me more.'

'We don't have much time,' said Maruo. 'My life, my father's life, the village and its people depend on your Aunt Rosa showing up at my doorstep.'

Zandi could see that Maruo was deeply troubled.

'Do you have any means that can carry your Aunt Rosa to my father's bedside before it's too late?' Maruo pleaded.

Zandi took the car keys and they pulled and dragged the naked Aunt Rosa into the back seat. 'The chicken ... the chicken ...' Aunt Rosa mumbled.

'I always thought they were made up stories about the people and the village of Bakgatla,' said Zandi as she drove them away from Nongoma. 'All this time when Aunt Rosa told us stories about a manservant who fell in love all those years ago with the Prince of Bakgatla, your father King Lamar, she was actually talking about herself, I mean himself, Jabu Solomon KaNgwane.' She shook her head and glanced back quickly at Aunt Rosa' s naked body.

'I know,' said Maruo. She was feeling relieved. She had convinced them to come back with her. What would her father think? What would happen next? 'The fact that my father killed his own father to protect a secret love, my father's love for his manservant, for your so-called Aunt Rosa ...' Maruo was looking at Zandi's profile. Zandi's beautiful eyes were focused on the road. 'Do you believe that love is capable of murder?' said Maruo.

Just less than an hour from the village of Bakgatla, Aunt Rosa rose from her sleep. She screamed when she realised she was naked. 'Oh no!' she cried. 'I haven't seen that thing in a long time. Somebody give me something to cover this bloody curse.' She ripped off the car seat covers and made herself a little skirt. Her ready-made breast wool hung down to cover her round belly.

'When were you planning to tell us the truth Aunt Rosa – Argh! I mean Uncle Solomon?' said Zandi. She stopped the car.

'We have to keep on moving Zandi, please,' pleaded Maruo. 'My father doesn't have much time.'

But Zandi was opening the door and getting out of the car.

'What are you doing?' Maruo screamed. 'Come back!'

'I think I am going to be sick,' Zandi said. And she fell down.

'Oh! No, no, no!' Maruo opened her door and rushed round to Zandi. 'You can't do this to me. Not when we are less than an hour to Bakgatla.' She breathed into Zandi's mouth and pumped her chest. 'Come on!' She tried again.

Aunt Rosa also got out of the car. 'Is she alive?' she asked, looking down at Zandi. 'Tell you what. Give me your clothes and I will run as fast as I can to King Lamar's bedside.'

Maruo immediately took off her dress and gave it to Aunt Rosa. But Aunt Rosa's dick was hanging like an overripe banana, so Maruo had no choice but to also hand over her nice red underwear. 'Run!' And like the speed of air, Aunt Rosa ran.

Maruo struggled a bit to get Zandi on her back, and then she sprinted in the direction Aunt Rosa had taken.

'I can't believe I'm hanging on a naked woman's body like a brush running through a horse's hair,' Zandi murmured.

Maruo smiled and put her down. 'You bastard,' she said.

'You dog,' said Zandi.

They laughed and walked a few miles. They joked about Aunt Rosa's sunburnt dick. 'I can understand where Aunt Rosa is coming from,' said Zandi. 'Who wants to own a piece of that stick.' Clouds gathered, and a shooting star moved across the clouds. They came to a tree and stopped to take a quick break.

'I am not worried when I am with you,' said Zandi, and took Maruo in her arms. 'Aunt Rosa used to say that when I come of age, ready to get married, something wonderful is going to happen.' Maruo blushed at Zandi's words. 'It feels like I have known you forever and yet it is only few hours,' said Zandi. She played with Maruo's pubic hair.

But then a horn blew loudly nearby. 'My father!' said Maruo, and pulled away from Zandi. She ran towards the village of Bakgatla screaming, 'Papa! No!' She ran and ran. 'Papa, Papa!'

Maruo was welcomed by a hue and cry of women throwing themselves on the ground. Villagers were hitting the ground with their fists. When Maruo looked around, she saw green trees that had been dry when she left. She saw her uncles interrogating Aunt Rosa. 'She is with me,' Maruo declared. She stopped her uncles from hitting Aunt Rosa with sticks.

'What happened to your clothes child?' her uncles enquired. 'Lord help us. Maruo, cover your body,' someone said. 'What is wrong with this child? Can't you see we are mourning the death of Queen Zama, your mother?' another one said.

Maruo rushed to the palace. She found her father well and awake and sitting next to her late mother. 'Papa, what happened?' She threw herself on the floor. Her younger sisters covered her naked body with a cloth.

'Two minutes we were bidding Papa goodbye, another minute Mama fell in Papa's arms,' one of her sisters explained. 'We thought we had lost them both, but it turned out Papa has come back to life.'

Maruo cried for her mother the whole time the funeral arrangements were being made. 'I don't understand!'

After the funeral, King Lamar and Maruo found a chance to talk. Maruo was worried about Aunt Rosa and Zandi. King Lamar assured her that he would do everything in his power to find them.

'Do you also promise not to tell the villagers about your sexual preferences Papa?'

'I have lived my whole life defending a lie, child,' said King Lamar, taking hold of his golden cobra head stick. 'Life without the one you truly love is nothing but a painful experience.' He put on his shoeshine shoes and proudly raised his head. 'I have walked that road, and truly speaking I am not there anymore.'

Maruo blocked the door that led to the outside world. 'What about honour, Papa? You promised we would have wealth if I brought back your lover.' She looked straight into her father's eyes, demanding answers.

'You are acting like a fool,' said King Lamar. 'I did not raise you to complain.' He put on his tiger printed jacket. 'If the villagers decide to take away everything from us, we will figure something out.' King Lamar pushed Maruo aside with his stick, and then he took a little journey around the village.

Rain had fallen and the land was restored to its beauty. The villagers were singing, and children were running around playing. King Lamar swung his stick, with a song playing in his mind. *Mangwane mpulele ke nelwa ke pula. Leha dile pedi, leha dile tharo ka nyala mosadi.* Maruo looked at him from a distance. 'I wonder what kind of love makes you want to give up everything you have worked hard for and disappoint everyone who looks up to you.'

Maruo's sister appeared at the door and told her there was someone waiting outside to see her. Maruo found Zandi admiring the garden. 'Some flowers you got here,' she smiled. 'Beautiful to the eye, and refreshing to the mind. What a combination.'

Maruo was not pleased to see her. 'What are you doing here?'

She looked at Zandi like she was some stranger. 'I thought you were captured and sent back where you came from.' Maruo folded her arms.

'Excuse me! After all that I have done, trusting you with my life and saving your life in the process. Is this the thanks I get?' Zandi pushed Maruo violently.

Maruo pushed back. 'Do you have any idea what your Aunt Rosa has done?' Mucus ran down her nose. She sniffed it back. 'I have watched my mother pray for this village to get better. And when it finally does, she does not get to see it. That's not fair!'

'Life is not fair Maruo.' Zandi tried to hug her. But Maruo pulled away.

Maruo's little sisters brought a jug of juice, glasses and a dish of freshly baked cakes. 'Are you two fighting?' one sister asked.

'No silly, they were just discussing old people stuff,' the other sister said, dunking cake in her juice.

'And how do you know, pumpkin face!' another sister joined in their argument.

'Because I heard Papa tell Mama that he is in love with a Zulu man.'

The sisters looked at each other and giggled.

'That's not funny,' Maruo warned them.

They held their little fingers on top of their mouths to stop giggling.

Maruo gave them a frightening look. But then she realised how lucky she was to have them, and she lowered her head and touched their little hands. 'That's very funny actually,' she whispered, and laughter broke out among King Lamar's daughters. Zandi joined in the laughter and enjoyed the view of the mountain tops. They all enjoyed the cakes and juice under the tree where the old stone lay full of wisdom.

Tar

MICHAEL AGUGOM

The first time I saw him come in – I remember it, because it was the day Mother mauled me with her stony words. She wanted me to take up a teaching job. She'd spoken to the headmistress of –

'Mother, I've told you, I have no desire to teach. Besides, I'm not trained for it.'

'You don't have to be trained. Look around you. No one on this island is doing what they desire, yet they're making money.'

'And how much exactly are they making?'

'Enough to get them out of bed every morning, to fetch them wife and start small family! What have you made with your so-called degree-certificate in engineering?! How much longer will I have a twenty-nine-year-old jobless and hopeless bachelor under my roof?! Count your teeth with your tongue, Tonworio.' She stormed out of the room and slammed the door behind her.

He made his entry under those circumstances.

I saw his head first. It burst through a puncture at the bottom of the termite-infested doorframe. He thrust more of his head in; squinted right and left as a thief would. And I knew: he's clever. I shifted on the bed and he retreated. I thought he was gone, but little did I know. His head again; I made no move. He had to decide on his own whether to come in or stay out. His skittish eyes looked me up and down; I pretended to be indifferent. More confident now, the rest of his body slipped out the hole: tiny, black, and cunning. And that mark on his side. He made up his mind and scurried left to the cupboard. Another occupant in our single room apartment.

Ebiye had said: Government is mouse. While it nibbles at your toes, it puffs air into the wound. A little pain and a little sweet sensation, at the same time. You are assuaged when you are supposed to be incensed. It is the way of authorities. I'd chortled. I'd argued with him.

It didn't take the mouse much time to have the map of our room in his head. The room wasn't much of a thing. Six by three, with a curtain that partitioned it in half. Behind the curtain were the bed, the cupboard and the clothes rail; on the other side, the table, the dead fridge, the plastic chair, the bookshelf and the TV stand. He came in and went as he pleased, as though he shared the rent with Mother. I called him Tar when sorrow became my garment, when Ebiye died in the pipeline explosion.

Ebiye was the brother my mother should have given birth to. He knew the front and back of my hand. And I knew his. When he returned from his fruitless sojourn in Europe and I returned from my fruitful university studies, I was the only one he confided in about what had made him unsuccessful. And he was the only one I told how I'd paid my way through school charging course-mates for impersonating them and writing their exams for them.

When Ebiye arrived in Albania, he realised he could not stay longer than a month: he had gone with a visiting visa. So he sought asylum, lying to the Albanian authorities that he was an environmental activist on the run from the Nigerian government. He ended up spending three years in asylum confinement. He lost hope of ever gaining freedom from that home and pleaded to be sent back to Nigeria. I was glad he returned home unsuccessful: his intention in going had been to peddle drugs. He would have been caught and injected with that chemical the rest of the world injects into convicted drug peddlers so that they return home and begin to rot alive. Ebiye could not have been successful; never, since our boyhood days had he stolen anything without being caught. After a year of being back, he did not begin to rot, and I knew he was telling the truth. I was glad to have him back. But six months later he died. We could have died together, but fate denied us that possibility. He had gone to scoop fuel from one of the broken government pipelines that run through the neighbourhood. No one could say exactly how the fire started, because only the explosion was heard. I would have gone with him that morning had I not suffered a hangover and overslept. As it was, it was the sound of Ebiye exploding that woke me up.

When Ebiye died, the sack of nails that was my head became heavier. I felt as though the nails were continually piercing my brain's membrane and I turned into an insomniac. When I couldn't sleep, Tar entertained me. I watched him make a grand tour of our room. I could see he knew where all the edibles could be found. The unwashed dishes were his favourite hangout. At night, he would eat up food remnants on the dirty dishes or gnaw at the wooden base of the cupboard. He loved to climb: on the bookshelf, on the cupboard, on the dead fridge. He was active and present. One minute he was at the corner of the bed, another minute behind the cupboard. Sometimes I would lie there, pretending to be dead, and watch him from between half-closed eyes. He would meander very close to me; but not too close to rile me.

Mother had gone away on omugwo for my new niece. Ebele, my reprobate younger brother, had just 'bore a whore' as he had been used to describe any female before he had gotten a girl of mixed race pregnant in his shop. He had believed her parents were based abroad and possessed plenty of foreign currency. But it turned out she didn't even know her father, an expatriate oil worker who had knocked up her mother and run back to his country. When Ebele found out he denied the pregnancy, claiming he hadn't been the only one shining the girl's shoe. Her mother brought thugs to his shop to burn it down, and they reached an agreement that when the baby was born, it would be tested to ascertain the father. In the end, no test was needed: the newborn female had Ebele's ears.

Ngonagbo brought me food. I felt ashamed I hadn't contributed a kobo to it. Ngonagbo had been my mother in our previous life. Mother had pointed that out so consistently it took an encumbering space in my memory bank. Mother called Ngonagbo 'our wife'; I was solemnly giving thoughts to making her my wife in our present life; my only handicap was lack of job.

'Have you had a bath at all?' Ngonagbo asked, opening the curtains for sunlight and sea breeze.

'Yes,' I lied. I had been indoors for two days, since Ebiye's death.

She opened the cooler: rice and chicken. 'Here, I hope you like it,' she said, and brought it to me on the bed.

I sat up to eat. She brought me a spoon from the cupboard. When she handed me the spoon, her hand trembled and she dropped the spoon on the bed. Something was wrong. I had a few spoons of the rice to calm my nerves. Her food was always no different from herself: wholesomely delectable. I made the mistake of looking up at her where she sat on the edge of the bed and I saw my fear in her eyes. 'Am I losing you too? You look like a drenched leaf,' I said.

It was taking her ages to gather her words. She got up and sauntered to the window, staring out at the rise and fall of sea-waves against sunlight. A scene I knew she had seen too many times to hold any grandiose ideas. Even though she'd opened the window, the room felt stuffy: her silence emitted too much heat. Whatever was taking such time to come out of her mouth could not be anything good.

'I'll be leaving for Onne tomorrow,' she finally said.

The sweet, buttery rice turned bitter in my mouth. I dropped the spoon. 'To return when?'

She turned to me and covered her face with a sad mask. 'I'm moving there.'

I asked her why by groping in her mind through her eyes.

'I've got a job at the seaport.'

'That's some good news,' I said. I thought I had managed to shroud my aching heart, but she's smart.

She returned to the edge of the bed and plopped down on it. 'I could come every weekend to see you. Onne isn't so far!'

'And when men with good jobs there ask you out?'

'Even if they do, it's up to me to consent isn't it? I'm going there to work, not look for a lover. Stop this men-with-job thing, Tons. You're not the only young man without a job.'

I didn't argue with her and when she left, I wrapped my dream of marrying her in a small cocoyam leaf and put it in the delicate hands of hope.

A few minutes later, Belema lumbered in as though on cue and started saying something. Belema is my neighbour. I could see his lips moving, lips that were the colour and texture of dry tar, but I wasn't listening. I wondered how any girl could stand kissing him. His eyes were bloodshot from smoking weed and his hairline was already receding, even though he was not yet twenty-five. He had always appeared thirty-something to me. When we teased him about the receding hairline he said it was a sign of wisdom, but I see where his wisdom lies: knowing when to take and never to give. He had made a career 'from cleverly grabbing money from the greedy,' as he justified his internet scams. Once, I asked him to change to a nobler career. He assured me he will when he's scammed the last greedy person on Planet Earth.

Belema had stopped talking. He sat on the plastic chair and took the cooler of rice. He examined it and said something else; he took the spoon and started eating. Ebiye, dead and gone, and Ngonagbo, leaving, were doing too good work eating my mind raw for me to fuss about the rice. I watched the rise and fall of the muscles at his temples as Belema wolfed my rice.

'Ol' boy! Ngo can cook-o,' he said between mouthfuls. 'I hope love potion no dey inside the rice?!' He was joking – only an insane lady would need a love potion for a jobless young man. He noticed I wasn't laughing. 'Ol' boy! I hope no problem? You look like fish wey men remove from water.'

'No problem,' I managed to say.

Having reduced the height of the rice, Belema took the chicken and left. He left the cooler in the washing bowl.

I lay back down on the bed. Tar scurried in. And another mouse followed right behind him; his friend I could easily tell. I wasn't surprised. His friend was on Tar's tail as he made for the cupboard. Maybe they are brothers, I thought. After a few seconds they were out again, scaling the doorframe.

We were sixteen when Ebiye became my brother. He earned it.

I'd lost Father to the disease that shrivels a man's genitals, and Mother was barely able to manage financially. Father's burial took a chunk of her savings. I was going to write my final exams to get into university. I had studied hard, but I discovered at the eleventh hour that that dream had been buried with Father's remains. I was sitting in my and Ebiye's lair, an abandoned shack a mile from the jetty.

Ebiye pranced in and sat with me before the vast sea, the sea that leads to the mainland and the bigger world beyond, the mainland I'd dreamt I would set foot on for the first time when I went university.

'Guy, how body?' Ebiye said, beaming his wandering eyes at me; those eyes that could see a fish twenty feet beneath the sea.

'Body dey inside cloth,' I said. I could not say I was feeling anything more.

'Wetin happen?'

'Nothing,' I lied.

He stared hard at me. 'Tell that to who doesn't know you. Come out with it abeg.'

'I won't be writing the exams.' Mother had begged whoever had ears for a fresh widow, dropped all she had scraped together in my palms. It was one thousand short of the total cost of registering for the exams. I had wept. 'Mumsy can't afford it.'

Ebiye stood silent, staring across the sea to our dreams; mine was on the mainland, his beyond the country. 'I'll travel beyond this sea; and so will you to your books,' he said.

I smiled to show him that my part of our dream was over.

'You'll write the exams, Tons,' he said and took off.

He was gone before I could ask where he was off to. We were supposed to throw our lines in for fish together, as we always did; to see who would catch something first, and the biggest fish.

Later that night, he came to our room and gave me the one thousand and a wild grin. 'I told you,' he said.

With my eyes, I asked him where he had gotten the money from. He made a sign with his finger to his lips. 'Just do me a favour: whatever happens, I mean whatever, don't mention that I gave you the money. Add it to what you already have and register for the exams. Promise me.'

On my way to school the next morning, a crowd of folks were noisily gathered at the front of Ebiye's compound. Some were entreating Ebiye's father to have mercy, others were egging him on:

'Have mercy, Papa Ebiye!'

'Papa Ebi, deal with him now lest he turns into an arm-robber tomorrow!'

'Don't kill him-o! It's just a thousand he stole, you want to kill him for it?'

I dashed closer and shouldered through the throng. I bumped my head against a woman's elbow, a bike-man slapped my shoulder for stepping on his toes, a buxom lady cussed me, 'You dey craze?'

I had mistakenly brushed her hips. I made it to the front. I saw Ebiye half naked, tied up, writhing on the ground. There were fresh slashes on his back. They were like bold red lines on a black slate. His father, a Defence Corps officer, was emptying a bowl of peppered water over him. Ebiye winced and groaned, with his teeth clenched. I could almost hear his heavy breathing.

'What did you do with the money?' his father bawled. 'I won't raise a thief in my house!'

Ebiye's swollen and teary eyes caught mine. In those eyes I saw ... With those eyes, he told me not to do what I was thinking.

The koboko lashed his back in quick succession, and he breathed in the pain without a plea or cry. And I watched. That long, flexible, leathery whip, used by the military for taming the unruly, came down on him more times, and I could feel every stroke lacerate my soul. Ebiye raised his head. The pain, the bruises, the trickling blood, the sweat, the shame, are something only a brother can endure for another brother. It made me shiver and tremble on my feet; tears fell on my lips and I felt their salty taste.

I held my schoolbag to my breast; the money was in it. I pushed my way through the crowd, who now seemed to agree that Ebiye had suffered enough punishment. I went to school and registered for the exams.

On my way home, I stopped by to see Ebiye. He was shivering in bed. I sobbed beside him.

'Wetin come dey do you?' he said, trying to smile. 'Why are you looking low? Were you the one flogged?'

'You should have told me, Ebi.' My voice shook.

'Tell you wetin? The money is for a good cause. I'll take more strokes for your sake if I have to. You won't remain on this island while I'm gone. Besides, if I hadn't taken it she would have spent it on one of her frivolities.'

'The money belonged to your step-mum?'

'And the witch sat there enjoying the show as I was flogged like Kunta Kinte.' He gave me a look, and raised a fist. 'Brothers forever!'

'Brothers forever!' We jammed our fists together. It remained our secret; our bond; my debt.

The night Ngonagbo left for Onne, I dreamt I was beaten into a stupor over her by two giants. She was sobbing when they stopped. She looked dishevelled herself. I couldn't tell if she was crying for me, or because of her own pain. I woke up perspiring. Then I heard the sound; it came from the washing bowl. I pointed my torch. Tar stared perplexed into the beam, then scuttled away behind the cupboard. He had been helping himself to some leftover rice from the cooler. I turned off my torch. Minutes later, the sound resumed anew. I paid him no mind: my mind was no longer in the room.

The next morning, Belema came in as he had two days before. Perhaps he thought there would be another cooler of rice. He said something about his laptop. I gave him an indifferent gesture, but he would not leave.

Tar came in and made for the cupboard and Belema saw him. 'Ol'boy, see that rat,' he exclaimed, pointing at Tar. 'That greedy bastard!'

I laughed at the irony.

'The yeye rat dey enter my room too,' claimed Belema.

'Not this mouse. He's too smart and always hungry.'

'How you sure no bi this one?'

'Because I know you're too selfish for him to survive in your room.'

'Selfish?! Something wey dey disturb me,' he said, emphasising a mouse's disturbance.

He didn't get the spite in my tone; I let it slide. 'What will you do about it?' I asked.

'I get rat poison already.'

'Who's ever stingy with poison,' I said.

'Wetin that wan mean?! You just dey insult me because I come your room. As you get sense, na rat you dey call *he*.'

'He has blood and feeds like us. Why shouldn't I call him *he*?'

'You don go crazy.'

'I think I am.'

'No. No bi think. You don mad.' Not upset or wounded by the argument but by the knowledge there was apparently no rice, Belema left.

When I tried to put on my trousers, I realised how much weight I had lost in the last four days. I had gone without food because I had only appetite to blow off blinding steam against the government, against Mother, against Ngonagbo – against everyone but Ebiye. I forced my mind to think of food and its importance if I wished to remain alive; to find food for that other appetite. At the door, I could not will myself to step beyond the threshold. I called out to Belema's little cousin and sent him to get me akara. Belema's cousin returned with it. I sat on the bed and ate a few lumps from the paper wrapper. The bean cake would have tasted better if my mood had not been as bad as a soured soup. I managed to reduce the number of lumps and set the remnants on the floor. I knew Tar would come, that he was somewhere in the room; if he wasn't, he would come in later.

I dozed off. Ebiye rose from the ashes after the explosion and walked towards me; then he disintegrated. Only his head remained intact. His head was on a decrepit gravestone. His eyes were blood-shot and blood drooled from his eyes, mouth and ears as he spoke. His words were stones tumbling off a cliff. 'Why did you abandon me? I'm your brother, Tons! Why did you leave me to blow up into shreds? What are you doing? What are you waiting for? Tons! Fight! Fight, Kill them, Tons! Kill the government – '

A sharp pain seared my fingers. I jerked awake. I saw Tar scuttle into a corner and then behind the cupboard. The akara wrapper had moved and the remnant was gone. I was sweating profusely and my fingers were bleeding. The biting pain in my fingers and the fury I bore in my heart burned in my soul. I hoisted myself out of the bed and went after Tar. I heaved up the cupboard and dropped it with a thud to crush him, but he dashed behind the bookshelf. When I lifted the shelf, all the books came tumbling down. Tar ran between my legs and out the room.

When I dragged my feet out of the door I felt a wave of hot air nip my skin. The brightness of day was blinding. I felt as though I was drowning in a warm pool. I marched next door to Belema's room. 'I need a little of that rat poison,' I said, barging in.

Belema was watching porn. He fumbled for the remote control. Too late. I had already seen the black man on the white woman.

'Wetin dey chase you?' he bellowed. 'I think say na my mother come inside.' He was panting heavily. It was difficult to tell whether from embarrassment or from the sensual effect of what he was watching.

'Sorry. You didn't lock the door.'

'Even if I lock-am, you for break the door the way you jus bash in. What's wrong with you?'

'Do you still have the poison, or not?'

He got up and fetched it from under his refrigerator and gave it to me. It was powdery, wrapped in cellophane. 'Ol'boy, I hope you no plan to drink-am yourself?'

'I'm not suicidal,' I said. 'Do you have any edible in this room?'

He pointed to his cupboard. I was surprised he admitted to having something.

I found bread and took a few slices. On my way out I said, 'Go out and get a girl. Stop punishing yourself watching these foreigners pretending before a camera.'

'I hear.'

I understood the sarcasm in his tone. I didn't care what he thought.
I left.

I sprinkled the poison on the bread. The poison smelt like goat
droppings. I dropped them generously at every bus stop of the room
and returned to bed and waited. Eventually Tar showed up, but he
was too clever to eat any of the poisoned slices. There had never
been so much food littering the whole room like that. If it were I, of
course I would have smelled a rat. If you hurt a friend so bad, and
he doesn't come to fight you or at least confront you, rather he brings
you food, and grinning broadly – don't dare eat. You would be buying your ticket to hell with your own money. I cleared out the slices
and threw them in the small waste bag at the door.

I was sitting on the plastic chair when Tar came in again and went
behind the cupboard. He thrust his head out from there and gazed
at me. He was telling me with his eyes: he's smarter than I am.

'Bloody thing!' I howled, and threw my shoe at him.

He retreated.

'This room won't contain us,' I bawled. 'Sooner or later I'm going
to kill you. Better leave, selfish bastard! Your death don near!'

After a while he came out of his corner and challenged me again.
But I had lost strength for his lark. He scurried to the waste bag and
began to forage in it. He brought out a slice of the bread, paused,
gave me another look, and scuttled away with it. I returned to bed.

With my nose, I combed the room for Tar. Belema said I'd find him;
but I couldn't. His decomposing smell was everywhere, but he was
nowhere. I returned to bed exhausted, consoled by the thought of
having done him in.

Mother returned a day later. I heard her familiar footsteps in the
corridor; I heard her coming into the room, but I pretended to be
asleep. I didn't want a barrage of questions and a reminder to count
my teeth with my tongue.

'Heaven! Tonworio! What's this smell?'

I tossed in drowsy pretence.

She slapped my arm. 'I'm talking to you! Get up and stop the pretence. I'm your mother,' she bawled.

'It's Tar.'

'What tar?'

I faced her but I didn't get up. 'The smell,' I explained.

'A rat has died in this room and you –' She stooped closer, bringing her nose to me almost clinically. 'Good God!' she yelled, cupping her nose with her palm. 'When was the last time you had a bath, Tonworio?'

I returned to my pretence.

'Chim-o! Tonworio, are you alright?!' She shook me.

I said nothing.

She dashed out of the room and began to sob in the corridor. It's good she sobbed. I had a dream before Ebiye died: I was at my own funeral, I was being interred, and Mother was glowering at my remains in a very cheap wood coffin. Everyone I knew started wailing except her. She was grinning down at my remains. You know that grin, that expression of bliss, the one a woman has on her face when she beholds her newborn child for the first time.

Mirage of War

S VAN ROOYEN

War.

One word, simple, complicated. It sensitised my mind and got my cock throbbing. I stood watch on the dune. The sand swept over my feet, circles and curls and small wisps of pale gold, taken by the damp cool breeze, blowing from the bellowing ocean. Below my feet the earth keened, the rumbling breath of another wave clawed at the coastline, inching closer without stealth or speed. Soon the very ground I stood on would be swept out to sea, only to be carried back by the wind, the never-ending sand in the desert, brought back to life. Like this conflict. Engagements and tranquillity, dissension, mutiny. The pacification, ceasefire, truce, and calm, forced by my hand or another's.

It was over. Till the next time.

Dirt, soot and dried blood caked my face. The soft morning mist pushed and pulled the warming desert air, its tug of war lifting my lapels. My brothers gathered in small groups. The wind carried the silent melody of their voices as the chaplain presided over the empty, unmarked graves.

Missing in action.

Taken.

Lost.

And so was I.

Ten years since I'd been home. Not that it had ever been home. Except in De Wet's arms. A lifetime ago. For a few hours we had breathed each other, touched each other, listening to the music of the night as the flames lit our faces, danced across our bodies heated by youth and love. One night.

On the fields of war I hid my emotions, my guilt, in silence. The soldiers' words, actions, broke me. My inability to understand 'normal' became the commitment in my masculinity, the force in my thrusts, as I took confession in his body then his blood. I saw his face in every tear, heard his voice in every whimper of pain. Not 'stop', not 'no', as I ripped at his sack, forced pleasure and release. It was power, power over the man beneath me as I pulled out and made him crawl over his own mess to lick my boots. I was evil, their evil.

'At thy call we shall not falter.'

A father, my father, had found his two sons entwined in the dawn light. De Wet and I had returned from bush school the day before. As an early birthday present, Pa had presented his twin boys, us, with our grandfather's old windbuks. The air rifle had a solid handle, hand-carved from something that looked like ironwood. It was heavy, but the warmth radiating from it seemed natural in my hands. From the look of the rusted metal barrel it had been neglected, but Pa assured us that with a bit of cleaning and oil the Crosman167 would shoot again. That was what we had spent our day on.

The late summer rays drew long pink and orange lines across the horizon as we set off to play. Small knapsacks packed with cold chicken, boiled eggs, and a few apricot jam sandwiches. De Wet had snuck out a half-bottle of port along with a box of stolen matches to make a fire. Out in Springbok the nights quickly turn cold, the arid sand only holding onto the heat of the day for a short while. In bush school, our night marches had taught us to rough it like real men, dig a hole deep enough to hold the wind at bay, build a fire close by.

Not the same hole, as I found out by accident when my sleeping bag caught alight. Keep your pack mates close. Desert hyenas and small jackals scavenged, and toes and fingers were easy to nibble on. I'd shot at a few dassies and, while it was fun, De Wet made a big fuss. It was his nature. My nurturer. We spoke about our dreams, the future. Our future. I took solace from the cold in the boy beside me, in the shared heat, the giggles and drunken hiccups.

'Lief jou.'

Dawn broke, its bloodstained tendrils demanding blood in return.

I found myself on the midnight train to Pretoria, shipped off to war, my sixteenth birthday murdered. My mother wailed on the station platform. Wet, sticky heat seeped through my green sweater, spun and knitted by her weary arthritic hands. The shirt underneath rubbed against my wounds with every step, provided me with the evidence of the beating I had taken for De Wet. Then my own. The cattle whip had snapped on the forty-sixth lash, the final four meted out by our father's two huge fists to De Wet's face after his son had ripped the blood-soaked leather away from him.

His father, not ours. Not mine.

The woman that cleaned my wounds as I bent over the kitchen table mumbled about a winter with frost, a girl that was shunned, touched by a boy as she should not have been. The aroma of sweet tea drifted from my mother's breath.

'It was winter, Stan. Cold.' Her hand trembled on my flesh. The haunted memory moved through the room as grisly words fell from her lips. The crisp night air from the open kitchen door was like arctic chill on my hot skin, my mother's fingers icicles, scraping every nerve ending raw. I bit my tongue until blood ran into my mouth, holding in my scream as another piece of ripped flesh was soaked and cleaned. She took my silence as a sign. 'Your father –' she shuddered, 'Henk found her on the pass after the storm. He needed to survey the damage, check the west boundary.' Her hand tapped slightly on my lower back to say she was done. I straightened up. She drained the steel basin and came back to sit at the kitchen table, hand drifting to the tube of the ointment she'd just spread over my weeping wounds. 'She'd been out in the cold the entire night. She was holding her coat and wrap tucked in the ball of her arms.' My mother looked up at me. 'You,' she whispered, 'still connected to your cord, sleeping in that cocoon.' I watched her, holding my breath as the room lit by an old gas lantern seemed to dim, growing dark. My vision swam, the edges closing in like a tunnel. *Breathe, Stan. Breathe. None of this is true.* The breath I took brought understanding. Somehow I knew that De Wet had known when he'd kissed me. 'Henk took you, brought you home to me.' She blinked back tears, cleared her throat. The sound reminded me of the injured wildcat I'd once found out on the pass. Whimpering from pain, close to death. 'We didn't want any trouble. The farmhouse was too far from the hospital to make the journey at night.' My mother, no – *Maria*, Maria touched the locket on the fine silver chain around her neck, the locket that cradled our photos. 'I'd given birth to De Wet only two weeks before. Henk put you into my arms, named you, gave you my late father's name. A friend helped us forge the birth certificate, made it look like De Wet's. Good enough, you know.' I turned away. 'Stan,' she whispered. 'We loved you as a son.'

They had loved me. Once.

Enough to keep me.

Not enough to tell me the truth.

In due course, I began to find my feet in the war. My battalion, my brothers with a more traditional counter-insurgency methodology, evolved, adapting with our increased use of native troops. I became a predator. I became the alpha of my pack.

I became Malan.

On the fields of blood and sand, I was haunted by the vastness of eternity. I asked myself the unforgivable questions. Would our actions echo across the centuries? Would strangers hear my name long after I was gone, wonder who I was, how bravely I had fought, how fiercely I had loved?

There was one love, had been once.

In my uniform pocket, that day on the dunes, a single envelope slept. In the newsclipping it contained, a dull photograph showed graduating doctors at Wits. De Wet, his long, lanky frame, stood proudly with his fellows, his light, shoulder-length hair a dull fading grey. His eyes were hooded under thick, dark lashes, the photo hiding the crystal sapphire depths of his eyes.

So De Wet had lived his dream, to heal with the hands his father had given him.

De Wet was my heart, empathy and love, unconditional acceptance, and forever the dreamer. Nurturer to my protector, light to my dark.

Prey to my predator.

That night in the veld I had used him, forsaken our brotherly love.

Betrayed my family. Abandoned a future that was never mine.

I had kept away after that, never sending my forwarding address, always moving from one battalion to another. This single envelope reached me, sent directly to the 32nd battalion via a political contact, six months too late.

Dr De Wet Hougaardt Malan
1-Mil Hospital
Pretoria
22 April 1975

Specialist Major Stanley Malan,

I have asked my supervising, Brigadier General de Beer, to officiate this letter and prioritise it due to its content and sensitivity.

I regret to inform you that I have had news from Besmarie Farm, of the passing of Henk and Maria Malan. I have taken a leave of absence before deployment to attend to this matter.

This news will reach you later than I would have hoped, due to the ongoing operation.

I trust as a brother you will understand.

Dr De Wet Hougaardt Malan

I turned away from the setting sun and the calming churn of the ocean waves lapping at the Skeleton Coast. We would be on the move again, the Buffel outfitted for ground coverage and our pseudo operations, false covert missions, planned over the next twelve months. But first, Operation K, three thousand kilometres and thirty days on foot. *Bush time and the mirage of war.* The mind of a broken man can be a beautiful playground. Where some see a maelstrom of destruction, I would see the order and normality. The world had a broken foundation. For harmony to exist, anarchy needed to snarl, and fuck every rat's nest. Comrade, rebel, even... brother.

1975 came and went. Operation K in full flight, blood to bath in, honours to survive. Operation Savannah, Ebo, the Bridge. Bravo Group battlefield tactics in Operation Cobra.

1976 was almost uneventful, underground retaliation and crossbred operations all kept silent from the records by my hands. Genocide none would ever speak of.

1977 escalated 32 Battalion into gods, following Operation Silver, Kropduif, and then Seiljag. More death and decay on both sides. I lost fifteen brothers in one night.

Revenge.

Not just a word but a code name. Operation Rextill. 1978.

On the eve of the spring solstice, dressed in bush fatigues, I took what was taken from me at Katima Mulilo. I stood in the summer monsoon, drops of desert rain pounding down my face and my body. Stripped naked I knelt in the gathering pools of rainwater running dirt and despair from my soul. Screams echoed in the humid air of the night. The water tracked rivers in the dirt below my knees. I braced my right hand beneath me, the pools of water cold as sleet on my heated flesh.

The body was willing.

I drew a shuddering breath, spat in my hand and reached for my aching cock as I watched my enemy burn. I was always in control of my enemy's fate, but today fate took more.

As dawn drew near my team cleared out, our Buffel adorned with four mutilated corpses. Naked and stripped of name and rank. *Traitors.* Overkill? Not in my book. The trophy tied to the driver's door hung limply by what used to be his neck, a large belly cut exposing the insides. The Zulu on my team had once told me that it released the spirit, saving the killer from insanity and pollution. Owethu smiled down at me from his perch on top of the Buffel as he checked the rope knots holding crates of ammunition. I looked over the defectors. Lieutenant de Jong, the magistrate, loved money more than his battalion. Lieutenant Baker, 32nd division Foxtrot battalion, the company's best sniper. Captain van Jaarsvelt, the faggot, had seen better days, someone had chopped his excuse for balls off and stuffed them into another body's mouth, unknown, some rich white family's prodigal son, wanting a claim to the diamonds buried beneath their feet.

As the convoy left the smouldering village, my brothers were smiling, playful banter and bottles of brandy passed around or lifted to the lips of those that could not drink themselves. Henry was calling in the mission. Breda was telling us about his wife giving birth, and how every time he nailed his ass down on this stupid bench he wondered if we would ever make it out from this steel womb.

The diesel fumes inside got to everyone eventually.

Gift's tobacco pipe scented the fumes. The big gentle giant had been part of the battalion for over six months and he had yet to say a word or give us his real name. He cradled little Tom's head in his lap, the new boy we'd lost last night. We would mourn. *I would mourn.* At least I had his body to take home this time. I was a brother not an invisible ghost, for now. Tangible human, not mysterious wind.

War put me on display.

Gift's eyes widened, his hand reaching out to take hold of Breda as the Buffel tilted left then right. The sound of metal scraping drew deadly silence from my men, as our vehicle went over on its axle, Tom's body going airborne before landing on the bent metal bench. Gift seemed frozen in place, body pinned to the wall by a piece of reinforced floorplate. His eyes were fixed to where Breda had been sitting, nothing but pieces left behind. Henry was reaching for the radio. I felt wetness drip from both my ears. I was looking at Henry, his mouth moving, but no words penetrated my mind. The world around me grew brighter than the sun, heat singed my body, as piercing sound ruptured my skin, the very air I breathed, exploding.

Then nothing.

Briefly, the eerie melody of rushing blood, deep thumps of my heart roused me from my slumber.

Then nothing.

I let insomnia take me, spent hours, days and weeks in the memorial rose garden at 1-Mil, remembering. Slivers of memory, silent black and white films, others vivid with screams. 1-Mil Hospital. Dr De Wet Malan. Pretoria. 22 April 1975.

'Baaco, Wilson, Sam, Dayu, Gift, Owethu, Breda, Henry, Tom,'

I whispered at the yellow roses. 'I lost you too.' I tried to lift my useless right hand to rub at my burning eyes.

I held the nine sets of dog tags, rubbed the long, rectangular aluminium ovals, end over end.

Serial number. Religion. Blood type.

'Name and rank, soldier.'

Their voices echoed.

My only answer, home, brother.

Serious complications. I was tired of the words. Dural tear, sepsis and surgical nerve root damage. Never discussed with me, but whispered in the ward. The military-printed, patient privacy curtain did little to muffle voices and the tears of the doctor who had made the mistake. Something about an Oxford scale, his left foot, my left foot, against gravity. They had withdrawn the L5 nerve root to remove the disc and shrapnel fragments. *Partial paralysis.* This I knew already. Severe muscle wasting. I couldn't listen anymore.

Permanently damaged.

No more.

'Surgically damaged!' De Wet's voice.

I writhed on my gurney, my prostrate body twisting. Spasms wrenched my impotent legs, water and shards of glass pissed down on me.

'Shit for legs,' I moaned. Pain, sharp and beautiful, wrapped me in her arms, held me, while the world around me greyed.

'Too little, too late!' he was shouting.

He ripped the stained white curtain from the rail and tossed his doctor's bag onto my bed. 'Get dressed,' he mouthed at me, then continued his rant as he pushed and shoved at the two older gentlemen dressed in pressed white doctor's coats, hovering at the end of my bed. The vultures fled, as De Wet listed medical councils like a litany from a madman.

When I had dressed my top half, the shouting had turned to low octave murmurs, whispers. Then the single heavy door closed at the end of the ward.

De Wet stood next to my bed. He looked tired, worn. His face was older, knowing. I had missed so much, missed him. Guilt no longer part of my honour, I looked up at him with hope.

It seemed so simple.

'Come home.'

I could see the longing in the clear crystal depths of his eyes. Dark blue shards misted over, became silver with tears. He held my gaze, my soul trapped in a snare I couldn't escape. 'I'll take care of you, as you have always taken care of me,' he said.

I couldn't speak, couldn't make the words right themselves to utter even a greeting.

He took the brown tracksuit pants from my shaking hands, knelt down, and helped me dress.

He spent the next two hours completing forms, collecting braces and medicine. Then he helped me into his bakkie. It was late afternoon. He never spoke a word, just kept his eyes on the road and drove.

We shared the sandwiches and coffee he'd packed in a small basket on the middle seat. Our eyes conversed, telling a thousand stories.

At dawn, he opened the rusted gate to Besmarie, the squeak of the hinge betraying our arrival to the ghosts. We drove up the dirt road, slowed at the whitewashed fence, and looked over at the two new headstones, then moved on. De Wet parked underneath the kweper tree and we looked out onto the farm.

He took my hand, interlaced what was once ripped apart.

Scorned but never forgotten.

Not Malan. Just me. The mirage of the forgotten war.

Perilous Love

JENNIFER SHINTA AYEBAZIBWE

Her back against the tree, Tibahitana watched the distant silver sedan make a slow curve along the opposite hill, leaving a trail of reddish-brown dust on its snail-like journey in the early December afternoon. She estimated its speed at fifteen kilometres per hour. There had been an excited air of anticipation at home as the household awaited Tukwase's return from Germany. Accompanying him would be his wife Katrin and her best friend Ilsa. Tibahitana hadn't seen her brother and sister-in-law since their wedding three years ago. Their mother had insisted that they have it here on the farm, and Katrin had conceded on condition that her family and friends be flown in at her and Tukwase's expense. It had been a beautiful but expensive wedding; so expensive that they were still paying off the debt.

From the flurry of activity as the car approached, it was obvious that not much happened in Rubindi, their sleepy village in the Mbarara district of western Uganda. Even the dogs were excited. Maps, the matriarch, famous for her aloof composure, lay under the orange tree, tail wagging with contained eagerness. The other dogs danced and barked a ring around her.

Tibahitana followed the movement of the car as it curved and wound its way along the bendy road from her vantage point, losing it to shrubs and patches of bushes. At one point, the car struggled to proceed. The dirt road, rugged at the best of times, was impassable when it rained, and they had received a good dose of rain earlier in the week. Fortunately for the car and its occupants, the sun had reigned in the last two days. Tibahitana could make out a couple of people running towards the car and after a brief exchange at the driver's window, they started to push. Thank the stars for Kigatwa and Mujuni, the inseparable village bums. She lost sight of the car at the very last bend, but could easily follow its journey in her mind as it slowly drew closer and eventually came to a stop near the simple brick house in the large family compound.

Tibahitana ground out her cigarette and joined the welcome party. Introductions were made, hugs and kisses exchanged, bags and suitcases carried into the house. Muhirwe, who usually worked the banana plantation, did most of the carrying, smiling shyly at the group of strangers when anyone thanked him. His understanding of the English language was limited at the best of times. He could barely make out what Katrin and Ilsa were saying because of their foreign accents.

'Did you have a good journey?' someone asked in the commotion

'It was great until we got to Kampala,' Katrin said. 'The traffic was crazy!'

'Yes, the traffic is rather overwhelming, isn't it?' Bamwine said. Allocating chairs on the verandah, she motioned Katrin to come and sit on the one closest to her. It was never too early to inquire about the grandchildren she was waiting for – young people cared too much for their freedom nowadays. The white metal chairs squealed on the cement.

'Are the renovations at Entebbe complete now?' Tibahitana asked no one in particular as she made herself comfortable against one of the corner poles, sitting astride her chair and ignoring her mother's disapproving eye.

'I don't think so,' Tukwase replied. 'Lots of barricades everywhere.'

'And dust,' Ilsa offered.

Tibahitana watched their guests silently. Her brother's wife was very tall but graceful. She looked relaxed in khaki cargo shorts, a navy Levi's t-shirt, and leather sandals. Her blonde hair was tidied back in a loose bun. Tiba looked for signs of pregnancy but noticed none; she knew what would be going on in Bamwine's head and was glad to have the attention away from herself for a change. The thought made her smile. She couldn't wait to catch up with Katrin. They had struck up a good friendship over the years thanks in most part to modern technology. The regular lengthy emails they exchanged were her only connection to the outside world on most days, and were what kept her sane in her self-imposed exile. Tukwase looked happy, his hand in Katrin's, as he switched from Lunyankole to English, with a smattering of German. Married life clearly agreed with him.

Tibahitana's eyes moved to Ilsa, and lingered. Her skin was a milk chocolate brown. She had thick, untameable hair, most of which she had forced very unsuccessfully into a ponytail. Her large deep-set hazel brown eyes, very light compared to Tibahitana's dark hooded pools, followed the conversation with interest. Her cotton shorts and colourful, loose, sleeveless tunic showed off strong arms and long legs. Lovely calves, Tiba thought. She put Ilsa's height at slightly below her own 170 centimetres. Then she felt Ilsa's eyes on her.

'Would anyone like something to drink?' Tibahitana spluttered uncharacteristically, getting up suddenly. 'We have water, granadilla juice, freshly made by me this morning, some cold beer, unfortunately only Club Pilsner ... oh, and some banana wine, very cool and refreshing, we got it at the little shop you passed on your way here, over there.' She pointed with a furrowed brow. She was babbling and embarrassed and quickly left the verandah to fetch the drinks everyone had requested.

Tibahitana cursed as she bent over her mountain bike with intense concentration. She'd hoped to do a few kilometres in solitude before the sun came up, but her beloved Mongoose Teocali Comp had chosen that morning to pop a tyre.

'Good morning,' Ilsa said.

Tiba was so lost in her task that she hadn't heard Ilsa approach, or her greeting.

'Good morning,' Ilsa said again. Her mellow voice carried farther than she had intended in the morning silence.

Tiba looked up in surprise. She hadn't expected anyone to be up for at least another couple of hours. Ilsa looked fresh-faced in shorts, a vest and hiking boots.

'Good morning. Sorry I didn't hear you …'

'Do you need help?' Ilsa came closer.

'Ummm … could you hold the bicycle upright?' Tiba said gratefully, and tried to down-play the excited little leap her heart had given at the sight of Ilsa.

Ilsa squatted next to her, close enough for their shoulders to touch, close enough to smell the cool morning air on Tiba's skin. Working together, they soon changed the tyre.

'Wait here,' Tiba said abruptly.

Ilsa was happy for a chance to take a few breaths, clear her now intoxicated head and take in a few eyefuls of her host Tiba's athletic frame was clearly defined in the cycling tights she wore. She moved with the agility of one accustomed to physical activity. Her lithe legs ended in incongruously delicate ankles now perfectly snug in thick socks and sensible hiking shoes.

Tiba disappeared into the house, interrupting Ilsa's appraisal, but returned all too quickly with her old but equally capable bike. 'You can have the Mongoose,' she said to Ilsa. 'Ride with me.'

They rode in silence for the first five kilometres, Tiba leading the way along the village trails she knew like the back of her hand, Ilsa following unquestioningly. The last two kilometres were uphill, and their breathing quickened as they focused on navigating the less used path. It got even rockier when they rounded the bend to the top, but the view was worth every ache. The valley went on for miles, painted gold by the rising sun. The silence was broken only by the incessant chirping of the birds and the soothing gentle flow of the river in the distance.

'It's beautiful,' Ilsa said softly, hungrily taking in the view and her own deep breaths.

Tiba nodded.

They dismounted, walked to a couple of rocks positioned for the best view, and sat without talking for what seemed like hours.

'I love coming here,' Tiba said.

'It is beautiful,' Ilsa said again, unable to find the precise words to describe the beauty and silence. 'Have you always lived here?'

'No.' Tibahitana's answer wasn't very revealing, and she smiled apologetically. 'We should head back,' she said. 'I have to take the goats out to the field.'

They hardly saw each other for the rest of the day. Ilsa spent most of the afternoon lounging lazily on the lawn, basking in the sun and catching up on some reading. Tiba busied herself with farm chores: cleaning out the chicken coop, feeding the pigs, taking the goats and cattle to the river for their twice-a-day drink. All through the day Ilsa found her thoughts constantly returning to Tiba; unbeknown to her, Tiba was having as much trouble thinking of anything else.

'We're heading out to the trading centre for dinner.' Tukwase was a shadowy figure in the doorway of Tiba's small face-brick cottage at the back of the main house. 'Katrin would like to show Ilsa the sights.' He struggled to make out Tiba's face on the couch in the dimly lit cottage. Only a candle flickered on the table in the lounge. A small stereo crackled softly on the windowsill, which Tukwase knew was more for company than for anything else. 'Wanna come?'

'Sure, gimme a minute to change.' She had just had a bath in an attempt to soothe her tired muscles after the busy day.

She got into the back seat of her battered 4x4 Pajero, which Tukwase had borrowed without asking. Ilsa was also in the back, and Katrin was in the front with Tukwase.

'Better suited for the terrain,' Tukwase said, and they all laughed.

'Is Mom OK spending the evening alone?' Tiba asked.

Her brother nodded, and they were on their way.

The trading centre was situated about five kilometres away from the farm, in a valley surrounded by swampland. It wasn't much to write home about: two long rows of shops on opposite sides of the main road, a petrol station with one pump at one end and a clinic in the middle. Most of the shops were small. Some were aimed at tourists and stocked with handmade trinkets and souvenirs, but they were all mostly closed by six in the evening. Mama's Bar and Grill, the most popular restaurant, was sandwiched between a hardware store and a butchery.

The group walked into the restaurant to much cheer. Tiba and Tukwase had known Mama Mwebesa – now old but just as formidable – since they were babies, a fact she was all too happy to remind them of every time. She gave Tukwase a bone-crushing hug first, fussing about how thin he was, and then turned and hugged Katrin. Holding her at arms' length, she exclaimed: 'The last time I saw you, you were a worried bride. I think married life suits you very well!'

Katrin laughed, more at the memory of herself fussing over the wedding menu. If she'd known then what she learned at the wedding, she wouldn't have worried. Mama Mwebesa was a fabulous cook who also dabbled in magic: the woman could literally make rabbits appear out of thin air. She had saved the wedding after their caterer from Mbarara town bailed out at the very last minute. Katrin could never thank her enough, and told her so again.

'These are my children,' Mama Mwebesa said, waving the thanks away kindly.

Katrin introduced Ilsa, who also got a big hug and was graciously welcomed to the village. Mama Mwebesa promptly insisted that the night was on her and she would have no argument to the contrary from anyone. They were seated in no time, with beer and platefuls of roasted goat meat and an assortment of local vegetables: gonja, boiled dodo with fresh butter beans and the bitter but tasty katunkuma.

'It's a kind of plantain,' Tiba offered, noticing Ilsa examining the gonja with interest. Ilsa looked up and smiled thankfully at her, and Tiba noticed once again how Ilsa's eyes danced when she smiled. She quickly moved on to the next item. 'This, we call katunkuma,' she said, popping the bean-sized, bittersweet, dark green vegetable into her mouth. 'From the eggplant family.' Ilsa held Tiba's eyes, quite happy to listen to her talk about vegetables all night. 'The unassuming greenery here is dodo,' Tiba continued, feeling a little shy and breaking the eye contact, 'it's known to the rest of the world as amaranth, doesn't look like much but it's packed full of delicious goodness.' She was rewarded with a laugh from Ilsa.

They all enjoyed the spread, Ilsa and Katrin possibly the most. 'You should make this for me back home babe,' Katrin said jokingly to Tukwase. She knew though, that getting the ingredients in Hamburg would be next to impossible. The restaurants that called themselves African all tended towards North African and West African cuisine.

Tiba got up to go and smoke. Outside the air was balmy, and amphibian mating calls enveloped the valley. Tiba drifted back to her childhood holidays in the village, all the trouble she and Tukwase had gotten into. The place hadn't changed much: the only difference was her brother's prolonged absences.

When she went back inside, she found Mwebesa showing Ilsa some moves. They were dancing to 'Yellow', the latest single by assorted Ugandan artists. Tiba sat quietly watching and declined when Tukwase and Katrin gestured for her to join them on the dance floor.

'Do you like her?'

Tiba hadn't heard Kobusingye come over and stand next to her. She looked up and shrugged. 'How have you been?' she asked instead of answering Kobusingye's question.

'OK,' said Kobusingye. Settling on a vacant seat, she said accusingly: 'I haven't seen you around these parts in a while.'

'I have been a little busy…'

Tiba and Kobusingye had had a fling many moons past, soon after Tiba had moved back to Rubindi. They had both quickly realised it wasn't working and ended it, but had remained good friends. Kobusingye was one of the few people in the village who didn't think Tiba was strange, Mama Mwebesa being another one.

'Bamwine must be overjoyed to have Tukwase home,' Kobusingye continued conversationally.

'I think we all are. Gives the place an air of festivity.' Tiba came off nonchalant, but Kobusingye knew how much she loved and missed her brother.

'She's beautiful,' Kobusingye said, as they watched Ilsa throw her head back and laugh at something Mwebesa said, her yellow summer dress blowing bubbles around her.

'You're up early,' Tiba said, pushing her bike around the house into the compound on her way out.

'I'm not a late sleeper,' said Ilsa.

Soon they were riding away again, albeit on a different route. Again Tiba led and Ilsa followed, grateful for the sturdy build of the bicycles as they navigated the rocky terrain. They bounced and twisted downhill on the narrow path, the silence only disturbed by grass against bicycle spikes and chattering birds announcing their presence. Ilsa's breath came out in short misty puffs that quickly disappeared into nothingness. In front of her, Tiba's movement seemed effortless, her rhythm barely broken by the uneven path.

Tiba finally stopped. She pushed her bicycle through a clearing, and Ilsa followed suit. They came out on the other side to a sparkling river and a swarm of butterflies on the bank. Hundreds of little colourful delicate wings ascended to the heavens in silence. Ilsa was quiet for a long time. When Tiba looked over at her, there were tears flowing freely down her cheeks. Against her better judgment Tiba walked over to Ilsa, took her hand, and stood close to her, saying nothing. Moments later, Ilsa was smiling. She looked apologetically at Tiba. 'It's so beautiful here,' she said.

They left their bicycles resting against a thorn tree and walked over to a makeshift bench someone had erected. 'I grew up here, but left after primary school,' Tiba said. She picked up a stone and threw it, rippling the still surface of the river. 'My father is remarried, so I lived with him in Kampala until I finished varsity. I only came back here permanently a couple of years ago. I fell in love with the place and with farming all over again, quit my IT job, ended a three-year relationship that wasn't really going anywhere ... and the rest is history.' She breathed deeply after the uncharacteristic long monologue and looked down at her sneakers.

'Must have taken major guts,' Ilsa observed gently.

'It's the craziest thing I've ever done in thirty-six years, and I would do it again in a heartbeat.'

Ilsa smiled with admiration.

'It would have been near impossible without my mother though,' Tiba added.

'Bamwine seems amazing,' Ilsa affirmed.

They sat in silence, watching the river shimmer as the butterflies brushed it playfully and ascended over and over again. In the distance, the sound of animal hooves on gravel signalled that the village was now awake and in motion.

'I can't place your accent,' Tiba said tentatively. She had been puzzling over this since the afternoon of their first meeting on the verandah.

'My mother was German, a professor at Oxford, and my father was a Luo diplomat. They met in England and I was born there. We left for Germany when I was ten.' Ilsa made shapes in the soft earth with her finger as she spoke.

'Did you ever visit Uganda?'

'Not a lot. My father wasn't close to most of his family, except for his older sister in Kampala. But I had plenty of extended family on my mother's side in Germany.' Ilsa looked up from her drawings in the earth. 'What are you doing?!' she exclaimed.

Tiba was taking her tank top off. She exposed smooth dark brown skin and a toned slim frame, evidence of her days spent digging ditches and shovelling poop. She kicked off her shoes, impatiently shook off her denim shorts, and jumped into the river. 'Are you coming?!' she shouted, splashing at Ilsa.

'Are you ready?' Tiba asked her trainee in the round thatched kitchen. The day before, Tiba had showed Ilsa how to make fire in the single entrance firepit she had moulded out of clay, coaxing the embers out of the dry twigs, with Ilsa looking over her shoulder in deep concentration, her brows drawn together in the way they tended to do when she was focused.

Ilsa knelt on the stone floor and repeated Tiba's steps, giving a loud whoop when the dry leaves came to life.

Tiba taught her how to feed the chickens and collect eggs. They had multiple hilarious accidents before Ilsa got the hang of milking a cow. Next was tree climbing: Ilsa carefully followed Tiba's instructions as she stepped and dodged up the thick trunk of the mango tree at the bottom of the banana plantation. They sat on a branch and gorged on mangoes like greedy children, peeling them with Tiba's pocket knife, sheltered from the late December heat. They took long walks in the evenings, serenaded by a cacophony of toads, and spent lazy afternoons under the incongruous giant pine tree in the compound, Bamwine's brainchild.

One afternoon, they took a blanket to the hilltop. A gourd of banana wine, which Ilsa had grown to rather enjoy, was placed between them. They shared a straw Tiba had snapped off a tall patch of grass, and some berries plucked off several trees on their way.

'What does your name mean?' Ilsa asked.

'One is not better than the other,' Tibahitana translated, and they giggled like schoolgirls at the irony..

Ilsa reached out and touched Tiba's short spiky locks, sides trimmed to a mohawk shape, tentatively. 'I like your hair,' she said shyly. And then suddenly, 'I want to stay. Here with you.' Ilsa hadn't tested the words on herself, so she was just as shocked as Tiba by the passion with which she uttered them.

Tiba was quiet.

It had been three weeks of blissful country existence. But the guests would depart for Kampala in three days, where Tukwase and Katrin would part ways with Ilsa and head north to Morocco on the last leg of their journey, Ilsa was to spend a few days in Kampala with her aunt and cousins before flying to Germany after New Year's day. Ilsa's words were such seductive words. Tiba wanted them. And yet …

'It's dangerous,' Tiba said with a sigh, her eyes on a faraway cloud.

They were lying face up on the intricately patterned mat, heads resting against folded arms, the valley laid out below them. Smoke rose lazily in the distance, a cow mooed somewhere, breaking the silence.

Ilsa sat up and hugged her knees: 'I don't think I care.'

'I do,' Tiba said sadly. She couldn't let anything happen to this woman.

'What's the worst that can happen?' Ilsa said defiantly.

'Jail time, up to fourteen years,' said Tiba, anger in her voice.

'It's not fair!' Ilsa declared, with a petulance uncharacteristic of her thirty years.

'I know,' Tiba said gently.

'What we want matters!!' Ilsa shouted, scaring away a flock of red-headed lovebirds in a nearby tree, and Tiba began to feel the first stirrings of hope.

Ilsa slowly lay down on her back again. She gently slid her fingers through Tiba's calloused ones and laid her head on Tiba's shoulder, and Tiba protectively pulled her closer. The loud beating of Tiba's heart drowned out the village sounds and whatever was left of her fears.

Clouds gathered suddenly: a storm was brewing.

They stayed put.

Maimuna Doesn't Know

WILFRED JEAN-LOUIS

Café Mansour is on a busy street facing old town Mombasa. The late afternoon sun colours the sky above with orange hues. Colourful matatus race across the road, weaving between tuk-tuks and bicycles, blowing their horns and pumping loud music. 'Ferry! Ferry! Ferry!' their conductors shout. The street is lined with parked cars. The small yellow and red Bajaj tuk-tuks zoom by against the evening traffic to pick up their next passengers. Street food vendors are setting up shop and hungry pedestrians stop to buy mahamri and mkate mayai. The smells of fried eggs on bread, heated sugar, coconut and cardamom waft and mix with the smell of the patrons' cigarettes.

Two men in long white kanzus are walking towards the café, side by side.

'Eish! Today work was tough,' Idris says, wiping his forehead. A Swahili of Arab descent, Idris has a hooked nose and almond-shaped eyes. He carries his phone in one hand, and a black backpack slung over his shoulder.

'Agreed,' says his companion. 'It was hellish.' Abu is tall and slender, with shoulder-length black hair. 'And I've got three more imports to clear tomorrow. The agents got business when I was in the mosque.' Abu carries his leather-bound document folder under his armpit. 'Did the bank grant you leave for your exams?'

'HR sent the confirmation this afternoon,' says Idris.

'So you finally get to go to Nairobi for that wedding,' laughs Abu. 'I already had a long message of apologies written down in case my exam leave was turned down. She's such a cow though, keeping me in suspense for two weeks. She said, "Your email got lost in a flood of messages." What flood? She's an assistant for crying out loud.' Idris is waving his arms around. 'The most she gets are forwards from her manager.'

'Baas baas,' Abu says soothingly, patting Idris's back. 'Let's have coffee. I was kneeling next to the speaker in the masjid. I've a headache.'

The café's padded metal seats scrape on the floor as they sit. Abu stares into the little menu that divides the table: a small piece of wood with a slit across, in which a white, laminated paper with the café's offerings is secured. 'I feel like proper coffee today. The sufuria one that's burnt a bit,' he says.

'That should sort your headache out,' says Idris. 'Let's ask for a big pot.' He says this without looking up from his phone.

The waiter, a light-skinned, portly man, also wearing a kanzu, takes their order. An elderly Arab man sits at the table next to theirs, reading a book.

'So Idris,' Abu asks softly, 'how are things going with you and Salim?'

Idris looks up from his phone. He puts it down on the table. He leans in towards Abu. 'I told Salim this morning that he needs to get a new kanzu for masjid on Fridays, and all he says is, "Allah (praise His name) doesn't care about how shiny my kanzu is. My presence before Him, and my gratitude to Him for all the good tidings He has brought us, are enough." Then he says he has to spend the weekend with his wife.'

The waiter returns with a tray that holds a medium-sized bronze teapot and two little white teacups. A small silver jar of sugar, with a teaspoon handle sticking out, gleams in the evening sun. 'Karibuni!'

he announces. His forehead has a few drops of sweat on it from the humidity.

'Shukran,' Abu and Idris say.

Abu puts one of the little white teacups in front of Idris, lifts the pot and pours the black coffee. 'Gosh, your Salim is so devout,' he says. 'But a weekend with his wife? What will you do now?'

Idris sighs and looks away onto the bustling street. 'A year later and I still can't grasp the idea of being his second, when in fact he met me before her. It is degrading being downgraded from first to economy class.'

Abu rocks his head back and laughs. 'Or worse – the bus!'

Idris smiles. 'But we're OK. I've a free weekend on my hands now. I can finally clean the bloody apartment. The other day Salim jumped onto the dining table when he saw a spider. When I heard the noise, I first thought the cat had jumped down off the shelf again. I came out of the kitchen and saw Salim standing on the table shouting "Achaa!" and pointing at a cobweb in the corner. The cleaning lady seems to be losing her touch. But I couldn't help but laugh.' Idris picked up his phone and opened the gallery, swiping right a few times. 'Here's a photo I took of him at that moment.'

Abu lets out his hearty laughter, as loud as it is infectious. Several people walking by on the street look sideways towards the sound.

Idris grins, 'I know, right? This one I must print and put in our memories album.'

'Naam,' says Abu. 'With a caption underneath that says *Brave Heart*.'

'Or *My Hero*.'

Abu is pressing a white napkin to his forehead. 'You're killing me here,' he laughs. The elderly man at the next table smiles to himself, and continues reading his book. 'My Latiff isn't really scared of anything,' says Abu. 'Probably just the thought of me being away from him for more than a week.'

Idris lowers his teacup. 'That's a sweet thing for you two. Salim seems very comfortable spending time with Maimuna. I'm trying to get used to having four days to myself. If he weren't so possessive, I'd have another husband to fill his gap.'

'Oh you two,' Abu giggles, and lifts the pot of coffee towards Idris's cup.

'Is Latiff well?' says Idris.

'He's fine,' says Abu. 'I'm hopeful that engineering firm accepts his application. He's quite bored of government.'

'Inshallah, he will get the position,' says Idris.

'Be thankful that woman doesn't know you exist,' says Abu.

'I know. Maimuna doesn't know I exist.' Idris sighs. 'One less irritation for Salim. I am saved as Clearing Agent in his phone. He's paranoid about her ever finding out. But his sister still visits me – Fozia. She's like a sister to me too. She insists that Maimuna is just a formality. You know how these Arabs are. I can be thankful Fozia's OK with Salim being gay.'

Abu tilts the pot towards his own teacup. 'She called Maimuna a formality? That's harsh.'

'Right?' Idris smirks. 'She picked up that sarcasm in the UK. Salim can't stand it. It's refreshing to listen to the both of them talk. Fozia always has the last word. Some of Salim's questions deserve those remarks though. Allah (praise His name) granted me a slightly daft man.'

'But a man, nevertheless,' says Abu. 'Some of our brothers are still single and lonely, wrecking good relationships.' Abu smiles mischievously at Idris. 'Did you hear about what happened with George and Hamid? Heh! Those two have issues.'

Idris stirs his coffee. 'I did hear,' he says. 'Imagine that! Embarrassing Hamid and his wife in public because George is jealous of her. What shame! She came before George ever knew Hamid. I heard she almost took him to the Kadhi's courts for a divorce.'

'How did you know that?' asks Abu, raising his eyebrows.

Idris leans in smiling. 'Salim told me. Who probably heard it from Fozia. She's a lawyer and a gossip. She must have picked it up in the hallways.'

They laugh loudly. The elderly man at the next table looks up from his book at them, then looks back at his book.

'Ssssh, we're distracting the babu,' says Abu, wiping a tear from his eye.

Idris leans back in his chair. The sun reflects off his glasses' metal frames. 'It's a mess for Hamid,' he says. 'He had to shower her with a trip to Dubai and ...'

'And ... ?' asks Abu, leaning closer.

Idris leans in again, grinning. 'And a PREGNANCY!!' he announces.

Abu gasps. 'NOOOO! Are you for real??' He laughs loudly again.

Still grinning, Idris leans back with his teacup in both palms. 'Salim couldn't hide his glee when he told me that. Sometimes I think men are worse gossips than women.'

'Except that they call it discussions.'

'And they have them in their cars with khat.'

'Yes!' they call out in unison, high-fiving each other.

Three women at a table behind them turn to see what the noise is about and quickly turn back again. But one of them moves her chair closer to their table.

'Allah will bless them with a good child,' says Abu.

Idris looks at his phone briefly, then puts it down again. 'If Maimuna gets pregnant, which I'm sure she will eventually, I pray that she gets a daughter. Salim wants a son, but I feel a daughter is more suitable. Maimuna will be more occupied with a daughter, and that means more time for me with Salim.' He smiles at his own logic.

'Latiff's family has been hinting about an arrangement between him and his father's friends' daughter, who I hear is quite the snob,' says Abu.

Idris leans in and whispers: 'I think the lady behind us wants to listen in.'

'Let her,' says Abu. 'You know what happened the other day?' He lifts the pot and pours more coffee into their cups. 'I went with Latiff to the family residence for dinner. One of his cousins made this odd joke about my small body. He said, "Harun has buibuis that can fit Abu". Harun is the cousin's wife. We laughed it off, but I think he knows.'

Idris's eyes squint into the evening sun, which is lighting the entire street in brilliant orange-pink, reflecting off the white walls of the buildings, bathing the street in dazzling light. 'Interesting,' he says. 'Has this cousin ever approached you away from the family?'

Abu leans back, checking his phone. 'No. But I see him looking at me when he thinks I don't notice. He's closeted, or curious. Or both.'

'At least you get to dine with the family,' Idris says. 'I stopped after Salim and Maimuna's wedding. I feel out of place when all they talk about is how beautiful, or fortunate, or amazing Maimuna is. I don't blame them. She's really stunning. But that should be me instead.' Idris sighs, sipping his coffee.

'I can imagine how that must feel,' says Abu, patting Idris's hand.

The old man at the next table raises his hand, summoning the waiter.

Idris lifts the pot, shaking it a little before dispensing its last contents into Abu's teacup. 'On a lighter note,' he says, 'one of the tax agents who comes to the bank is hitting on me. It's a bit flattering. I thought he was just being silly, but turns out he is rather into me. He's dark, a Luo man, who got transferred down to Mombasa from Nairobi.'

'How does he know about you?' Abu looks up from his phone, smiling. 'You're not exactly the most feminine gay out there.'

'His gaydar is as good as a ship's sonar. He says he knew as soon as he interacted with me. Perhaps it's my handwriting. I might have put a love-heart on my letter 'i' instead of a dot,' says Idris, feigning an innocent look.

'You still write that way?' exclaims Abu. 'I thought that behaviour was left in high school.'

'I can't help it. It slips out sometimes,' says Idris. 'Anyway, he's actually good looking. He's shorter than me, but muscular. He joked that he carries the ships' containers himself.'

'And …'

'Yes, and he has a good bulge,' Idris says, putting his palm on his smiling mouth as if scandalised by the very thought.

The old man closes the café's leather booklet that houses the bill, and stands up. 'It's haram to look at somebody else's down-there in public,' he says, glancing at them sidelong. Idris and Abu look up with shock and amusement, Idris leans back into his seat, his eyebrows raised high; Abu looks cheeky as he returns the old man's glance with a smirk. Then the old man walks out into the street, vanishing into the sea of people.

'Did he just …?' asks Idris.

'He did!' says Abu.

'Another round?' Idris raises his hand to summon the waiter.

Abu is rubbing his chin, staring at his phone. 'No, thank you.' He looks up at Idris. 'My headache's healed, and I've to leave soon.'

'Yes, the traffic to Tudor is quite chaotic,' says Idris.

'And the earlier I get home, the better.'

The portly waiter returns with the bill in its leather booklet. 'Shukran,' he says when Idris pays, gathering their teacups and the empty pot. When Abu gets up, there is a gentle scraping of the chair the lady eavesdropper sits in and soft giggles from the other ladies. 'They must know, silly ladies,' Idris says to himself.

It's a short walk down the busy street to where their different matatus are. Abu turns south at the small city roundabout. Idris watches him walk towards a white matatu and enter it. Satisfied, he pauses to put on his sunglasses, then walks on.

Abu alights in Tudor, and walks down an estate road towards his apartment, a neo-Swahili style block with long, rectangular, sliding windows and small balconies sticking out. He climbs the stairs to the very top. The grille of his door is open, and he can see a pair of sandals. He smiles. Inside, a fan is beating the humid air down with its currents. Lying on the sofa with Ali Smith's *There but for the* on his face is Latiff. Abu looks Latiff up and down, excitement and warmth brewing in him. Latiff is wearing a plain white t-shirt and blue boxer shorts. His hairy legs are stretched out across the sofa, one leg crossed over the other. Between his t-shirt and his blue boxer shorts, Abu can see the scar on his torso, a relic of an appendix removal procedure. One hand lies limply on the sofa, the other sprawls over the book. He is breathing slowly.

'Someone had a long day,' Abu mumbles, then he pats Latiff's hand. 'I'm home,' he says.

Latiff's hand removes the book to reveal a bearded face, and glasses sitting atop it. 'You're home, habibi,' he whispers. He leans up and pulls Abu down, kissing him. Abu's heartbeat increases its pace. They kiss again. Latiff closes his eyes. Something stirs below his torso.

'Not now,' Abu whispers, smiling. 'I've just stepped in,'.

'I'm sorry about yesterday,' says Latiff. 'The job hunt is frustrating. But it was unfair of me to lash out at you. I want to make it up to you in any way you like.' Latiff is speaking softly, unbuttoning Abu's shirt. 'And I know you like this.'

'This, among other things,' whispers Abu, his hands at the elastic of Latiff's shorts.

Idris gets off the matatu and walks to the kiosk. He ran out of milk this morning. The kiosk, a red one with soft drink branding on the side, has a hanging banana leaf – a sign that khat is sold there. Idris used to pick up a bunch for Salim every Friday. But ever since Salim moved out to live with Maimuna, there is no need. When the kiosk owner asked why he didn't buy it anymore, Idris told him he quit.

Idris climbs the stairs of his apartment in one of those 1980s, government standard, civil servant's houses, now being sold off by the state. The neighbour's cat is sitting on the top step. 'Silly cat,' Idris says. He puts down his paper bag of milk, unlocks his padlock, opens the grille, then the brown wooden door behind it. The apartment is dark. He opens one side of the curtains, and slides open his window. He switches on the overhead fans, and walks to the kitchen to put the milk in the fridge. The apartment is quiet, save for the plastic base of the fan making a knocking sound. He switches on his white kettle, and goes to his room to change.

His bedroom too is dark inside closed curtains. It smells familiar. Salim's empty cologne bottle is lying in Idris's clothes. A warm wet tingle glows on Idris's left cheek, followed by another slower one on his right. 'You should be here with me,' he says quietly. He rubs his arm across his eyes and picks out his home t-shirt, a plain white one with the bank's logo on it. He throws himself facedown onto his side of the bed, and sighs deeply into his pillow. He rolls slowly onto his back, holding the duvet, and stares at the ceiling. His phone rings from the living room, but he doesn't move. A breeze blows through the window, moving the closed curtains. The ceiling fan blows a downdraught of wind gently over the middle part of the bed. If you were here with me, you'd be snoring, Idris thinks. The other side of the bed has been vacant since Salim left. Idris turns and looks, expecting to find a man sleeping there. Instead, he sees a sea of duvet, a pillow and a side table that has an empty ashtray on it. Salim used to smoke before he slept. Before he had sex. After he had sex. When he woke up. When he was having breakfast. When he was driving. When he was working. A year later, the smell of cigarettes is gone.

Idris gets up and walks to the living room to get his phone. In the kitchen, he opens the window. It is a humid evening, dark now at 8 pm. A moment later, the grey and white cat silently slides through. 'Silly cat,' Idris says. 'How did you get there?' The cat meows, lifting its tail. It jumps down to the floor where its dish of water lies. 'Would you like a meal, silly cat?' The cat is bent over its dish, licking the water noisily. 'Look at me talking to you,' says Idris. 'I've become one of those single cat ladies.' He warms his spaghetti and sauce and sits down in the living room. The ceramic bowl sits on his lap as he checks his messages. He swipes down. There is a message from the flirtatious tax agent: *I'm out tonight at the German beach bar. Would be good to see you there.*

Idris stares at the message. Then he tilts his head backward. 'It beats staying indoors,' he moans. *Thank you for the invite. I feel like I want to stay indoors tonight.* He presses the 'send' button and puts the phone down. The cat purrs away on the next seat.

Idris is about to put his fork into his bowl when the phone lights up. *Did you have a good day?*

The sender is Salim, and inside Idris something stirs. A warmth courses through his chest. He smiles. *It was long. Met up with Abu at the masjid and had coffee with him afterwards. How was yours?*

He puts the phone down. He scans through the television channels looking for something to watch. He lifts his fork to his mouth. The phone's screen lights up again: *I will behave myself, I promise you.* Meanwhile, a notification of another message appears and disappears at the top of the screen. Idris sighs. He would have to shower, find clothes, and smell good in order to go out; a lot of work, after a particularly long day.

He looks at the new message: *Mine was long too. Heading out now for a couples' night with Hamid and his wife.*

The warmth in Idris's chest cools. He frowns at the message. 'That couple used to be us,' he says. *OK great. I'm sleeping early tonight. Be safe, I love you,* he types. Then he erases it. *That's nice. I'm going out with friends. It's been a while. Be safe. I love you.* He presses the 'send' button.

'We should go out after dinner,' Maimuna says, standing in front of her mirror, carefully wrapping her white and blue silk hijab around her head, holding the long tail of her glossy black hair. It falls elegantly onto her shoulder. She turns towards the bed. Her husband is sitting staring at his phone, his eyebrows furrowed as if reading a deep, philosophical article. His white linen shirt is open, exposing his hairy chest, his thin, golden chain hanging loosely around his neck. His right index finger swipes down on the screen, and he looks up at her.

'Your wish is my command, your highness.' Salim smiles at her, and looks back at his phone.

Maimuna smiles and looks at the mirror. 'Allah, you're so great. I love this man more and more each passing day.' She raises her rouge coloured lipstick and applies it slowly.

Salim stands up and buttons his shirt, looking down, making sure he buttons it correctly. He walks towards his wife and hugs her from behind. 'You look and smell divine,' he says. 'You're going to drive all the men crazy.'

She coos, and turns to kiss him briefly. 'Shoo, put on your shoes now. We need to go or we'll be late.' She puts on her stilettos, looking at herself in the mirror. It is true what is often said about her: she commands presence in any room. Her slim white and blue abaya flows down, capturing her curves minutely. She delicately picks up her matching blue clutch and walks to the door like a supermodel on a runway in Milan.

Salim slides into his moccasins, looking at his phone. He reads: *That's nice. I'm going out with friends. It's been a while. Be safe. I love you.* A small pang of jealousy impales him. He is stuck with his wife and two other young married couples for their now monthly tradition of fine dining, where they discuss everyday things. Idris is going out with his friends to drink and dance.

'Where did you want to go after dinner, habibi?' he calls after Maimuna, who is gracefully descending the stairs of their newly built apartment.

'Let's go to the German bar,' she says.

Abu lies panting beneath Latiff, his arms around Latiff's muscular back. He thought he heard his phone ring, but he doesn't care at this moment. Latiff pushes forward into him and Abu lets out a moan. Despite his stockiness, Latiff is a talented lover. Latiff smiles down at Abu as he pushes down rhythmically, beads of sweat on his chest and forehead. Abu puts an arm around Latiff's neck and kisses him. Nothing else in the world matters in this moment in time.

Idris throws his phone behind him. Abu is not picking up. Idris is kicking his legs in the air, wriggling. 'Fuck! Why won't these slip on?!' he mutters. He is wrestling on his black skinny jeans. Tonight, he will dress up as if he were a male model in a fashion magazine photo shoot. The jeans finally roll up past his thighs. His phone rings. 'Alright, I'm coming downstairs in two minutes,' he says. His regular taxi is waiting. He stands up, leaning forward to pull his jeans all the way on. The zip is short, but easy to pull up. He exhales and sucks his stomach in, managing to button the jeans. He sprays Tom Ford's Portofino around his neck, puts on a loose fitting white V-neck t-shirt, straps on his Casio watch, and slides into his sneakers. 'I'll be back late, silly cat,' he says, lifting the cat from his bed onto the circular, woven cat bed in the living room. He locks his grille and descends the stairs in small, light steps, slowly but urgently.

'How are you today?' asks the taxi driver. He has a bald patch on the back of his head, and wears his usual flower print shirt that has a missing button in the middle, exposing his white vest.

'Let's go to the German bar tonight,' says Idris.

He sits in front next to the driver, phone and wallet in hand. Diamond's Ngololo song plays from the cab's speakers. It has a casual yet upbeat tune to it, and Idris is tapping his foot as the song plays. An ideal soundtrack for the night ahead. They make their way north. The traffic has subsided and is flowing. As they drive over the bridge, Idris can see that the tide has come in. The glimmering waters reflect the lights from the villas and apartments around the creek. The air gets cooler the further they drive, nearer to the oceanfront. Majestic palm trees are lit with fairy lights in soft hues of orange, green and purple, standing out against the blue-back night sky, dotted with stars.

'Eight hundred, please,' says the taxi driver. 'Shall I bill you now, or on your return trip?'

Idris has one foot out the door already. But he stops and opens his wallet. 'I'll settle it now,' he says. 'Keep the change. Maybe buy yourself coffee to help you with the night.'

The taxi driver smiles. 'Shukran,' he says.

Like most establishments by the oceanside, the bar's roof is made of makuti: dried reeds and leaves of palm trees. Fairy lights wind around the flame trees in the parking lot. Little garden lamps light the path towards the entrance. Euro-dance music is playing. It reminds Idris of his university days, clubbing in Leeds. A young white couple, German judging by their accents, speak violently as they get searched. In the background, the ocean's waves are crashing on the shore. The bouncer searches Idris and lets him through.

He wangles his phone from his pocket. *I'm here. What side of the bar are you in?* he types to the tax agent. He scans the crowd. It is the end of the month, and the bar is full of locals and tourists alike. The wait staff wear blue jeans and white t-shirts bearing the bar's logo. Idris advances towards the main counter, brushing against the shoulder of a patron walking in the opposite direction.

His phone vibrates. *At the patio on the left. Smokers' area that overlooks the beach.*

'Another smoker,' Idris mumbles. He orders a light European beer, and walks gracefully with it towards the smokers' area, feeling nervous and excited. Sitting on a wickerwork chair, looking out onto the ocean, is the tax agent. Dark, with his meaty body, he is wearing a fitting maroon football t-shirt and blue jeans. His left hand holds a cigarette, his right hand a large smartphone. Where are his friends? Idris wonders. The tax agent is at a table for two, alone.

'It's nice to see you again, Ounda,' says Idris.

Ounda stands up and hugs Idris briefly. 'I honestly thought you wouldn't come,' he says in his deep voice. He pronounces 'come' as 'kham', revealing his Luo origins. Idris puts his phone and wallet in his pockets, and sits down. He feels as if he's doing something illegal, like drugs, in public. 'You look amazing,' Ounda says, leaning forward and looking Idris straight in his eyes. Ounda's eyes are very white, with brown irises.

Idris feels himself blushing and he looks down, then back up at Ounda with a small smile. 'You look good yourself,' he says. 'Where are your friends?'

Ounda laughs, a deep, manly laugh that belongs in a country club more than in a beach bar. 'They left,' he says.

Salim drives north in his sleek, Lexus IS250. Maimuna presses the 'next' button on her phone, and the car's bluetooth music system softly begins to play Nancy Ajram's 'Fi Hagat', the mellow violins and violas opening the song drowning out noise from outside. The car is a concert chamber, and Maimuna swishes her arms like a concert-master. She then resumes messaging on her smartphone. Salim gives her a sideways glance and smiles.

That used to be Idris. The last ride Idris had with him was after he returned from his honeymoon in Thailand. Idris wasn't happy. No matter how many times Salim tried to explain the circumstances, Idris wouldn't listen. He was hurting too much.

Salim turns off the highway and into the beach bar's parking lot.

'This should be a great evening. I can see Mustafa parking his car on the other side,' Maimuna says. One of the couples from the dinner invited themselves to the night out. Maimuna was pleased.

The two couples walk towards the bouncers, and after being searched, walk into the bar. Maimuna and Aisha request hashish bongs, and the party is led outside to the smokers' area. A palm tree with purple fairy lights is next to the table they are given. Salim looks around. He freezes – Idris. Opposite Idris is the back of a short, meaty man, possibly a rugby player.

'I'll try the new passion fruit flavour,' Maimuna tells the waiter. 'Will you smoke with us, my love?' she asks Salim.

Salim turns to her. 'No thanks, I'll smoke my cigarettes.'

'Suit yourself! Aisha and I will smoke together. Honestly you men are too responsible nowadays.' She laughs.

Mustafa is occupied with his phone. Salim looks at his, and types a new text message.

'So I ended up retiring from rugby,' says Ounda.

Idris is transfixed by Ounda's hairy, muscular arms. The veins are subtle yet visible, and he can see the lower half of a tattoo underneath the right sleeve of Ounda's shirt. Idris can feel his heart's pace increase. 'Such a brave man,' he says, his voice a tone higher than usual. He feels giggly and light. He takes a sip of his drink and leans in towards Ounda, smiling. 'It's a miracle you recovered from that injury.'

Two couples walk onto the patio. A tall, beautiful woman in a white and blue abaya stands out, accompanied by – Why Allah, of all nights?! Idris's heart skips a beat, and there's a familiar, tingly feeling in his stomach. He keeps his gaze on Ounda's arms, but he feels Salim's gaze fall upon him.

Ounda's phone rings. 'Excuse me, do you mind?'

'Sure, no problem.'

Idris's phone lights up: *Didn't expect to see you here. Who is he, and where are your friends?* the message reads.

Idris looks up. Salim is blocked from his view by the other couple. Maimuna delicately holds the hashish pipe. She is so beautiful. 'Idiot. You can't be possessive with me when your wife is sat next to you,' Idris says under his breath. *Fancy running into you here. He's a friend. He works at the tax authority. His friends just left.* His message chimes at Salim's table.

OK, comes the reply.

'Sorry about that.' Ounda is back. 'Where were we?'

'Excuse me,' says Idris. 'Bathroom.' Standing up, he sees Salim clearly.

Salim sees Idris stand up. He says, 'Excuse me. I have to go to the bathroom.' Maimuna and Aisha barely notice, deep in conversation with each other. Mustafa is occupied with his phone.

Idris has just stepped out of the cubicle. There is Salim leaning against the bathroom counter, handsome in his white linen shirt. Otherwise, the Gents is empty. Idris approaches the counter, washes his hands and holds them under the drier. The drier emits a dull whine as hot air gushes out onto Idris's open palms. 'I thought you stopped going out after you got married,' he says when the drier turns off.

Salim turns and looks at Idris. His light brown eyes are gleaming under the bathroom's sepia light. He can't speak.

Idris's world is now silent, all the noises of the bathroom and its environs silenced by Salim's presence. He glides towards Salim. His ears feel hot, and his heart starts to beat rapidly. He looks into Salim's eyes, and hugs him. At this very moment, Idris has no care for anything in the world. He can feel Salim's arms wrap around him, and pull him closer to his chest. Salim's smell and embrace still intoxicate him. He inhales deeply, smelling Salim's Dunhill cigarettes and the heavy woody scents of his cologne, absorbing his body's warmth against his. Salim kisses Idris. A current flows through him, like electricity. The kiss is familiar, light in the beginning, then progressing into a deep, wanting one, sucking the air out of Idris's lungs. Salim puts his arms around Idris's waist and holds him tightly. 'I have missed you,' he whispers.

'So have I,' says Idris. 'He's just a friend.'

Salim looks at Idris with inquiring eyes, a sense of alarm building in him. 'It's a date, isn't it?' he says. He lets out a long sigh, and releases Idris from his embrace. Idris is looking at the floor, playing with his hair. 'Salim.' He looks up, his face flushed. 'I have to go back.'

'Promise me you won't go home with that guy,' says Salim. 'I'll visit you during the week.'

'I have to go now,' says Idris. 'I shouldn't keep my friend waiting.' Idris holds the door open for an elderly Indian man coming in. 'And you shouldn't keep her waiting either.'

Ounda is smoking his cigarette and looking out at the ocean. Idris smiles at him. There is a second beer bottle next to his quarter full glass

'I hope you don't mind a refill,' Ounda says. 'And I was wondering if you'd like to watch a movie at my place afterwards?' He looks down at his drink, and then back out at the ocean again, not making eye contact with Idris.

Idris stares at Ounda, heart racing. He has just seen Salim return to his table. He saw him kiss Maimuna on the cheek.

'I have a feeling it might be more than just a film?' Idris says.

Ounda leans forward with a big smile. 'It will be the best film you'll ever watch, I guarantee you.' His bright eyes are twinkling.

Idris looks at the little bubbles rising from the bottom of his beer, then out at the ocean.

My Body Remembers: A War Cry

ZUKOLWENKOSI ZIKALALA

Aweee Mama weMama we Maa!
(Mama weeMaa)
Awee Mama weMama we Maa!
(Mama weeMaa)...
Thul' ungakhali!
Sul' inyembezi!
Awe Mama thul' ungakhali!

Not as startling as the boom of my dad's voice when he disturbs my morning glory musings to have me do the garden. But the sound of you and your comrades, Buzwe, rushed out to meet us when we were still in Central Block making our way to the Great Hall stairs.

Your singing interrupted a conversation I was having with Vatiswa about how the Jacaranda blossoms, our warning alarm for the up-coming exams, were still not out yet. We had just come from an African Literature lecture where the two of us ganged up on Stacey because she antagonised our lecturer and us by saying Tyler Perry's *For Colored Girls* was 'melodramatic and uhh just badly done.' If she hadn't been gifted with one of those high pitched voices that hits a nerve like a siren when she speaks, I probably would have kept my cool. This woman's been whining all semester and everyone in class is tired of her. I think Vatiswa and I will make good friends, especially since she became a vocal ally in class against Stacey.

Today was the first time Vatiswa made an appearance this whole semester. I didn't even know who she was when I got to class this morning, but there was something familiar about her: by this I mean I knew she was a student at the university. I'm usually the first to arrive, but today I encountered this familiar stranger wearing a long orange head-wrap that revealed her dark face. She has full cheeks, a nose that makes her look like she's smelling something, and beautiful large eyes. I thought she was in the wrong class – but I wasn't going to tell her that. So I just said hi and looked for a desk with a leg rest across from where she was sitting – just so I could steal glances at her. She did not seem concerned about my presence. The fact that she also did not have any stationery laid out in front of her almost confirmed my suspicion that she did not think there'd be class in the venue in a few minutes. But when Prof arrived she whipped out a brown A6 Moleskine notebook from a small sling bag which was hanging on the side of her chair.

Buzwe Mabala, I fear you think you are here to study a BA (SRC) and I've teased you about this before. I see the nerves of Campus Security rise and fall, following the intensity of your crescendos. It is the last day for students to vote and you have been campaigning for weeks. I am not all about that 'have-your-say' blah blah.

We arrive on the stairs outside the Great Hall and you're standing at the top of the ledge facing us, well actually facing your comrades, leading them in song. Hands clapping, betwixt the rhythm of feet stomping the ground, betwixt tenors and sopranos beautifully woven into baritone. Most of the radicals are clearly young 'conscious' politics students having their bit of the First Year Experience.

'Do you mind if we chill on the stairs a bit, while you update me on what I missed from last week's lecture? If you're not rushing any-where that is?' she says.

'Yeah sure, but can we sit away from the tent. I don't feel like explaining to these guys why I'm not voting,' I respond as I lead us to an unoccupied spot facing the bushes which is right across from where your crowd is gathered, Buzwe.

'Vele, why aren't you voting?' she asks, digging in her bag.

'I don't care too much about all the stuff these kids are promising all of us. I'm too lazy to stand in lines – it's just such a tedious process. You, are you voting?'

'Aha! There we go …' She holds up a cigarette that is bent near the tip. 'Me? No, I don't care about this place,' flicking the tobacco in place with her middle finger, 'I just want my degree bruh. I've spent too much time here. Do you have a lighter on you by any chance?' her eyes squinting as she completes the delicate task of fixing her stick.

'No sorry, I don't smoke.'

'Alright, I'll be back just now, lemme ask these guys for a lighter real quick.' She points in the direction of you and your band of sing-ers. And as if on cue your flock shouts:

Amandla!
Awethu!
Amandla!
Awethu!

This back and forth reminds me of when we used to have war cry practice in high school. On Thursdays we'd assemble at the bottom fields, where the male teachers and other old boys would groom us into becoming men of honour. Most of the teachers were old boys in any case. Even though I was in grade 9, assembly still made me anxious; we were no longer the main targets for bullying, but I'd seen quite a few boys from my class being forced to surf on the bus to Gandhi Square. Grade 9 privilege meant that we had the second and third stands from the bottom to sit on, where the mid-morning summer heat would still catch us, piercing the insides of our skulls. Most of the grade 8's had to sit on the grass. Even the thought of taking your school blazer off in this sun, despite the heat, was blasphemy.

I remember vividly how charismatic boys from different groups would shout profanities across the grandstands, making the rest of us aware of their presence. Fellow grade 9's antagonising the newbies and reckless laughter coming from all sides. Late seniors throwing their bags up at those in higher stands and then parting us like a scythe cutting long grass as they made their way to the top stands to join their mates. Purple faced boys with chapped lips – obviously on that pimple removing chemical. Tall boys, fat boys, buff-boys, lanky boys, boys trying-to-get-away-with-personalising-and-stylising-their-uniform-boys, hostel boys who didn't shower boys, and cute, rodent-like grade 8 boys. And then you Buzwe. Head boy. Standing in between your two deputies. Alpha of Alphas. Three satyrs lost in the fantasy of leadership, with bashers instead of garlands crowning your heads.

The old high school Buzwe is a personal legend that I nibble on in my memories. Your height did not make you stand out for you were not much taller than I was. Your skin was a glowing shade of brown that captured the sun's orange light. In line with the rules in the school code of conduct, your short hair was brushed and trimmed around the edges with sideburns ending near the middle of your ears. Your full-colours blazer wrapped a muscular body, only revealing the tough hands of a rower. Your ironed grey pants lightly pressed against your thighs and calves, and your posture was display enough of your athleticism. You and your deputies and a few other prefects would trot around at the front sharing private jokes, occasionally stopping either to confiscate an item or to drill a boy – 'scraps' we called them – who did not have the correct uniform on.

I remember how Mr Booysen tried to get us to settle down one morning. He barely had any chin; instead he had a vertical line below his mouth, a feature which explained his asinine tendencies. How he'd stand on the podium, holding onto the microphone hoping that some force from the ether would cause us to settle down. Realising that this would not happen, his vibrato would shrill into the grandstands demanding that we shut up, a routine that went something like...

-Gentlemen.

-Cacophony continues.

-Guys, could you please settle down.

-A sudden loud outbreak from some group where all the matrics sat.

-Ey!! Would you shuddup!

-The noise simmers down, prefects hastening the silence from everyone ...

-Silence.

'Jeeezus guys! Why does it seem that we never learn? Always it is the same thing with you.' He'd be sulking now, and would look up to where the matrics were situated: 'Vosloo, Gumede, you too Batemen, everyone takes from you matrics, yet you're noisiest!' He would shake his head and pause so that the weight of his disappointment would affect us. Switching to his cool laid-back mode, easing his way back into the brotherhood. 'Today we won't take up too much of your time ...'

We were learning a new song, something about being men with iron hearts and fighting and winning. It was an important song because we had to link our arms around each other's necks when we sang and move from side to side very slowly. I think we also sang it with the pipe band once. The fact that when Mr Booysen sang it alone first, his eyes were closed and his right hand was on his iron heart, was also an indication of the song's importance.

I remember when Robbie Van Wyk, one of your deputies and good friends, whispered something in Booysen's ear before taking the podium. He was another 'beast' according to most of the seniors, the typical water-polo achieving type that's also in the A team for rugby, with his full-colours blazer, and blonde curly hair and broad shoulders. I don't think he was all that bright.

'Okes, I don't think you realise the impact and *lark* the gravity of the words here. You guys are singing with no heart whatsoever ...' His lips would be extra puckered every time he made the 'O' sound and he raised his right hand to make an 'O' shape. The little smirk on his face and the accompanying sniggers from some of the prefects and matrics every time he said something at assembly, baffled me throughout that year.

He then proceeded to make the same sonorous rants: speeches that the old boys, the old boy LO teachers like Mr. Booysen and prefects (during orientation week) make. Yes ... that jingle, no different from what we heard on Armistice Day when we wore roses and the choir boys would lead sepia coloured tunes that attempted to stir a nostalgia that I did not share. You know the speeches too for, as Head Boy, you had to read them out again and again: *the spirit of the boys, the blazers that they fought and died for, the blood that will be shed on that field on that weekend's rugby match, for the pride and glory of showing our might, honour, integrity and valour – our pillars of strength!* Yes that romantic shit that even now has old boys still crushing on that school. You also had to pray the prayers.

'Yeah!!!' some of your fellow matric comrades screamed out. Assembly was really about matrics. There was loud applause and the Holy Spirit of Our Sacred School for Boys descended on us.

This is the myth that my faculties were forced to take in. Coming from Soweto, my mom always makes sure that I remain grateful for not going to a school like the Sepetsela High we saw on *Yizo Yizo*. I could not code-switch as well as the other black boys from the suburbs, and so I wore the humiliation of 'coming-from-the-dusty-streets-of-the-ghetto' on my tongue: when I stammered in class, or when I said 'determaiind' instead of 'determined'. Or at the finance office when that lady would bark at me about my dad having to come and collect my report because my fees hadn't been paid in months. I thus could not partake in institutional pride. High school memories always leave a sour tone.

I wonder if you and Robbie van Wyk are still in touch. He came back in my matric year to teach Afrikaans and LO and I'm assuming you haven't been there since you collected your results. First thing I noticed when I perused your wall on Facebook was that you removed all your High School pictures. You now have pictures of Bantu Biko, Sobukwe, Sankara and all those men we now valourise. Men we educate ourselves about, spreading our own myths in pubs and taverns downtown while drinking Black Label and smoking land. You now sing a new song to syncopated beats that exist outside the linear nodes of antiquity that our white liberal High School fed us.

I am now just watching you and your fellows disrupting the order of the day, singing on this pavilion. It is clear that our histories are not framed but are written on the stomp, step and belting of your bodies. Ancestry is in progress right now. Even as you sing many of the students continue to walk on, making themselves transparent. But kancane kancane, psychologically, your loud visibility is sensitising us to the asphyxiating sulphurs in this tower of knowledge.

I search for Vatiswa, but I guess she eventually got caught up in the euphoria because she is nowhere to be seen. I have a bit of time before my next class so I'll wait.

My mind turns to whether you saw us when we first arrived on the stairs, even though you are singing in this heat. I wonder if you see me now. Look my way Buzwe. I also want to be led by you in public like the others, not just when you take the lead in fingering my bumhole on my bed, or when we suck revolting moustaches. I enjoy

the stuffed conspiratorial moans warm on my neck when we're together, but I am no longer trying to rub our escapades out like our
high school selves, my body remembers too much.

What your band of followers does not know is that you have
hidden your pretty. You have taken on the radical tongue, where your
'Rs' and 'Ls' trill against minds within your reach. Your face retains
its malleable nature within the crowd. I always fondle it when you
lie beside me on my bed on lazy Sunday afternoons, while the hard,
rough edges around your palms and thumbs graze and comb the
tiny hairs on my body before I ride your penis again.

'Sorry for taking long!' Vatiswa's sudden voice causes me to gasp
for air as I remember to breathe again.

I turn to look up and you are standing right next to her.

'Buzwe meet my new friend ...'

'Oh I know Buzwe!' I quickly interrupt her getting up to give you
a hug.

'I go way back with this guy Vati, in fact he is the one who has
my Linguistics textbook.'

'Yeah, we're in the same class.' I respond

'We also went to the same high school, but in different years,' you
say to her as you swing taut arms my way. We do a bit of a twalatsa
remembering to give each other the customary slap of high 5 instead.

Reading this awkward moment Vatiswa rolls her eyes.

'Arghh abafana! Do you boys need a moment?' she teases. 'Heh!
Meanwhile wena Buzwe, you've been blaming me for it going
missing. When were you going to tell me you're sorry?' Her stance
changes and she folds her arm underneath the one handling her
cigarette, large eyes blinking in disbelief.

'Angithi I was going to get to that. Anyways I'm sorry,' you say,
playing into this coy drama with me as your audience.

I smile like an idiot.

'Mmhmm!' she responds, whilst pursing her lips. Then turning to me, 'I was just telling him about that girl from class, konje what's her name?'

'Stacey.'

'Shem even her name needs to be decolonised! She knows nothing about Black popular culture. Babe can you believe that she said *For Colored Girls*, the movie, was badly done? I was so touched,' she says leaning in towards you.

'You're lucky you're not in the same TUT with her,' I say sitting down, so I can hide myself in my bag, or my phone, just somewhere.

'How do you guys deal with her in class?' she asks me. 'Ngathi she's one of those who always have something to say.'

'Hayi we just deal hey,' I sigh

'And wena, are you not in that class?' you taunt her.

'Hayi Buzwe, you know I am in that class.' Blushing.

As you two forget that I am there, your sweet nothings fade away. I pretend to read an urgent message on my phone.

What do you think when you fuck me? You were my first, you know this. It was you who taught me the language of intimacy. My legs dangled in the air that Sunday afternoon, and my face suppressed an awkward laugh as I watched your face, with your eyes closed, bobbing back and forth with the occasional grunts.

It's funny how people can just trample on the bunions of an invisible man.

'Tjo! Sorry Vatiswa, but I urgently need to go. My mom is outside my building waiting to drop off some food,' I say, my fingers moving fast over my tangled earphones.

'Oh sure dude, no worries. We can do this some other time.'

'Bye guys …'

'Eh chief, I'll come through later to get my textbook,' you say, and for the first time your eyes catch mine.

'Sure, no problem, just let me know when you're coming.'

I salute and then walk off.

Gregory Porter's 'Painted Canvas', comes on and plays in my ear, a bluesy type of tune. Like beer housed in those blue barrels at funerals, weddings and unveilings, I am fermenting right now. You and I did not walk out of the high walls and cobble-stoned quads, having become men. We did not walk out of there with iron hearts, with the pride and the dignity of being made men, whatever that means. We're not old boys, we're black boys. We play different tunes with our tongues to crowds, to teachers, to friends, to taxi drivers, to pastors and parents, to ourselves. Yet the bangs of your desires have no song. But I know this: you will come to my room later to collect your textbook and then probably rock my soul in your bosom, maybe one last time.

This Tomorrow Was Christmas

JULIET KUSHABA

The first time I entered church after I said 'No' to the Pastor who had come to our house to do the job of a go-between, I felt as if my skin was peeling off when my eyes met with those of the Pastor's wife. I could imagine many other stares on me, all of them accusing me. I could not help thinking how the Pastor's wife must have told everybody that cared to listen, how the entire story of the Pastor-go-between and me went; how I refused to marry a man from one of the most affluent families in the village, how I had denied my widowed mother the numerous cows the suitor's family was willing to give her for my bride wealth and so on. And I knew how women's talk in this village got lifted from home to home as though the carriers expected a huge payment after its delivery. I was wearing a heel not too high compared to the ones I usually wear especially when I am in the city, but my legs connived with my heart and shook me up till I settled myself on a seat next to the entrance. This was after several chunks of light and darkness since the time I had uttered the 'No' answer. My mother had not spoken with me for three days following the incident.

But I thought or rather hoped that that was going to be the last time I would ever worry about village women's talk. I even thought it would be the last time for me to conflict with my mother over my decisions or the lack of them on this matter. But tomorrow, the same thing could have happened and maybe another tomorrow, and many other tomorrows a lot more of this could have happened again if I had not swallowed a courage pill.

This particular tomorrow was Christmas.

'My friend,' I announced to my mother and my siblings, 'will join us for Christmas!'

'That's lovely, Siima.' It was my twenty-four-year-old brother, Jeff who spoke first.

'Oh, God! What a surprise!' my mother said, holding both her hands up to the sky.

My mother started moving up and down, smiling by herself, as she made her preparations for Christmas. It was clear the news was caressing her heart.

'It's going to be the best Christmas ever!' My kid sister, Meeyi, said and jumped to me for a hug.

That afternoon, the family was moving out for 'Secret Christmas Shopping' as we called it; each one of us buys some items secretly which are presented to the other family members as Christmas presents. So that afternoon, everybody prepared amidst a cocktail of joy; shopping, Christmas and a visiting friend!

There were five of us riding in my dead father's old Suzuki through the Gatagata Township. 'Is your friend tall?' 'Big-bodied?' 'Light-skinned …' were some of the questions I had to answer from my full-blown-mood siblings, and I knew it was so they could figure out their 'secret shopping' items. The air in the car and outside tasted of Christmas. There were lots of people on the streets. Young and old, all busy with their part of preparations for the day. We all bought a few more items than we usually did on other Christmas days.

Nobody had dinner that night when we got home. Everybody was busy wrapping and putting names on the presents hidden in their bedrooms. My mother was busy moving some things from the guest room, creating enough room for my friend. I had just stepped in to help her after I completed my wrapping job when my sister Aine called from her room.

'Siima, your phone is ringing. It must be your friend!'

I ran to the living room to answer to the call. It was my friend.

I had to create room for Meeyi and Aine as they ran past me, out of the house to pick up my friend from the road lest they knocked me down. Meeyi's blouse was unbuttoned and as she flung out, it looked like a flag rippling in the wind with its multi-coloured flowers all over. Our home was about 250 metres from the highway so we always walked there to meet our guests who did not know home.

'Would you like me to escort you?' Jeff asked. He and I are eight years and one month apart. As children, we were always more fond of each other than of any of our other siblings despite the fact that there was a big age difference. This was because we had so many things in common; we each had a short sixth finger on our right hand, we were the only left-handed children of the five, we liked pumpkin when all the other children dissed it ... But we had grown particularly close after a Pastor had given me this terrifying prophecy which I have since lived with like an extra body part. This man of God prophesied that someday I would get raped and have a baby boy who would become a burden not only to me but to the entire society. The family cried, lamented and prayed about it. But Jeff decided to do something extra to protect me. He appointed himself my body guard. He started escorting me, almost everywhere I went as long as it was an isolated place, or darkness was beginning to fall. He would stand a few metres away from where I was doing whatever kind of business I had to do and then he would come to me and we would walk back home together. It always felt safer with him.

'No Jeff, I think I will be alright,' I said. It was evening but I knew I would be safe with my other two siblings.

I followed behind them and I was surprised when I saw them standing spellbound. I expected them to have helped Nyonyozi cross to our side of the road but they just stood a few metres from the road. Staring. I moved closer, wondering whether Nyonyozi was still on the bus, but she had rung me to say that she had arrived. I briskly walked closer to find out what they were looking at and from where they stood, I could see Nyonyozi. She was looking at them, and she did not think they were my people as I was later to find out from her.

'Is this your friend?' Aine asked.

'Yes, her name is Nyonyozi.' Aine covered her mouth with her hands when I answered. Meeyi did not ask any questions. She just gaped. I became a bit nervous. Neither of them crossed the road with me.

Nyonyozi must have noticed that something was wrong. But she is a closed-up, reserved kind of girl and so when I got to her, she just turned and looked at me. I knew she was waiting for an explanation. But I had none. I opened my arms for a hug and although she gave me one, I could tell from all the tinges in that embrace that I had lost something.

We crossed the road and joined my siblings. They were still looking awestruck. They greeted Nyonyozi and walked a few feet behind us. I did not speak with them again; I allowed each one of them sufficient pause to enable them to swallow their thoughts and any ugly words they might have had. They reciprocated the pause.

As we approached home, we could see from my mother's hand gestures that she and Jeff were having an animated talk but as soon as we got in their view, they both lapsed into silence. They were seated under the big miyembe tree-shade in front of our house and neither of them moved from where they sat, although ordinarily they would have come to meet the guest. My mum was seated with her legs stretched before her on her favourite green, purple and white five-metre straw mat which she occasionally used. The mat was spread between the plastic chair on which my brother sat and another vacant chair opposite him. She looked like she had had a sudden attack of stroke.

Nyonyozi greeted her but no sound came out of my mother's mouth. All she did was nod her head as though she had been dumb her entire life and all she had ever known was sign language. Jeff offered a handshake and stayed silent. We stood there. I was still carrying Nyonyozi's luggage in my hands and she, her handbag. It felt annoyingly awkward. Everybody was quiet, and the only sound which could be heard was of a squawking bird in the tree above our heads. I wanted to dissolve. By this time, the sun was beginning to set as I became increasingly uncomfortable. I did not know whether to just take my friend into the house and let mother be or to keep standing there and wait for her to recover from her apparent stroke, when she suddenly broke through my thoughts;

'Eh! My daughter Siima,' she said in her sharp voice, looking at me sternly, 'so all this time you have been exciting us about "*my friend … friend … friend*", this is the kind of friend you meant?!'

I could see from the anguished look on Nyonyozi's face that she was hurt by my mother's words. But for me it was double pain for although I had known this was bound to happen, I had not anticipated the magnitude. The fact that Nyonyozi was being embarrassed by my people and in my presence made it worse for me. I felt the words tear my flesh like they were jagged iron, each word cutting into a deeper layer than the one before. I felt them as they cut into every layer that made me human.

My little sister ran into the house and returned with two gift boxes, well wrapped in blue with a beautiful purple and gold ribbon across each box. She sat on the mat, next to mother and started unwrapping the boxes. Everybody turned their attention to her, allowing my head some space to deal with the reality until she spoke. 'See, these are the secret Christmas presents I had bought for your friend.' One was a sky blue shirt with three light vertical red stripes on the side of the chest pocket which appeared like they were disappearing into the shirt. The other gift was a set of men's socks.

'I am sorry,' Nyonyozi finally spoke. I guessed the words were directed to my little sister, Meeyi, because Nyonyozi walked to her and held out her arms.

'I am sorry. I made you spend your ...'

'It's not your fault, Nyon ... Your name is Nyonyozi, right?' my kid sister said, still in the embrace.

'Nyonyozi.'

I was still trying to figure out what to do to save Nyonyozi any further embarrassment when mother added, 'Here! See? It's our language that failed us. Nobody voiced the word "girl" at all ... but we knew it was *a friend* who was coming,' She glared in the opposite direction as though she was talking to herself.

'Now, pull your ears so you can hear me clearly,' the voice was very firm and I became quite terrified, 'if you still wish to be called my child ... are you listening Siima?' I nodded. 'Do not step in my house with that girl. What would a girl of thirty-something still be doing not bringing a suitor?!'

I turned and looked at Nyonyozi. She was still the same woman I loved; her hips were still as spacious and her waist as fragile. I knew she was still as calm and as intelligent as she had always been. And as if she felt my eyes on her body, Nyonyozi raised her head and looked at me. Her dark and lovely eyes seemed to look into the depths of my being, searching for understanding. I knew if I did not clear this, she could decide never to put her feet again across this place I wanted her to call home and it would be my fault.

'Mother, Nyonyozi and I are married,' the words were almost caught between my breath and my teeth. 'We got married two years ago and tomorrow is our anniversary.'

I had to keep Nyonyozi.

Stowaways

ALEXANDER K OPICHO

He does not have time to care about his sick wife whom cancer has made to look so emaciated, scaring him to look at her, as if she is a walking corpse. Nor about the leaking roof of their main house. He only wants to take Chepkemoi to college. The money is meant for nothing else. It is clear in the mind of his heart. The money is earmarked for the college education of his last born daughter, Chepkemoi. He shoves his wife out of his way, pushes her aside violently. She falls on the old couch without a sound as he walks out of the house. Where is Chepkemoi? He wants them to leave for Eldoret now! Eldoret is where he can easily get a pocket-friendly college for her. He calls her in a harsh voice, twice, and then Chepkemoi appears. He commands her to pick up her bag of books as if he hates her.

In just a couple of minutes, they are already half a kilometre away from their home. He is walking in long paces and Chepkemoi is running. He leaves her far behind. She regularly sits down to mend the broken strap of her shoe. He muses within himself that he cannot stop to wait for her; that could look like he is degenerating into cowardly acts. Waiting for Chepkemoi would amount to sympathising with petty things. You can get education without having shoes. Moreover, education is better than shoes.

Chepkemoi runs faster to try and catch up. But the loose broken shoe confounds her. At last, she chooses to carry her shoes in her hands. She is swifter now, fast. She runs ten yards in front of him. The ankles of her strong legs knock against each other as she maintains her lead. He realises that Chepkemoi has well-rounded, swollen buttocks. Sharp emotions pang him. He does not want to lose his daughter to the unknown world.

A mobile phone rings loudly from Chepkemoi's hip pocket in a ringtone like the call of a toad. She put on a pair of blue jean trousers that morning. She pulls out the phone while maintaining the walking pace that will keep her in the leading position. She looks at the avatar of the caller on the screen. She carefully rejects the call and returns the phone to her pocket, swiftly slipping it in as if her pocket is too big for the phone.

'You only know how to buy those foolish toys from China, but you cannot look for education.' The angry voice from behind her terrifies Chepkemoi. She keeps mum. Giving any response to her father's irate outbursts can result in what she does not want. Instead, she increases her walking speed as a sign of her loyalty and apology.

Somewhere in the bottom of her heart, Chepkemoi's mother feels more motherly love for Chepkemoi than for her older daughters, Chepkirui and Chematui. In fact, nowadays she doesn't love Chematui at all, especially when she remembers how her husband had to beat her as if he were beating a cattle stealer from another tribe. For no reason other than that the girl got pregnant and could not identify the boy who was responsible. Her husband remembered the school fees, the money he had paid for Chematui, only for Chematui to succumb to pregnancy. And without even a good score of marks in any subject. Not mentioning her inability to speak good English like the girls on the television news. To make it even worse, he imagined the boy might be from a foreign tribe other than the Kipsigis. These thoughts sent him amok. He looked for Chematui in the kitchen, but he did not find her. Only his wife was there, and she still doesn't know where Chematui was. Her ignorance earned her beatings as if she were an antelope in the hunter's trap.

Her husband is a man of temper. But good luck! he recovers soon. He cannot stay irate from cockcrow to chick roost. The longest he can be temperamental is half an hour. She perseveres through his volcanic behaviour. After he recovers, she goes for him with one of her powerful weapons. The power of the tongue. She knows how to frame her words before delivering them to her verbal victim.

'My husband,' she said that day. But she did not succeed in getting his attention. He was looking in the other direction. She continued: 'You want to kill me for nothing. Why do you want to cause mayhem on my body when you are aware that I am already weak?' Still he did not look at her. He was panting and sweating as if he were a warrior on an active battlefield. 'You have to know that going to church on Sundays or going to school will not make a girl be a good woman. A girl needs circumcision. This will control her blood from driving her crazy like a she-goat.' She artfully aims a pinch at him with words like these. However, she only finishes the last words from a distance. You cannot not predict what her husband can do.

He did not become violent. He just gasped and breathed violently on hearing these words, as if he had been stung by a female wasp. But immediately he regained his composure. He responded to her sting with the astuteness of a seasoned verbal warrior. 'I am not a fool to start with circumcising girls in my home. You! Give birth to boys first!'

The challenge of giving birth to a baby boy still harrows her like her cancer. She is an eyesore in the community. She has wasted her husband for being unable to give him a son. Her husband's age-mates have sons and daughters. They have traditionally circumcised their sons and daughters under Kipsigi customs and rituals. Is this what makes her husband volatile towards her? The village medicine woman lulled her into sweet and foolish daydreaming. The woman's only craft was inducing her to give away her money. She predicted that her last pregnancy would be a baby boy. But she gave birth to Chepkemoi.

Chepkemoi had all the features of a boy. Four of her fingers were equal in length. Her forehead looked exaggerated. It was only the thing between the legs that confirmed that the baby she had given birth to was a girl. Chepkemoi. She named her without ceremony because her husband was so disappointed.

What makes him love Chepkemoi now with such energy that he is lavishing on her the luxurious gift of a college education? Maybe it is a domestic trick only known to men.

Chepkemoi is tired, but how can she safely tell her father? Being tired at such a time will be taken as lack of appreciation, as frailty or betrayal. He does not like people who complain when they are working, bound to do a certain task within a limited time. Should she ask God to give her more energy or should she ask her father for a short rest? Mostly, she just wants a mug of cold water straight from a spring or well, or even from the rivulets like the ones at the far end of her father's farm. The thirst she is feeling cannot be quenched by just any water. Anyway, all problems have an end, Chepkemoi thinks within herself as she soldiers on.

She has finished asking her father if they are trekking from Kericho to Eldoret before she remembers that asking is dangerous. She punctuates her question by violently slapping at her lips with her hands. She increases her speed to lead by an elongated distance.

'No, we shall not trek up to Eldoret,' her father says. 'It is far and risky. We cannot cross Luo land on foot.' This is the time of elections. 'We are in a different party,' he says. 'Ours is the Democratic Antelopes. Theirs is the Revolutionary Tilapias. They can suspect us to be spies only to lynch us.'

He is speaking with an air of calmness and fatherly love, so Chepkemoi allows herself to ask another question: 'Where shall we get the bus?'

A loud and rough roaring sound comes from behind them. It is a lorry. It looks like a prison lorry, but it is not one. It is being driven by a white man.

'Move aside!' her father commands her. Chepkemoi has already waved to the lorry driver to stop, but she moves aside. Father is pressing her into the depths of the bushes. The lorry swerves to the side of the road and stops. The white driver waves to both of them to get in. 'You are a small child who is very immoral, mannerless, foolish and useless!' her father is cursing as they run towards the lorry. Why had she waved to the lorry?

The white man greets them in Kiswahili. They get in the front, in the driver's cabin. Chepkemoi is sandwiched between her father and the white man. This is the first time in all her life she is sitting near a white man. She feels warmth, and a good smell comes from the sweat of the perfumed white man. He brushes his arm against Chepkemoi as he wipes the steering wheel. To her surprise, Chepkemoi discovers that a white man has a tough skin. She has always believed that a white man's skin is a soft skin.

The white man does not start the lorry. He takes out a wooden snuff horn from his breast pocket, knocks out a screw of snuff, and presses it up into his sharp and long nose. He does not sneeze! He returns the snuff horn to its cradle in his pocket and starts the lorry. Chepkemoi chuckles and suppresses her laughter. She presses her hands on her mouth as if she is about to sneeze. She steals a look at her father. He always goes into fits of violent sneezing when he uses snuff. Her father's face is wearing an expression of surprise. Maybe he thought all white men are Christian missionaries. Maybe he didn't expect a white man to commit such a heinous sin. Then her father begins searching his pockets with a sad face. The white man takes out the snuff horn again, and holds it out to Chepkemoi to give to her father. She shrinks herself back, shaking her head, no. A girl accepting a gift of snuff from any man on behalf of her father is automatically and irreversibly submitting to marriage with the snuff donor. This is an active custom among the Kipsigis people. More so, this is an old white man when there are a lot of Kipsigis young men, including her boyfriend. Chepkemoi is very relieved in her heart by her father's swift and timely receipt of the snuff horn. With both his hands cupped in acceptance, he looks like a Pentecostal churchgoer in prayer.

Their lift in the lorry does not last all the way to Eldoret. They get dropped at the junction near Tenwek mission hospital. The white man branches away towards Kisumu, and Chepkemoi and her father stand at the junction to wait for another vehicle.

They haven't waited for a long time before a minibus appears. Loud and raucous music blasts out. It is branded and tattooed all over in all different colours. Calligraphic writings are drawn across its metallic body. Words like Al-shabab, Tornados, Saddam, Baghdad Boys, Sweat Of The Poor, Bob Marley, Second Wife, and so forth are all over the body of the minibus, which stops without their having to wave to it.

Chepkemoi enters the minibus first. There is only one vacant seat, so she stands aside to make way for her father to go ahead and sit. But he declines. He lets her have the seat. She sits without arguing. The minibus is already moving. 'Let it continue, you she-man!' curses the tout, ordering the driver to continue to play the music. It has no melody that can touch Chepkemoi's heart. It is Kanungo e Teko, Luo cultural music by Tony Nyandundo or whoever. All in all, it is nothing but thunderous noise. Why is the tout at the doorstep of the minibus madly gyrating his waist to such sounds? Why can't the driver play Kalenjin music, good and soft songs like 'Where are you baby'? Nice and melodious, sung by a woman whose name is Chelele.

The middle-aged man next to Chepkemoi is crying. He is in a military uniform. He must be an area sub-chief or a district officer, most probably from the Nandi community. Only Nandi men qualify to be appointed as village administrators by the government. Why would a man in military uniform and with the crown on his barrette cry? Does it mean that the government is also crying? The man groans and writhes as if he is in unbearable pain. 'Ndaret,' he mumbles. 'Ndaret. Ndaret. Ndaret.' Over and over. Ndaret means snake in Kipsigis. It means the same in the Nandi language. From the other passengers, Chepkemoi finds out that the crying man is a village administrator. One old lady whispers in Chepkemoi's ear that the man was bitten by a black snake when he was clearing the bush at the fence of his land. Chepkemoi tenses up. She struggles to make herself small so that she won't have body contact with the victim. She makes a space between herself and the snakebite victim lest the serum flow into her body. She realises she is sweating, and she feels like she may vomit. She wants to get to Eldoret this very minute.

The minibus stops, and two short, crude-looking traffic policemen get in. They look like seasoned ruffians. Their uniforms are not orderly, and violence is written on their faces. They behave as if all the people in the minibus are criminals to be harassed. Each man brandishes a long gun, molesting every passenger. Chepkemoi's father has already moved out of their way, but one of them whacks him a slap on his cheek. The other wallops him, and he staggers. He almost falls down. He releases chocolate coloured mucous from his nose, mixed with the snuff he sniffed. Before he can recombombulate, one of the policemen has handcuffed him. They pull him out of the minibus.

'Why are you so rude that you just stand in the bus the way you like? Is this your mother's kitchen? You useless man do you smoke marijuana? Let us go.' Chepkemoi is shaking, not knowing what they will do to her father. She follows them outside. 'Are you a second or third wife to this man in handcuffs?' Before Chepkemoi can answer, the other policeman points to her feet and laughs. 'Why haven't you got your shoes on? You have very small feet, like the wings of a baby pigeon.'

Chepkemoi's father corrects the first policeman: 'She is my daughter and is not a prostitute.' But he gets slapped, pushed by the barrel of the gun to walk faster.

'You move on, good liar!' the policeman says. 'We're going to remove your testicles.'

Chepkemoi begins giggling, but out of fear and confusion, as she runs behind them. They enter a wild woodlot, away from the eyes of the public. But the driver, who had run after them, arrives on the scene. He implores the policemen to forgive his passenger. One of the policemen is wildly searching the pockets of Chepkemoi's father.

'Where is the marijuana you smoke?' he shouts.

But before Chepkemoi's father can respond, the driver intervenes. 'This man was standing in the vehicle because he had to give the village administrator a place to sit. The administrator was bitten by a black snake.'

'Sympathy for snake-bite victims or even good heartedness is not an excuse to break the Kenyan law,' the two policemen reply. But one of the policemen takes a bribe of some money from the driver. And Chepkemoi sees that the other is holding a brown lump of something that looks like a lot of banknotes. The policemen now change their attitude and remove the handcuffs from the wrists of Chepkemoi's father. The policemen ricochet into playfully kicking and mocking the driver and Chepkemoi's father. They kick the driver as if he is a swine. 'Run away, you marijuana-taking liars' they scold. Chepkemoi's father leads them in the running this time, followed by Chepkemoi. The driver walks after them looking very disappointed. He clucks like a wild turkey when he is sure the policemen are not in earshot.

The tout, also now dejected, and looking worried, welcomes them back to the minibus. Other passengers are looking on in expectation. The driver takes the steering wheel. When the minibus has started, Chepkemoi's father stoops and whispers to her in a shaking voice: 'The school fees money is gone. The policemen cunningly took it from me. I did not even notice until just now.' Chepkemoi does not say anything. She looks up at his face. He is struggling to suppress the threatening tears.

The snake-bite victim is still mumbling, 'Ndaret. Ndaret. Ndaret.'

They arrive safely at Eldoret. Chepkemoi's father feels openly haggard. His face is pale, and full of expressions of tiredness. What is he to do? His plans from home squarely depended on the money he had. He could have done some shopping for personal effects for Chepkemoi. He also had an idea of buying himself a wristwatch, and an African hat made from the papyrus grass of Lake Victoria. All has gone to the dogs. Now he can do nothing. Gone are the days when a civilian like him would fight the policemen and even arrest them. What if the government gave the civilians some guns? Guns must be made available to civilians so that in situations like this one can personally enforce justice by using his or her gun. 'I beg your pardon?' says Chepkemoi to her father's mumbling. He does not answer. He just keeps on walking, keeping to the left side of the road lest he gets knocked down by a stray motorcar. He hates the motor-bicycles most. Why did the Chinese put their silly motor-bicycles in each and every corner of his country? Why couldn't those two short police-men fight the Al-Shabaab, the Al-Qaeda, and the other bad men of Islam instead of robbing an old man? 'My hard-earned cash!' he says aloud. He clicks his tongue. He longs to meet one of the policemen in his village at a drinking spree. He will pull off his testicles and stuff them in his stupid mouth. His mind and his heart grow heavy. What will he tell the college big man so that he will accept Chep-kemoi for two weeks while he waits for the money to be paid to him by the tea factory? Raucous sobs from behind him interrupt the flow of his feelings. Chepkemoi is crying uncontrollably as she walks.

'What is it? Stop crying and tell me!' he roars.

'My mobile phone is gone! Imagine! It was a Samsung Galaxy! It had all the features!' She names them between sobs: 'Facebook, Twitter, Whatsapp, Instagram, M-Pesa money transfer! Even Pesa-Pap banking!'

He feels no sympathy for her torrential shedding of tears. 'Keep quiet and walk faster. Maybe that tout in the minibus stole it from you.'

They get to the main reception of the Afro-Development College in Eldoret at exactly six in the evening. They are invited by the receptionist to sit on the cushioned chairs. There is a good velvet carpet under the chairs. This is when Chepkemoi's father discovers that their feet are grimed with the red dust of the highlands. His feet are as brown as a brick. He steals a glance at Chepkemoi's feet: they are browner. The usual conspicuous scars from the jigger-bites in her childhood are nowhere to be seen under the brown veneer of dust and grime. The receptionist is sitting behind a computer screen. She finishes talking on her mobile phone, then invites Chepkemoi's father to talk.

When Chepkemoi saw the phone of the receptionist, sad feelings of loss had gone deep into her heart. She feels worthless and sub-human. Life without a mobile phone is worse than life in hell. She does not even hear what the receptionist and her father talk about. She is awoken out of her reminiscing about her mobile phone when her father pulls her to come along into the office of the principal.

Mr Namugongo is a middle-aged man, slender and tall. On his face, he has time-worn glasses with colourless frames. He looks like the type that does not always finish the food on his plate. He has an air of self-heroism around himself, expressed in the way he pronounces English words. As he moves around his office he looks at everything in a pose of panache, as if he is tired of umpteen successes in throwing arrows at enemies during the tribal clashes.

He has stayed around the college till evening because there is political violence in town. Mr Namugongo tells Chepkemoi's father that the rowdy riff-raff of youths has been vandalising properties. Rampant rape has also been reported. Two days ago, there was a forceful mass eviction of poor people, and five hundred internally displaced people from the Gikuyu community were hiding in the church at Kiambaa on the outskirts of Eldoret. Then Kalenjin militia set the very church on fire. One mother among the people who were burning in that church tried to save her baby by throwing it out. But when the attacking militia discovered that the baby was a boy, they threw it back into the burning church. The five-month-old baby burned to death along with the rest of the people in there. The people in the church were members of the Democratic Antelopes, but the militia belong to the Revolutionary Tilapias. They are in conflict over the faked results of the presidential elections.

Then Chepkemoi's father narrates each and every sad incident that has befallen them on the way. Mr Namugongo does not interrupt. Chepkemoi is sure he will not accept her. Immediately when her father finishes telling him that he will bring the money in a fortnight, Mr Namugongo raises the landline phone from its cradle. While he is calling, he shouts, 'Rispa! Rispa!' Is he calling the policemen to come and arrest them for disturbance?

A tall and slender brown woman enters the office without knocking. She has her head in a fantastic coiffure. She is in a sleeveless dress. Her breasts point sharply, as if they are competing with one another. 'Here I am sir.' The woman's voice pierces through Chepkemoi's heart like an electric shock. A strong sexual impulse waves through Chepkemoi's nerves.

'Rispa is one of the students doing a certificate course in gender studies,' explains Mr Namugongo. It is the course that Chepkemoi has also come to do! Her father had wanted her to do cookery or midwifery, but she refused. Mr Namugongo tells Rispa: 'I want Chepkemoi to stay with you in your hostel room for two weeks.' Chepkemoi's heart palpitates with suppressed joy. Rispa takes Chepkemoi's hand and leads her out into the night.

Chepkemoi does not waste her time with worries about where her father will sleep. Neither does she remember that she has forgotten her torn and loose shoes in the principal's office. She is now in college! She is happy. Rispa leads her by her hand for a distance. In the safe darkness, away from the eyes of people, Rispa pulls Chepkemoi to her.

'I will call you Memo,' Rispa says. It sounds nice. Rispa gives Chepkemoi a long kiss. Rispa's breasts are touching Chepkemoi's. Rispa's thighs feel warm against hers. Chepkemoi smells a sweet smell. She feels different from what she feels in the loving arms of her boyfriend Kemboi. She allows Rispa to lead her. Her heart is throbbing.

The faint whistling of the hornbill comes into the ears of Chepkemoi early in the morning. It is from a distant forest. She thinks she is at home in Kericho, sleeping under the rough thatched roof of her mother's kitchen. But she opens her eyes and everything is different. She is in a well-furnished bedroom, under covers of shawls that look like leopard skin. Is she in the ward at Tenwek hospital again? She was once admitted when she broke her left hand falling from the tree she had climbed to get a piece of well-dried firewood. Chepkemoi discovers that she is in the loving arms not of a boy, but in the slender, long, and soft-brown arms of Rispa. They have slept on the same bed under the same covers. What happened? Chepkemoi secretly touches her thighs. She does not find herself with any undergarment on. Rispa is also naked, and very hot, like a cooking stove. Chepkemoi does not feel anything bad about all this. She feels good. When she steals a look at Rispa's face, she finds her very lovely and delicate. She loves her. She wraps her arms around Rispa. They sleep till ten in the morning.

The principal was crushed by the sight of Chepkemoi. He gave the girl's father a thousand shillings for transport back to his home. Chepkemoi's father thought that the principal was doing this kindness out of being a good Christian. How can a man who is not your tribe be so kind and understanding, as well as generous? But Mr Namugongo was thinking: How can such a humble man be the father of such a beautiful girl?

Mr Namugongo comes from the Babukusu community in the western part of Kenya. In his village in Bungoma district there is a poverty of women, leave alone girls. In his village such beautiful girls as Chepkemoi are married to village rich men or chiefs, or the rich sons of paramount chiefs. He has even been thinking that Rispa is the most beautiful girl they have on the college campus. He has now come to a new dawn: Chepkemoi is more beautiful. She is short and physically perfect. Her legs curve out artfully. She is not very brown or very dark. Her bosom is well rounded and juts out like the eaves of a house. When she talks, her face welcomes you to a wonderful natural gap in the upper row of her front teeth, attended by two flickering dimples on each cheek. Mr Namugongo does not want to guess what she could be in bed. 'To hell with that thing called a woman in my house!' He curses himself for having married that heavy-weight ugliness at home. She does not know why he is giving Chepkemoi's father that money! But he will say that the old man deserves maximum hospitality.

They part at the main gate of the college. Mr Namugongo turns left. Chepkemoi's father goes straight, towards the car park, expecting to get the last minibus from Eldoret back to Kericho.

Silent and alone in his thoughts, Mr Namugongo walks towards his house. He does not use a car often. It is economical to walk in the evening. He calls it using his footsubishi – from Mitsubishi, the Japanese-made lorry known for being good at covering long distances. He thinks about Chepkemoi as he uses his footsubishi home. His erect penis pulls at the front of his trousers. Good luck! It is in darkness! The people he meets can't notice. He pockets his left hand to secretly mitigate the effect of his penis on the front of his trousers. It could be good if he was with Chepkemoi this very moment! He could tell her that she is not going to pay any school fees. He could tell her that she is the student leader. He could give her a part-time marketing job, so she could earn some money. Such a beautiful girl is even supposed to be given a full-time job. The time for fearing his wife is over. It is now time for a second wife. Moreover, his wife has only had one son against five daughters. What a waste in life! Mr Namugongo clicks loudly, but to himself. 'This is my time to marry,' he mumbles. Is Chepkemoi still a virgin? Or is she already aware of the world? Seducing a virgin is distasteful. He went through a trialsome love-hunting when he was a boy. It was very difficult to procure a date from that girl, now his wife, regardless of the money gifts he made to her. But this time round it does not matter what he will go through. What he wants most is sex with Chepkemoi. And at most to know if she will accept to live with him as a second wife. Mr Namugongo is tortured by these feelings of lust until he enters his compound. Without knowing how, he has arrived at his home. He enters to the welcome of the ugly face of his wife.

Chepkemoi learns the word lesbian from Rispa that morning. She is very annoyed that their English teacher at St Monica's in Londiani parish never taught them such important words. Were her four years of being a student in secondary school a total loss when now she is discovering that love between two girls is known as lesbian love? 'People of the same sex who love one another are generally known as gays,' Rispa tells her further.

Chepkemoi giggles. 'How can a boy love a boy and yet they have nothing between their legs?'

'Don't worry about that, Memo,' Rispa says. 'Focus on our love.' But she instructs Chepkemoi not to share with anyone about their relationship. 'We have to keep it a secret.' Chepkemoi is surprised. But Rispa tells her that they can be arrested and taken to prison if they are found. Chepkemoi is also surprised to learn that in Uganda the president has allowed lesbians to be burned in public. 'Mob justice,' says Rispa. Chepkemoi feels worried, but she swears to Rispa that she will never leave her. 'Don't worry,' Rispa tells her. We will hatch a plan to stow ourselves away to Europe or America. There people in same-sex relationships are tolerated. And there we will be married.'

Staying Afloat

UNOMA AZUAH

I stood near the window of my brother's one-bedroom apartment, watching rain fall in a pounding frenzy on the village of Anthony. I'd left the window slightly open and moisture settled on my face. Waves of rain cast a grey shadow on our neighbourhood. The streets were empty of people and flooded with water. Everywhere there were pools of floating garbage. My job interview with Mr Oderin, the editor of the *Newsvine*, was for the next hour. He had warned me that I must not be late. Thirty minutes later, the rain stopped. I took my shoes off to wade through the flooded streets, cringing at every tingle of my feet. I could upset a floating snake, or step on a nail. It was a relief to get into a bus.

'Sidon well!' the conductor shrieked.

I was half sitting on the seat, trying not to wake the chubby lady sitting next to me. She was snoring. But when the conductor gave me a sharp jab in my thigh with his elbow, I moved closer. The smell of fresh fish lingered around the sleeping lady. 'Papa Sunday, no touch me o …' she mumbled.

'Oshodi Eko! Mile Two!'

The yell from the bus conductor announcing where we were going woke the lady up. She wiped the drool dripping down her chin with the edge of her wrapper, sighed, and sat back to make herself more comfortable. I looked out through the misty window. A throng of civil servants were waddling through puddles, shoes in hand. A sharp itch on my wet leg made me reach down to scratch. My heart was pounding violently. These days, I wake up with panic attacks. Two weeks ago, I was laid off from my job.

It had been a stress-free two years as a bookstore cashier. My boss even gave me a one-room accommodation in his boys' quarters. But the wonderful two years suddenly came to an end two sunny Saturdays ago. I had taken my bath, applied my lily scented body lotion, and sprayed myself with my tester perfume. I was all dressed up, ready to head to the bookstore, when Hezekiah, my boss's houseboy, peered through the torn curtain of my door and told me that my boss wanted to see me.

'What does he want me for?' I said.

Hezekiah's face said nothing. The stupid boy just grinned at me. He was always giggling or grinning. Usually I didn't mind, but that morning I found it irritating. I wanted to wipe his grin off his face.

'Do you know why he wants to see me?' I asked louder.

Hezekiah grinned.

Hezekiah had been nice to me, though. Late at night and also early in the mornings, he would sneak out steamy, delicious meals from our boss's kitchen for me. His kind gesture helped me save money on food, and I was grateful to him. The downside was that I often had to share my little room with stacks of plates until Hezekiah was finally able to fetch them. My boss constantly needed Hezekiah for one thing or the other. If they were not in Hezekiah's room chit-chatting, Hezekiah was in the kitchen cooking for him. If Hezekiah had been a woman, my boss would probably have married him. Something that got on my nerves was Hezekiah's constant questioning about why all my friends were girls. 'Don't you like men, Ihuoma?' he would frequently ask me. 'Why don't you have a man to take care of you?' I would laugh it off.

I pushed Hezekiah aside and made for the main house. My boss was at the eating table, bare-chested. As he reached for his orange juice and napkins, his drooping belly swayed back and forth. The aroma of fried eggs and toasted bread made me drool, but I swallowed my saliva. My boss invited me to sit next to him.

'Hezekiah! Bring a cup and a plate for Ihuoma!'

'Yes, sir!'

I was too anxious to eat, but also too hungry to turn down the food. I took two quick bites of the toasted bread stuffed with fried eggs and reached for the cup of cocoa. My boss coughed, and then he announced that he had been duped out of one hundred and fifty-one million naira. He was getting ready to pack up and head to the UK to be with his family. He was not exactly sure about when he was going to leave but he would give my last salary to Hezekiah for me. I was to check in a couple of weeks.

I choked. My boss stroked my shoulder and told me to drink some water. I coughed and gulped some more cocoa. It helped, and I cleared my throat some more.

Mr Donatus, my boss's driver, came in with a parcel. Mr Donatus was a tall man with a strong odour of dry sweat. His deep-etched tribal marks sank into the folds of his wide grin. He nodded when I greeted him. 'Good morning sir,' Mr Donatus said to my boss, and gave him the parcel. Without saying another word, Mr Donatus stepped out.

My boss opened the parcel, and in it was wads of dirty naira notes.

I was snapped out of my reverie when the bus slammed into a deep pothole and dirty water splashed up onto my forehead. It trickled down my nose, and I could smell the stench of old faeces. I instantly wiped my face with both of my palms before that stuff could trickle into my mouth.

As we got closer to Mile Two, the traffic was less hectic. Over-grown grass straddled both sides of the road and there were fewer pedestrians. Through the window, I could see a solitary teenage girl with a tray of oranges on her head. 'Buy oranges! Sweet oranges!' she wailed.

'Canal! Canal!' the bus conductor called out.

I tapped him on his shoulder to let him know that Canal, which was opposite the *Newsvine*, was my stop.

The receptionist told me to wait for Mr Oderin, who was at a board meeting. There was another lady sitting opposite me in the waiting room. She smiled at me, and I was almost sure she winked at me. She asked me who I was waiting for and when I told her, the smile on her face instantly disappeared. 'Who are you here for?' I asked her. She ignored me and furiously chewed on her chewing gum. Ten minutes later, a young man in a dashiki walked in and asked the lady to follow him. After what felt like hours, the young man came back to fetch me.

He ushered me into Mr Oderin's office. The windows were closed and the air conditioning hummed in the background. Mr Oderin was pacing around the huge table in the middle of his spacious office. I greeted him. He kept pacing around the table, waving his hand at the dusty chair close to the door. I sat down and waited. He finally stopped pacing around the table, walked towards me, pulled out a bunch of keys from his pocket, and locked the door. My heart skipped. I felt my eyes open wider. I looked at Mr Oderin, and I looked around his office. He stretched out his hand to give me a handshake. A strong smell of sweat hovered around my nose. There were brown rings of sweat on the armpits of Mr Oderin's blue shirt. Then he went and sat on his rolling chair. He placed his hands on his desk, facing me.

'Did my wife see you when my personal assistant got you from the reception area?' he said.

'Why? I don't know your wife. What does she look like?'

He pointed above his door to a picture up there on the wall. It was a picture of the lady in the waiting room.

'Yes!' I said. 'She saw me.'

'Leave through our back gate after this interview.'

'Why?'

'Just do as I say. My wife makes unnecessary trouble, but *she* loves women more than I do.'

'She does?' I could feel myself smiling. 'But why would she make trouble?'

'Don't ask me questions. I am the person conducting the interview.'

I instantly wiped the smile off my face.

'So, what qualifications do you have?' said Mr Oderin.

'I have a BA in English and I have two years of working experience. I have also done some freelance writing for some newspapers here in Lagos.'

'You have beauty and brains. Yes?'

There was that smile on my face again. But it disappeared when I saw Mr Oderin's hand making a strange motion around his groin area. He seemed to be slowly unzipping his trousers. All of a sudden, Mr Oderin stood up. He dropped his trousers and hurried across the office to me with his trousers around his knees.

'Drop to your knees and suck me!' he said. His manhood was flapping back and forth.

'What!' I yelled. I could smell alcohol on his breath. Wasn't it too early in the morning?

'You think you can just walk in here and get a job – just like that? You must be kidding,' said Mr Oderin. 'I can drop down for you,' he went on, 'if that's the way you want it.'

I covered my mouth with both of my hands. I could hear the rain. Mr Oderin dropped down on his knees and started pushing up my skirt. I wriggled out of his grip and ran across the office.

'What's wrong?' he said. 'Do you think your private parts are a gold mine? Do you know the number of ladies that actually beg me to have them?'

'I am sorry, sir,' I said from the other end of the office. 'Just let me go. I don't want the job anyway.'

Mr Oderin let out a loud yelp and made to grab me again. I bolted away. We ran around and around his office. Mr Oderin got out of breath. He paused. He loosened his tie. His trousers had slipped down around his ankles. He dragged his trousers along the floor as he stumbled after me again. There was nowhere to run, so I backed myself against the wall and threw punches at him. He grabbed me. I struggled to get loose, but he held tight. His manhood was breathing on my buttocks.

Then I remembered the trick I'd played on one of my lecturers in a similar incident when I was an undergraduate at the University of Nigeria. During drama rehearsals I had learned an improvisation skill: a barking dog, a hooting owl, a cockerel, and a cat. Out of my mouth a dog barked, an owl hooted, a cockerel crowed and a cat meowed.

Mr Oderin released me with lightning speed.

'I am no ordinary human being. I have powers! I can show you more!' I broke out into piercing laughter.

'No, no, no! I am sorry. I will give you the job,' stammered Mr Oderin, grabbing the Bible off his desk. He held onto his Bible with one hand and grabbed onto his trousers with the other hand, struggling to pull them up with his one free hand. When he succeeded in pulling up his trousers, he stammered, 'Would you be so kind as to sit down.' When I sat down on the chair close to the door, he put the Bible back on his desk and buttoned up his trousers.

I told Mr Oderin that if he didn't keep his word and give me the job I would make sure he had a car accident within six days. And if he still didn't give me the job after that, he would be afflicted with a strange illness in six weeks' time, which would cause him to die six months later. He asked me to start work the next day.

The rain had lessened to a drizzle as I stepped out of the *Newsvine* office. But I was barely out of the gate and in the street when somebody lunged at me from behind. I was knocked down and held down. Terrified, I hit, kicked and delivered pounding blind blows with all the power I had in me. After a short wrestle, I was able to grab onto a hairy thing. I yanked hard, and it came away in my hands. It was a woman's wig. Then the weight on me was lifted. It was Mrs Oderin. She stood up, adjusted her dress, grabbed her wig back, and hurriedly replaced it on her head.

'Ashewo! Idiot! Husband-snatcher!' she yelled.

A small crowd had gathered around us. I picked my bag up from the ground, brushed off the mud on it, and rushed away. But Mrs Oderin followed me, still calling me names. 'Thief! Oloshi!' I frantically flagged down an okada. The motorbike's wheels left a trail of mud on Mrs Oderin's face as we zoomed off.

When I got to work at the *Newsvine* the next day, there was a note from Mr Oderin asking that I cover an event on Opebi-Allen Avenue. It is one of the busiest streets in Lagos. Most high-end companies and offices are located there. Elite homes are also located there. When I got to the address, the event was what seemed like a birthday bash. I approached one of the ladies I saw, who told me it was a convention party for the Women Against Violence society, and escorted me in. The president was in her office taking an important call from the Commissioner of Women Affairs, she told me. She invited me to sit in the large living room and said she would call the vice president to meet me while I waited. A lot of women were milling around. Most of them were quite attractive, and I tried not to stare too hard. I flipped through the bundle of magazines laid out on a side table. I was excited about my first major assignment. Getting a personal interview with the president of the Women Against

Violence society would be a dream come true. When the lady came back with the vice president, my mouth fell open. It was Mrs Oderin.

I leapt up and bolted out of the living room, and out of the house. I ran towards the gate. But the tall, gap-toothed gateman was scowling at me as he proceeded to lock the gate with a gigantic padlock. 'You want to go to madam good-good, or you want to go bad-bad?' he said. His breath reeked of stale cigarettes. I eyed him, and then gauged the height of the brick wall surrounding the premises. It was too high.

I picked my way back to Mrs Oderin's side. For some odd reason she was calm as she pleaded with me to come to her office. She wanted to talk to me about something important, she said. She didn't convince me: I could have sworn that she had plans to assassinate me. But I made a quick sign of the cross and followed her through the house to her office.

The office looked nearly empty. Except for the chair beside a huge table in the middle of the room, there was only one other chair and a side table with a lamp on it.

'Make yourself comfortable!'

I sat on the chair closest to the window and looked down at my knees. It was consoling that the window was slightly open. Mrs Oderin perched herself on the arm of the chair I was sitting on and gawked at me. She apologised for attacking me at *Newsvine*. 'I thought you were one of the girls that throw themselves at my husband,' she said.

'You would rather have them throw themselves at you?'

'Well, I don't mind,' she smiled. 'At least I am discreet about it.'

I took a closer look at her. Except for the scary-looking lashes and her dishevelled wig, she was not bad looking. Curvy. She ran her long fingernails through my Afro and caressed my back with her other hand. I didn't try to stop her. 'You could have asked me nicely. I may have obliged you,' I said.

There was a knock on the door. Mrs Oderin sat up instantly and straightened her cream blouse. A tall lanky woman who looked as though she was in her early fifties came in. Her make-up was heavy, making her face look like a mask. Despite that, she was a gorgeous woman, with a warm smile.

'They said there is a journalist here waiting to interview me?'

'Yes,' I said.

'You are the one?' she asked, with an even wider smile. 'What's your name?'

'Ihuoma.'

'Nice name!' she said. 'Folake, please send her to my office when she's done with you.' She closed the door gently behind her.

Mrs Oderin dragged the other chair closer to mine and sat next to me. She held my hand. 'I really like you,' she said, and kissed my hand.

A lot of images ran through my mind: my former boss's sagging belly, me choking at his eating table, the smell of sweat in Mr Oderin's office, the fight in the street with Mrs Oderin. I pulled my hand away.

'Why?' she asked with pleading eyes.

'I'll pass,' I said. 'I am just not interested.'

The rain started again. It felt as if pebbles were dropping on the roof of the building. The room got darker. Mrs Oderin kept her eyes on me, but I stood up and made for the door. Maybe the president would be a better bet.

The president didn't want us to use her office for the interview. She asked if I minded going to a more comfortable place, and I didn't mind. With a large umbrella, she led me to her car, and around to the passenger's side. Then she went around to the driver's side and half got in. She was about to fold up her umbrella, which she held above her, when the gateman ran out into the rain and held it for her. She thanked him, and then fumbled for her purse inside a large handbag wedged between the gear lever and my seat. She gave him a one thousand naira note. His echoing 'Thank you ma! Thank you ma!' rang through the rain.

Just a few houses down the same street, we pulled into a modest house with well-trimmed hedges. The president said it was her guesthouse. Inside was a lavish, well-furnished living room. I hesitated before stepping onto the rug and pulled off my shoes. She dropped her handbag on the longest couch in the room and excused herself. Right opposite me was a minibar. I sat back and inhaled the most pleasant rose fragrance I've ever experienced. Within minutes, Madam President was out. She had on a yellow, free-flowing gown.

'Are you hungry?' she asked.

'Not really. I wouldn't mind a drink though.'

'Wine, malt, soft drink?'

'Wine will be perfect.'

'White, red?'

'Red.'

She invited me to her bar, and told me about all the types of wine, their history, and why older wines taste the best. I was impressed with her knowledge of wine. She poured some wine for me and we settled into the interview. She told me to take my time. She would drop me off if it got too late, or I could sleep over. For some reason, I couldn't look straight into her eyes. The radiance of her beautiful face seemed too bright to behold. Maybe it was the wine, but I hadn't drunk that much. I tried to pull myself together.

Her name was Gloria, which she insisted I call her. She was a single mother who had been to school and lived in the US for years before deciding to come home and give back. Gloria asked me about myself, where I was from, what I had studied at the university, how long I had been a journalist, my plans, and if I enjoyed my job. My eyes darted around. They went everywhere except to her face. At a point, I started slurring my words. She asked if I was alright. I didn't respond, so she knelt before me and held my face. I don't know where

I found the courage, but I gave her a lingering kiss. I think the light in the room dimmed at that moment.

When I left the next morning, I was wasted. Gloria desperately wanted to take me home, but I refused. I was too embarrassed to spend another minute in her presence. But I loved the glow in my groin area. I wobbled my way to Opebi-Allen junction to find a bus back to Anthony. There was no bus in sight. I had reluctantly decided to go back to Gloria's cosy guesthouse when a car swung towards me. Its horn blared so loudly that I covered my ears with both hands. It was Mr Donatus, my former boss's driver.

I must have passed out in the car, because the next thing I knew Mr Donatus was gently pulling at me to get out. We were at my brother's apartment in Anthony. I looked around for my handbag. My notebook was the only thing that stared back at me form the car seat. I had no money with me. I remembered refusing to take the thick fold of money Gloria had offered me. I panicked. I didn't want to see her again, not so soon. Maybe in a few days when I would have cleared my head, I told myself.

Mr Donatus was already zooming off when I waved at him to stop. I could get my salary from Hezekiah, I'd realised. Mr Donatus frowned when I asked him to drop me off at his boss's place. He had errands to run and I had delayed him enough, he said. We were barely at my former boss's gate when Mr Donatus took off again, with one of my legs only just out of the car. I wanted to yell at him, but I changed my mind. He had done me a favour.

I almost knocked my knuckles out at my former boss's front door, yet nobody responded. So I decided to try Hezekiah's room. I hadn't quite reached his door when I heard groans and moans. At first I thought somebody was hurting Hezekiah. But I listened, and it sounded more pleasurable than painful. Did Hezekiah have the nerve to bring girls to his room? I tiptoed to the window. I took a peek. I saw my boss. And Hezekiah was kneeling.

Going Home

ALISTAIR MACKAY

Nothing. For about the tenth time in as many minutes, Nick leaned back into the couch, yanked his phone out from the front pocket of his jeans, and checked for messages. Irritating, compulsive behaviour. A month in New York and already he missed home. He should be out exploring the city. And of course there would be no messages. It was nearly 7pm, which meant it was well after midnight in South Africa. So much for the neighbourly global village. Time zones, the last great heretics against an ever-compressing world of technology and instant gratification. His presence and engagement in his new life were required.

Most days Nick was happy with the distance. Home reached out to him from that little black screen every morning and offered an interested audience for his thoughts. But by late afternoon when his friends were heading to bed on the other side of the world, Nick was in his stride and exhilarated to be in the magnificent be-whoever-the-hell-you-want-to-be-ness of the city without having to report back on it. But exhilaration is exhausting. Lying on the couch, flipping between vapid reality shows on TV, half-reading the news on his laptop, and consulting his phone, Nick was in no mood for his cultural insights. He needed downtime from epiphanies.

He'd run into Dustin on the subway the other day, and Dustin had looked happy to see him. They hadn't seen each other in – what?

fifteen years? Not since primary school. But Dustin's 'we should get together sometime', that always-unfulfilled promise between strangers who'd once shared a life, sounded genuine. Time for some good old-fashioned Facebook stalking. It couldn't be too difficult to find the guy. They would have loads of friends in common. Aaaand yes!

Nick smiled as he started up a message. Weird to be messaging Dustin. Nick didn't even like South African expats. They either turned out to be racists who assumed you shared their views because you'd also left, or they made up for feeling third-world provincial by acting all posh and pretentious. *Great running into you on the train the other day* Nick began, scanning through Dustin's pictures. He looked so different from the scraggly, shy kid Nick vaguely remembered from school. He was hot now, and well built ... Although he was often at galas and gallery openings, so there was a risk he fell into the second category of expat douchery. At least he was coloured, so he probably wasn't a racist asshole. *You're looking great*, Nick wrote. *New York agrees with you.* The message showed up as read. Did Dustin have nothing better to do on a Wednesday night than check Facebook? Nick wrapped up: *At any rate, I thought it could be good to grab a drink sometime. Let me know when you're free.* They hadn't really been friends when they were kids, and Nick felt good reaching out to Dustin now, who was probably lonely and homesick in the big city. *Sure*, came the immediate response. *Shall we get that drink tonight?*

Nick checked the time for an excuse. Too early to pretend the night was over, but meeting up now required all the effort of showering, changing, being charming in real life. He really just wanted to hang out on the couch, maybe send some texts with the vague promise of company in the future. He walked to the window. The street below was full of people in a silent movie – walking and laughing with each other, walking and talking seriously into their phones, sitting at the outside tables of the bar across the road and regaling one another … Nick couldn't hear a thing. The double-glazing of windows and the deep drone of air-conditioning units silenced their lives.

The bar Dustin had chosen was a warm, quiet spot in Chelsea, with exposed red brick walls and the kind of dark leather booths that make it feel like everything is going to be alright. Deep, rich hues and masculine lines were counterbalanced with small tables and close, intimate spaces, somewhere between a gentleman's library and a womb. Dustin had done well: Nick liked it. It was a good choice, also, because it reminded Nick of Cape Town. If he ignored the accents of the bar staff and pretended the beer in his hand tasted like Black Label, he could be in any of the bars on Bree Street.

'I've been here three years this month,' Dustin said. He had been telling Nick the story of how he ended up working in finance.

Maybe looking Dustin up had been a mistake. He definitely had a bit of that pretentious twang Nick was worried about, enunciating his words as if Queen Victoria had been personally involved in his education. He seemed so smug about how well he knew the city, too, laughing when Nick let slip he had never heard of whatever restaurant was supposed to be so cool. Dude doesn't have to prove anything to me, Nick thought, fighting the urge to roll his eyes. Dustin's gestures were a little camp, too. He pursed his lips when he listened to Nick's stories and crossed his legs like a girl. Nick tried not to let it grate him – as it had at school, he now remembered – because Dustin had grown into an incredibly good-looking guy. His scrawny frame had filled out. His arms were lean but ripped. His biceps made the sleeves of his bright turquoise t-shirt tight when he moved them, and his chest stuck out just enough to cast a shadow.

So Nick tried the expat thing. It was what he was there for, wasn't it? To create a little bubble in which they were the insiders? 'I mean, what kind of country doesn't have a ground floor? You walk into a building and BAM! – first floor. And Fahrenheit! I can't bitch even about the heat in the subway. I say, "Jesus, it must be forty degrees down here" to the lady sweating next to me, and she looks at me like I'm simple.'

'Yeah. I guess it's strange not to use the metric system.'

This wasn't working. They were talking about units of measurement for Christ's sake. Being from the same country wasn't enough to feel at home.

Nick would have left already – he'd drunk the requisite drink and stayed for a polite half-hour – but a strange sexual chemistry kept him there. Strange because Dustin was so obviously gay. The whole effeminate thing really pissed Nick off. Could these gays not just be normal men? Why spend your life in a big act? But there was something seductive about Dustin. Maybe because he was coloured. Nick had never slept with a coloured guy before, and had always wanted to. He loved their warm, brown skin like deep tan after summer. He loved their cheekbones and their blunt, direct attitude. He loved the idea of crossing that divide. It would feel like relief. Dustin had dimples, too. Nick went mad for dimples.

Nick locked eyes with Dustin in the way that always got him laid. 'Are you seeing anyone at the moment?' he said.

Dustin smiled. 'I'm not, Nick.' He looked down at his hands and tapped the table. Then he got up to get them both more drinks.

Nick watched him. Dustin's movements got so much more relaxed when he was at the bar. He stood with the comfortable slouch of someone talking to a friend, and laughed easily when the barman made some joke that Nick couldn't hear. Why was Dustin so damn aloof and uptight with Nick? Did he think that was being sophisticated?

'I can't believe you're single,' Nick went on when Dustin sat down again and handed him another beer. Dustin tilted his head in acknowledgement of the compliment but would not take the bait. Nick powered on through: 'I see you like dating macho okes.'

As soon as he said it, he knew he'd overplayed his hand. There's no subtlety in revealing you've gone through someone's Facebook photos. Now he'd been made to sound creepy and overly familiar. Dustin was giving him nothing, just sitting there like a condescending blob. His face was impossible to read.

Finally, Dustin shifted in his seat, broke Nick's humiliating silence. 'Are you still in touch with anyone from school?'

'I still see a lot of those guys,' Nick said. Reminiscing was better than having his flirting rejected. 'Remember Chris? He shared a digs with me at varsity. And I'm still good mates with Gugu and Thabo. Do you remember them?'

'Of course I remember them.'

'What about you, man? Are you still in touch with anyone from school?' Who did Dustin used to hang out with? Nick couldn't remember. Dustin was one of those quiet kids. 'It's funny, I don't think we really saw much of each other at school. We were in maths together. And soccer, I think?'

'I didn't play soccer.'

Nick laughed. Nah, Dustin hadn't played any sports. No extracurriculars, actually. Not enough money? Parents couldn't afford the gear?

'I didn't enjoy school much, Nick. As you know. It's not the greatest place for someone like me.' Dustin took a sip of his whiskey and stared at the glass in his hand. He wanted to say something else.

Nick waited. The silence was less uncomfortable this time. It was almost beautiful seeing Dustin's sadness. No more performance. No witty comebacks required. Nick wanted to lean over the table and kiss him. He felt his cheeks flush. So what if Dustin hadn't had many friends at school. Why coax an uncomfortable story out of him and ruin the evening? It was hardly Nick's place to be playing therapist. 'Right,' Nick said at last, 'I get that. It makes sense.' He leaned back and ran his fingers through his hair. 'I loved school, you know. But it's not for everyone.'

Just like that the moment vanished. Nick had avoided an awkward outpouring of emotion, and Dustin seemed to be relieved as well. His movements became more fluid and less controlled with each new story they told each other, and he was warming to Nick's sense of humour. The more Dustin laughed at Nick's jokes, the more Nick liked him. The booze did its job of silencing the critical mind and blurring out life's many shortcomings. Dustin glowed with angelic light. His smile made Nick's chest tingle. It was those magical dimples. They were going to be good friends. He had found someone to connect with far from home. Someone so handsome it was dizzying to imagine him naked.

Dustin sighed. 'Well, since I'm going to be hungover at work tomorrow anyway, would you like to come home with me?' Nick grinned at the handsome face offering good news and focal stability. He was adrift in warm colours and background chatter. Yes, Nick would very much like to do that.

'I hear this area's very cliché gay,' Nick said, punching Dustin on the shoulder and stumbling a little. 'You're going to have to try be less of a fag.'

Dustin was taking a ridiculous amount of time to find his keys. 'Don't worry, Nicolas,' he said. 'You don't have to live here.'

Nick counted the stairs in his head. Maybe a simple, mechanical task would restore his mental equilibrium. He was getting a bit too loud and obnoxious for himself.

Dustin's space was beautiful, all granite countertops and clean lines, with the historical character of the building shining through in an old fireplace and wooden floors. Dustin had clearly made some money, and had unexpectedly good taste.

He poured them each a glass of red wine. He passed the bottle to Nick. 'A little taste from home,' he said, winking and raising his glass. Nick's eyes filled with tears when he read the label – it was hands down his favourite wine in the world. How did Dustin know? He was a genius! A sensitive and kind soul. Nick had struggled to find any South African wines in New York, let alone this beauty from the Hemel en Aarde valley.

Nick put down the wine, wiped his eyes with the palm of his hand, and grabbed ahold of Dustin's head. He pulled Dustin into him and kissed him. Dustin's tongue kept to itself like the servant at an extravagant party – tentative and weak. Nick would have to take control here. He bit down hard on Dustin's lip, pushed him against the red brick wall, and ripped his t-shirt off over his head. Dustin's abs cascaded down in undulations of maple syrup and shadow. A trail of soft black hair beckoned. Nick put his hand into Dustin's pants. Soft. Nick rubbed for a second or two. Nothing. That's not what would get this bottom-boy going. Nick unzipped his own jeans and stepped out of them. Rock hard and ready to be serviced. He put his arms up behind his head and waited for Dustin to kneel. Nick's smirk always worked on guys like Dustin, guys who needed direction and force. The arrogance got them off. Dustin hesitated. But then slowly he got down onto his knees. He looked up at Nick. He had the strangest expression in his dark eyes. Not just hunger and lust. Something like … anger? Dustin began to kiss and suck. Nick groaned, and shoved Dustin's head down all the way onto his cock. Guys like Dustin just needed to know who was in control. Half-choking, Dustin struggled against him, and pulled back against Nick's hand. He gagged, wiped his mouth with his wrist.

'I can't do this, Nick.'

'Of course you can,' Nick said, pushing Dustin's head back down, hard.

'Get the fuck off me!' Dustin roared, and staggered up to his feet.

Nick stepped back. 'Sorry, sorry' he mumbled, lifting his hands in a truce.

'Who the fuck do you think you are doing that to me?'

Nick chuckled. 'It's what you invited me up here for, isn't it? My bad.'

'You think it's funny? You think it's OK to treat me like that again?'

'Hey! I thought you were into it.'

'Don't play dumb with me Nicolas. I'm not going to tell on you to the teachers.'

Teachers? What the hell is he talking about?

'Remember when we were in grade seven?'

'Uh, kinda. Why?'

'You and that prick Thabo. You pushed me around. You torment-ed me. Shoved my face in the dirt. Called me a stupid fag – '

'Oh come on man, we were teasing you!' It was all friendly, wasn't it? Dustin must have been misremembering. Or had they had been a little rough? Kids can be mean.

'You made me kiss your dicks. You made me tell you how much I loved doing it or you'd tell the whole school I was a fag.' Dustin had crossed his arms tightly across his chest and was kneading his biceps compulsively. They didn't look big or impressive anymore. Dustin looked frightened, like the same small boy looking down at the floor. Nick could see it now. 'You even pissed in my mouth, you fuck.'

Jesus. The memory punched Nick in the solar plexus and spread to his chest. Cold, dark shame. Here was that crying boy, looking up at him, on his knees in the dirt, behind the music school.

'You don't remember? Oh, that's nice. I spent years in therapy trying to work through this shit and you don't even remember it.'

'What the hell is wrong with you, Dustin? You were down there blowing me just now.'

'I don't fucking know. I thought it would be cathartic or something.'

'To blow me?'

'I wasn't exactly planning on doing that. Or inviting you up here. I don't know, it just kind of happened. I thought we'd gotten past it at drinks. I thought maybe I could prove to myself I'd let it go.' He looked up at the ceiling and let out a short, unsmiling chuckle. 'I thought the whole reason you contacted me was for some sort of atonement.'

Nick couldn't look at him any more. Memories were falling out of the deepest reaches of his mind and knocking everything out of place. Some nasty kid was intruding on Nick's straight A childhood, possessing his body, and using it to push the other kids around. This brat tormented people at the slightest sign of weakness, and hated them for accepting what he hated about himself. Anger and fear rose up in his throat again, long forgotten and deeply familiar. It was difficult to breathe.

Dustin sat back down on the kitchen floor. His lips looked raw and his eyes were red. 'You looked me up, you paid for the drinks. I figured you were lonely and needed a friend,' Dustin said. 'Here's my chance to be the bigger person, I thought. Forgive and forget. I assumed you would have become a nicer person by now. Especially when I realised you're gay.'

Nick sat down on the floor too. 'I'm not a bad person, Dustin,' he said. His heart was racing. 'And actually I don't like labelling my sexuality.'

Dustin turned to look him straight in the eyes. He did not blink. 'I don't care if you think you're a bad person or not, Nicolas. This isn't about what stupid story you tell yourself to make yourself the hero. You fucked up my life. You were an asshole. And you still are.'

'Oh come on. I'm sorry about all that kid stuff, but this isn't the same. I thought you liked it rough, and I was trying to get you in the mood. What do you expect me to say?'

'I was hoping for a genuine sorry, but I guess you aren't.'

'I am sorry.'

'You're not. It was stupid of me to hope for it.'

The clock on the oven said 2am, then ten past two, and still no words seemed like they could fix it. At a quarter past, Dustin rolled his head back, closed his eyes, and sighed. 'I think you should leave.'

Nick stood up and buttoned his shirt. His fly was undone but his cock had shrunk back into his boxers, hidden and soft. He zipped up and gathered his things from Dustin's sleek granite countertop. Phone, keys, wallet. Dustin picked up his t-shirt from the floor and pulled it back on. It was the same bright turquoise colour, Nick now recalled, as the flag of the house the two of them belonged to at school.

Dustin opened his front door. Nick stood at the threshold. He couldn't leave it like this. He stuck out his hand. Dustin looked at it.

'Look, Dustin,' Nick said, trying to make his voice sound breezy, 'I know I'm not – '

'You don't know what you are,' Dustin said, and he closed the door in Nick's face.

Nick climbed down the stairs in a daze, adrenaline thundering through his veins. The lights in the stairwell shone so brightly his eyes ached, rammed full with every scuff, angle and texture of that dead space. The streets of New York were deserted. Drunks and the homeless shuffled about in their own little worlds. Nick's phone vibrated in his pocket. It would be Dustin saying goodbye, showing mercy with a small bow to conversational custom. Nick needed that goodbye to feel normal. To feel like himself.

But it was the flurry of texts and instant messages from South

Africa coming in. Six hours ahead on a Thursday, his friends were either just getting to work or firing off messages while stuck in traffic on their way. *You have fun last night? What did you get up to? Have you made any friends yet?* his sister asked. *We're missing you, buddy!* Thabo said. *But I hope you're having a blast over there. I'm gonna look at flights to come over in December. It's been too long, man!*

Nick turned off his phone. His featureless reflection looked back at him in the black, empty screen. He descended slowly into the subway. The air that had been trapped in there all night was damp and unbelievably hot for 2:30am. He was sweating like a marathon-runner by the time he got to the right platform. A group of drunk students swayed, laughed and gossiped loudly about a friend they'd seen earlier on. 'Come on!' one of them shouted from down the platform. 'How long is this train going to take? I need the air conditioning. It must be a hundred degrees down here!'

Àwúre Ìfẹ̀ràn

RAFEEAT ALIYU

'Gigi, are you sure this is a spa?' Noura asked as Gigi drove past the gates of a mansion and found a suitable space to park.

'Trust me,' there was a wide, easy grin on Gigi's face. 'Let's go.'

A young man dressed all in white opened the front door, led them to a room and motioned for them to sit down. 'Fatoki will see you shortly,' he said, before leaving them alone.

'What's that about?' Noura frowned then she shrugged her shoulders. It was her first week at her new job and Gigi had surprised her with a spa date to celebrate new beginnings.

Noura eyed her friend. She could see from the way Gigi bounced on the chair that she was definitely hiding something.

'I can't hold it in anymore,' Gigi said. 'We are here to get you your love charm.'

Noura's nostrils flared, 'What?'

'Remember the bet you lost?' Gigi laughed, completely missing the change in Noura's mood. 'Don't think you can get out of it so easily.'

Of course she had lost the bet. She had failed to correctly guess Rokhya's honeymoon destination. But that did not matter, Noura had only agreed to the stupid bet to shut Medina up. She had no intention of seeking any love charm. Imagine someone like her visiting a babalawo. Jumbled images of all the Yoruba movies she had watched

219

flashed through her mind. Red cloth on walls, gaudy skull and bones paintings, calabashes filled with orange-tinted sacrifices, a middle-aged man dressed in white probably with some chalk markings on his face and beads around his wrists and neck. Noura shuddered; Gigi had tricked her and she wanted nothing to do with it.

'This is ridiculous.' Noura rose to her feet. She should have seen past Gigi asking her to spend the day. She could have been at home watching the latest episode of her favourite zombie apocalypse series.

'Nouratu,' Gigi called her by her full name.

'I don't need a love charm. Come and take me home.'

'Now that we are here why don't you just see this through?' Gigi changed her tone and became conciliatory. 'Are you even listening to me?'

Noura pursed her lips, tapping her foot impatiently against the tiled floor. She had not noticed it at first, the wall on her left, but obviously it had touched her subconscious because now she realised that the wall held an interesting piece of art. The mural's borders resembled ankara print, geometric designs in cool colours: black, blue and a yellow-brown. In the centre was an oval shape painted black with swirling spots of ochre. Tiny legs projected from this dark shape; it looked like an insect crawling somewhere. It was strange but the more she looked at the mural the calmer Noura felt. Her anger slowly faded and Noura finally faced her friend.

'If you're uncomfortable we could go,' Gigi pouted. 'I got too excited with this but Baba is really good.'

The way the edges of Gigi's lips reached for her chin made Noura smile. 'You could have just told me where we were going.'

'If I did would you have come?' Noura's smile put Gigi at ease.

'No,' Noura replied truthfully. 'But I did go to this so-called Baba's website ...' In her attempt to convince her to visit this place, Gigi had sent her a link to Fatoki's website. Curiosity had led Noura to click on the blue line.

'It's nice isn't it?' Gigi's eyes widened comically.

'It is, I also watched his videos on YouTube.'

Despite her scepticism, Fatoki's credentials impressed Noura. Not only had he lectured at a prestigious university in the UK, but he had given lectures around the world in several countries ranging from the US to Brazil, South Africa to Japan. The picture on his website showed a middle-aged man wearing a suit and glasses, he looked more like a political aspirant than a babalawo.

'I wonder how you know him Gigi?'

Unease flashed across Gigi's face but it was gone so quickly Noura wondered if she had imagined the entire thing. It must be from her job, Noura thought. Gigi had worked as a researcher in the embassy of a country that was small but rich, and her career brought her into contact with all sorts of individuals.

'I came to get my horoscope read,' Gigi responded. 'Although it's not really called horoscope here … ah, here he comes.'

Noura's head spun and she saw Fatoki in person for the first time. He looked exactly like his picture except taller than Noura had imagined. He was wearing trousers and over it a plain white shirt in the traditional style. She felt she would have fainted if he had come out wearing jeans!

'Baba,' Gigi greeted, bending her knees slightly in respect. 'This is my friend I was telling you about, Nouratu.'

Fatoki stretched his hand out and Noura regarded it warily. Was she not supposed to kneel down as per tradition? She took his hand. 'Noura. Nice to meet you sir.'

'Your dear friend has told me a lot about you.' Fatoki pumped her hand, 'It is great to finally meet you.'

Noura did not know how to respond to that but Baba was not one to waste time. 'You will have to excuse us Gigi,' Fatoki said before he led Noura out of the waiting room.

They did not walk far; there was a small study to one side of the hallway. Noura's head was already reeling from the experience. She was really meeting a babalawo in an office. She took a seat opposite Fatoki, with a large mahogany desk spanning the space between them.

'Make yourself at ease Noura.' The fact that he said her name the way she preferred it took Noura's tension down one notch.

She smiled. 'This is a lovely ... establishment you have here.'

Fatoki returned her smile. He sat opposite her and Noura noticed the mural on the wall behind him. Similar to the one in the living room, this painting was all earthy colours – black, brown, ochre with a bit of yellow to brighten the mix. Everything about it seemed traditional, from the motifs that Noura could not place to the colours. Fatoki craned his neck to look behind him.

'I see you like my daughter's painting.' The pride in his voice was evident.

'She is an artist?' Noura could not help the note of surprise in her voice.

'She is.' Fatoki's smile was proud. 'I am one parent who will not complain when my child draws on my walls.'

Noura snickered, slightly relaxed. 'Baba,' the appellation came surprisingly easily, 'I am sure Gigi has told you about me. I am in a relationship with a man that I do not love.'

Fatoki nodded, 'She has but it is better to hear this from you yourself. What exactly do you want?'

'I want to fall in love,' Noura blurted out. As soon as the words left her mouth she raised a hand up to her lips.

'There is no need to be ashamed,' Fatoki assured her as he rose from his chair. He walked towards a shelf that resembled those in the Chinese medicine shops Noura had seen in one of the badly written martial arts movies she had loved as a teenager. There were rows and rows of tiny drawers that presumably held things like love charms. Fatoki pulled open one of them and the smell of traditional black soap slowly filled the room. Noura recognised that smell and swallowed.

'Do you speak Yoruba?' he asked.

'Yes,' Noura sat up straight as she answered.

'That is good,' Fatoki took out what looked like a small bar of the soap wrapped in brown paper. 'You should be comfortable enough to read the incantation.'

Noura bit her lip. She was not sure about that at all, she had always considered incantations to be deeper parts of Yoruba language that she would never need. There she abruptly stopped her train of thoughts. Wait a minute, who said she was going through with this charm anyway? Visiting the Baba was one thing but actually using the love charm?

'I will print it out for you,' Fatoki returned to his seat. 'This is black soap, pounded with something to help you find love.'

'Can't I get black soap from anywhere?' Noura asked.

To her surprise, Fatoki was not upset by the question. 'You can get black soap anywhere, but not this special mix and it would not be complete without the magic words.'

'So I am to have a bath, and then what?' She could not help the scepticism that crept into her voice.

'After the spiritual bath you will meet someone to love,' Fatoki was unperturbed. 'I must warn you that this soap is very potent.'

The sound of the printer working jarred the silence in the room. Fatoki handed the sheet of paper to Noura., 'These are the magic words.'

She had said she could speak Yoruba, not read it. Noura frowned at the piece of paper, at the dots below the 'o's' and the accents on the vowels. She easily recognised some words, but others took several pronunciation trials. She sat cross-legged on her bed studying the incantation, the warmth of her mum's dinner still in her belly.

That was one of the advantages of having her mother as a neighbour. When Noura had decided to move out of her father's house there was a huge uproar. Her father had been furious but despite that could not take time out of his busy schedule to reproach Noura. Rather it had been Uncle Bola who had tried to dissuade her. When all attempts had failed, her father and his relatives went primal, using her mother as the bad example. 'That woman was too independent.' 'That woman never submitted to her husband the way she should have and now her daughters are following her lead.' It was the modus operandi when it came to her extended family: they always bad-mouthed her mother first, then Aida who was a single mother. After the defaming came the pleas but Noura was set in her decision.

After their mother Khaira left their father when he married a second wife, Noura and her sisters had immediately wanted to run away to be with her. Being children, it was not feasible so they vowed that when they got the chance they would leave their father and stepmother. They romanticised the notion of finding their mother and reconnecting with her.

Noura always imagined that when she left her father's house it would be to her husband's but when she reached twenty-five and was making enough money to move out on her own, she leapt at the chance. It was just her luck that she found the perfect boys' quarters with a single bedroom, a quaint parlour and tiny kitchenette in the same estate her mother lived in. That meant delicious meals and more time spent with her mother than Noura had ever hoped for as an adolescent terrified by her mother's departure.

For the tenth time, Noura tried reading the incantations. She screamed in frustration when the words jumbled across her tongue and reached for her phone.

'Hey babes!' Gigi's voice sounded cheery above the music thumping in the background.

'Don't babes me,' Noura said. 'Come and fix this mess you've put me into.'

'Are you referring to the love charm?'

'I can't believe I'm considering it.' Noura chewed her bottom lip.

'Yes!' Gigi cheered. 'Do it!'

'But the incantations are hard.' Noura fell back onto her bed.

'Just take them with you to the bathroom and say the words slowly,' Gigi advised. 'But how are you going to meet the love of your life at this time of the night?'

Noura sighed. 'I called Taofiq over.'

'OK …' despite the music and the telephone line, Noura could still make out the uncertainty in her friend's voice. 'Yes, you said you wanted to love him. Sha be careful babes … ehn?'

Noura waited as Gigi carried out a conversation on her end. 'Sorry I have to go now.' She laughed as though someone was tickling her.

'Say hi to Michael.' Noura assumed Gigi was with her latest boyfriend.

'Ah, yes will do,' Gigi answered. 'Call me when it works.'

She let the phone rest on her ear after Gigi hung up. It was barely nine o'clock on a Friday evening and Gigi was already out catching fun. Gigi never introduced her to the people she dated and Noura figured it was because Gigi changed men as often as she washed dirty plates. They had been similar in that way but Noura had calmed down when she met Taofiq. She and Gigi were the early bloomers in secondary school, chasing boys and not giving a toss what anyone had to say about it. Aida thought the aggressive boy craze was a coping mechanism Noura developed after the divorce. Inhaling deeply, Noura lifted herself off the bed. She slipped out of her t-shirt and harem pants on the way to the bathroom. Taofiq would be here any minute. It was time to test that bar of soap.

On my way.

Taofiq had sent that message over an hour ago and Noura was tired of waiting. She had bathed, surprised by how moisturised her skin felt after the black soap, before opting to wear something provocative. As she slipped into the sheer red babydoll she had picked for herself while buying lingerie for Rokhya's hen party, Noura wondered if sex with Taofiq would be different after she fell in love with him. On a whim she asked the question of her sister.

A second later, Aida's reply came, *What are you talking about?*

Noura yawned and sat on the edge of her bed. *I have had my spiritual bath.*

What? Lol! Rokhya better not hear of this. Noura could picture Aida roaring with laughter, she could also see Rokhya's disapproving face framed in a colourful hijab.

Seriously, if I fall in love with Taofiq that's it right? Noura typed.

Having second thoughts? Aida replied.

Nope! If she typed it, maybe she could convince herself. *How is my baby?*

Cheikh is fine and asleep. Do you want me to call?

The gentle tap on her door caused Noura to spring off the bed. She hastily wrote a reply to Aida as she rushed the few steps towards the front door.

Not now, talk tomorrow. Noura hit send as she reached to open the door, a reprimand for Taofiq on the tip of her tongue. A cool night's breeze hit her as the door swung open. Noura's eyes grew to the size of headlamps when she realised that the person standing before her was not Taofiq. Her lips parted, she stood still, observing this stranger. Noura was rooted to the spot, but within her it was as if a circus had launched a grand performance. Her pulse raced and her breath quickened, her heart danced to a furious beat while her stomach performed backflips. Further down between her legs a forest fire raged and all of a sudden her legs could not support her.

She lost her grip on the door as her knees pulled her down towards the ground but the stranger intervened. That only made the things worse, as the stranger's hand holding Noura up burned her waist. She felt light-headed being this close. Noura stared into eyes framed with long dark lashes and a colour that was red and gold.

Such pretty eye shadow, Noura thought.

'Are you all right?' the stranger cleared her throat. Her voice had a slight accent that Noura associated with Great Britain.

Noura willed her legs to cooperate, she tried to stand but her knees still felt wobbly. 'I am fine.' She leaned against the doorframe. 'Can I help you?' This voice was not Noura's. Nouratu's voice was sensible and slightly high-pitched – who did this raspy, seductive voice belong to?

'You're Noura Kanjuni right?' The stranger shifted from one foot to the other. 'You left your scarf at my dad, Odusina Fatoki's house. He sent me to give it to you but today has been busy for me. I'm sorry to pass by so late …'

Her lips were moving but Noura could not really hear her. Instead Noura was studying those lips, lips that were full and slathered in a bright orange colour. Her eyes shifted to the long kinky twists that sat on her head in a doughnut and made her face look long and elegant.

Noura's eyes sought Fatoki's daughter's large eyes, that regarded her as she explained why she had stopped by at such an odd hour. Then Noura's eyes continued their journey, travelling along the length of her neck, appreciating the way the tank top she wore fitted against the curves of her body and the way her shorts showed off fleshy thighs.

When Noura's eyes came back up to her face, she noticed Fatoki's daughter staring at her expectantly. Looking down Noura saw the outstretched hand holding a silk scarf.

'Than …' Noura's mouth was filled with saliva she swallowed. 'Thank … you.'

'My pleasure.' Fatoki's daughter gave a lopsided smile that looked so adorable. 'Good night.'

As she made to leave Noura found her voice and called after her. 'What is your name?'

'Oh I am sorry,' she apologised. 'I'm Bewaji.'

'I'm Noura,' Noura breathed. It did not occur to her that Bewaji already knew who she was.

'Nice to meet you Noura.' Bewaji coughed. 'Good night.'

How can someone be so beautiful? Noura thought as she watched Bewaji rush towards the front gate. It was only after the tall figure disappeared and the strange feelings her appearance had evoked diminished, that Noura realised she had just met a stranger while wearing nothing but see-through lingerie.

Soon after that, Noura noticed that the scarf was not even hers.

It did not work.

Noura had waited for Taofiq but he did not show up until the morning after. Things had not gone according to plan even though Taofiq was the first man she had set eyes on following her spiritual bath. She stared at Taofiq while he apologised, giving excuses as to why he had not shown up. Noura studied his strong face and square jaw that sported a day-old beard. He wore trousers and a black jalabiya that emphasised his broad shoulders. As he explained why he had missed their date, Taofiq elaborated with his hands and looked at Noura through half-closed eyes, licking his lips intermittently.

Yes, Taofiq was good-looking. No, Noura's feelings towards him had not changed at all. There was still the same indifference; the spark just was not there. Noura considered another bath, especially since Taofiq was right there but then dismissed the thought completely. Clearly love charms did not work.

'I am so sorry baby,' Taofiq pulled her into a tight hug and stroked her back with his large hands.

Noura stepped out of the hug. 'I waited all night for you,' she complained.

'I was at a meeting, I told you,' Taofiq said. Then his phone started ringing and he glanced at the screen. 'I need to take this call baby.'

She watched calmly as he rushed out the front door and closed the door behind him. He would say it was work but Noura was sure he was seeing someone else. She wondered why the thought of Taofiq cheating did not really bother her. It must be the lack of love. At this point their relationship felt more like a contract than anything else. Noura continued the weekend cleaning she had started before Taofiq arrived. Thirty minutes must have passed before Taofiq came back in.

'That was work,' Taofiq held up his phone. Noura smiled at her correct estimation of Taofiq's character. 'I am needed urgently.'

'Sure,' Noura dragged a damp cloth over the centre table in her parlour.

'Are you still upset with me?' Taofiq took her hand and pulled her up to her feet. He wrapped his arms around her waist and held her close once more.

'No, I'm not,' Noura mumbled.

The kiss Taofiq gave her before leaving was short and sweet; it also cemented the fact that nothing had changed in her feelings for him. After cleaning to her satisfaction, Noura called Gigi to whine. She gave up when her friend did not answer the call, imagining that Gigi was resting after the party the night before. She settled with messaging Aida, the only person other than Gigi who knew of her visit to Fatoki.

So nothing changed at all? came Aida's message.

Nothing. Noura replied

Even the sex? Aida asked

That didn't even happen. Noura groaned as she stuffed a chocolate cream biscuit into her mouth.

How do you feel otherwise? Aida asked

Noura paused to consider Aida's question. Honestly she felt relieved. In the end she could not imagine being in love with Toafiq despite his positive qualities.

Have you gone out today? Maybe it'll work on someone else? Aida added after a lapse of ten minutes.

From her older sister's tardy reply, Noura guessed that her nephew was keeping Aida occupied. Someone else ... Unheeded Noura's mind went to Fatoki's daughter. She had thought of Bewaji often since their awkward introduction but there was no need to mention that to Aida.

Doubt that would happen. Noura responded.

I'm taking Cheikh to a birthday party want to join us? Aida inquired.

Noura declined the invitation. She did not feel like attending a party with rowdy three-year-olds even though she loved her nephew.

The next time she went to Fatoki's house, Noura was alone. At Gigi's insistence, she was here to inform him that what he had given her had not worked. Or so Noura told herself. If she had admitted the truth, it was really because she wanted to see Fatoki's daughter again. Even through the ups and downs that came with her job as a UX designer moonlighting as a project manager, Noura could not stop thinking about that encounter. Sometimes it felt like she had imagined it all. At the most inappropriate times, Noura would vividly remember the way she had felt that night and all of a sudden she would start trembling. Sitting through meetings with clients and briefing them about progress so far in the sprint, Noura would recall the red-gold of Bewaji's eye shadow and that would be enough to render her inarticulate. Skin flushed, Noura would stutter her way through focus groups and lab testing sessions.

Now she slammed the door of her car and headed towards the front door and pressed the bell. Last time, she and Gigi had not had to wait long for someone to answer, but this time was different. Noura pushed the button again; there had to be someone at home. She looked over her shoulder – surely the mai-guard would not have let her in if no one was home.

Hearing the door open, Noura turned and warmth flooded through her as she recognised Bewaji. Noura did not mean to stare but her eyes scanned Bewaji's face.

'Hello, Bewaji, is your father around?'

Today Bewaji wore a white tank top and shorts. She had no make-up on. In defiance of the simplicity, her face glowed. It was incredible to Noura.

'No he is not.'

Noura could not help the crestfallen expression that graced her face; she was disappointed. Now she had no reason to cross the threshold.

'Um … he should be back soon,' Bewaji rushed to add. 'Do you want to wait for him?'

'I would love to wait for him.' Noura beamed.

Noura let Bewaji lead her into the house. They walked down a hallway and Noura noticed Bewaji was taking her to the same room she and Gigi had waited in before. That was not what she expected but Noura decided to bide her time, so she sat down on the same chair as before.

'Can I get you something to drink?' Bewaji tossed thick braids over her shoulder, the move exposing the butterscotch of her rounded shoulder.

Noura stared at her. It took a while for Bewaji's question to penetrate her consciousness. 'Yes please,' she breathed. 'Some water.'

Bewaji's hips swayed as she walked out of the room. All of a sudden the prospect of waiting alone seemed grim and Noura shot up from the chair.

'Hold on,' she called out to that back. Bewaji looked over her shoulder and Noura held back a gasp. 'If you don't mind, can I wait with you?' Noura twisted her fingers as Bewaji regarded her. 'I mean it would be boring to wait here on my own.' As soon as the words left her mouth Noura cringed inwardly. Could she have sounded any more desperate? Bewaji's small smile caught her unawares, making Noura feel instantly lighter.

'I don't mind, Noura.' The way she said her name raised goose bumps along Noura's skin.

Leaving her handbag behind, Noura followed Bewaji through to the kitchen. She leaned against the cool tiles of the kitchen wall, seeking respite from the heat that suffused her.

Noura did not understand why she could not take her eyes off Bewaji. There should be nothing sensual about rinsing a glass with water at the sink, but the water gliding off Bewaji's smooth hands entranced Noura. Her fingers tingled with the need to see if Bewaji's skin was as velvety as it seemed. These sensations would have confused Noura if she had stopped to really think about what she was feeling. She swallowed, not knowing what was going on, only that it felt good.

'Here,' Bewaji offered the water, startling Noura from her reverie. Noura's hands shook as she accepted the glass.

Noura thanked Bewaji and drank the water, hoping it would dampen the fire raging inside her. Then she remembered part of the reason she had come here in the first place. 'The scarf you gave me is not mine.'

'Really? Dad was pretty certain it was.'

There was an awkward silence during which Noura turned the glass in her hands over and over again.

'Are you the artist?' Noura blurted out.

Bewaji's head jerked back in surprise, 'Yes I am.'

'Your father told me about you,' Noura said. Again she did not like her choice of words after she had said them but she continued, 'You painted the mural in the waiting room too.'

Bewaji nodded. 'Are you interested in the arts?'

'Very much so,' Noura replied. She could not draw a stick figure, but Noura appreciated fine art. 'You need to tell me what message you were trying to convey in that mural.'

'The one in the waiting room shows a dung beetle.' There was a small smile on Bewaji's face. 'It is supposed to symbolise patience.'

Is that why looking at it calmed me down? Noura thought while staring at Bewaji with wide eyes and raised eyebrows. So this was the artist daughter Fatoki was so proud of. Noura appreciated that her talking about art seemed to ease the tension in the room.

'I was painting before you came, if you are interested...' Bewaji offered.

'Of course!' Noura replied without waiting for her to complete her sentence.

This time she kept her eyes averted when Bewaji led the way to the dining room that was just next-door. She was immediately drawn to the work in progress, evident by the tins of opened paint and the stepladder before it. Everything else in the room had been pushed to one side so the space around the mural was free. Noura observed what seemed to be a pile of pots tilting precariously on the far right of the painting. It was silly that to Noura the pots did not look like cooking utensils at all, rather their shape brought to mind the figure of a well-endowed woman.

'What does this signify?' Noura found herself asking.

Bewaji rubbed the back of her neck with a hand, 'I am not sure how to explain it.'

'It looks like there are stars in the pots.' Noura moved closer to the wall to investigate the yellow swirls of light in the dark pots.

'Well...' Bewaji began, the doorbell ringing stopped her short. Her eyes travelled to the clock on the opposite wall.

'Oh wow, it's two already? She's early for the first time,' she muttered more to herself than to Noura. 'Excuse me.'

Bewaji rushed out of the room. Noura bit her lips, wondering who this 'she' was who was interrupting them. She gulped down the cold water, emptying the glass. There was a high-pitched squeal that she heard easily even though the dining room was quite a distance from the front door. She heard the chatter before Bewaji reappeared with a woman, their hands entwined.

Who held hands out of secondary school? Noura thought as she waited for an introduction.

'Baby girl, this is Noura,' Bewaji motioned towards her. 'Noura, this is Ubeyi.'

'Nice to meet you.' Noura waved at Ubeyi, lips pursed. Ubeyi stood shorter than Bewaji. Her wavy Peruvian weave reached bra-length and was curled at the ends and her face was perfectly made up, eyebrows drawn in a perfect arch and lips a pink pout. Noura found herself wondering if Bewaji called all her friends 'baby girl' and held their hands like that. As Ubeyi greeted her back, Noura was filled with a sudden urge to leave.

'I should be on my way.'

'Have you given up on waiting for my dad?' Bewaji stopped her.

Noura bobbed her head, 'I'll just come back, I should have made an appointment first. Don't worry,' she stopped Bewaji from escorting her to the door, 'I can let myself out. Have fun with your friend.'

When she reached the kitchen, Noura paused and twirled on her heels. She rushed back to the dining room.

'I was wondering,' she asked Bewaji, 'is it OK if I have your number?'

'So is that your new catch?' Ubeyi asked, arms crossed under her breasts and eyebrows raised. She had watched closely as they exchanged numbers before Noura scuttled out the room.

Bewaji rolled her eyes. 'I haven't been here long enough,' she shrugged. 'Besides I am not looking for anything now.'

'That's what they all say,' Ubeyi rolled her eyes too. She leaned against the dining table. 'She is fine sha.'

'And as straight as a ruler.' Bewaji turned her attention to her mural and with a pang realised she might not be able to complete it today as planned. It was hopeless to work in front of Ubeyi; her secondary school friend would keep her distracted.

'Are you interested in her?' Bewaji tried to keep her voice flat as she sat on the dining table next to Ubeyi. Then she helped herself to the bottle of fresh juice her friend had brought with her.

'Abeg don't finish my juice, I am on a juice fast,' Ubeyi warned while making no effort to snatched the bottle from Bewaji's hands. 'Plus you know I am happily married.'

Bewaji smiled. They had come a long way from cuddling each other on the top bunk. She had been a few months shy of her thirteenth birthday when Bewaji realised that what she felt for her best friend Ubeyi was more than just 'like'. But even after their shared kisses and curious explorations, Bewaji had convinced herself that it was a phase and nothing serious. She had never expected to still find women attractive after graduation. Yet here she was; here they both were. Ubeyi now lived in Ajah with a wife and a kid they were raising together. Bewaji would never have pictured the possibility of that future, especially in Nigeria.

Having fully accepted her sexuality outside the country's borders, Bewaji found herself wondering what the queer dating scene in Lagos was like. For reasons unknown, her treacherous mind honed in on Noura's startled face.

Pub 360

H W MUKAMI

I had been sitting in the bar for some while, when I noticed a woman walking towards the pub. The bar was almost empty, my only companion a woman who was a regular in the pub, sitting alone at the counter, so I watched the newcomer with interest. She looked comfortable: the sneakers on her feet looked new and good and her gait was upright and easy. I wondered idly if this was her first time wearing the sneakers for whatever sport she played. She dug into the side pocket of her shorts, pulled out a thin wad of cash, glanced at it and replaced it in her pocket.

She stepped in, looked my way and sent me a little wink. I responded with a small wave and a smile. She looked around challengingly with a boldness that reminded me of a lioness, then headed straight for the bar. She was dressed in neat African tie and dye shorts, and a black oversized t-shirt. 'A cold beer please,' she ordered at the bar. I watched her gaze fall on a woman sitting two stools away, drinking a beer so cold the glass was sweating. She looked to me as if she was in her late thirties.

The woman flinched as the visitor moved to the bar stool next to her; but she didn't look up. She toyed absently with the little pool of spilled beer forming under her glass, her face as long as a night in a cold cell. Then she raised her head and stared ahead of her absently,

237

but still did not turn or acknowledge the visitor. She was not so new to these parts.

It wasn't a very classy pub but it had proven safe and welcoming to a woman drinking alone. The music was smooth and soothing. The windows were small and coated by a thin film of dust. There was no air conditioning, not that it seemed to matter to the regulars. One wall of the room had a long piece of wood drilled into it to make a shaky but usable counter. The woman sipped her beer, sighed and stared at the outdated calendar on the wall ahead of her. Her dark eyes had a glassy faraway look; they seemed to fall sightlessly on the scanty display of dusty bottles of local and exotic wines and spirits.

'Hi, I am Ashuni but you can call me Ashu,' the newcomer said, extending her hand in greeting. Her voice was thick and syrupy as though it came straight from her throat.

Then something happened; the drinker dropped her tense shoulders like a coat falling from its hanger, her whole back straightened and her neck turned as if by remote control to confront the intruder. She looked more relaxed, her face looked smoother, as if she had just removed a mask. I hadn't seen that in her silent history of drinking in the tiny Pub 360. In the past, I had seen her brace herself against the voice of a man, but this was certainly no man. Like an angel she smiled, showing a mouthful of impossibly white teeth against her beautiful black face; tiny crow-feet wrinkles sprayed at the corners of her eyes as she blinked at the other woman.

'I … um.' The answer died on lips that had started to tremble. The two women stared at each other for a full minute. It seemed to me that they stared in amazement and understanding. Their breath appeared quickened and their eyes locked and held. It was a fascinating sight to behold, and although I was seated in the far corner of the tiny pub I felt the exchange of two female souls hold, lock and rock. Surprisingly I felt no jealousy; just a deep pleasure that such a meeting had taken place in my presence. I stared; it was chemical and biological and spiritual and sexual all at once, right in front of my eyes, and yet no physical contact had happened yet, not even a handshake! I felt a little excluded from their little world; who wouldn't? I did not want to take a sip of my drink and miss it. I was mesmerised.

'I am Oluchi, but my closest friends call me Chi. Not that I have many close ones but, I am sorry I –' She looked slightly away and blinked rapidly in embarrassment, then shyly and awkwardly held out her hand.

'It is such a pleasure to meet you Chi,' cooed Ashu as she took the offered hand and held it in a firm grip without shaking it, then took her left hand and covered the grip intimately. In a move that visibly took Chi by surprise, Ashu pulled herself from her stool and took the stool closest to Chi's own, and whispered something into her ear. And just like that, Chi leaned into her new friend's shoulder. It may seem fanciful, but it seemed to me as if her scent made her feel something she couldn't explain even to herself.

The barman muttered inaudibly under his breath and his brow creased. He looked disturbed. I guessed he thought alcohol was starting to get to Chi. 'May I offer you a drink, please?' She said in a begging tone. 'Have a drink with me, my treat.' Chi cleared her throat. I noticed that she was struggling to come to terms with what was going on. Maybe she was more drunk than I had thought, yet she was only on her second bottle. She looked like a little child lost in the woods. She shivered and I wondered if it was caused by a cold beer on a colder night, or whether she felt she was on dangerous ground. A short gasp seemed to tear from her lungs to her full lips. She tried to cram it down with pursed lips and looked helplessly at the tall, beautiful creature sitting beside her. It was as if she was summoning her absent sense, Oh for heaven's sake woman, stop being ridiculous! She shifted on her hard bar stool as a tiny bark of laughter escaped her.

I watched as Ashu moved in again and wrapped her arm companionably around Chi's waist, not seeming to meet any resistance; the older woman was proving to be a promise of unexpected pleasure. At that moment, Chi looked vulnerable and alone to me, something which Ashu must also have noticed, because her right arm rose to pull Chi into her welcoming arms. I wondered whether she had done this with lots of other women, for fun, comfort or friendship. But something told me nothing like this had ever happened to her before. What was so special about this particular woman drinking alone in a tiny low class pub? She was pretty, attractive even but not a striking beauty. Her eyes held a timeless childish mischief that it seemed Ashu found hard to resist. I watched her eyes light on Oluchi's full dark lips which twitched and curled hesitantly into a half smile as she corked her head to one side challenging, gaining more courage where barely seconds ago I had seen fear, emptiness and too much pain for one woman.

They locked their arms and held each other. Chi's muscles relaxed, she sighed with released tension and contentment. Ashuni, who I though of as the daring one, breathed into her new friend's ear, and she was greeted with the naughtiest giggling she had ever heard.

'Ahem, hey!' the barman said in a voice that suggested he couldn't take it anymore. As if being pulled out of an enchanting fantasy, the two women froze and turned towards the angry growl of the barman. His face was puffed in pent-up rage and disgust and his eyes hard and cold like a pair of black marbles. 'Whatever it is you pair of black whores are thinking of doing in my bar, you better think twice. You can go and perform your free pornography to other clubs but not here, you are starting to make my other customers uncomfortable. You are watching too many foreign videos, you shameless copy cats. This is Africa; so clear your bills and get your dirty demonic selves out of here.'

The two women looked around the deserted pub for the said

customers but saw only me and my warm wine, the waitress, and a beggar seated outside the door. I didn't look uncomfortable, and nor did Maggie the waitress; so the women appeared to understand that they were being thrown out unceremoniously. It was still early evening and the usual customers had not started to come in yet. Besides, it was still early in the month and it was usual to have only one or two drinkers dropping in now and then or none at all. Business was bad for everyone.

Ashu and Chi stood up, and just like that, cleared the bill. Their unfinished frothy drinks stood dejectedly at the counter as the pair walked out with their heads shaking, clearly embarrassed. Who had done wrong? Was it so wrong to feel, to be who you are? It was as if I was reading these questions on Ashu's face. 'Maggie, get 'em back in here please,' I said to the waitress. I stood up, and wearing my mad smack on my face, walked to the counter. 'Johnny,' I told the bartender, 'I have never known anyone who lost their job for shutting their mouth. Son, you just lost yours.' I watched in deep satisfaction as his jaw fell almost to the bar counter. I got my palm wine from my usual corner table, jumped behind the bar, threw my head back and took a deep warm swig. It was time to right a wrong, and I had to start somewhere.

My pub was a small one; sometimes it paid the bills and sometimes it didn't, but I was proud of it nonetheless. I was not about to let any paying customer be treated with disrespect by a disgruntled, moody and biased barman, not on my watch. I told him to hand over his apron, get out of my pub and come for his wages the following weekend. Then I took the high stool like a queen reigning over her domain. Time for damage control and fun! I knew what being different meant and how it felt. Luckily, the cute couple of Ashuni and Oluchi had not gone far. The night was dark and cold and thanks to Johnny, we had not had a chance to order them a taxi, as was our custom. They looked uncertain at first, then surprised at seeing me and not Angry Johnny behind the counter. They looked around for any sign of him and obviously decided that no sign was a good sign. I beckoned them over, and gave Maggie an early leave for the night; I was feeling in high spirits and absolutely pleased with myself.

'I do believe you beautiful ladies did not finish your drinks.'

These two looked independent and fun, my type. I was not going to miss out, not for any mean barman.

I missed spending time with women, talking quietly and intimately – so magical, fun, warm, and companionable. I was going to take a chance and let those two get to know each other better in my pub, so that they would have good memories of the place. I trusted my judgment in firing the barman. It was probably a sign from above; Pub 360 needed a change. Johnny's attitude was bad for business. How could he insinuate that the beggar outside the pub was better for business than this couple of innocent lovebirds who were bringing much needed cash? I had felt the jab of the insult with them. At first they appeared nervous, I had preferred to keep the ownership of Pub 360 a mystery lest some freeloading customers took advantage. They eyed me with some suspicion and doubt. 'Ladies I must apologise for my barman, who is from this very minute out of work. Drinks on the house!'

Chi asked for a double tot of whisky, which she knocked back dry and straight, then grimaced as it burned a fiery path down her throat. It probably warmed her in ten seconds flat. Ashu said she preferred her beer warm and I poured myself another warm glass of local palm wine. We allowed a little awkward moment to pass as the different brands of alcohol coursed simultaneously through our systems. Afterwards, the atmosphere thawed remarkably and we were relaxed. I started by introducing myself, and I made known that I was lesbian too. As I didn't have any living family, I had a problem socialising with people and making friends, let alone keeping any new ones. I liked keeping to myself anyway and liked my own company.

With the help of alcohol, I narrated all this to the new friends I was so determined to make and keep. They huddled protectively, intimately and freely next to each other. They listened, and sipped, and listened. I talked about how I was orphaned in my early teens. How independent I had learned to be – changing electric fuses in my house, painting furniture, cooking, farming, and everything. I was trained as an orthopaedist and worked in many hospitals for close to fifteen years. Each waking day and night, I saw enough blood, torment, pain and human suffering to last me a lifetime. It was enough; I had to quit or lose my mind. Pub 360 was the place I had to find myself in, somehow.

I had no idea where all that had come from, and how I could speak my soul out so freely to strangers. I discovered I had just found kindred souls right there. 'Oh I can see how that works, I will drink to that!' bellowed Ashu and we all burst into uninhibited girly laughter. The spell was broken. I think they sensed a need in me to connect with other ostracised women, and right there they opened their hearts to me.

In a matter of minutes, we sized each other up and understood the meaning of it all. Clearly a long-term pact had been made and sealed in guiltless alcohol. They both started talking at once, giggling, laughing and not giving a care, as if we owned the world.

And we did; the world in Pub 360 belonged to us that whole night.

Pyrrhic Victory

OLA OSAZE

One hot sticky night in July 1997, Brent and I were halfway through a 12-pack of Icehouse when we first schemed about making fake money. I was all of 21, fresh out of college with no immigration papers in sight, and newly liberated from my controlling mother. Brent and I spent that summer putting our counterfeiting plans into action.

While a starless indigo sky stretched endlessly overhead, he took me to the five-storey grey building sitting on a small street in Charlotte's financial district. His third-floor office was empty of people save for us. Dotting the office landscape were black Dells perched atop long grey desks paired with black ergonomic chairs. A quiet hum filled the whole room.

'It's back there,' he said, pointing his slender, pale forefinger.

Brent and I followed the hum to a small room at the far end of the open space, to the monstrously big machine that occupied almost every inch of the room.

'So many buttons and knobs and things,' I said, looking at the white copier, my words a whisper of awe.

Brent calmly slid a $20 bill into the feeder. He fiddled with a couple of buttons and pressed the giant round orange one with 'Start' etched on it. The machine whirred and buzzed to life, its trays moved with purpose from up to down. What it spat out was an exact replica of the bill except for the addition of white paper borders.

'See.' Brent's beam was partially obscured by his blond whiskers that curled over themselves and dangled on either side of his mouth. 'An exact copy,' he said pushing it into my waiting hand.

I fingered it, turned it around to its underside.

'What do you think?' he asked, excitement elevating his voice an octave higher.

'It's so real' I whispered, turning the note over again and examining it.

Brent laughed.

I looked up suddenly. 'Can we really get away with this?'

In response, he grabbed a pair of scissors from the adjoining table. One of its royal blue, plastic handles had a dent in it. With eerily steady hands, Brent cut the replica out of its white background and held the lone $20 copy up to the light. There was no security thread running from top to bottom. No watermarks either.

'So it's not an exact copy,' I said peering up at the blue-green inky reflection of light seeping through.

'No one will do this to a $20 bill. If we go to McDees or to Walmart – not the one you used to work for,' he quickly added, 'no one is going to verify the authenticity of a $20 bill. They may do that with a $50 bill and of course a $100, but a $20?'

He left the question hanging in the air, the answer already offered.

A contrasting image bubbled up to the surface of my mind and formed words in my mouth. 'Well, they may not double-check authenticity *for you*,' I said thinking about those moments when white sales people trailed me through the aisles of their stores.

Brent gave me a sly look before plucking the $20 from my hands and pocketing it. I followed him from the copy room to his desk, peeking momentarily through the giant windows that yawned over the freeway below where car lights danced and glanced off the tarmac.

I thought about my mother. Brent had rescued me from her that summer, on a night much later than this one. Our home had been a hotbed of words fashioned like swords. It was a home in which the meshes of window screens bit into my flesh when I grabbed them, shook them, and screamed through them for help. As we left, I kept expecting her to come thundering down the driveway towards us, picking up jagged pieces of gravel and pitching them at us, because that's the kind of crazy she is. In the back seat of Brent's car was my suitcase, bulging with all the clothes and books and shoes and miscellaneous items I'd managed to toss into it, in the limited time I had between her falling asleep and Brent's arrival.

She'd seized my Nigerian passport and birth certificate the night before. I'd looked for them in the minutes before Brent's arrival but all I found was a wad of cash in that pillowcase she stuffed at the back of the bedroom closet. She thought no one knew about it although I'd known about it for a long time, which is why I'd looked in the first place, but she must have hidden my documents elsewhere. I chucked the cash into my suitcase in anger. I chucked it in my case the same way I'd grab whatever change she left lying around when I lived with her: a *fuck you* kind of way. Stealing was my way of getting back, of standing back up after being felled by fists, belts, soup ladles, shoes, sticks, hangers and other so-called instruments of discipline she employed.

But I was finally free of her.

The apartment complex where Brent lived, where I was about to live, was quiet and dark, the lanes leading from the gate to the buildings, deserted. Streetlights stood tall and isolated with an almost majestic beauty as their yellow lights haunted the asphalt streets below.

In Brent's coupé, I felt for my neck, my arms, chest, stomach, and thighs. I felt the welts that were still there. Some were already turning dark blue because they were older. All over my body, pain sang a tormented melody. But my heart – it raced and raced with the joy of the free.

But mother wasn't going to make escape an easy feat.

'Move back home and I'll give it back to you!' she screeched into the phone not long after I fled her home.

I slammed the phone back into its cradle on the white formica counter in Brent's kitchen. Outside, the day was coming to life like any other day. The garbage truck was roaring up the street on its early Tuesday morning run. Birds were chirping their morning songs amidst the loud hum of cars. Inside, my world was tilting off its axis. I grabbed my bag and keys and headed out the front door, the clatter of the morning rush hour filling up the entirety of my brain, preventing me from thinking about the rage gathering like a storm cloud in my stomach. I did not want to think about it. Instead it followed me down the stairs of Brent's apartment building, it whispered in my ears as I went from sidewalk to bus station to bus to Walmart, where I took my position in the women's department. I walked to the lingerie section and punched at the racks of bras and panties causing several of them to drop to the floor. I stepped on them, wiped the underside of my shoes on them. Still the burning in my chest hadn't abated so I took a stroll to the men's department, where my favourite pilfering took place. I went to the boxers' section and grabbed four of the silk ones off the racks. I didn't even look to see what they looked like. I just took them and did a nonchalant shuffle back to my department where I jammed them into my bag behind the checkout counter. She was waiting for me when I emerged from behind the counter. The hammer had been hanging over my head all damn morning; her presence was the first indication of its desent.

'Ade, can you come with me please?' Though it was phrased like a question, it was really a command, and her being the manager on duty made her command a mandate. Her hair was puffed up in its usual gravity-defying blonde halo, which slowly wilted over the course of the day. The white polo shirt she wore was neatly tucked into her khakis. Perfectly ironed pleats ran down the middle of each leg. With two fingers she beckoned and I followed.

When I entered her office, two other middle-aged white people swivelled their heads to watch me walk in. One was the head of my department and the other the head of security.

'Sit down,' Mimi, the manager on duty, ordered me. I obeyed and plopped down on the one available chair with the heaviness of one who knows what fate awaits them.

'Your mother called us this morning,' she paused and fixed her ocean blue eyes on me like she expected this interaction to mimic a *Law & Order* episode, one where I'd confess everything, words gushing out of me like torrential vomit. 'She says you're here in America illegally. That we've hired an illegal alien.' She said the word *illegal* like it tainted her. 'Is this true?'

I sat back in shock. She'd threatened all kinds of things before, my mother. But this was cold, calculating evil.

'She's not well,' I replied when I eventually found my tongue. Even then the voice that came out of me was a deep croak of shame. I felt ashamed that it was my own flesh and blood that'd placed me here, in this metal chair. That these three white strangers were a witness to my shaming, made the moment all the more surreal. 'She's not well. I'm sorry she made this crank call.'

The silence that ensued seemed bloated with all my wishes that they would believe me.

'Of course she's not well. What mother would do such a thing to her own child?' Mimi finally said, fixing me with a steady gaze, causing me to wilt under her stare.

What mother indeed?

'Just bring us your birth certificate and social security card, so we can verify that you are indeed a citizen. I know you showed a replacement social when you started but just indulge us and bring in the actual card.'

She was referring to the flimsy sheet of paper I'd manufactured on one of the computers in the UNC computer lab. I'd modelled it after the receipt Social Security Administration issues after you apply for a replacement card, which is what I'd showed Mimi when she offered me this job. My real social had 'Not eligible for employment' in black block letters typed on it – I couldn't very well show that to her, could I?

I was instantly seized with another hankering after leaving Mimi's office, so I grabbed my bag and swung by the men's department again. The white and grey linoleum tiles sparkled in the artificial light of the store. I waved at my buddy Kenneth as I marched past the electronics department. He stood there with a half smile and puzzled expression on his face. The glass doors of the store entrance slid open with a swoosh. I went through them, my breath a block of ice in my chest because I was worried that someone had seen me grab those button-ups in men's. I hadn't exactly been careful. I crossed the sidewalk and the parking lot, which put me in front of the bus stop where I sat down woodenly on the bench. Even though the sun had eaten through the earlier overhanging clouds and was now beating down on my skin, I felt nothing but cold.

When the bus eventually came, after I'd boarded it, I did not look back as Walmart was left behind. I knew I would never return.

After making our first copy at Brent's office we tested it at McDonald's. From the drive-through window came smells and sounds of potatoes frying in bubbling vats of oil and round clumps of meat searing atop red-hot metallic surfaces. The young black woman working the window chewed her gum with gusto, blowing pink elastic bubbles, popping them and sucking the pink blob back into her mouth. She was nodding her head to Tony! Toni! Tone's latest,

'Lay Your Head on My Pillow', playing from a radio somewhere in the depths of the fast food restaurant.

'That'll be $2.08,' she piped.

I looked at the crisp $20 note in my hand. I pushed it into Brent's dry hands. He smiled though his hands shook, which surprised me. There was nothing I could do with my shaking hands except lay them down on my thighs and study them in great detail. I noted how the brownness of my skin was just a few shades darker than the leather of the car seat and how the seat's coldness had caused goose pimples to dot my thighs.

'Uh huh,' I heard her say to Brent's 'thank you.'

My gaze stayed on the goose pimples, millions of them, like tiny mountain peaks, texturizing the part of my thighs not covered by my jean shorts. I smelled the fries. I heard the crinkling of paper that encased them, the car window winding through its crevice, and the gearshift crunching from P to gear 1. Then and only then did I look up, spotting the wad of cash in Brent's hand – the one clasping the steering wheel. His hazel eyes caught my black ones communicating information, a current of knowledge being transmitted between us. Our experiment had worked. Nervous laughter bubbled out of our throats. As we drove out of the McDonald's parking lot, the harsh afternoon sun glinting in our eyes, our bodies suffused with adrenaline. We didn't need to say it aloud. It was a given that we'd do this again.

We met at a friend of a friend's party. He was a 25-year-old college dropout who'd taught himself how to write code, an unrepentant hustler and a proud fag. I was a 19-year-old girly girl, slugging my way through Organic Chem again, cowering under my mom's control, and trying not to fall for Adrian, the Black butch dyke who worked at the BP station near campus.

At that party, plastic red cups in hand, amber coloured beer swirling inside, our drunken conversation went the way of:

'I'm a bad influence,' he said, all cocky and smiles. 'Just ask Craig.' He jutted his head at the lanky, skinny-as-a-rake, four-eyed party host who'd just introduced us.

'He's not kidding. Ever need to create fake docs, steal shit, embezzle shit? This guy is your guy,' Craig said, patting Brent's shoulders, laughter squeezing out between words. 'Just don't let him talk you into anything without weighing the pros and cons first. Carefully.'

'Hey!' Brent said, an exaggerated look of hurt on his pale face.

'It's true. Brent here can talk himself out of any situation –'

'Well, that's true,' Brent quickly piped up, chuckling, before taking a big swig of his beer.

'But when the shit hits the fan, don't count on this fool to do a damn thing about it,' Craig said, first looking at me then eyeing him knowingly.

Brent got momentarily serious. 'It happened once.'

'Yeah. Once and it got me fired and almost arrested, asshole.' Craig playfully punched him on the shoulder.

'How was I supposed to know they switched security guys last minute? Plus getting fired from RadioShack was not the worst thing to happen to you. And I did make it up to you,' Brent said with a lecherous smirk.

Craig gave a wink and flashed a quick smile. 'That will be the one and only time,' he said before making his way into the heart of the party where people, with red cups of their own, were swaying on the dance floor.

'What was all that about?' I asked though my mind was already turning over a million different scenarios, but mostly I fixated on one phrase: *fake docs*.

Brent didn't answer right away. He finished off his beer and took a peek at my already empty cup. 'You want more? I'm headed to the keg. Craig talks too damn much,' he said collecting my empty cup. He laughed, shook his head as he went to fetch us more beer.

We talked for hours, seated on the front porch, watching drunken revelry happen around us. Well *I talked* and he listened. Maybe it was the beer's fault I spilled it all – my parents' divorce, my dad's upcoming nuptials back home to a woman almost half his age, and the subsequent rages that mom rained on my body. I even told him about being undocumented.

I must admit what fuelled my curiosity about him at first was the tidbit Craig had let loose, intent as I was on figuring out a solution to my problem. But what kept my interest in him was his audacity.

'Here,' Brent said weeks later, pushing a North Carolina ID card into my palms. 'Don't ask,' he said shaking his head in answer to my raised eyebrows.

The card was warm. As if it'd just been spat out of the device it'd been made in. I bent it one way then another, marvelling at how real it looked. That weekend I went with him and Craig to Scorpio's, brandishing it with shaky hands I hoped the bouncer wouldn't notice. It was the first time I'd stepped into a gay club. The first time I got to make out with a woman in a club. We'd been sneaking looks at each other all through the drag show and eventually made our way to a single stall bathroom where we sloppily made out. I sank my hands into her tight black curls and nipped at her coffee-hued neck.

That was the last time I saw Craig until the night I stopped by Brent's apartment to find them arguing heatedly.

'You said I'd get half, $500 total but now it's $250?' Craig said, his brown face flushed an almost maroon red. 'Muthafucka, you always pull this shit. Stealing from my pockets. Do you know how much I was counting on that money?'

'After the risk I took to get these out? And the security guy I had to bribe to keep his mouth shut? This is all you get.' Brent stood tall. While not as tall as Craig, he was broader.

'You didn't tell me that before. Now you spring this shit on me after I gave you the connect and hooked things up?'

'Take it or leave it.'

Craig looked at him then at me, then at him again. He looked at the ground, at the carpet that lay there, where the anger that had held his body rigid now seeped. He let out a small laugh. He laughed some more, shaking his head before looking back at Brent.

'This is the last time. The last time,' he said, sauntering out of the apartment, but not without giving me a final glance that made me remember his warning at the party last year.

'Did you steal this stuff?' I asked in the wake of Craig's departure, in the midst of the tense silence that now occupied the room.

Brent shrugged, handed me a Stella while he took a long swig of his. He snatched the phone hanging from its cradle on the wall, punched in some numbers and barked, 'It's here,' after a few moments.

After hanging up, he took another long swig. 'You shouldn't be here right now,' he said, eyes swinging to the door and back to me.

So I gathered my things and walked out, feeling a mix of fear and excitement.

After I took refuge in Brent's home, the day he had me walk a cart full of DVD players, stereos, speakers and amps out of an electronics store with a wink to the security guy watching the entrance, was the day he stopped asking me to leave.

'Just act like you're the kind of bitch that can drop that kind of money in one go,' he prepped me the night before as I sat on his plush beige couch, the one he said he got as payment for something he'd done for someone or other.

He was standing with a beer in one hand and the remote to his large TV in the other, flipping and flipping until he landed on our favorite show: *Law & Order*.

'But Brent –' I was nervous and thrilled at the same time, but nervous was winning.

'Don't. Just don't. You waffle you get caught and …' he tailed off looking at me, 'deportation and all.'

'What if the alarm goes off? What if that security guy isn't on duty?'

'It won't. And he will be. Now stop freaking out. I thought you wanted this? All that talk after you moved in and after you left Walmart, about wanting to break your mom's hold over you and put some cash in your pocket. Well, here's your chance.' He'd lectured and I, the willing ingénue listened, drowning my anxiety in beer and *Law & Order*.

When I lived with my mother I'd steal her vodka right before bedtime and replace what I'd stolen with water. I drank the vodka to loosen up the knot known as my body. Without the vodka the knot would remain a knot and fear would once again win, at the expense of my sleep. When I was ten and visiting America for the first time with my parents, the family friend who hosted us left piles of quarters on his desk. Cash. In the open. In my mind he was asking, no, begging someone to steal from him which I did repeatedly. At Walmart I can count the number of days I *didn't* stuff my bag with goodies on one hand. In Nigeria, I'd rifle through my friend's mother's things, keeping trinkets and jewellery that caught my eye. I was no stranger to stealing but stealing for higher stakes was a more terrifying feat.

In the store, my palms were so slick with sweat they slid down the handle of the cart. My teeth chattered so much I could hear them. Tremors overtook my body. I imagined what lay beyond the sliding glass doors. I imagined Brent's coupé parked and waiting just beyond them, even though I knew he was actually waiting in the adjacent parking deck. The security guy in his blue uniform, his shaved dome reflecting the light from the fluorescent bulbs overhead, looked me up and down. I imagined what he saw: a skinny black girl with braids down to her shoulders, eyes round and wide, face with fat cheeks, wide nose and thick lips. I wondered if he saw the tremors, the forced nonchalance of my wink. If he did, it did not deter the doors sliding open and my going through them.

When the wheels of the cart clattered onto the pavement, I gunned for the deck, too terrified to look back because I was certain someone with the authority to slap cuffs on my wrist was watching. I plunged forward, my teeth gnashing. Only when I saw his green coupé with him sitting in the reclined driver's seat, a proud papa smile on his face, did I feel like it was all worth it.

When he thrust the crisp notes into my waiting palm the next day, the proud papa smile was still there. Dumbfounded, I looked at all that cash. It was then I realised I hadn't done it for the money. All that bloody fear and anxiety was just for the adrenaline fix. Brent's approval heightened that rush of power and all of it felt far better than the money.

Within weeks of our McDonalds experiment, I watched Brent buy a pair of $4 socks with a fake $50. The blonde waif working the check-out at JC Penney's at the Four Seasons mall didn't even run the bill under the purple light that I could see plain as day under the counter. She just grinned a goofy grin while Brent laid it on thick, his fagginess dialed up. He was 'Oh honey' and pearl-clutching and lisping while waving his hands in the air like he was Just Jack. I stood by the rack of bras, looking interested in one particular number when really I was studying him, trying not to laugh at this caricature he was putting on.

'Next time you try it,' he said afterwards as he treated me to a steak and shrimp platter at the Red Lobster across the street from the mall. I shook my head in response and dangled a piece of shrimp close to his face, giggling at the expression of disgust on his face and at his usual muttering against shrimp, something about them being the cockroach of the sea. This was a leftover from the hold his Seventh Day Adventist parents used to have over him, a hold I witnessed up close when Brent took me up to the mountains of Boone, North Carolina, to the house where he grew up. Along the way we wound our way through the Blue Ridge Parkway and took in endless mountain ridges strewn with the red, brown and yellow leaves of fall. We went shopping in boutique stores in the main square of the small mountainside town, titillated by the shocked expressions on the faces of white shoppers, many looking like they wished miscegenation laws were still in effect. I met his quiet diminutive mom who had an air of saintliness about her. His father was also quiet, but his aura was more of a raging fire.

Something was simmering there underneath the surface. When Brent introduced me, they regarded me coolly, not saying the things relating to race that I know they must be thinking. When we eventually sat down to dinner, not a word was uttered at the table. Except for, right after his mom cleared the table and brought out the pie, his dad asked, 'Are you still a queer?' I nearly choked on a chunk of apple and crust. The hacking seemed to last for hours, but no one seemed to notice, so intent were they on Brent's response to his dad's question.

'Look at the time,' he finally said, elbowing me in the ribs and gesturing towards the door with his head. 'The traffic heading back to town will be brutal. We should get going now.' His mom and dad looked at us as we gathered our things, our pride, and ourselves and headed out the door.

'We'll pray for you my son. God will forgive you your wicked ways,' his mom said, looking at me with what must have been the same look the missionaries gave the natives in colonised Africa.

Brent was mostly silent on the four-hour drive back. He barrelled down those curvy roads at an alarming speed, regaining a bit of his original confidence with each passing turn. Thirty miles outside of

Charlotte, when we got stuck in an epic go-slow, he told me about being Seventh Day Adventist, about the dietary restrictions, the ultra-conservative doctrine, the racist underpinnings, and his absolute disgust for all of it.

'The day I told my dad about dropping out of college was one of the happiest days. Really. Just seeing the look of utter disappointment, that pain … it was one of the highlights of my life,' he said and I could see for him it was a pyrrhic victory.

Back at the Red Lobster, Brent bit into his burger and used a finger to mop up and lick the blob of ketchup and cheese that'd plopped onto his plate.

'You keep yourself locked up in these ideologies. I always tell you hustling is a frame of mind.' He was saying this because I'd just told him that if I flashed a $50 bill the sales person would use both the black marker and the UV light to verify authenticity, whereas his being white excluded him from that treatment.

Deep down I wonder if he knew how clichéd he was, rebelling against his ultra-religious background by living this life. If he was a cliché, then what was I?

'I paid for that meal with a $100,' he said on our way out, chuckling. I looked at him with widened eyes and glanced back, frightened that someone had heard us. We weren't quite out of the restaurant yet and he was broadcasting to the world that we'd paid with fake money.

'Brent, you're a jackass,' I hissed, walking quickly ahead of him, pushing the doors open and rushing to his car.

'Bitch, you act too damn scared' He was still chuckling as he opened the door and we got in, 'What did I tell you? It's a frame of mind.'

I didn't say anything, but looked out the car window at passing cars. Two voices in my head were duelling for my attention. I wanted to silence the one that screamed about caution. Till one day he insisted it was my turn and I agreed. I decided to go lowbrow, opting for the Target we visited often, where Brent pawned fake notes with an air of arrogance every time.

'Just do it already,' he whispered hotly behind me after following me on a third loop around the store.

I looked at the gym shorts in my shopping cart. $12.99 wasn't enough. I grabbed a black bra and dumped it in there, which brought the total to about $25. Feeling better about that sum I led us to the check-out lines. I scanned the faces of the cashiers, looking for those with bored expressions on their faces, those who looked like they no longer had fucks to give and were eager for the end of their shift. Spying one who seemed to be staring off into space, I gunned my buggy in her direction.

'What's this?' The stout black woman, her ponytail forming a stiff cone behind her, asked while flashing the UV light on the $50 I had just given her. Brent, standing behind me, was clad in his office drag while I was wearing one of my spaghetti strap numbers. This one had cost me nearly $150 at Dillard's. Surely we oozed money. Surely this was enough to fool her into taking the $50 note at face value?

'What's this?' She looked at me, waving the $50 in the air. 'You trying to pay with fake money?' I shifted uncomfortably while Brent suddenly developed a keen interest in the latest issue of *National Enquirer* on one of the shelves. A tired looking security guard perked to attention and came over from his spot by the entrance.

'Are you?' the woman persisted, bolder now with the security guard by her side.

'What the hell are you talking about?' I finally found my tongue and tried to exude the energy of one used to getting her way, like Brent had taught me.

'Let me see that,' the security guard snatched the note from her hand and peered at it then he tossed it back at me. 'That's fake!' He regarded me for a moment then his eyes shifted to Brent. By then it was clear that Brent and I were of the same party, despite his sudden obsession with the magazine rack.

'You two should follow me.' The security guard started to come around to where we were standing and lots of possibilities, all with horrific outcomes, flashed before my eyes. I looked at Brent who stood, his arms dangling helplessly by his side. He moved his lips as if to say something but no words came out. It dawned on me he was going to be useless and suddenly I was angry at him for leading me haplessly towards the very same outcome I was trying to avoid – apprehension – but mostly I was angry at myself for letting myself be led haplessly. It was this anger that lifted my knee when the security guard's cold rough and calloused palm encircled my arm. My knee lifted with a swiftness I had never before known. It connected with something soft, something vulnerable, and the guard doubled over, a howl escaping his lips loud enough to distract everyone standing nearby. In the midst of the ensuing fray, I felt another cold hand – smooth and soft this time – on my arm and looked up to see Brent's face right before my own. He was dragging me away from the register and the howling guard and his attendants who were now bending over him. He dragged me out the entrance just as the cashier looked away from the fallen guard to see we were no longer in front of her.

'Hey!' She yelled at the same time Brent's car keys slipped from his shaking hands to the ground. Without thinking I scooped them up, unlocked the door to the driver's side, and pushed Brent through.

'Move!' I grunted and jumped in after him. How I managed to slam the door shut and slip the key in the ignition I do not know. I sped out of the parking lot as the cashier and another security guard ran out of the store looking for us.

'Never again,' I said aloud while Brent silently white knuckled the dashboard, his green coupé piercing the black night as I tore down the freeway towards his apartment.

Images raced through my mind. Had I seen a camera at the entrance to the store? Did they have footage of us? I thought about how things would have been different if Brent had paid, remembering the jolly white check-out girl who'd been taken in by his Just Jack impression at JC Penney's; the black woman at McDonalds; the many cashiers at other stores, even Target, who took money from his hands without question. I saw Craig's brown face contorted in fury when Brent had switched terms on him that night.

Then I looked at Brent, white as a sheet, trembling beside me and saw the deluded white boy for what he was.

I parked askew in front of his building, opened the car door with as much force as I could muster and just walked, leaving him, his green coupé and his apartment complex behind.

'Frame of motherfucking mind, my ass,' I pushed the words through gritted teeth as I crossed the street, staring boldly as the night unfurled before me.

Nine Pieces of Desire

IDZA L

Bibi usually tells me that if you do something very wrong, Allah will not hesitate to strike you dead. He will call you by name, just like he did to my sister Latifa. She was barely three years old, Latifa. When she died, she almost carried my mother's entire happiness to the grave with her. After the burial, Ma had my other sister Amina leave for Lamu as soon as she could walk on her own two feet. A visit every Ramadhan, but no more.

'Your mother did not want to tempt death with the two of her remaining girls so she had Amina go to your aunt in Lamu,' Bibi told me.

We were born three girls, one after the other. Ma often says I was the first one to come but Ba says no, it was Latifa. Bibi doesn't remember. She was the only one with Ma during the delivery, her bad ears being her shield against the screams. Bibi, perhaps drained out from Ma's seventeen-hour labour, put one stroke on Latifa and one stroke on me so that they could never know who the first-born was.

'It is not easy to give birth to three girls,' Ma usually says.

'It is not easy to give birth, that is all,' Bibi answers her.

Ma barely lives. She is sad and has infected both Bibi and me with her sadness. So we walk around with a certain natural heaviness in us which, once very foreign, soon became familiar. I learnt long ago how not to lose myself to laughter, lest it cause Ma more pain. Even when the times were joyful, like during Ramadhan, I had to be careful to approach happiness with the stealth that Ma and Bibi approached it with.

'Don't tempt fate,' was Bibi's favourite reproach.

I do not blame Bibi. She does not have much with which to resist the sadness. Her husband, my grandfather, never came back from Dubai where he went to work more than ten years ago. Two of her sons soon followed to look for work and to know what had happened to their father. It has been five years since we heard from them. The last of Bibi's sons, Uncle Ali, wants to go too. Bibi will not have it.

'Isn't it enough to kill me three times?' she says. 'Let me die first, then you may go. It won't be long now.'

But Uncle Ali will go, I know it. I can see it in his restlessness. Sometimes I see it in the way he looks at us, like someone who is about to go on a journey. Other times his intentions reveal themselves in how he sighs when anyone mentions Dubai. From time to time, he comes home and whispers into Bibi's ears about his plans: stories of a new agent he has found who charges only half what his brothers paid and many promises to call when he gets there.

But Bibi shakes her head no so vigorously, you'd think she was about to go mad.

'Isn't losing a husband and two sons enough?' she says.

'You have not lost them. Do we take other people's lives before we know they have died? They will come back. Insha'Allah,' Uncle Ali says. 'Have faith Ma.'

'I know it. I know their sweat does not fall on this earth anymore,' Bibi says.

'But what are my sisters for? They will be with you and they will take care of you.'

'Your sisters have their hands full with their husbands, can't you see? They don't own even the hair on their heads. Don't go, I plead with you.'

I often think of my sister Amina. I try to imagine her life in Lamu. I wonder whether she says her prayers every day or if she forgets like I do sometimes. Does she get lazy sometimes? Ma has a photo of her in her bedroom. Save for the broad nose and the kinky hair, she doesn't resemble me at all. Even less now I presume, for I was told that she has relaxed her hair. Mama would never allow me to do that to my hair. Everything to her is haram. Sleeping is haram. Laughing loudly is haram. Eating is also haram.

I fear Ma. She looks at me as if I'm a ghost.

'You look just like her,' she says.

'But how, Ma? Wasn't she three when she died? I am ten now.'

'What kind of questions are these?' she asks, her cold eyes revealing her anger. Much, much later she adds, 'I know because I am her mother.' This is her apology for her outburst and I gladly accept it.

Ma wears her sadness around her like a colorful hijab, inviting everyone to notice it. I have not yet learnt how to drown myself so completely in sadness like her, but I know how to be quiet. I have perfected the art of quietly doing things, a way of adopting a busy presence like that of birds. Nosy neighbours insist that I was not raised by Ma, that it is Bibi who deserves that credit.

Ma has nightmares sometimes. I dread the days when she has them for I am always the victim. Before Uncle Ali put a lock on my bedroom door, Ma would come into my room and pull at me, screaming, thinking me to be Latifa.

'May Allah curse whoever dug that well. May their feet have worms and may their children be beggars all their lives. May Allah shorten the days of their lives!'

'She would never hurt you,' Bibi assures me after leading her away. 'She just thinks you're Latifa.'

I don't know what to believe. Mama wakes up the next morning as if everything is normal and doesn't notice the red marks. At lunchtime she asks what happened to my face. I run to my room and cry quietly. Mama doesn't like tears. She prefers her sorrow dry.

In the late hours of the afternoon, when Bibi is taking her afternoon nap and Ma is reading the Quran, I sneak away to the two adjoining rooms that Grace's family calls their home. Ours is a Swahili house, built in the fashion of Arabic houses. It is a rectangular house with a long corridor. It has nine rooms facing each other on either side of the corridor. Our part of the house, the front part, is separated from the tenants by a grille which is never closed. On it hangs a curtain through which we can see the tenants but they cannot see us. Bibi says it is good this way: the tenants must not feel like they can get away with anything in a house that is not even theirs.

'Remember the camel and the tent?' she tells Ma.

I know she is talking about Grace's father. Bibi cannot stand the loud prayers that he has in the middle of the night, every night. He is a pastor. Sometimes he will not stop praying till the small hours of the morning. Mama is reluctant with the eviction notice, however. Apart from being our oldest tenants, they are the only ones who pay rent on time.

'Allah knows how much we need it,' she says.

It is Grace's mother that Ma can't stand. She has forbidden me from going to their room. She says that they touch, cook, and eat pork all the time. I know this is a lie because I asked Grace, and she said that they only eat cow meat, and even then only on the last Sunday of every month when her father hosts the church elders in their room.

I sneak away in the afternoons when Ma is busy with Allah and Prophet Muhammad. Sometimes she keeps reading her Quran until the shadows on the walls have disappeared and Grace's mother has lit the lamp.

The teachers' strike is on so Grace didn't go to school today or the past week. Her two brothers are in school because unlike Mto-mondoni Primary School, where Grace goes, Greenfield Academy is private.

'Are your teachers on strike too?' Grace asks when she sees me.

'No. Have you forgotten today is Friday?'

'I wish we also had a free weekday like you people,' she says. I notice that her mind is elsewhere.

She asks me if I am doing anything. I tell her, as she can see, I am not. She suggests a walk and five minutes later, after a reluctant nod from her mother, we are on the road leading to the Chief's offices.

'Didn't your mother tell you not to go to the Chief's place?'

'When is Amina coming?' she asks, ignoring my question.

'Not far, it is Ramadhan soon.'

'I can't stand Amina.'

'Why?' I ask as if I don't already know.

'She thinks she is better.'

'Better than who?'

'Than me and you. What did you think?'

I don't like this side of Grace. She reminds me of a picture my English teacher had on her phone. A neck had three heads sitting on it and the hair of each head was tied into a bun at the top so that it looked like the hair belonged to all of them. I asked Teacher Leila how this was possible.

'Is she a jinni?'

'If it is a jinni then we must all be jinnis,' she said. 'We all have many sides to us. Let no one cheat you that they are always wise or happy. Some days one is happy, some days one is sad. Those are the many heads we all have.' I did not understand her.

When we get to the Chief's place we find that we cannot go in because the watchman is there.

'There will be no swinging for us today,' Grace says. 'Let's go.'

'Where to?'

'Come!' she says in an excited whisper. She grabs my hand and starts running. I am forced to run along with her. She leads me to the place where I come for my madrasa classes. It is empty today save for three boys in green kanzus who are playing pebbles. One of them is screaming, 'Haram! Haram!' incessantly as if he were rehearsing a chant. We walk past them without a word.

'Let's go in,' Grace says when we get to the door of my classroom.

I say no. I don't want to seen by the Imam, who thinks I am the best behaved girl in class. Grace ignores me and walks inside. The room has a raffia carpet spread from wall to wall, and a few books are scattered all over. Grace walks up to some of them and reads the names written at the top.

Leila.

Shaman.

Nuru.

By this time I am worried because soon there will be a call for prayer and the compound will not be as deserted.

'Grace, let's go home.'

She signals at me to go to the back where she is now sitting cross-legged.

'Is this how you usually sit?' she says. 'So that the boys get a little glimpse of your thing?'

She then starts laughing. Her laughter is like my mother's anger. It starts low, as if it is apologising, then gains speed and rises up her throat until she has tears in her eyes. I sit next to her. This close to her, I catch a whiff of a smell that tells of a skipped shower.

Bibi says that a woman can be lazy in anything but not her body. She takes long, hot baths at night and prescribes them as medicine for any sickness. Bibi's bath is an event in her day. Sometimes I think it is all she looks forward to. She fills her basin with half hot water and half cold water. She then adds all sorts of things in it. Once, when

I asked her why she only puts a few drops of olive oil in her bath-water, she said, 'We don't waste gold, do we?'

'Grace, you have not showered today,' I say.

'What's the hurry for? Today is not over.'

'But a girl is supposed to shower in the morning and at night before sleeping. Cold bath in the morning and a hot bath at night.'

'Who said?'

'Bibi.'

'I will shower later, you don't worry.'

We sit in silence for a while, and I am afraid I have offended her. I start to tell her that we should go because I cannot hear the voices of the boys who were playing pebbles.

'Do you have a boyfriend?' she asks.

I laugh and tell her no. 'Do you want Bibi to kill me?'

'And you?' I ask.

She shakes her head. She then stretches her legs in front of her before crossing them at her sides as if to put them away. Then, watching me, she brings her bent knee slowly, slowly as far as it can go between my legs. Her gaze holds me captive so that I am both here and not here and I am afraid of moving even the slightest inch. My stillness registers as assent to her because she is now moving her knee further in with the urgency of someone who really needs to pee. I find myself opening my legs further apart, keenly aware of a thrill that is building up in my middle part. I surprise myself by sighing when Grace's knee goes just short of grazing my panty. I move my body slightly nearer her and push my legs further apart. Grace gets up, scans the room quickly, and gets on top of me. I barely register this when we hear the sound of laughter coming from the windows. I quickly throw her off me and look towards the window. I see nobody.

Grace recovers first. She stands up and makes for the door. It takes me two, three seconds to join her on the murram road that leads to home. Neither one of us says a word to each other.

The next day, Ma neglects her Quran in the afternoon to attend to the more urgent task of going to the market. Bibi has a visitor. I stay in my room the whole time, bored and looking out of the window, counting the people walking. There used to be a dog I would play with, a dog Baba had, whenever I would get bored. After a while they said it had rabies and that it had to be killed. Baba said that the dog had bitten one of the tenants and because of that bite the tenant might die. The dog had to go.

The front door shuts and I hear Bibi call my name. She tells me to go to her room and wait for her. I step in and marvel, not for the first time, at the darkness. You would not guess that the sun shines in its entire splendour just beyond the curtains. But this is how Bibi has always been. She has her own way of doing things. Bibi walks in soon after and wipes her hands on a towel. She is not the cleanest person in the world, at least not like Ma who washes her bed linen every day. Bibi's bed is rumpled, yet in this room there is a sense of organised mess. Bibi takes my hand and leads me to a mat placed beside her bed. I sit down and wait for her.

'Did you know the Imam was here today?' she asks.

'Yes, I heard him,' I say.

'He wanted to speak to your mother but he didn't find her. Why she went to the market at this time, I don't understand,' she says. 'The best time for the marketplace is when the sun is either coming out or going down. Never at two o'clock in the afternoon.'

I smile and nod. Bibi talks of Mum as if she is an errant child.

'Mariam,' Bibi says.

'Yes?'

'Allah was so kind as to bless me with three girls, just like your mother. The seed of girls has been planted in our wombs. Even in you, I'm sure. If there is one thing I have learnt when bringing up girls, it is to watch them very, very closely. Nothing is lost on girls at your age. Especially if they are clever like you. Do you hear?'

'Yes,' I say.

'My dear girl, when Allah created humans, he had ten pieces of desire in His hand. He gave nine pieces to women and only one piece to men. My mother's sister, Aunty Khadijah, once told me something important about girls. She said there is a certain age in a girl's life when she has to be protected from other girls. At that age, the company of other girls is dangerous. There is a type of madness that moves around in their bodies like blood, and they pass it on to each other like a disease,' she says.

She goes silent for a long while and I soon realise that she is using the silence as a weapon, just like the women in our family have been known to do. It is my cue to start crying. As the tears start falling, Bibi continues talking.

'Be careful of other girls, do you understand me?'

I nod my head. I now know that the Imam must have seen.

She continues, 'At a certain age, when a girl starts to notice boys, and wants to be noticed by boys, she is veered towards forming friendships with girls. But never, ever earlier than then.'

'Mariam, the Imam told me he saw you and Grace yesterday at the madrasa. If it is true, I am afraid I will not allow you to speak to that girl again,' she says.

I break out into loud sobs. Bibi seems shocked at this but I no longer care. I am incapable of keeping my sorrow dry. For some reason I remember Baba's dog, the one that was killed. After it was killed, everyone waited for the tenant to die. The tenant never died. It seemed that the dog had never had rabies in the first place.

Pampers

OLAKUNLE OLOGUNRO

When your baby brother Cheta was born in the hospital, that place that smelled strangely of liquid soap and disinfectant, your father bought a big pack of Pampers for his shit and pee. 'Cheta's Pampers is wet,' your mother would say whenever he cried, his face scrunched up and legs in the air. She felt his buttocks and said, 'Give me another Pampers from the bag.'

At that time, the news around school was about homos, or ndintu – ass bursters. That was what all the boys in your class called homosexuality, boys like Chuka, Emeka, Michael, Odika, boys who wore smartly ironed uniforms. During Christian Religious Studies or Science class, they asked questions related to homosexuality.

'Excuse me Ma, was there condoms during Jesus' time?'

'What did homosexuals use in that period?'

They asked these questions with suppressed laughter, and your Christian Religious Studies teacher, Mrs Akindele, a portly woman with a tired gait, stared at them sternly and continued with her story of how Jesus raised the dead or healed the sick.

Your Science teacher, Mr Orji, bushy-haired, thick-lipped and unmarried in his early forties, would stop whatever he was teaching – cells, osmosis – and start a long talk about the evolution of men from apes, saying, at the end of it all, that it was nonsense packaged in the box of education to make it acceptable. Who did not know that it was God who created the earth and everything in it? Except homosexuals, though. They evolved from the apes God created, hence their disgusting lifestyle.

'But,' he would say, 'don't write the Biblical story of the creation for me if you want to pass my exams. Write what I teach you.'

What amazed you, really, was the newspaper story that birthed the talk of Pampers. This was not one of the homos-will-roast-like-popcorn-in-hellfire stories. It was that gay men had to wear Pampers. You snuck into Cheta's room and took a Pampers from the pack. It felt soft and firm, like bread from the bakery on Uka Street. Why did gay men have to wear Pampers?

The boys, Odika leading the pack, told the story that a gay man, a fucking faggot, had gone to have sex in a hotel with another fellow fag, and when they finished, the fag's intestines spilled out through his yansh, and the other fag had to rush and get Pampers for him to wear so his intestines wouldn't drop to the floor. The word 'fag' hung in the air long after the boys were done with their story, and their words – 'How on earth can a man choose to find love in another man?' – haunted you.

'Don't touch me o! I'm not ready to wear Pampers,' the boys would joke in class.

'Let those gay people catch you, your Pampers will be extra large, you will see.'

'Abegi, free me. My Pampers size never dey market.'

You laughed at their jokes, but fear lodged itself in your heart and a visceral dread tightened your throat. What would happen if you, at last, had sex with someone else who liked boys the same way you did? Your intestines would spill out of course, and you would have to wear Cheta's Pampers. Your punctilious mother would notice that the Pampers were going missing and she would know that you had stolen them. And then your parents would know that you liked boys more than girls. What would they say? How would they react? Your fear bunched like wool, wrapped you up until you felt listless and limp, your palms constantly sweaty.

Nouhoum came to your school in the first term of SS3, the term when your school – once tall and beautiful, with purple and white paint and immaculate louvres – had begun to age like an old woman, shedding paint and missing louvres, like teeth.

Your class was a cocktail of Igbo names like Raluchi, Onuekwusie, Fanasi – Yoruba names like Yewande, Molara, Adura – and a sprinkling of Biblical names like Timothy, Mary and Rebecca, so you found his name odd, Nouhoum Amadi, exotic even. It seemed to you the kind of name nobody answered to, something found only in dust-covered, long forgotten library books. And this – the exotic obscurity of his name – filled you with wonder. Later you would learn that his mother, a squat, dark woman with hips like brackets, was from Mali and Nouhoum, who spoke flawless English and French, was born in Mali to a Nigerian man, but named after his maternal grandfather.

Nouhoum – with skin the colour of roasted groundnuts, a jaw shaped like the letter V, and slender fingers – did not join the other boys to joke about homos like you did. He did not say the word 'fag' with the insulting superciliousness of the other boys, or laugh about the gay man who was burnt in Onitsha, or another one who was stripped and made to walk naked, his penis swinging like a pendulum, while whip-clutching people shouted at him, saying that he was a disgrace to other men, that this was why many ladies remained single because there were no real men to marry since all the handsome men were ndintu. Nouhoum stared at the boys, an eyebrow arched slightly. He never laughed. He never even smiled. Every time someone said something like, 'Na Pampers you go wear last-last,' you glanced at Nouhoum.

It was on a Wednesday afternoon, one that was ablaze with heat, that Nouhoum stopped you as you arranged your books in your bag and prepared to go home. You stared at him when he stood in front of you, his tie lopsided, and his smile gentle.

'You live on Obollo Close, don't you?' he said.

'Yes,' you said. You felt pleased that he knew something – anything – about you.

'I live on Uka Street, in that green two storey building beside the bakery,' Nouhoum said. 'I always see you when you come for bread.'

'OK.'

'Are you going home now?'

'Yes.'

He walked with you, and a myriad thoughts rioted in your mind. Perhaps Nouhoum liked boys in the same arousing way you did. Perhaps he would, when you got to Factory Street which was always deserted during the day, kiss you and tell you he loved you, and you would act surprised at first, before saying with a smile that you loved him too. And then again, you thought, as he spoke about how boring Government class was and how he really preferred English Literature class, that perhaps you were being too silly, that he only wanted to be friends – ordinary friends who went to school together and back home together.

When you turned into Factory Street, Nouhoum said something funny about a woman who walked past, her weave-on sitting on her head like damp sawdust, and you laughed aloud, your head thrown back. Your laughter had just begun to fade when Nouhoum said: 'Okhai, I like you.'

You stared first at his face, then at the dense cluster of withering nondescript flowers on the ground beside his feet, and you felt your thoughts melt, replaced by a liquid happiness. To hide this joy from him, you stared above his head, at the sky bleached to a powdery shade of blue, bereft of clouds, and in your suppressed happiness you thought that the sun was tilting.

'Are you ...' you started to say.

He nodded, as if to say he understood things you did not, as though he knew saying the word 'gay' felt sticky on your tongue and difficult to unfurl.

'I want us to be more than friends,' he said. There was a theatrical feel to his words, something strapping boys with sprouts of hair on their chins said to coy giggling girls, their tone bloated with false American accents: 'I want us to be more than friends.' But Nouhoum saying those words made it seem real, true. And you felt something burst open in your chest, something deliciously warm in that region where your heart thumped.

You learned about Nouhoum, things you did not know before. His father, he told you, left his mother for their maid when he was seven, and his mother had remained unmarried since. He said, too, that he did not like custard because it made his chest heavy. You laughed at him and told him that despite his foreign name and flaw-less French he was still a bush boy, because custard was everybody's favourite, even old people. And he did not eat sardines because the smell of fish nauseated him. Most times, you would stare at him and laugh as he held your hand in his. He was like a book, each page revealing new things. As the days wore on you stored bits of him in your memory, because you always wanted to remember, because with Nouhoum you had the sensation of arriving home from a long, weary journey.

It was Nouhoum who unravelled the mystery of Pampers to you. You were in his mother's house, where a portrait of her in an Ankara headwrap hung on the living room wall, in his room where the wall was painted a muted green and a standing fan stood in a corner like a dutiful servant. It was a Saturday. His trousers were off, and even though you had kissed his lips, rubbed your hands over his erection, you could not let him unbuckle your belt.

'Why?' he said, nibbling your earlobe and running a finger in little circles around your nipple. You wanted him to do more than that. You wanted him to slip into you. Small needles of pleasure scattered round your body to your feet, pricking you. Would you feel the same sporadic bursts of pleasure you felt when you touched yourself in the bathroom, the fragrant smell of Lux soap masking the raw smell of your semen? What would Nouhoum do if your intestines spilled out? Would he run out and buy you Pampers? Or would he tell you to hold them in with your hands until you got home and could steal from Cheta's pack? You shrugged his hand away from your buckle and attempted to slip away from him, to ease the discomfiture that surged inside you.

'I don't want to wear Pampers,' you said.

'Pampers?'

You told him then, the story of the two men in the hotel, and the one whose intestines spilled out. You stared pointedly at the standing fan as you talked.

Nouhoum laughed when you ended the story, loud laughter that seemed unlike him. He said, 'You know things like that never happen, right?'

There was, in his tone, an assuredness that made you peel your gaze from the standing fan and fix it on him.

He told you, his arms on your shoulder, that gay people never wore Pampers after sex. 'Come on, Okhai,' he said, 'how can you even believe that nonsense?' He told you about Surulere, the last neighbourhood he lived in before his mother moved here, the area where people who hated homosexuality had used the word Pampers until it had an ominous pallor. 'I think they realised that no matter what they do gay people will still continue to thrive. So they needed something to discourage people, and poof! – innocent Pampers was roped in. It's an unplanned lie. Your intestines do not drop out of your buttocks like that.'

He traced a finger across your collarbone when he finished speaking but you nudged his finger away. You needed time to process his words. An unsettling peace, like a butterfly, flitted in your belly, coming and going. Then you unbuckled your belt and Nouhoum held you to his chest, silently.

When he slipped into you, you felt like you were two selves. As his thrusts intensified, one self was being pleasured, the other was worrying – Would your intestines fall out? Did you have enough money in your wallet to buy Pampers? What size would you wear, Large or Midi?

Nouhoum slid out of you, took off the condom, and you felt strangely bereft, as if someone had sunk the boat you were sailing on to escape from a dark room to paradise. He held you in his arms again, and you smelled yourself on him. You wanted him to take you on the boat again, to row and row until you arrived in paradise. He traced the curve of your lips with his hands and said, teasing, 'So ...?' A spontaneous sound burst from you, and he waited, amused, for your laughter to quieten. 'Do we still need Pampers for you?' he asked.

My Dad Forgot my Name?

VICTOR LEWIS

No, but he could not call me by my name that day.

If he had, it would have been a strange sound among the other less than domestic sounds surrounding us: the heavy breathing from the wide screen TV displaying an acrobatic simulation of sex and the thump-heavy house music. It would have been a strange sound indeed to add to that cacophony. And I suspect that the last thing he wanted to be at that moment was a father, on that day when I ran into him at the spa. A man who I had just finished having sex with in one of the cabins behind me walked by and then turned around to say, "You two look alike." We stood. We stood, facing each other, my father and I, in a dimly lit corridor at a spa. Time stood too.

The man moved on, adjusting his towel suggestively and perking his derrière to make it appear more inviting. Other habitués walked past us and some turned around to look at us. Maybe the atmosphere we stood in had a force field that attracted the instincts of others; did they sense that something was not quite right between us? Or was it just that in that atmosphere gravid with the energy of over-heated testosterone, desire thick as muck, with failure, expectation, long-ing, urgency, fear and hidden hungers, reality is twisted? The music, which I never paid much attention to usually, thrummed through the labyrinth of passages around us. Today it added a menacing note to the shadowy figures who moved through the passages, naked but for the towels around their waists. It was desire city and all the city lights were on. My desire and my father's desire added to the high wattage. The TV monitor on the corner wall where I came face to face with my father squelched with multiple actors in an artificial, unbridled, fucking and sucking scene. It felt like death, but I did not imagine my end to be like this. Nor does the grim reaper as rendered in popular imagination with cloak and scythe, have anything on my Waterloo. Life beyond this point is a black hole.

The ghostly light from the screen fell on my father's shoulders and framed the back of his head as the scene changed to a darker close-up of a pair of naked men gorging on each other's tumescent body parts. Nothing on the screen just above my father's head even remotely resembled sex. At least not the kind I indulge in. I don't believe sex is a spectator activity, but those men on the screen were doing it to be seen; as if they expected applause at the end.

My dad didn't look like my dad. He was my dad, obviously, but to me he appeared taller and stronger, with a sort of predatory majesty. He seemed more potent, physically vital and present, than I had ever imagined or experienced him, as a child – or even as an adult for that matter.

And my dad was completely naked but for his towel draped over his shoulders like a boxer in training, his bollocks hanging proudly free for all to see. I couldn't look down, even though I was dying to see if my father had a big cock, or whatever. He too appeared to be transfixed by my presence, but I could not read his expression. He either was a master at a poker face or he was not at all bothered by the situation we were in. He observed me coolly, unwaveringly. You could say that for once I had my father's undivided attention. After a short while I realised that I was not breathing. I let out a heavy load of held-in air loudly, as I continued to gape at my father. His elongated frame which all four of his children had inherited, was now, due to time and beer, fuller in the middle. His chest was a decent swell of pectorals covered in tightly knotted greying hair. The skin on his shoulders and neck appeared smooth and nutty brown in the dim lighting. Does my father work out? I wondered. I had never before seen my father completely naked. We were not the kind of family that went to the beach. Nor were we in the habit of being undressed in each other's company. In fact, I don't think I had ever wondered what my father's body was like, or even if he had one in *that* way. Of course, he had one, but to me he was just my father. A parent, male or female, is beyond that sort of animal gaze; a sleight of consciousness making exempt the parent from ruminations connected to desire and sex. My father is, dare I think it, handsome. Good looking in the sort of way that would appeal to your mother, if you were to take him home to meet the family. He has safe looks − strong dimpled chin, decorous, clean-living looks − a look that would appear not to have thought a bad thought, ever! But a sexual being with hunger in his eyes, in his whole body − my father? I know the look; I sometimes feel that way too. In him I see a reflection of my own inner upheaval and fear that I am doomed to a lifetime of sex devoid of real intimacy and the joys of a fulfilling monogamous coupling.

All that and more hung heavily around him, along with his wet towel. My father and I stood face to face in a time freeze. How long had he been here? Had he already had sex with someone? Who? The end of the world, the end of my life as I knew it, had my father's face and smile on it. My father was an Opportunity Sexer!

My father was one of those men I like to think of as 'opportunity sexers'; men who only have sex when the opportunity presents itself, men who are not at liberty to choose freely, men with other lives elsewhere. I have also often wondered about what happens all the other times when the urge gets too strong? How do they manage those feelings? Maybe they exist absent of feelings until the opportunity presents itself. What a conditioning! My mind whirred at an unnatural speed. In fact, it was not me thinking. It was the drunk and stoned alter ego that I changed into when I stepped out of my clothes at the spa. That person was busy, in a detached but deeply panicked, bowel-tightening sort of way. Someone rounded the corner and our eyes met. He looked at my father, first his face and then he unabashedly placed his eyes lower, below my father's navel. I felt something very strange, as if my intestines were trying to strangle themselves. I was speechless. Even if I had been in possession of all my wits, what would I have said: Don't look at my father like that? Or, look where you are going, slut?

Instead, I continued to appraise my father. My father played semi-professional football as a young man so his legs were well developed and still strong. What am I searching for? I asked myself, not sure if I had said it out loud. Had he just had sex with the same guy I had been with? The one who had commented how alike we looked? How come I had never run into him before? Was this his first time? Of course, mum was away with her sister. My mind continued at speed to nowhere.

Earlier, when I arrived, the taxi stopped close to the entrance of the parking lot of the spa and I thought I saw the same make and colour of car that my father calls his business car, in the parking lot. My father owns three vehicles. The one for daily use and city business is an SUV which made my mother laugh when he bought it – she said, 'Finally a car that can drive itself' – because of its ridiculous size and profusion of gadgets. He also owns, which I suspect to be his pride and joy, a somewhat older model of a rather grand looking Mercedes Benz saloon car that gets frequent valet treatments, and which he drives when he visits other family members and men of a similar age and class to him. Mercedes Benz is the prestige brand for cars in Anglophone West Africa it seems. And prosperous West

African men of a certain age living away from home need their familiar talismans. But what would my father's car be doing parked at the parking lot of a spa frequented by men who go there for sex with other men? My instincts were dulled by alcohol, a lot of blow, a lot of puff and a simmering, toxic self-disgust at finding myself where I had vowed not to go again after the last visit; the possibility that this was my father's car had not even occured to me.

I wouldn't go to the bath house if I had a partner, I tell myself whenever the thought of a visit fueled by need makes itself very present in my reality. But living in a small provincial town with only one bar that is considered 'gay friendly' – it has a rainbow flag in a prominent place on the promotional banner – rather than an outright safe space for men who have sex with men, drives me back to the one place where I would rather not be when I desire some human company of the same sex variety. Anyhow, so called 'gay friendly' establishments always make me slightly uncomfortable as I am made to feel that I have to behave in a certain way, as if my custom is merely tolerated, which to my mind defeats the intention. Maybe it's just me. The other extreme, with a large void in between, is the spa: ready sex, men walking around half naked – and some stark bollock-naked, carrying deep denial around with them like crosses; staunchly, and braced for sex with multiple strangers and then washing it all away till next time when the desire gets too strong. Sometimes that desire is in ferment and turns sour. Not the sourness of bad hygiene or anything as superficial as that, but a churning tumult of your essence, a ferment of deep denial combined with self-loathing that rises out of your very being to assail your sensibilities. To be sober and clear eyed and not dulled by alcohol and weed is to be slimed by that invisible viscous cloak of bad energy.

I am a private person; a deeply sensual soul who craves the familiar to aid total surrender. At the spa I am a completely different person. I always feel lost to myself, right out of my body and out of touch with the part of me that is only usually accessed via sex, a part of me that I must shut off like a faucet, but that is still primed for the cold animal satisfaction without frills, that the spa offers. Here, sex is a sort of necessary evil, like medicine: good for you but it tastes like shit and sometimes makes you feel even more sick. I don't have the kind of body that men drool over. I don't possess a big cock or any of the other things that attract people looking for instant gratification. But I have an imagination and a sense of fun that plays out over time, teased out by gentle charm and quirky intelligence. At the spa, this is not immediately apparent if no one is ready to engage with me beyond the quick exchange and release of bodily fluids. I am not knocking the spa but it is not the place to go looking for a man to spend quality time with, or a man to enjoy sweet treats with: coffee and cakes at overpriced cafés.

Evenings at the cinema or long candle-lit, home-cooked meals for two that would end up in the warmth of naked intimacy are not part of the deal either. To me, sex should be an oasis from everyday life where you temporarily put your critical faculties on hold.

Sometimes an encounter with a stranger at a spa is bad energy masquerading as sex, which leaves you soul-drained and used rather than refreshed. What you also get sometimes is an encounter with a man in conflict with his own sexuality who will use you as a psychological punching bag to release some of the nasty energy driving his own unresolved issues.

But to the spa I must return again and again. The alternative is even less gratifying: Porn? That is like watching a sport you are good at but having to sit on the sidelines to watch two show-offs who, by dint of them having nice bodies and large appendages, pushed themselves to the front of the queue and got chosen to represent humanity at the games of the gods.

A spa where men go to have sex with other men is a world unto itself, a world without women, family; a sphere where all thoughts of women and their associations are expunged from the conscious mind. A friend once commented that 'real' gay men don't go to spas. 'Spas are for married men and men with female partners; men in hiding from their nature; men who are caught in an eternal conflict of practice and identity,' he said. 'Men who would not kiss you but offer you their most intimate parts for you to suck on, men who would bend over and be fucked and readily fuck you, but not feel at liberty to divulge details about their identity. Men who navigate and juggle a double life like a game only a particular kind of man can play.' My father is one of those men. What do those men tell their wives, girlfriends or partners after they have had a part of themselves that only they know about, touched by a perfect stranger? Can they wash the stranger cleanly off till next time?

Maybe that's the point: to wash it clean away in a willful ritual act of purge and cleanse after the urge is sated. My father is one of those men? Am I one of those men? My failure is my father's failure too. I am the same as my father. And I should also add to that list, gay men who are out of the closet who go looking for temporary release as it is the only evil in town that vaguely resembles what they might be looking for.

As a child, I never really had any direct physical contact with my father. My father worked, and so did my mother. But the way he had it set up made my mother's job as a librarian less important. The bulk of child care, including disciplining four children, fell to my mother. She accepted it. On some days, a rare occurrence, when he wasn't out on some wheeler-dealer business, my father would drive us to the park and whilst we played with other children and mum was busy talking to other mothers around the sandpit or swings, he would hover around the children's play area, watching us with half an interest as if we were somebody else's kids. Looking back now, my mind seems to register my father's distance towards me as puzzle-ment at the fact that I liked to draw and be creative in my room rather than play football or be active outside, or that I enjoyed, along with the twins, helping my mother in the kitchen. But my father was not the ball kicking type of a father either, though he played football as a young man.

I am the youngest and I have been made to understand that my mother's pregnancy with me was a surprise. They would have been happy with Adamou and the twins; one boy and two girls were enough for a young couple to be getting on with. Once when I was younger, around my late teens, my mother told me that I was the spitting image of my father at that very same age, just around the time they met. My mother also told me that when she first met my dad she had put him down as a man who would respond to the at-tentions of other men. But she later came to realise that he was just shy and as it turned out, had no real experience with women. I was not a shy teenager but I was a bit reticent and did not actively seek to interact with others. This I believe led to my mother's attempts to reassure me about what she would have observed as shyness. I had known, since I was fourteen years' young that I was only going to end up being involved sexually and romantically with a man. I told my mother this soon after that talk, just before I left home for the first time to go to university. And she promptly told me not to tell my father. Adamou, the eldest had left home in a blaze of anger and ugly words spoken in a ferocious whisper late one night that awoke me and my two sisters when I was about eight years of age. The cause of the, so far, unhealed rupture in our family life is still a family no-go area. My mother's sister did ask my mother about it once; her reward for asking the question was a slap. My mother quickly apologised and then dissolved into tears. I saw the action as desperate. But what was she so desperate about outside of protecting her family's privacy?

The last time I saw my father was three months before at my sister, small Abiodou's, wedding ceremony and party. She is so named because she and her twin were born on Christmas day and 'small' because she is younger by eight minutes than big Abiodou. When I saw him that last time, something had compelled my critical eye to be engaged while he sat rapt listening to big Abiodou's remarks. She makes an outsized effort to mark her out from her identical twin sister, so she was decked out in Efik bride drag. Her individualist efforts are legendary in the family, so no one seemed to mind or notice that there was a woman bedecked in multi-coloured beads and two-foot-high head dress covered in paste jewellery combs giving a rather humorous and intelligent speech at a white wedding, about choice and the freedom to choose one's own family.

My father had looked clean-cut and sort of brushed down in his new custom-made suit. He looked much different from my mother who is bespectacled, petite and a little tight around her mouth. Because of her petite stature, she always manages to look chic without much effort. To a stranger they looked like they belonged together. But to someone who knows her, she appeared closed in and wrapped up in many secrets in her pale gold lace n'docket and wrapper; whereas my father appeared, at that family gathering anyhow, to look well, open, prosperous, apparently wearing his age well and operating on well-oiled pistons. His greying hair was cut to a number two buzz, I imagine to minimise the effects of a receding hairline. It always surprises me how in fact, my dad is quite fleshy for someone who appears to be so slender. I know I give that impression as well. Someone once commented that they expected me to be bonier to the touch. I like the look of my dad for obvious reasons: I look like him and whenever I get the chance to be in his company it gives me some sort of comfort that I have a rough idea what I would look like in my early sixties if I manage my body well. Growing older and being successful has endowed my father with an air of authority and an appeal that were I to meet a man like him at a bar, I would be happy to get to know him. I watched my father closely because he intrigued me like a stranger, a familiar stranger.

Back at the wedding celebrations, there was a point while watching the live band when I happened to lock eyes with my father. He had turned to look at me because as I imagine it, he would have felt the piercing rays of my scrutiny. He had been checking out the lead singer as I was – a young bombshell of a male, with cascading locks, happy to be in the spotlight. When our eyes met, he had shaken his head in an open approving way as if to say: isn't he great? Was he meaning the performance or the man? Later on, my father took to the dance floor with big 'Biodou – as we had taken to abbreviating the names of the twins. I watched in amazement as big 'Biodou attempted to teach him some hip hop moves to Naija Pop. What riveted me about their dance lesson was how it was not a dance lesson at all. My father got it every time. No matter how complicated the move, he interpreted it to suit his long frame with an ease that forced me to remove myself as far away from the dance floor as possible, to better observe them unobserved and properly check out my father. He had an aura about him of a man with a very rich inner life and he did not mind putting some of that on display. Other people watched too. They looked brilliant together, the Calabar bride and the clean-cut, urbane older man dancing to highly infectious, Nigerian Pop music. The father of the bride looked radiant and happy just to be, it seemed. We had exchanged pleasantries over the course of the afternoon but later drifted towards one another for a chat and a drink like two adults rather than father and son. I would not know what it was like to feel like my father's son. I cannot recall with anything like a memory of a time when I had a playful physical contact with my father. It was not rough or unpleasant when we were together either. It just did not happen. When I was much younger, he would have carried me in his arms from the house to the car and from car to the house on a few occasions as I remember it. That's about all the close physical contact: practical, necessary actions.

After we got our drinks, as usual, he teased me about the 'small provincial one church town' that I called home. My father spoke to me in an open, almost flirtatious way. He laughed right into my face and touched me, with both hands on my forearms, he threw his head back to laugh when I asked him if he had been taking dance lessons. It wasn't funny. But he laughed in response to the compliment. Like someone trying to cover up a blush or something. I found myself enjoying the light of his easy charm.

Faced with my naked father at a spa where men go to have sex with other men, for want of somewhere to place my eyes, I chose to observe his lips. The growth around his mouth made his lips look defined and strong. There was a faint smile. Two of his upper front teeth were visible in a small inscrutable smile. His nose jutted out of his face like a dare and his eyes looked quite defined as if outlined with kohl. My father has long lashes for a guy, I observed in a way designed to kill the moments and suspend time. His strong chin was carpeted with a trendy three or four-day stubble. He looked younger and more alive somewhat. He tilted his face towards me as if in expectation, expectation of what? The realisation did not make me feel any different from what I was already feeling, a strong feeling of transgression, as if I were doing something that I shouldn't be doing, but couldn't help because I was not the only player, and was more than happy to have company on the journey down to hell. I boldly appraised my father with desire vibrating in my every fiber. I felt cut free from all responsibility. The feeling that is conjured by the words: My Knight awaits, persisted; the feeling of having arrived at some sort of conclusion and then what? There is no life beyond. If this is death, it is sweet.

'Son' he finally managed to gather himself to say. I presumed he called me 'son' because he did not remember my name. My father always called me by name. 'Dad', I replied. My father opened his arms as a man would to congratulate his son for a job well done or to say goodbye before a long trip. I walked right into my father's naked embrace. The taste of his mouth was like, like dark brown, like stout mixed with something sweet; like ice cream made with Guinness. My father's tongue searched my mouth voraciously. His fleshy lips pulled on my lips with adult hunger. It was bliss, the surrender I had always known was mine at the right touch, the right chemistry. I snapped out of the dream when I realised I was grinding boner for boner with my father. My father!

I can still remember his smell. A combination of cologne I remember well from my childhood, desire and sweat. I pushed him away, blind with a feeling like rage as I ran first one way and then the other, trying to gather myself to find a quick way to the locker rooms to get my things and get out of there. My towel fell to the floor. I ran naked without looking back. He did not attempt to stop me.

Out on the deserted streets, I realised that my underpants were trying to escape from one of the legs of my trousers and my trousers were inside out. I retrieved my underpants and carelessly stuffed them in my pocket.

I started to shiver from the cold after having been in a warm space. My phone rang whilst I waited for a taxi. I ignored it. By then I was clean sober. Awake to what just happened. No use hoping to wake up from a dream. There was a radio on in the background; voices from waking reality coming from the taxi office. I badly needed to use the toilet. I waited. Thankfully the taxi pulled up. 'Brosia?' The driver called out from his car. I got in the car and my phone started to ring. 'Are you not going to get that?' The driver asked looking half amused by my erratic behavior and I guess by my appearance as I noticed his eyes were looking straight at my clothes in disarray. I stomped on the disconnect button so hard the driver looked at me sharply. They would have seen it all, taxi drivers on the late-night shift at weekends: difficult drunks, lover's fights, couples that could not wait to get home and then a man with inside-out trousers stomping on his phone with force. I had a strong urge to throw my phone out of the speeding taxi when we hit the motorway. I looked out of the window with suicidal interest. It would be so quick; the end, oblivion. 'Your door number?' The driver said. His voice jolted me from deep within. I handed him quite a lot of cash. He protested. I walked away towards my front door and my father sitting on my doorstep.

'What are you doing here, dad?'

'I am here to finish what we started earlier,' he replied. That was what I wanted him to say. He was in control like he had never been with me as a child. I entered the flat and my father followed me in; the whole time smiling faintly. I am a sucker for quiet authority in the bearing of a prospective partner. When we got inside, my father said, 'You left in a hurry,' regarding me with grown-up amusement, my outside-in trousers. My father stepped up to me and wordlessly helped me out of my jacket. He squeezed my neck with his large hands whilst he did it. He unbuttoned my shirt and kissed me in the middle of my chest and then on my neck. He was in complete control. I responded as naturally as breathing. I felt like a pure being. I made up my mind to die. My father unbuttoned my trousers and pushed them down as he pushed me to the wall. I was happy. I waited to touch my father tenderly. He took me by the hand and led me to my bedroom. I lay down calmly waiting for my father to finish divesting himself of his expensive looking sports clothing. He still had the half smile on his face, a confident almost cocky smile. I watched my father taking off his final garment. He took off his watch and placed it on the table. He parted my legs with his knees as he hovered over me and then lay between my legs and pulled the covers up to our necks.

I woke up in the afternoon. Voices from daytime TV drifted to my room from the sitting room. Used condoms littered the floor, interspersed with hastily torn packaging as far as the eye could see. My lips were swollen. The membrane securing my tongue to the floor of my mouth was broken; it felt sore. My neck, chest and face buzzed from the memory of the strong, urgent kisses. I felt pure bliss. I woke up slowly to the reality of the day in front of me. My naked father appeared in the doorway as if he had heard me think. 'I love you, Alieu' he said. I wanted him again. I long to die.

Aqua Speaks

JAYNE BAULING

She never intended it to be a secret name. It's just that there are few spaces for saying it in her present life. The men watch her. Their eyes make her conscious of being the first woman forester on the plantation.

'Best you let us give the orders until they get used to you,' her fellow foresters say.

She wonders how long it will take.

After Saasveld, it is strange to be among men only. It is not as if there are no other women on the plantation. Jongiwe and Ben have young wives. They work in town and only get home after the foresters have knocked off for the day. She never sees them. Then there is the clerk Nomvula in the office, dull in her brown or navy clothes, seemingly a stranger to joy. Too, there is an older woman who cleans the office; she wears a domestic's overall and a doek around her head, and is married to one of the workers. Off-duty, even on the hottest days, she dresses in a baggy jersey and shapeless skirt, always with a blanket or towel wrapped round her lower body and thighs for extra modesty.

Thando wears khaki, the same as her colleagues. The men working under them wear overalls. They stare at her arms where they emerge from her shirt's short sleeves and she wonders if it is their slenderness or her shapely biceps that make them do so. She is proud of her arms, but she knows there is no admiration in the stares. If the men meet her eyes, her famous giraffe eyes, there is nothing of friendship in theirs.

She only covers her arms, donning the required protective gear, when she is allowed to give a chainsaw safety demonstration, a sop from her colleagues before they get to the business of explaining that these procedures are orders, not guidelines.

Pines please her with their symmetry and their bracing smell, so she is gratified to be here and not posted to one of the eucalyptus plantations. *Pinus patula, Pinus elliotii and Pinus taeda.* Sometimes she chants the names softly to herself like a charm. Other times she says them loudly, to impress non-forestry people with her knowledge, showing off.

When summer brings sweltering conditions, heat trapped by the trees, she shaves her head, swaps trousers for shorts and folds her pale fawn socks down over the tops of her brown work boots. She knows she has good legs. The men stare even more. If she stares back, some look away, but a few hold her gaze a while before spitting into the dirt and resuming work.

Returning to her allotted plantation house in the evenings, she passes Nomvula's small house, always closed up even in the heat. The woman must lock herself in as soon as she returns from the office. Thando wonders what she is afraid of, to constrain herself so.

The houses are set far apart from one another, in a cleared area a kilometre down the red dirt road leading from the main plantation entrance. The sun has baked their green corrugated iron roofs almost white, and the stoeps are polished cement.

At the house, she examines herself, picking ticks off her skin. Her voice mostly goes unused overnight, unless she is called out to a fire. Then her task is to give assistance, driving vehicles, or helping with hoses while Jongiwe and Ben direct the fire-fighting team.

'What if there's a fire one of the weekends it's my turn to be on duty?' she asks them.

'Call us,' Jongiwe says. 'We'll arrange it so that at least one of us is never further away than town.'

'Just until the men get used to you.' Ben is appeasing.

Here she must be ordinary Thando Ngobeni – Thando Ngobeni number six-thousand-and-something, she used to joke in the places where she could tell the other name.

Sometimes she is able to laugh at her teenaged self, inland schoolgirl in love with the blue-sea sound of the word aquamarine, taking it for her name, Aquamarine Gal. She wrote it inside the back covers of her exercise books, whispered it to her friends, said it boldly in snug circles.

She had never seen an aquamarine then, never seen the sea. On quarterly family trips to the provincial capital, she would linger outside jewellery stores in the mall, gazing at the shine and sparkle of their window displays, tiny tags all turned over to hide the prices. There were never any aquamarine pieces, but plenty of tanzanite – earrings, rings, bracelets, pendants, whole necklaces.

Tanzanite's blue was like a poem or a song, but somehow Tanzanite Gal didn't sing along with the colour. As for the more obvious gold, diamonds and platinum, she rejected them as over-used, especially in the context of bank cards, the kind that marked their possessors as high-flyers, inhabiting a world she saw on television.

She only modified the name during her forestry training at Saasveld in the Cape. She was seeing the ocean for the first time, finding it mostly grey and turbulent, only occasionally as serenely aqua as she had imagined it.

That wasn't why she changed it. She already knew Afrikaans, coming from Mpumalanga, but at the college and in towns like George and Mossel Bay she heard and spoke it to the extent that she began to think in it as much as in SiSwati or English.

Again it was the sound of a word that compelled her. Avontuur. Adventure. In Afrikaans the sound held mystery and bravado in equal measure. She became Aqua Avontuur.

It is the name of someone who dares.

She could tell it to the girls at Saasveld, whatever their background. They called her Aqua in front of their male peers and the staff, and it didn't matter. They moved in a pack and the bold name proclaimed her. She was happy then, high on her own existence, falling in and out of love.

Only now, with it all left behind, does she fully realise it.

Her student practical postings were to Cape plantations. She reverted to Thando Ngobeni and knew she made little impact on her mentors, those generous in sharing their knowledge or men resentful of the responsibility and irked by her gender.

Now she is Thando again, with no one on this plantation who knows the other name, no one to tell it to, and her Saasveld friends and lovers posted to plantations in other provinces but possibly sharing with her what she slowly comes to recognise as loneliness.

Home is near enough to visit on her off-duty weekends. Her father turned his back on her the day she told the truth about herself, her brothers too, so there are only her mother, her affronted grandmother and a few friends from school who remember her as Aquamarine Gal. She tells them she is now Aqua Avontuur.

'You should stay away,' her mother says.

'Why?' Defiance flaring. 'So Gogo can't come after me with a sjambok again?'

Recalling the day her grandmother attacked her with whip and fists, intent on *beating it out of her.*

'You know this business of curing girls like you?' Her mother is awkward, embarrassed to be talking about it. 'Even your brothers talk like this now. I am afraid for you, Thando. You draw attention to yourself, calling yourself this Aqua name, showing your skin, kissing Sindi, *sies*. Child, I wish you had chosen work to take you to the cities where these things are accepted.'

There are fires on the plantation as the heat climbs and the rains fail. She tries out a khaki cotton-knit vest instead of her short-sleeved shirt. Her shoulders are smooth and shining, a rich brown. She likes them, turning and bending her head to kiss the right one, its hard curve.

Ben doesn't react, but Jongiwe sucks in his breath when she arrives at the plantation office for their daily planning session. With its wood floor that smells of polish, and white walls covered in charts, the office is at the entrance end of the cleared residential area, and they all walk to this morning meeting. It is very early, the rising sun hidden behind the dark walls of surrounding forest, the air still cool. Birds call, but otherwise the plantation is quiet at this hour, its vehicles and machinery idle.

'Go back to your house now and get your shirt.' Jongiwe is urgent. 'The men can't see you with your shoulders bared. The shorts are bad enough. I should have said something then – '

'Why?' She faces him, bringing her hands to her hips.

'What is the problem with her clothes, Jongiwe?' Ben wants to know.

'Don't you understand, Thando?' Jongiwe ignores Ben. 'You know our culture. A woman who bares her shoulders and thighs? The men on this plantation are older, traditional – '

'It doesn't matter,' she says.

'If they see you like this, they could get ideas – '

'I don't care. I don't like men,' she adds, briefly exhilarated to be ending the silence she has kept since coming here.

Jongiwe sucks in his breath a second time, understanding her.

'Maybe best to take Jongiwe's advice, Thando.' Ben is tentative, apologetic, not really understanding. 'At least until they get used to you.'

'Always that story,' she mutters.

She wants to defy them, but she understands that Jongiwe is neither condemning her nor defending their culture. Simply, he is trying to prevent trouble at work.

Leaving the office to go and change, she passes Nomvula arriving for work. She keeps the same hours as the foresters. The look she gives the vest is shocked at first, but then nearly wistful.

Thando thinks she must be in her late thirties although she dresses older, in those sensible, conservative garments with their drab colours. In Aqua mode she has tried a friendly greeting more than once. The response is always hushed, a mix of politeness and timidity. She has the idea that Nomvula is frightened of her when she is Aqua, that she finds Thando safer.

Thunder and lightning mock the foresters with their empty promise of rain. The lightning strikes trees, and the dam from which they draw water to fight the resultant fires is drying up.

'Thando?' It is Nomvula on another morning, hesitant in initiating conversation. 'I've heard something. The workers, they're saying it's you. Stopping the rain, causing the fires. They say you bring bad luck.'

'I'm a witch now?' Thinking of the other things she has been called, at home where they know what she truly is. 'Lightning, the witch's curse. Do you believe it, Nomvula?'

'No. But I am afraid for you, Thando. You have too much . . . too much life, sometimes, when you forget to hide it.'

Thando is afraid for herself too, because she is Thando, Aqua Avontuur put away but ceaselessly clamouring for release, Aqua who draws the danger Thando fears.

'Not lightning this time, I think,' Jongiwe says as they stand around with red eyes, and parched throats after a hot wind has swept another fire along the forest floor of dried pine needles, scorching the lower parts of the trees, flames blown along too fast to climb to the upper growth. 'The signs were there, where it started. Those women caused it, out there on the edge of B5.'

'Accidentally probably. Carelessness.' Ben's gaze ranges over the blackened undergrowth, searching for the red flicker, the drifting smoke wisp that will mean their job isn't done.

'What women?' She hears how hope lifts her voice.

'Living in the open.' Ben is embarrassed. 'Getting custom from the truck-drivers who take our timber out. You know?'

'Sex-workers.' Jongiwe is blunt. 'The police evict them, but they always come back.'

They come back this time too, to an unburnt clearing close to the road used by the timber trucks. She finds them one evening after work, with the sun still shining strong and gold through the trees. She has changed into cut-off jeans, sandals and a vest in the style of the khaki one she still yearns to wear for work. This one is the colour she thinks of as aquamarine, a light, clear greenish-blue. Her head is freshly shaved and she has put on lip-gloss.

Maybe she will make a friend.

The women laugh at her when she appears among them. Her shy greeting is met raucously. Her breath comes sharp and shallow, but she persists, posing beside a tree, smiling so hard it feels false, flirting with her giraffe eyes so that they can admire and envy her eyelashes.

They're supposed to like her, to want her company like wanting fresh air after hours indoors. This is how she has imagined it.

There is a tight ache in her throat and her eyes burn.

'We know who you are,' one taunts, wearing the same uniform as all the others, high heels, short skirt, tight top and false nails. 'The workers talk about you to the truckers, and they tell us.'

'So you like us, forester-lady? How much you got? Imali? We charge extra to go with a girl.'

'Miskien it's a boy really. See those cute little muscles?'

'See those little titties?'

'No, please. You don't…I mean, I thought…'

She shrugs and turns. There's no point in pursuing it, in telling them of the ache for company that has brought her out here. Futile to try, when they have no friendship to give her.

Aqua came to find the women, Thando walks away from them.

'Get a man, Sisi,' one of the women calls after her. 'A man to fix you.'

Their jeers rise, louder than the swelling evening birdsong piercing the air, and reaching a pitch that makes her think of baying dogs.

The only tenderness is the amber sun's, warm on her back in its brief benevolent hour. She follows her long shadow home to the residential area.

Jongiwe's house stands open to the evening air as she passes. She smells meat cooking and hears him and his wife, calling to each other from different rooms. Ben's doors too are open. His small children are playing with a smiling cream labrador on the stoep.

Nomvula's house is more modest than the foresters'. It is closed and silent, her small grey-brown car outside, loneliness within.

Thando considers entering the fenced garden and knocking on the door, but she is wholly Thando now, afraid of further rejection.

At their office meeting in the morning, Jongiwe talks about the need for speed in harvesting the trees affected by several of the recent fires.

'Because they'll start dying from the bottom up. I've got a meeting at Head Office, but you know what has to be done, Thando. Ben can direct the men for you,' he says.

'Ben is silviculture,' she reminds him. 'I'm harvesting.'

'It's just until they get used to you,' Ben says.

Thando is on the point of accepting it, as she always does. Nomvula arrives, dressed in dull olive-green today. At noon she will go home for a solitary lunch, the same as Thando does unless there's an emergency. Then she will return to the office until four-thirty or five, go home again and be alone.

'No.' It is Aqua who speaks. 'They need to get used to me now. Today. They need to get used to taking instructions from me.'

'Listen, Thando – ' Jongiwe starts.

'No,' she says again. 'And I'm not Thando. Let me tell you while you're all three here. The name I like is Aqua Avontuur. That's what I want you to call me, until I tell you I'm someone else. Spread the word.'

Nomvula claps her hands together softly. A smile lights a lamp behind her plain face.

She says, 'I used to tell people to call me Miz N. I wish I hadn't stopped.'

Aqua copies her, her palms meeting.

'Hey, Miz N,' she says.

'Hey, Aqua.'

The Authors and Editors

ADAIR, BARBARA | SOUTH AFRICA
Barbara Adair has written numerous novels, articles and short stories. Her novels include *In Tangier We Killed the Blue Parrot* (2005, Jacana) and *End* (2009, Jacana), both of which were shortlisted for writing awards. Her writing has appeared in *Sunday Independent, Sunday Times, Weekender, Horizons, Selamta, Sensitive Skin Magazine, New Contrast, From the Grand Canyon to the Great Wall: Travelers' Best, Worst and most Ridiculous Stories From The Road* and *Queer Africa*.

AGUGOM, MICHAEL | NIGERIA
Born in Nigeria, Michael Ndubuisi Agugom worked as a TV presenter and producer with the largest TV network in Africa. His fiction has appeared or is forthcoming in *The Capra Review* and *Referential Magazine*.

ALIYU, RAFEEAT | NIGERIA
Rafeeat Aliyu is a Nigerian writer of speculative fiction and writing queer romance is a challenge that she enjoys tremendously. 'Àwúre Ìfẹ̀ràn' is an excerpt from her forthcoming novella featuring magic, true love and family in the dynamic city of Lagos. When she is not writing, Rafeeat enjoys making homemade ice-cream, listening to kizomba and watching old-school wuxia films.

AYEBAZIBWE, JENNIFER SHINTA | UGANDA
Jennifer S Ayebazibwe is a 32-year-old lesbian woman, born and raised in Uganda and now residing in South Africa. She is passionate about storytelling and the documentation of lesbian experiences. When she is

not telling stories, she writes the odd poem, studies economics, politics and philosophy through Unisa in the evenings, and spends what's left of her free time with her wife and daughter, the loves of her life.

AZUAH, UNOMA | NIGERIA

An English professor and guest lecturer/writer at various universities, Unoma Azuah is listed as one of the top Professors in Affordable/Private Colleges and Universities in the USA. Her writing awards include the Urban Spectrum award for her debut novel *Sky-high Flames* and the Snyder-Aidoo book award for her novel, *Edible Bones*. She studied at the University of Nigeria, Nsukka and she has post-graduate degrees from Cleveland State University and Virginia Commonwealth University.

BAULING, JAYNE | SOUTH AFRICA

Jayne Bauling is a South African writer whose Young Adult novels have won several awards. Her short stories for adults and youth have been published in a number of anthologies. She has twice made the regional shortlist for the Commonwealth Short Story Prize.

DORE, AMATESIRO | NIGERIA

Amatesiro Dore is a 2009 alumnus of the Farafina Trust Creative Writing Workshop and 2015 Fellow of the Ebedi International Writers Residency. He has been published in *AFREADA*, *Afridiaspora*, *Bakwa Magazine*, *Brittle Paper*, *Chimurenga*, *EXPOUND Magazine*, *Farafina*, *The Kalahari Review*, *Kwani?*, *Munyori Literary Journal*, *Naija Stories*, *Omenana*, *The Ofi Press*, *The ScoopNG*, *Vanguard Newspaper* and *YNaija*. His work was the Most-Read piece published by *Bakwa Magazine* in 2015.

ETAGHENE, YVONNE FLY ONAKEME | NIGERIA

Yvonne Fly Onakeme Etaghene is an Ijaw and Urhobo dyke poet and performance activist. She has published four collections of poetry, released one poetry album and produced four solo art exhibitions. Etaghene has written and acted in two solo shows: *Volcano's Birthright{s}* and *GUAVA*, performed on two continents. In 2015 she won the Joseph Henry Jackson Award in short fiction. Her novel *For Sizakele* addresses identity, intimate partner violence, queer gender and relationships.

ILAMWENYA, NANCY LINDAH | KENYA
Nancy llamwenya is a short story writer, poet and teacher. She enjoys all types of fiction, but has a particular soft spot for African literature. In 2015 she was mentioned as the best African entrant in the Umoja Writing Competition. She uses her work to teach the intricacies of Africa: the immense wealth of wisdom, practices and possibilities in this well endowed continent.

KUSHABA, JULIET | UGANDA
Juliet Kushaba is a sexuality scholar, mother and feminist. She writes both creative fiction and non fiction in an attempt to fulfill this duty.

L, IDZA | KENYA
Idza L is a Kenyan writer. She is interested in writing stories about women and the lives they live.

LEWIS, VICTOR | SIERRA LEONE
Victor Lewis skates close to the edge most of the time and leaves everything, repeat, everything to the last minute; mostly he manages to get things done. He thinks that being queer is freedom: freedom from ordinariness, freedom to create his very own reality. If he were to list ten of his favourite things, the list would include the colour indigo, African women and dancing the tango in Buenos Aires.

MACKAY, ALISTAIR | SOUTH AFRICA
Alistair Mackay grew up in Johannesburg and has worked for a marketing strategy consultancy, as well as on the communications team for a political party. He has a regular column on *MambaOnline* that explores personal journeys through SA's urban gay culture. He also contributes a monthly political branding column on *Marklives*. Alistair has a politics degree from the University of Edinburgh and is currently doing an MFA in Creative Writing at Columbia University.

MAGANO, THATO | SOUTH AFRICA
Thato Magano is currently pursuing his MA in Political Studies at the University of the Witwatersrand and is a member of the WITS Fees Must Fall movement. He is co-partner at *Vanguard Magazine,* a womanist

platform for young black women in South Africa, speaking to the intersectionality of queer politics, Black Consciousness and pan-Africanism. He is a co-founder and Strategy Director at Ponelesego Youth Development Projects.

MARTIN, KAREN | SOUTH AFRICA

Karen Martin is a writer, artist and editor. She has an MFA in Creative Writing from Syracuse University. Through her Highveld Reading and Writing Studios she provides mentoring to other writers and teaches literary craft. Karen has initiated and developed several projects for Gay and Lesbian Memory in Action (GALA), including the award-winning *Queer Africa: New and Collected Fiction*.

MOHAMED, BISHARA | KENYA

Bishara Mohamed is an interdisciplinary artist who works with numerous materials and processes which have a relationship to her ideas. She is a visual artist, writer, educator, filmmaker, performance artist and public speaker. Her creative work has the thread of dealing with the dreamy, nightmarish landscapes of history, myth and memory and the narratives, creatures and objects that occupy that space.

MUKAMI, H W | KENYA

H W Mukami was born in November 1978 in a cold, remote town in Central Kenya. 'Pub 360' is a story about overcoming challenges, love, hope and change. When H W is not crafting some killer manuscript, she can be found repairing simple electric gadgets with her son, treating bone fractures and joint dislocations at the local health centres, photographing landscapes, seascapes and giant baobabs, or playing with her neighbour's smart dog, Smart.

MULGREW, NICK | SOUTH AFRICA

Nick Mulgrew is founding associate editor of *Prufrock*, Deputy Chair of Short Story Day Africa, and publisher of uHlanga, a poetry press. In 2014 he won the National Arts Festival Short Sharp Stories Award and in 2015 he was shortlisted for the White Review Short Story Prize. Nick has written a poetry collection, *the myth of this is that we're all in this together* (2015, uHlanga) and *Stations* (2016, David Philip), short stories.

OSAZE, OLA | NIGERIA
A trans person of Edo and Yoruba descent, Ola Osaze grew up in Nigeria
and now resides in the US. Ola is a Voices of Our Nation Arts workshop
Fellow, and has writings featured in *Apogee, HOLA Africa*, Black Public
Media, Black Girl Dangerous, *Black Looks*, Autostraddle, *Transatlantic
Times, Trans Queers: A Transfags Sex Journal,* and anthologies, including
Yellow Medicine Review, Queer African Reader and *Outside the XY:
Queer, Brown Masculinity.*

OLOGUNRO, OLAKUNLE | NIGERIA
Olakunle Ologunro's writing has appeared or is forthcoming in *Litro*
Online, *Praxis Magazine* Online and *Novel Afrique.* He was shortlisted for
the 2015 AMAB-HBF Prize and the 2015 Awele Creative Trust Awards. An
alumnus of the Farafina Trust Creative Writing Workshop, he lives in
Lagos, Nigeria.

OPICHO, ALEXANDER K | KENYA
Alexander Ernesto Namugugu Khamala Opicho was born in 1974 at
Bokoli village in Bungoma district, Kenya. He studied Governance at the
university. He is currently researching the rights of minorities in devolved
governance for his PhD thesis. He lives and works in Lodwar town in the
northern desert corridor of Kenya. He has published more than a hundred stories, both in print anthologies and online.

PAULET, EMMA | SOUTH AFRICA
Emma Paulet is completing her Honours Degree in English at the
University of Pretoria. Her poetry has been published online and in
Inclinations, the annual creative writing publication of the Inklings
Society (UP).

TEYIE, ALEXIS | KENYA
Alexis Teyie is a Kenyan writer and feminist. Her poetry is included in the
Jalada Afrofuture(s) and Language issues. Her short stories have been
published in the Short Story Day Africa *WATER* anthology and *Imagine
Africa 500.* She has also featured in *Q-zine, This is Africa, Black Girl Seeks*
and *African Youth Journals.*

THAFENG, MATSHEPO | SOUTH AFRICA
Forty-year-old Matshepo Thafeng has been telling stories since her primary school days. While she was growing up, she read everything in sight, and in her first year of high school her English composition was placed on the staff room wall for everyone to read. Matshepo studied drama and speech at the Market theatre laboratory and later graduated from Unisa in 2012 with a BA in Communication Science.

VAN ROOYEN, S | SOUTH AFRICA
S (Sanet Nel) van Rooyen believes that events that profoundly affect our lives happen mostly by accident. She is driven by empathy and defined by past hurts that have made her the person she is today. One of her deep loves is for her homeland, Mama Africa, and when she dreams of her it is always in her mother tongue: *'It's always vivid with the colours of my homeland.'* Dirk B.

WILFRED, JEAN-LOUIS | KENYA
Jean-Louis Wilfred is a postgraduate business student in Nairobi. He has written for a financial news website and worked with the creative artsorganisation that pioneered Kenya's first queer anthology *Stories Of Our Lives.*

XABA, MAKHOSAZANA | SOUTH AFRICA
Xaba, Makhosazana co-edited the first anthology *Queer Africa: New and Collected Fiction* (2013) which won the 26th Lambda Literary Award for the fiction anthology category in 2014. She is also the author of *Running & other stories* (2013), which won the SALA Nadine Gordimer Short Story Award in 2014 and two poetry collections: *these hands* (2005 and 2017) and *Tongues of their Mothers* (2008). She is currently working at GALA on several book projects while pursuing her PhD at Rhodes University as a Mellon Scholar.

ZIKALALA, ZUKOLWENKOSI | SOUTH AFRICA
Zukolwenkosi Zikalala was born and raised in Pimville, Soweto, by his parents Constance and Gordon Zikalala. He is an African Literature Honours student at the University of the Witwatersrand, and a writer and scholar in the making. He is also a Mellon Mays Undergraduate Fellow (2015 cohort), where he is being exposed to the world of academia. Creative writing has always been a passion of his.

Note from the Editors

The journey for *Queer Africa 2: New Stories* began in September 2015 when we prepared a call for submissions. When the deadline for submissions came at the end of January 2016 we had received 95 stories from 13 countries. In the call for submissions we invited writers to submit their 'literary translations into English' of previously published stories. Unfortunately, we did not receive such a submission. Our intention was to include stories from Francophone and Lusophone countries, as well as in other indigenous languages of the continent.

Once all the submissions were in, we removed the names of the contributors so that we could read all the stories blind. It took just over two months for each of us to read all the submissions. Over a weekend in April we met to discuss our individual choices. Interestingly there were seven stories which we both agreed met all the literary criteria we were looking for. We then decided on a process in which the person who had ticked a story as 'yes' would motivate to the other person why the story needed to be included. This became a very detailed and engaging process because we quizzed and pushed each other for clarity on why a story deserved selection until we both agreed on whether to include it or not. We wanted to engage in this process as a way of being fair to the writers. Once we reached agreement on the 26 stories, our ball park goal having been 30 stories, we then chose the stories we were each going to work on refining with the writers, based on our interest in the themes and writing styles. It was only after this step that we returned to the original submissions in order to reveal the names of authors. Again, we did this in order to be fair to the authors as some of them are known to us. We are therefore very proud of the writers who dreamed and wrote the varied and thought-provoking stories anthologised here.

We both had fulfilling and fun-filled learning experiences working with the writers. The support and facilitation work ranged from as little as changing the title of a story, to detailed changes on the story lines and story tones, to points of view and narration styles.

The differences between the two anthologies are a testimony to the growing excitement in the continent. Notably, there was no need to extend the deadline of the call for submissions as we received 95 submissions. While *Queer Africa: New and Collected Fiction*, has 18 stories from 6 countries, in *Queer Africa 2: New Stories*, there are 26 stories from 7 countries. Some of the authors' country-identities show the nature of the African diaspora represented in this book. The countries represented in this anthology are Kenya, Nigeria, Rwanda, Somalia, South Africa, Sierra Leone and Uganda and in cases where some of the authors identify as citizens of more than one country, mostly the USA was the other country and in some cases, South Africa. While we deliberately included previously published stories in *Queer Africa: New and Collected Fiction*, all the stories in the current anthology are new. It has taken just over a year to select and assemble this anthology, while it took three years for the previous anthology.

This second anthology affirms our intention as expressed in the Preface to the first book:

It is our intention with this anthology to productively disrupt, through the art of literature, the potent discourses currently circulating on what it means to be African, to be queer and to be an African creative writer.

May you be excited and provoked, entertained and inspired by the queer African creative visions we bring you here.

THE LANGUAGES USED IN THE STORIES

Africa accounts for an estimated 2 000 of the approximately 6 500 languages spoken worldwide. For many of the authors contributing to this anthology the rhythms of their mother tongues and languages of the African diaspora come through in varied and interesting ways because English is their second, third, or even fourth language. This contributes richly to the stories they tell.

Many Africans are functionally literate in numerous languages, and hearing different languages regularly spoken around them is a norm embraced with pride. When bringing the stories for this anthology together, as editors we decided that words in African languages should not be glossed or italicised. This is, after all, fiction from Africa, written by multilingual Africans.

Having become intimate with the stories over the past months, our feeling is that the stories are written in such a way that words or phrases in Arican languages do not detract from the text and its meaning. However, a few explanations may enrich the reading experience.

A number of the Nigerian authors have included dialogue in the vernacular in their stories, e.g. 'Pampers', 'Tar', 'Iyawo', 'Staying Afloat' and 'The Day He Came'. While unfamiliar to some readers, the meaning is not difficult to follow.

Many of the stories are referential of the rich African oral folktale tradition and their authors have succeeded admirably in translating this oral tradition into writing. Two of the stories that seem to us to embody this tradition are Matshepo Thafeng's 'The Stone' and 'Stowaways' by Alexander Opicho. The words of an isiZulu lullabye 'Thula baba', in 'The Stone' are well known and loved by many South African children, black and white, and further add to the emphasis on the oral, despite this being a story printed in a book.

The multilingual nature of the authors – and Africans generally – is obvious from the close to twenty different languages used sparingly in the various stories, among others Arabic in 'Maimuna Doesn't Know', Afrikaans in 'Aqua Speaks' and 'Mirage of War', Swahili in 'The Voice Is the First to Go' and isiXhosa (among others) in 'My Body Remembers: A War Cry'. 'Is It Love that Has Me?' by Bishara Mohamed from Kenya, uses the Somali worda 'hooyo' for mother and variations of 'khaniis', used to desribe gay people.

An author who uses code-switching to great effect is Thato Magano. His 'A What?' illustrates the facility with which young South Africans in particular have made many of the official South African languages uniquely their own. Phrases in Tsotsitaal, a vernacular language spoken mostly in the Johannesburg area, e.g. 'eintlek vele', are a mix of Afrikaans and isiZulu. 'Eish', 'shem', 'mxim', 'hawu' and 'neh' form part of the vernacular used across South Africa. In addition, the two main characters in the story sometimes slip into isiZulu with words like 'ukubekezela' and 'istabane', and Setswana, with phrases like 'kgale o e nyaka' and 'etletse dilo tsa bana wa bora'.

We trust that readers will agree that, far from detracting from these stories, the moderate use of the writers home languages contribute to the uniqueness of this anthology, written by Africans.

THE EDITORS
MARCH 2017

Acknowledgements

To the staff of Gay and Lesbian Memory in Action, thank you for the many ways in which you contributed to the book in particular, during the initial stage of distributing the call for submissions at all the events you attended. We acknowledge and thank the former director, Anthony Manion, who commissioned this book and oversaw the early stages of its development and John Marnell who contributed his various skills during the development of the call for submissions.

We are grateful to Barbara Boswell whose perceptive and intellectual introduction to the book contextualises the stories so aptly.

Special thanks go to Colleen Higgs, our publisher at MaThoko's Books, for her oversight and ongoing support and encouragement, and to copy editor Gill Gimberg for the incisiveness she brought to the texts. Thank you to Danielle Clough for the eye catching intricacies of her artwork on the cover design and to Monique Cleghorn for her book design.

We wish to acknowledge the authors who contributed with enthusiasm their imaginations which sparkle throughout this book, without whom, the call for submissions would have fallen flat.

Finally, to our editors, Makhosazana Xaba and Karen Martin, who managed this project from the beginning to the end, in particular – read through the 95 submissions, selected the final 26, and brought their creative talent in working with the authors – thank you. We are immensely grateful.

The publication of the book was made possible by the core support from Sudentenes og Akademikernes Internasjonale Hjelpefond (SAIH) and The Other Foundation.

CARETAKER DIRECTOR, GETTI MERCORIO AND
INCOMING DIRECTOR, KEVAL HARIE